Spanish Pursuit

by

Patrick Shanahan

Published by New Generation Publishing in 2020

Copyright © Patrick Shanahan 2020

First Edition

The author asserts the moral right under the Copyright, Designs and Patents Act 1988 to be identified as the author of this work.

All Rights reserved. No part of this publication may be reproduced, stored in a retrieval system or transmitted, in any form or by any means without the prior consent of the author, nor be otherwise circulated in any form of binding or cover other than that which it is published and without a similar condition being imposed on the subsequent purchaser.

ISBN 978-1-80031-597-6

www.newgeneration-publishing.com

New Generation Publishing

1

The early morning sun warmed the expectant faces of the passengers as they stepped from the train, the women in their expensive dresses and vertiginous heels, the men in sharp suits and crisp shirts. I scanned the crowd as it wound its way along the platform towards the station exit, looking for a familiar face. It was the third train of the morning that I had stood and watched, but there was still no sign of the person I was waiting for. I glanced at my watch – ten to eleven. I pulled my mobile from my jacket pocket and hit the keypad.

"Ces, where are you?" I asked as soon as he picked up.

"*On my way, geezer. Where are you?*"

"I'm outside the pub opposite Ascot station. What's happening?"

"*Wall to wall traffic on the M25.*"

I let out a frustrated sigh.

"The M25? What're you doing on the M25? You didn't say you were driving. You're supposed to meet me here at half-ten."

"*Mate, keep your wig on. I ain't driving. I was blagging some bird, weren't I?*"

"What? On the M25?"

"*Not on the motorway, you nobhead. In Essex, last night. There was a pileup on the way back home this morning. Whole place was gridlocked.*"

I stared at my mobile in disbelief, deja-vu washing over me. There was always some sort of gridlock in Cecil's life, especially when he was supposed to be at any event I'd organised.

"So you went out last night? Great. I could've gone out too but I decided not to because I knew I had to be somewhere this morning. You only had to do one thing, Ces... get yourself here and yet again –"

1

"*Leave it out with the fucking lecture, geezer. I ain't in the mood for it right now. I'll be there. I ain't that far behind 'ya.*"

"So how long you going to be?" I asked, a tiny wave of optimism daring to suggest that he might only be ten minutes or so away.

"*Hour, hour 'n a quarter. Just getting to Waterloo. There's a train at –*"

"An hour and a quarter! You're joking, aren't you?" And then I realised he wasn't. "I'm not waiting, Ces. I've sorted the tickets and the hospitality, and I'm not standing outside Ascot Station like some sad-sack waiting for you when I could be in the enclosure enjoying a cool glass of champagne. I've paid out five hundred quid for this deal, half of which you still owe me by the way and –"

"*Chill, geezer. Leave the tickets at the gate. We'll catch 'ya there.*"

"What?"

"*I said, leave the tickets, mate and –*"

"No, I meant, who's we? You said 'we'"

"*Me, Jas and Carlos. The crew.*"

I hesitated as this new information sank in. "Sorry? Jas and Carlos? What are they… who said… you're with Jas and Carlos? Now?"

"*Yeah, mate. They fancied a day out with the boys.*"

I took a deep breath. Not only was Cecil late, but he had added another issue to the equation.

"Hang on, Ces, I've only got two tickets. I told you when I bought them there were only two left. How come you've got Jas and Carlos with you?"

"*Simple, ain't it. Was in Fad's last night before I did the old Essex mumble and invited 'em. They was up for it.*"

"But I just said, there are no more tickets. I got the last two for the hospitality deal."

"*Mate, we can blag a couple more.*"

My next deep breath was more of a desperate gulp for oxygen as I fought to clear the swarm of thoughts that had invaded my head. Around me, a steady stream of racegoers were making their way to the course, untroubled by nothing more than dreams of picking a winner or two, their enthusiastic chatter fuelling a sense of the excitement to come. I decided that I couldn't let Cecil's unexpected introduction of an additional complication ruin the day.

"Listen, Ces, it's great that the boys are coming down, but any blagging for tickets is your problem. If you get them in, we can all meet up for a beer, but I haven't paid all this money to waste the two tickets I have got. Make sure you tell them."

"*It's cool, geezer. They know the mumble. You go on ahead. Leave my ticket and we'll see 'ya in there. Yeah? No need to hang about for us.*"

I didn't share Cecil's confidence about acquiring tickets as easily as his 'blagging' reference suggested.

"You sure?"

"*Yeah, I just said, no prob. You go and get the party started. We'll catch up.*"

I checked my watch – almost eleven. There was no way Cecil could be at Ascot much before quarter past twelve if his timings were right. That was his problem, yet a sudden attack of guilt rooted me to the spot, especially now that I knew my friends were coming too.

"You okay with that? I mean, you'll find it all right?"

"*Geezer, its Ascot races. Half the country's going there. Not like we're on some expedition to the fucking Amazon rain forest is it?*"

"No, uh, I suppose not. Okay, first race is at one-fifteen. I'll find out where I can leave your ticket and text you. When you get there, just mention my name… Matthew Malarkey."

"*I know your name, nobhead.*"

I killed the call and contemplated how the day might change. Cecil's 'crew' were my friends, Carlos MacFadden and Jasper Kane. Carlos owned the bar that Cecil had been in the night before – MacFadden's, or Fad's as we knew it – and Jasper worked with me, his area of expertise being marketing, mine sales. Cecil, was my best friend, but a friend with attitude and a 'devil may care' approach to life. It was typical of him to spring a surprise. I didn't want to disappoint the other two guys, but their lack of tickets wasn't my problem. I dismissed all thoughts of how they might 'blag' it and headed off along the treelined hill that led to the racecourse. A bridge straddled the road to allow the crowd direct access. I made my way to the gates and approached a steward.

"Morning. Wonder if you can help. I've got two tickets but I want to leave one somewhere for my friend who's coming later. Where can I leave it?"

The steward smiled. "Let me have a look, sir." He reached out and took the tickets. He stared at them for a moment and then looked up, a frown creasing his forehead.

"These are for yesterday, sir?"

"Sorry?" I said, not quite comprehending the statement.

"You're a day late, sir. These are for the nineteenth. Today is the twentieth."

He handed them back. I grabbed them and stared at the date. The number began to blur in front of my eyes as the blood drained from my face. I staggered backwards and tried to focus.

"Are you all right, sir? You look a little pale."

I tried to respond but for some reason all I could do was focus on my admonishment of Cecil for being over an hour late.

"Sir? Do you want a seat?"

This time the steward's voice focussed my attention. "But I wanted Ladies Day. Today. This can't be right. What's the date?"

"I just told you, sir, it's the twentieth. It *is* Ladies Day, but your tickets are for Wednesday the nineteenth and today is Thursday."

"But I applied online. I'm sure I filled in the right date on the website." I reached into my pocket and pulled out the two blue lapel badges that I'd received with my tickets. I stared at the date in the frantic hope that somehow it would be the twentieth. It wasn't. I tried the desperate appeal approach. "Look, can't I use them today? They weren't used yesterday, so it's all the same, isn't it? Two more people isn't going to make much difference."

"I'm really sorry, sir. They're not valid today. Those are blue, today's badges are pink."

"But I've paid five hundred pounds for a hospitality package and I've got my mates... I mean, my mate coming. He'll go ballistic if we can't get in. Does it matter what colour they are?"

The steward shrugged. "I'd really love to help, sir, but we can't accept out of date tickets. I would suggest you call your hospitality company, see if they can do anything."

I turned and walked away, realising that it was futile to argue. It looked like Cecil wasn't the only one that needed to blag tickets. There had to be a solution. I called the hospitality company. They were understanding but said their venue was full for the day and in any case, they had no control over access to the course.

I had to think and think fast. A long expanse of black metal gates, with arched signs above indicating 'All Enclosures', separated me from the concourse in front of the grandstand. I stared at the crowd inside, eyeing their lapel badges, my mind in turmoil. Maybe the touts were an option, but I had never bought from a tout before and had no idea how much that would cost me. I already stood to lose five hundred pounds as well as disappoint Cecil who was expecting a day of partying. Maybe Cecil was my solution. I could just wait for him and see if we could blag four tickets. But I wasn't confident. And Cecil's use of the word 'blag' didn't make it sound like he had any intention of paying the going rate. Getting two on the cheap would be hard enough, let alone four. The other option was the ticket office if they had any left. But that would only get me in and I would lose out on the hospitality I had paid for.

I slipped the mobile back into my pocket and began to pace up and down, hoping the random to-ing and fro-ing would stimulate some positive decision making. It was probably the involuntary muttering that drew their attention, but on my third pass over the same bit of ground, I noticed that two girls were pointing in my direction. I hesitated, wondering why they were giggling. The taller of the two began to walk towards me, her spiked heels and tight skirt making her approach more difficult than it should have been. She reached into her bag and pulled out a pen.

"Can I have an autograph please?" she said, holding out her race programme and the pen.

I glanced over my shoulder, but it was clear she was speaking to me.

"Sorry?" I said. "My… my autograph. You want my autograph?"

"Yes. I know it's a bit cheeky with it being your time off and that, but my friend and I are huge fans." As she spoke, her friend sidled up alongside.

"Erm… I think there's some mistake," I said. "I'm not –"

"Your English is much better than when you're on television," the friend cut in.

"Television?"

"Yes, when you're interviewed after the match."

The match. My mind buzzed. What match? Interviewed? It was obvious they had the wrong person. I was about to explain this when I felt a tug on my right arm.

"Señor Cañizares. What are you doing out here? Come this way."

I responded to the tug and came face to face with a tall security guard.

"I… err, what am I… what d'you mean?"

"I'm one of the VIP area security team. I didn't realise you had arrived. I was just on the way to my break when I spotted you. You'll be mobbed if you stay out here."

And in that moment, I saw an opportunity, a way of solving my ticket dilemma. I knew I shouldn't entertain it, but what choice did I have?

"The VIP area? Err… yes… I was just waiting for my…" And then I remembered what the autograph hunter had said about my English. I had no idea who they thought I was, nor who Señor Cañizares was, but somehow I had to wing it. Señor Cañizares. Must be Spanish or South American or something. And an autograph request meant someone important. "Err… I wait for my… how you say? My team… my people, yes?" I said, trying to affect a foreign accent.

"They have their badges?"

"Badges, no. My… my friend has them… uh, has them… inside… in the VIP area. It's why I, uh… why I came outside but I forget their badges. Stupido, eh?"

The security guy glanced around. "Oh, I see. You've already been in?"

"Uh… yes, I… yes, I have."

"It's okay. Glad I caught you." He hesitated for a second. "Uhm, can I just say, I'm a big fan."

I smiled and said nothing. Best not to push it.

My lack of response focused him. "Your team. Give me their names. I can make sure they're escorted through." He pulled a two-way radio from his belt. I told him the names of my friends and he called them through. When he'd finished he said, "Now follow me before anyone else sees you. Oh, and it's best to wear your badge if you come out again."

I nodded. My thoughts were interrupted by a call from one of the girls.

"Can I get that autograph before you go, Ignacio?"

Ignacio. Señor Cañizares. I hesitated. The name sounded familiar when I put them together. I turned towards the two girls. It was a chance to find out who they thought I was.

"Err… yes. Sure. What you like me to write?"

"Your name please," said the shorter one.

"Oh, yes… of course. I mean, to who? To you two ladies? I write… what you say, my full name?"

The two giggled in unison. "Just say, to Becky and Debs, best wishes, Ignacio. That would be great," the taller girl said and handed me the programme and pen. "I'm Becky."

I began to scribble the message across the back of the programme along with an indecipherable scrawl that was meant to be a signature and hoped that they had never seen a copy of the real guy's autograph before.

"So, how you know me?" I asked, as I handed the programme back.

"Everyone knows you," Debs said as she checked the message. "You're always in the papers and on the telly."

"And I like Spanish football," Becky added.

Spanish football. I knew nothing about Spanish football but the name Ignacio Cañizares suddenly seemed familiar.

"I play in Spanish football? I mean, yes, err... sí, I play in Spanish football. You like?" I hoped that my feigned accent was working. Despite a recent trip to Ibiza, my knowledge of the language was at best, English tourist.

"Yes, my brother follows Madrid and we watch the matches on Sky."

The security guard beckoned towards me. "Señor Cañizares. We'd better go."

A moment of truth faced me. Ignacio Cañizares sounded big time. I'd heard the name, seen it in the media, but knew nothing about him. Plays for Madrid and regularly on television, according to the two girls. And I was about to steal his identity, even if only temporarily. Was it a step too far? I glanced at Becky and Debs. Their faces were filled with excitement at having met a superstar. They thought I was this famous footballer and so did the security guard. It could work.

"Señor Cañizares... please." The urgency in the guard's voice refocussed my thoughts.

I had to make a decision.

"Okay. My team, they come. You have the names, okay?" I dropped my out of date lapel badges into a nearby bin and followed him into the unknown.

2

The VIP area was filled with glamorous women, men in sharp suits and a team of staff ever present to top up champagne flutes and dish out canapés. Its main feature was a vast window running the full length of the room, from where guests had a spectacular view of the racecourse, its green strip of turf contrasting sharply with the long white rails that bordered its sides. To my left, a balcony that cast a long shadow over the crowd below was beginning to fill with hospitality guests in their racing finery, drinks in hand. Behind me, a bar stretched wall to wall, its seating areas as yet unoccupied.

I crossed the floor, trying to avoid eye contact with turning heads. I grabbed a glass of champagne from a tray and positioned myself in a corner. It was an ideal location from which to scan the room. It was almost full, an eclectic mix of people, some of whom I recognised from the media and some just there because they had the money to rub shoulders with VIPs. Once settled, I reached for my mobile and tapped out a text.

'Ces, you're not going to believe this. In the VIP area. Your names are on the door. 3 of you. Just go to the ticket office. Tell them who you are. If they say anything about an Ignacio Cañizares, just roll with it. I'll explain later. See you inside.'

Two minutes later, my phone buzzed.

'*nice one. knew ud sort it. b there in half hour.*'

For the next thirty minutes, I fended off the attentions of a number of my fellow guests, both male and female, the women being particularly attentive. Groups of waiting staff paced back and forth, champagne bottles poised, their aim it appeared, to ensure that no guest ever finished their drink. All except the most expensive champagnes and vintage wines were complimentary. And in those thirty minutes, I discovered the magnitude of what I had done. Ignacio Cañizares was a far bigger deal than I had realised, a multi-millionaire footballer with a price tag that matched his wealth. And yet I had barely heard of him, mainly because I had minimal interest in football and even less in Spanish football.

The free booze was helping to ease my tension, which had reached epic levels as I waited for backup. It had also helped me to perfect a Spanish accent that was now bordering on incoherent.

I was on my fourth glass when the lads arrived, each of them suited and booted. They had made an effort at least. Cecil approached, his hand outstretched, his gait more of a swagger than a walk.

"How you doing, geezer? You all right?"

I was still slightly irritated at Cecil so I didn't comment on his smart grey suit and open neck black shirt. "Just about. Glad to see you guys."

Jasper and Carlos followed behind. Jasper's grin told me what he was thinking.

"You seen the totty in here? How'd you pull that off, Matt?"

It was typical of Jasper to raise the subject of women straight away. Tall and good looking with a killer smile, an asset he could use to full effect when he chose to, he rarely had trouble getting the girl. His pale blue check suit, waistcoat and white shirt accentuated his early summer tan, an image that could only enhance his chances. I ignored his initial remark.

"You all get in okay?" I asked.

"Nae bother, Mateo," Carlos said. Carlos was the only one of the three with a tie, a red patterned design that stood out against his dark suit and pink shirt. It was knotted loosely so that it hung slightly to one side of the collar.

"Yeah, mate," Cecil said. "Just gave 'em our names like you said." He glanced around the room, a broad smile displaying his intent. "Let's get this party started then, boys."

"Lads, hold on, it isn't that simple," I said, aware that Cecil could blow my cover all too easily. "We need to keep a low profile. Just a nice quiet little drink in the corner and then we can watch some racing."

"Quiet drink? You having a laugh, geezer?" Cecil said, reaching out to grab a glass of champagne from a waiter's tray. "We got full hospitality, ain't we? Gotta get your money's worth.

Get on it, boys." Cecil's brash, egotistical, alpha male personality, his default position, was driving his mood.

Carlos and Jasper were not slow to react to Cecil's exhortation. Three glasses were raised in my direction. "Cheers, Matt."

I returned the salute half-heartedly, my mind still a long way off party mood, and said, "Guys, hang on a sec. Let me explain. The problem is we're not in the right venue. This is the VIP section. We're not really supposed to be in here. But without tickets…" I pointed at Jasper and Carlos. "I mean, without tickets for you two, it's the only option."

Cecil necked his champagne and asked, "So how'd you blag that, then?"

I paused while I contemplated the reality. "I didn't blag it. I was invited in. They've confused me with that Spanish footballer, Cañizares, and next thing I –"

"Cañizares?" Jasper said, his mouth dropping open. "Ignacio Cañizares? What, he's here?"

"No, they think I'm him."

"You know who he is, don't you?" Jasper responded. "Spain's number one striker, won the Ballon D'Or last year. There's talk of him going to Man United or Chelsea for over a hundred million. The papers are full of it. The bloke's on a couple of hundred grand a week at least."

I felt a clammy wetness creep across the palms of my hands as I absorbed Jasper's confirmation of Ignacio Cañizares's status, something I hadn't even considered when I made my decision to go with the security guard to the VIP area. Cecil interrupted my thoughts.

"Mate, even better. We'll get treated like rock stars. Might as well rinse it while we can. I've seen the geezer in the papers. He's married, ain't he, but always got some bird in tow? And there's plenty of hot chicks in here. Play it right and it could be a blinding little mumble."

"Yeah, now I think of it you do look a bit like him. Funny, I never spotted it before," Jasper added.

"A bit? A bit like him?" I waved a hand in a sweeping arc. "Everybody in here thinks I bloody am him. They keep staring at me."

"I wouldn't worry about that, mate. Half the people in here are hot looking chicks and it ain't no bad thing to have their attention," Cecil said.

A waiter approached with a tray of champagne. I grabbed a glass and took a huge gulp. Cecil and Jasper did the same, broad grins on their faces. Carlos had a more serious look.

"Boys, yer nae thinking. If they're expecting Ignacio Cañizares, either he's been in already or he's coming back. And he's not likely to have left before the racing starts, or why would he have bothered coming in the first place?"

"And?" Jasper said.

"No es complicado! If he –"

"Geezer, lose the foreign lingo and talk English, will'ya," Cecil cut in. "Don't take many glasses of the old bubbly to get you confused does it?"

Carlos had a habit of mixing his Scottish and Spanish roots when out drinking. Marginally shorter than Cecil and a good four inches shorter than Jasper, Carlos always gave as good as he got. His rotund physique and bald dome concealed a sharp, wise and sometimes abrasive personality. This time he simply scowled at Cecil and carried on.

"Listen, it's not complicated. If Cañizares is meant to be here then when he does get here or comes back, there's gonna be two of you." He pointed at me. "And he disnae wanna be here when he shows up."

The blood drained from my face. In my eagerness to find a way in, I had completely overlooked the possibility of the other guy showing up. My gut response was to make a fast exit but I realised that if I did that, we had nowhere else to go. And with no tickets I would have to come clean that I had screwed up on the date. In a scramble of confused thought, I stood rooted to the spot unable to utter a word.

"You all right, geezer?" Cecil's voice cut through my catatonic state.

"Uh… what?" I answered as I fought to comprehend Cecil's question.

"I said, are you okay? You're standing there like you just been hit by a death ray or something. You worrying about this footballer showing up?"

The word 'footballer' focused my thoughts.

"Yes, of course I bloody am. I've just blagged it in here by pretending to be one of the biggest football stars in the game, whose face is all over the papers and who could turn up any minute. Of course I'm frigging worried. What if I get arrested for impersonating a… a… footballer?"

Cecil and Jasper burst into howls of laughter.

"Don't be a nobhead," Cecil said. "There ain't no such offence. Worst happens, if they tumble who we really are, we get thrown out. Yeah? Who gives a toss? We still got tickets for the other venue, ain't we. We just need to blag these boys here a couple more and it's cool."

I took a deep breath. "It's all right saying that, Ces, but it's not that easy to find four tic… uh, two more tickets, is it?"

"Mate, you blagged it in here, didn't ya? Stop fucking worrying. Roll with it. We'll give it the old mumble, trust me. You're talking to me now, yeah?"

I glanced at Carlos and Jasper. Carlos rolled his eyes. Jasper shrugged. I turned back to Cecil.

"I'm just saying, Ces. Best be discreet, you know. Let's not draw too much attention to ourselves. That's all."

Cecil grinned. "I'm hearin'ya, geezer, but you gotta look the part. Behave like you're meant to be here, like that lot." He swept an arm through the air. "Plug yourself into their DNA, you with me?"

Kind of, but I wasn't comfortable.

Cecil sensed my apprehension. "You start giving out them nervous vibes, they gonna tumble'ya. And, mate, worst case, if we get our arses kicked outta here, let's make sure we've rinsed the freebies big time, first. They ain't gonna miss no booze in this place."

I swallowed hard as I considered Cecil's angle. Maximise the benefit of a lucky break in the VIP section, knowing there was the safety net of the other tickets if it all went pear shaped. But I didn't have the heart to tell him that there were no other tickets. And I had to get the two hundred and fifty pounds back that I had laid out for his ticket in the first place. The only way I could ask him for that was if he had the day out he was expecting.

"You listening to me, mate? We're wasting good drinking time here." Cecil's tone had taken on a note of urgency.

"Uh, yeah. Sorry, Ces. I was just, you know…"

"Mate, get a grip. I told'ya, stop worrying. You look like you could do with a livener." He turned to Jas and pointed to the bar. "C'mon, geezer. Let's get a round of shots. Get this party started and get a bit of life into this nobhead here."

There was no sense in trying to argue with Cecil when he was in party mood. He headed across the lounge in the direction of the bar, Jasper following in his wake.

3

It wasn't so much a sense of doom that had descended upon me. More an edgy apprehension, a nagging concern that if I didn't stay in the shadows and keep a low profile, something would go wrong. And I knew that Cecil was probably the wrong person to be with in a party atmosphere with free booze and good looking women. Subtle restraint was not his style.

I glanced at Carlos, hoping he could deliver some words that might calm my rising anxiety. He guessed what I was thinking but just shrugged and said, "You know what Cecil's like, Mateo. But he might have a point. You might be worrying a wee bit too much. Dinnae panic and see what happens. Go with the flow."

Don't bloody panic. Easier said than done when you are carrying a conundrum. The next voice, from behind, almost caused me to tip my champagne straight over Carlos.

"Ignacio. Good to see you. Remember me?"

My blank look inspired him to introduce himself.

"Rob Black... Daily Post. We talked after the Champions League Final in Rome."

The Post. The second last thing I needed, after Ignacio Cañizares himself, was a journalist. I shot a glance at Carlos. He narrowed his eyes and nodded, a signal I took to be part of the going with 'the flow' programme.

"Uh... yes, monsieur... I mean... err, Mister Rob... I see many people from your papers. But I... you know, how you say, sometimes I forget."

He slapped me heartily on the shoulder. "Understandable after that game. Great goal. But what a night. How did you feel?"

How did I feel? I'd not seen the game. I had no idea who played, let alone who won. Another glance at Carlos. He was displaying total ignorance, courtesy of a blank stare. I took a flier. Great goal must have meant a win.

"Err... you know, I felt good, incredibly happy. How you say in England? Over the moon... yes, over the moon. Big party after."

Rob Black frowned, then grimaced.

"Well, you looked pretty devastated after the game. A six one loss in a Champion's League Final is a bit of a crushing defeat."

Shit. Got that wrong then. I was saved from a scrabbling, confused response by Cecil's return.

"Get that down your neck, geezer," he said, as he handed me a small shot glass filled with something brown. "Cheers. Down in one, boys."

The pressure I felt made me want to relieve it. I necked the shot in unison with the lads. The instant hit caused a spasmodic facial reaction that did not go unnoticed by Rob Black. As I lowered the glass, I caught his quizzical look. I tried to form a sentence, but he got there first.

"So who're your friends?" he said, a smirk adding an undisguised disapproval to the final word.

"Err... Cecil is my... " I struggled for a description. If I was supposed to be an elite athlete, my entourage had to be credible. "... my... he's my nutritionist."

Rob Black's eyebrows did an uncoordinated shuffle that Cecil picked up on straight away.

"Yeah, mate. I look after his diet. Make sure he gets the right stuff at the right time. All about fluids, ain't it? Sometimes your top class sports stars gotta balance all that isotonic shit with something a bit more off the wall. That way the body can tell what the right intake is and can recognise the good from the bad. You load up on the good stuff all the time, your body got no way of knowing what's proper good. And then it starts rejecting the good stuff too. Bit like antibiotics. You stick a bit of the old toxic stuff in, and the body builds up immunity. Trust me, mate, this is revolutionary thinking. That's why my man's top of his game."

Rob Black stared at my empty shot glass and was about to ask a question, but Cecil beat him to it.

"Who the fuck are you anyway, geezer?"

Carlos provided the answer. "He's a journalist. Daily Post."

Jasper laughed. "A journalist? You boys like a drink. Fancy a shot? It's all gratis."

The shot had hit the spot, but the chemicals that drive anxiety were fighting for their place. I realised we had to lose Rob Black if I was going to carry off my deception for any length of time. And I couldn't afford any more of Cecil's rambling nutrition theories. Nor could I have Jasper plying him with drinks.

"Monsieur Black... err, I mean, Señor Black. I am sure you must be here because there are a lot of..." I turned to Carlos. "What is the English word for... famous?"

Carlos grimaced, and with that expression, I realised my error. Style it out.

"Of course... yes... famous. I think my English, it improve, you know."

Rob Black grinned. "So who are your friends? You got your nutritionist here but who are these guys?"

I didn't get a chance to respond and perhaps that was just as well.

"Mate, I know you got a job to do," Cecil said, "and asking questions is your mumble but..." There was only a momentary pause. "My client here's on his downtime. So, let's just chill, yeah, and give him some space."

Rob Black smiled. "Okay, but before I go, I gotta know who these guys are. I'm a journo. I like to know these things. Information comes in handy."

Cecil ran a hand through his thick head of hair. He nodded towards Jasper.

"This geezer's a personal trainer. Keeps our man toned and match ready." He turned towards Carlos and, unusually for Cecil's mental agility, a moment's hesitation occurred. Carlos noticed it.

"¿Qué pasa? Soy su representante."

Cecil shot a puzzled look at Carlos. "Do what?"

"I'm his agent."

"His agent. Yeah, the geezer's his agent."

In a haze of champagne and the instant shot, I was still trying to comprehend the entourage I had acquired when Rob Black directed another question straight at me.

"Right, so you have a new agent." He picked up a glass of champagne from a waiter's tray as he hovered near by. "What happened to José?"

"José? Err... uh... qué?"

"Yeah, that's it. José Aberquero? He was a nice guy. He looked after you."

"Uh, sí, but sometimes it is nice to switch... you know," I said, hoping Rob Black would change the subject. He did.

"Is this why you're going to Chelsea? Your new agent has some deal set up?"

Chelsea. In the fuzz that had clouded my head, I had decided that I was staying in Ascot and not going to Chelsea.

"Mate, he ain't going to Chelsea. Man U's gonna pay top dollar," Cecil chipped in.

Muffled laughter from behind Cecil quickly brought me some perspective. I shot a 'shut up' glance at Jasper and Carlos and pulled Cecil to one side.

"What did you say that for, Ces? That's only going to fuel his curiosity. I don't need that right now." Cecil seemed to be getting into the moment and that was dangerous. I needed low profile, not high profile, even though I was a temporary identity thief.

"Mate, gotta keep it real, ain't ya? If you're gonna pull off the mumble that you're some bigtime footballer, then you gotta cane it."

I didn't feel a need to cane anything and a sudden flurry of activity across the room near the entrance, confirmed that I should say as little as possible.

I tugged Cecil's jacket sleeve and hissed through gritted teeth.

"Shit. It's him."

"Who?"

"The... real... the proper Ignacio Cañizares. Bollocks."

His identity was unmistakeable. If I knew nothing about him before, I certainly had enough information to recognise him now. He was a total dead ringer for me. To add to the confusion, he was wearing a dark blue suit, similar to mine, and a white shirt, just as I was too. The only difference between us was our ties – his, plain yellow, mine, blue with a thin diagonal striped pattern.

Self preservation kicked in.

"Err, Señor monsieur Black, can I get you a... I mean, can we have a... a chat?" I grabbed Rob Black and spun him around so violently most of his champagne slopped over his shoes.

"Whoa, steady! What's going on?" he said, holding his glass out at an angle to avoid the slops.

Jasper caught the gist of what I was trying to do. "Yeah, Rob. Little chat, mate. Over there. Bit quieter. Could get an exclusive."

At the mention of 'exclusive', Rob Black's journalistic instinct kicked in. I pulled him towards a corner of the room where there was a large alcove on one side and a corridor that led towards the lavatories, on the other side. I had no idea what I was going to say. All I knew was that I had to get myself away from the real Ignacio Cañizares and get Rob Black out of the building before he ran into him and rumbled me. We ducked into the alcove and he turned to face me.

"So what's the story then?"

"Err… well, it's erm… how you say… hush-hush. I… err, can't tell you."

"What d'you mean you can't tell me? It's not a bloody story then, is it? You're not wasting my time are you?" His hard stare displayed his irritation.

"It's just that it's… " My mind scrambled for a word, as I tried to maintain the foreign accent. "Uh, secreto… I'm not to say something. You understand this, no?"

Rob Black smirked and drained the remnants of his glass.

"Look, I know I wrote that piece about you and that other woman, and I know that pissed your wife off, but it's all fair game. A bloke has to earn a living. So if this is some sort of windup to get your own back, I'm off. I got better things to be doing here." He turned to walk away.

I grabbed at his arm. "No, hang on, Señor Black. Wait… I, err, have a story, yes."

He turned back towards me.

"So?"

I glanced over his shoulder and beckoned to Jasper.

"Uh… just getting my nutrition… I mean, fitness trainer. Just… you know…"

Jasper approached. I needed assistance if I was going to get Rob Black off my case and out of the VIP suite.

"So… err, the story about Chelsea." I glanced at Jasper for reassurance. "It is no true."

Rob Black hesitated and then spoke. "And? Is that it? What's true then? You going to Old Trafford?"

"Old Trafford?" I looked at Jasper, who nodded. "Err… sí, Old Trafford."

"Yeah, Man United," Jasper said. "All that Chelsea talk's a red herring. It was never gonna happen."

Rob Black's eyes widened. He could sense an opportunity.

"What, straight up? A United move's a goer?"

His enthusiasm galvanised me. I could see a way of getting him out of the building.

"Straight up... I mean, for sure... err, sí. Manchester is expecting me but this news is no coming until, err... tomorrow."

"What, after your medical?"

"Medical? No, there is nothing wrong with me. I am fit and I –"

"Yes, after the medical," Jasper cut in. He nodded in my direction. "It's normal to have a medical before signing, you know that. These clubs can't take a risk where there's big money involved."

"What's the fee then?" Rob Black asked.

"Thousands... two, three thousand –" I said, but was cut off by Jasper before I could finish.

"Hundred and twenty million, give or take. Still negotiating." Jasper glanced at me. "It's his English... still learning the numbers. Listen, mate, if you want to be on an exclusive here, you better make yourself scarce before the other papers get wind of it. You've seen the speculation, haven't you... Chelsea, United? You want the headlines, right? Well, this is cast iron. Signing for United."

Rob Black loosened his tie. "Yeah... hundred and twenty mil you say?" He turned towards me. "Cheers. I owe you a favour."

I tried to hide the relief I felt that he was on his way. "You do. So no more write shit that upset my wife."

He winked, turned on his heel and headed at pace across the room, almost knocking Cecil over as he came towards us.

"What's that mug's hurry, lads?"

"It's nothing, Ces. We just wound him up with an exclusive story about our superstar here. Had to get him out of the building," Jasper said.

"Yes, but the real Ignacio Cañizares is my next problem," I added.

"Geezer, I wouldn't worry about him. Half the people out there will be seeing fucking double in an hour anyway, the way they're necking the old bubbles. C'mon, let's get out there and party."

"I'm staying here, Ces," I said.

Cecil face contorted into a look of sheer disbelief. "Geezer, you on fucking drugs? Staying here? What, hiding in an alcove all day? You're losing it, mate. There's booze on tap, birds getting pissed out there and there's bound to be a little tickle going on. But you wanna hide in a fucking corner? You paid two hundred and fifty quid for a ticket. Mate, walk in there like you own the place. You ain't no tourist. You gotta have attitude, ain't ya? You go out there like... I do this for a living, nobhead, what d'you do?"

"Yeah. Spot on," Jasper said.

I tried to dismiss Cecil's reference to the money but he was in full flow and hardly paused.

"And anyway, that footballer's got his hands full with some blinding bird. He ain't gonna be taking no notice of you. Worst case, if he sees ya, he's gonna think you're one of them dickhead lookalikes going through an identity crisis." He elbowed Jasper. "You should see the bangers on this one he's with."

"His missus?"

"Nah, mate. Trust me, that ain't his missus. He's all over her and she's loving it."

"Ain't his missus that supermodel?" Jasper said. "Some Italian girl. What was her name? Began with a... yeah, a C. She's big time. All over Hello magazine and that."

"Chiara. Chiara Rustichelli." The voice came from behind Cecil and Jasper. Carlos. I hadn't seen him approach. The two lads turned in unison.

"Yeah, spot on, mate," Cecil said. "How d'you know that stuff? I hadn't got you down as an'Hello reader... well, not with your fashion sense." He winked at Jasper.

Carlos ignored the jibe, knowing full well that Cecil was on another of his windups, something that often occurred between the two of them.

"How do I know this stuff? Simple. My two wee bar lassies, Hanka and Janka, read it and bring it in. They go on about what a beauty she is and what great clothes she's got. And, by the way, she just goes by her first name in the modelling industry. Chiara."

Jasper slapped Carlos on the back. "Bit of an expert then, mate."

Carlos grinned. "And I'll tell you another thing. That isnnae Chiara he's with," he said, revelling in his moment of expertise. "No, I've seen his wife's pictures and that's nae her."

"See, I told'ya, boys," Cecil cut in. "I got a nose for these things, ain't I? Anyway, listen, we gotta get back out there. We're wasting the day standing here and the races start soon." He turned to me. "You on it, mate? Just play it cool."

I took a deep breath. Cool was not my default position when there was a hint of trouble but I had no choice. I had to go with it.

"Okay, yeah. I'm good. Let's do it. But let's stay upwind of Ignacio Cañizares. I need to keep my distance."

"No problem, geezer. We'll keep over this side of the room. Anybody comes asking questions, Carlos can give it the old Spanish mumble and you say nothing. They'll just think you're a typical overpaid footballer, stuck up your own arse, yeah."

That wasn't how I'd envisaged my day and nor was it an image I felt comfortable with, but if it got me off the hook, then I had to play along.

4

We took a position on one side of a room that was now buzzing with activity. A sumptuous buffet had been set up on the opposite side, and the decibel level had gone up several notches as the guests indulged in more of the complimentary champagne, Pimms and other alcoholic beverages. A team of chefs were busying themselves behind an elaborate serving area, its bronze lighting rigs throwing a yellow hue across a variety of hot and cold dishes. Their tall white chef hats bobbed up and down in a puppet-like dance as they dished out the food. I hadn't noticed the service area when I'd entered, but then realised that a long, grey partition had been folded back to reveal its hidden secrets.

After twenty minutes or so I started to relax, the switch to Pimms, following several glasses of champagne, creating a carefree complacency. Jasper and Cecil were studying a race card. Carlos was studying the room. The occasional stares from several guests nearby had unnerved me at first, but then I realised their expressions of semi-recognition still required some confirmation from the celeb databases that occupied their heads. I was pleased they were racegoers and not a football crowd.

Despite the onset of complacency, I remembered to keep tabs on Ignacio Cañizares. The area was big enough to keep a considerable distance away from his party. He was near the main entrance, surrounded by a crowd, people who were quite clear about who he was. Two muscular, tanned blokes, their haircuts almost identical, shaved at the back and sides, save that one had a short ponytail, stood nearby scanning the immediate area. I realised they had to be part of Cañizares's protection team. Cañizares appeared relaxed, used to the attention. His female companion seemed happy and relaxed too.

And then things changed.

It was a sudden movement. And as he made it, I knew something was wrong. Cañizares's left hand shot out and grabbed the lady by the arm. He pulled her towards him, turned on his heel and dragged her to the far side of the room. His surprised entourage parted the ways, like traffic allowing an emergency vehicle through. When he reached the corner and could go no further, he stopped. The woman's expression had turned from utter surprise at the abruptness of the action, to sheer bewilderment. There followed some sort of intense exchange, punctuated by expressive hand gestures from both parties. Then the footballer turned to one of his protection team and appeared to whisper something to him. The guy looked back to where Cañizares had been earlier. I followed his gaze. Just a few metres away from where they had been standing, two women, dressed extravagantly even by the high standards of the rest of the clientele, had positioned themselves and were reaching for the champagne.

I glanced back at Cañizares. He was still very animated. His female companion equally so. He seemed to be trying to get a point across which she did not appear to understand. Alarm bells started to go off in my head. Something wasn't right. Then he moved away from the woman and began to walk across the room. In my direction.

I nudged Carlos.

"I'm just going... going to... the gents. Can you keep an eye on my drink?"

I turned abruptly and collided with a guest carrying a glass of Pimms. I stuck out a hand in a protective reaction and managed to flick the straw straight out of the glass. It somersaulted twice and landed in her cleavage. She stepped back in surprise, her sudden movement loosening her grip on the drink, which tipped forward splashing my shoes and the lower part of my suit trousers.

"I'm so sorry," I said. I grabbed the straw and stuck it back into her glass.

Her reaction was a momentary wide-eyed gaze that eventually cracked into a smile.

"Don't worry, darling," she said. "Accidents will happen. I admire your dexterity though. If it hadn't dribbled into my tits, I might never have known the straw left my drink." Her accent was cut glass English.

"I, uh... didn't see you," I said, feeling the flush rise from my neck.

"You didn't see me? In this dress? Darling, you disappoint me. I'm wearing it to be noticed."

She had a point. The dress was crimson with thin black edging on the sleeves and a neckline that plunged to her impressive cleavage. The outfit was complemented by a black lacy hat that somehow stayed attached despite its acute angle.

I glanced over my right shoulder and spotted Ignacio Cañizares standing just a few metres from Carlos. It was too close for comfort.

"Err, can I get you another drink," I asked the lady.

She smiled, a gleaming whiteness emphasised by the redness of her lipstick. "No, need. There's plenty more where that came from. I'm Arabella by the way." She held out an elegantly manicured hand. "And you are?"

"Uh… err, I'm Matt… Ig…" I hesitated, unsure of who I was supposed to be at that moment.

"Mattig? Is that Swedish or something?"

"Swedish? Err… no. It's… look, can I catch up a bit later. I have to… you know. The little boys' room." I pointed to my trousers. "I need to, uh… clean up."

I didn't wait for a response. I made my way towards the corridor where I had sheltered in the alcove. The lavatories were at the end. I hurried straight ahead without a backward glance. Once inside I stood still, hands on one of the sinks, leaning towards the taps, and took several deep breaths. On one side of the sink there was an array of toiletries – aftershave, hand cream, moisturisers, body sprays – and on the other side, a dispenser filled with tissues. I took one out and wiped the perspiration from my forehead. Then I splashed some cold water on my face and dabbed it off with another tissue. I breathed in deeply again, trying to calm my racing heart. The quiet of my surroundings and the deep breathing began to restore some calm. I raised my head and stared at the reflection looking back at me. My face was tight, eyes filled with some sort of dread. I started talking to the image.

"Get a grip, Matthew Malarkey. You can't hide in here all day. It's madness. You have to get back out there. Style it out. What's the worst that can happen?"

And then the worst did happen.

5

The worst happened in the shape of Ignacio Cañizares. At first, I didn't react to the door being flung open. I was too engrossed in giving a pep talk to my mirrored reflection. It was only when I become aware of a presence to my left that I looked up. And in that moment, I thought the mirror had moved with me. Standing stock-still, a look of shock on his face, was the famous footballer that I had been trying to avoid. His expression was even more surprised looking than mine. At least I had seen him across the room and knew what to expect. He had never seen me in his life.

I spoke first. "Hello." It was all I could think of.

"Hola." His reply was hesitant.

"I'm Matthew," I said. "You're the, err, footballer."

He tilted his head and furrowed his brow as he examined me up and down. "Sí, I am the footballer. ¿Y vosotros quiénes sois?"

"Err, sorry, no speak… I don't speak… erm, Español."

"Okay. I say, who are you?"

"Oh… err, as I said, I'm Matthew. Matthew Malarkey. A… a guest today."

"But. I no understand, you dressed as me… like me. Is it you are a… how is it, en inglés… sí, a like looker, no? I see them in Spain. They try to be in television."

"A like looker? Oh, you mean a lookalike." I laughed, anxious to distance myself from any masquerade and to cover my increasing nervousness. "No, it's coincidence. We just look a bit like each other, that's all. I'm nobody. Just a… as I say, a guest here."

"What is this… cocidence?"

"Coincidence. It's when two things happen by chance, accidentally, just luck, I suppose."

Cañizares grinned. "Ah, sí! Luck. Yes, I understand luck. We need at races."

"Uh, yes, we do. I hope you'll be lucky today."

He reached out and took my hand. "You also, amigo."

A nice normal guy it seemed, no airs and graces, no bigtime superstar. He moved to the urinals. I turned to walk away, a sense of relief that our encounter had turned out far better than I'd expected. He'd taken it in his stride. I felt confident that he wouldn't point me out to his entourage. I had just reached the door when I heard a call.

"Excuse. Señor Matthew."

I turned around. Cañizares was standing facing the urinal.

"I see you have no… how is it you say? Uh, no badge," he said over his shoulder. The people here have race badge, but no you. You, like me? You no wear because you are like famous person too? Sí?"

I felt the blood rush to my face. A quick scan through my memory completed the picture. Most, if not all the guests I had encountered, had the pink venue badge either on their lapels or attached in one way or another to their outfits. I had none. The ones I had brought with me were out of date and anyway, they were now in a bin.

My silence seemed to confirm what Cañizares was thinking. He smiled. "So perhaps you make mistake?"

"Mistake?"

"Sí. You go somewhere else in races but make mistake and you come here?"

I understood what he was getting at even if he hadn't put it very fluently. "Uh… yes, a bit. A mix up… with my badges, so they told me to come in here," I said, hoping that would be the end of it.

"Mix up? What is this mix up."

"Mix up… it's like a mistake… as you said. But all okay now." I smiled and turned to leave again.

"Señor Matthew, you do the like look… uh, how you said… the looker like, sí?"

"Erm… sort of."

"You do this looker like because you look like me, so you come here? Is this it?"

I swallowed hard, the feeling that I was about to be rumbled returning. "Err… no. The stewards told me and my friends to come in," I said, which was true, even though I had known the reason for their invitation. "I wasn't trying to be a lookalike, no."

He smiled at my response and then said, "You know, I have a little problema. I think you can help me, sí?"

I could see a trade coming. And I felt I would have to run with it.

"A problema?" I said.

"Sí, un problema. My wife she come here. I no expect –"

"Your wife?"

"Sí. I no expect this. She go on the fashion shoot in New York, so I no think she here. I think she is to be one day more." He zipped up and turned to face me. "She know I go races. Today she come here, and my business manager. They must want for to surprise me. ¿Entiendes?"

"Err, yes."

"But I have this lady who I come with today. She is, how you say it here? A girlfriend. She a television newswoman in my country. But my wife she will no understand, so it is a trick, you know… delicado."

"Tricky," I said, trying to be helpful.

"Ah, trick-ee. Sí. You know, two women, they will no be friends. My wife, she is Italiano. A hot woman. Apasionado, you understand?"

"You mean, passionate, maybe?"

"Sí."

I felt the question hanging in the air, but I had to ask it, even though I had a sense of the inevitable. "So how can I help?"

He smiled and walked towards the sinks, pushed a tap and hit the soap dispenser lever. Then he immersed both hands in the running water before answering.

"We can do the favour for each of us. You help me with problema, I say nothing about you in here, in this wrong place. Is good?"

It was neither good nor bad. It was just where I found myself. I glared at him for a moment and then nodded.

"So you go with my friend. She no understand that is not me. I take my wife and my business manager to somewhere else in the race. I get in all VIP places. Then no problema."

I gulped as the enormity of what he was asking sank in. "You mean you want me to pretend to be you with your girlfriend?"

He nodded. "Sí. Her name is Lorena. You do this and you show her a good day."

"Show her a good day? I don't even speak Spanish. How can I do that?"

"Is easy. You say you must speak en inglés. English, no? Is good because you in England. She like to speak English. She is good... speaker. She work in news, so... ella habla mucho en inglés."

Easy. It didn't seem that easy. 'Mucho en inglés' gave me hope.

"But she's bound to guess." I saw his quizzical look. "She'll guess... err, understand that I am not you." I noted too that Cañizares had a slightly deeper tone to his voice than I had. "And when I speak, she'll know."

Cañizares removed his hands from the sink and shook off the excess water. Then he dropped them into a mechanical hand-dryer that immediately roared into life like a jet engine. He raised his voice above the noise.

"Why is this? You look like me. It make me a fool when I see you and –"

"Fooled, you mean. It fooled you."

"Sí. I am the fool. So if I am the fool, then Lorena is fool too when she see you. Then you speak in the English, make bad, like me. Is easy. I no with her long time like my wife. Maybe one year. She not know... what you say... too much how I am still. Easy for you to be me, so."

A year seemed long enough to get familiar with someone, but I ignored it. And then I thought of something else. "But what about your bodyguards?"

"Bodyguards?"

"Your men." I pointed to the back of my head and tried to indicate a ponytail. "They could be a problem."

Cañizares laughed. "No, no problema. They do what I say."

He seemed to have everything covered even if he was concocting it on the spur of the moment. It struck me that he must be used to covering his backside, but then I assumed you had to if you were conducting an affair.

I should have walked away at that point, taken the hit, but I didn't want to let the boys down. If Cañizares was convinced by my look, then it should be possible to convince others. I probably wouldn't have to spend too much time with the girlfriend, I reasoned. She'd be focussed on the races, and if Cañizares tipped off his bodyguards, they'd be back up. If I didn't agree, I'd be kicked out with no other option. It was worth a gamble to save the day.

"Okay, but one thing though," I said. "You must try to speak English too... to everybody. Even if you do go somewhere else on the course."

He looked puzzled. "Why is this?"

"Because it's busy, lots of people here. They move around. If they speak to you and you speak Spanish, and then to me, it will seem odd if I speak English. So it makes sense if we both speak the same... hablo... err, hablar... in English. It's consistent."

"Consistent?"

"Yes. Look, don't worry. Trust me." I hoped he understood.

He pulled his hands from the dryer and rubbed them together. "Okay. What you say is good. And now, I give you five thousand English pounds for the, uh... horse."

"Sorry? For the horse?"

"Sí. For the horse... apostar. You know, you make the money for the horse, and you get more money."

"Oh, you mean gamble. Bet?"

"Sí, bet. My friend like to see money."

I swallowed hard. Five grand. But Cañizares hadn't finished.

"You do this good, and then I also take you to Madrid for weekend to watch match. You and tus amigos, sí? You fly to Spain, you go to top star hotel, and I give ten thousand euros for spend. You are my, uh... what you said? Like you are here?"

For a moment I was confused, the whole offer taking me into deeper territory. But if I was in, I had to be in properly. "You mean, a guest. We would be your guests?"

"Sí, at my cost. Okay? You will help with my problema?"

I had second thoughts. "Err... wait. Why don't you just leave with your friend? Avoid this problem."

"Is no possible. Lorena will no be happy. She look ahead for this big day. And my wife, Chiara, she make a surprise. We meet on end of week in Madrid, but now she here. She know I go to races today. If I not here she think I make story and get superstitious and –"

"Suspicious."

"Sí. Is what I say. She want to catch me. The papers, they make big story and picture. I must take care. Divorce, a lot of money. And the girl, Lorena, I like. If I leave before races, she think something, how you say… funny."

"Does she know your wife is here?"

"No, she no see her. I pull her away. I tell her that some people I no want to see come in. I was a bit hard… me entró el pánico."

I took a guess. "You panicked?"

"Sí. Lorena was mad with me but if she see Chiara, this make big problema. I no lose one if I no need. So you help me, you have good day here too with tus amigos."

Although he emphasised the last sentence with a smile, I felt the underlying threat. So I nodded. He smiled again, this time at my acceptance, reached into an inside pocket and pulled out four wads of banknotes, each one neatly held in a metal clip. He pulled the clip off one and handed me the cash.

"Five thousand English pounds. No matter if you lose. You… how is it? Entertainment… entertain Lorena."

I took the cash and put it straight into my pocket. And I had a question.

"Are you having a transfer to Manchester United or Chelsea? I need to know these things if I am to pretend to be you."

He laughed. "No, I no come to play in England. I stay in Spain. New contract with Madrid. Chiara no like the weather in England. Cold in London. Rain in Manchester."

The thought of Rob Black's exclusive flashed through my mind. But that was tomorrow. I had today to worry about. My impromptu business with Cañizares was done. I reached out to shake his hand, a gesture of agreement rather than any friendship.

"We have deal?" Cañizares said, his eyes fixed on mine.

"Yeah. Okay." I pointed at the sink. "Maybe we should use some of that," I said.

Cañizares looked around. "What is this mean?"

"The aftershave… err… perfume." I patted my face with both hands and then squeezed my nose. "So we smell the same, sí?"

"Ah, sí. Is good idea."

I picked up the aftershave bottle and sprayed a couple of light bursts either side of my face. Cañizares did the same. "It is no my… my, uh, normally perfume," he said.

"Normal. Maybe not but it smells like a good brand." And then something else occurred to me.

"Your tie."

"My tie?"

I pointed at the yellow tie Cañizares had on. "Yes, I need it. Take it off."

He looked surprised but said nothing.

"If your friend Lerona has seen –"

"Lorena."

"Err, sorry, Lorena. If Lorena has seen you with that tie, then I should wear it. We need to do this properly."

He winked as he realised what I meant, undid the tie and handed it over. I pulled off my blue tie, put it in my pocket and replaced it with Cañizares's yellow one. I turned to look in the mirror.

"How, do I look?"

"Perfecto, mi amigo," Cañizares said. "But you must clean your suit. You spill on it."

"Err, yes. Just Pimms… a drink. It will clean up."

"And you have pepino on your shoe."

"Pepino?" I looked down. A piece of cucumber was stuck firmly to the top of my right shoe. "Err… it's…uh… for luck."

6

Back in the main room, I sought out the lads. I made a beeline for Carlos. I found him studying a race card, a pen poised, marking off his selections. I tapped him on the shoulder.

"I'm going to need you, mate. Don't ask too many questions right now but stick close. You may need to do some translating."

"Nae problem, Mateo."

"And not into Scottish either."

"What?"

"Oh, nothing. Sorry. I'm just a bit edgy, that's all."

Cecil approached with what looked like a JD and coke in one hand.

"Got a blinding tip in the first race, geezer. War Envoy, two to one. Get on it, large." He stared at me for a second. "Where'd you get that naff tie?"

"Don't ask, Ces." From the corner of my eye, I caught a glimpse of Lorena in the same place that Cañizares had left her. She was chatting with the two bodyguards. And I had to blag not only Lorena but them as well. I grabbed a Pimms and then pulled Cecil to one side. It was time to unload the whole story.

And I did. The meeting with Cañizares and the fact that I had screwed up with the tickets. When I'd finished, he ran a hand through his thick head of 'Irish' hair – his term because it was so luxurious – and looked me squarely in the eyes.

"So that's your mumble, geezer. That's why you bin acting like a nobhead. Why didn't you just spill the juice from the offski? I'm your mate. I'm the geezer what looks out for'ya. So you fucked up on the tickets. It ain't an issue."

I breathed a sigh of relief. A weight lifted. At last, I could relax. A problem solved just by being straight.

"But, mate, we're in here now and we're staying in, yeah? So we still gotta blag it. Nothing's changed. Well, nothing that is except you just bin given five kay by one of the world's top footballers and told to do the old mumble with his bit on the side."

The mumble with his bit on the side. The words caused the pit of my stomach to churn like an overloaded cement mixer, and my moment of relief took an accelerated plummet towards the bottom of my emotional roller coaster. Cecil's summing up confirmed there was no significant change in our basic ticket situation.

"And, mate, you can't screw it up. It's a win-win. We're here, and you get this right, we got a blinding rock star trip to Madrid."

The cement mixer churned again. I scanned the room. Lorena, champagne in hand, was still in situ and full gesticulating chat mode. But I couldn't see Chiara. A positive sign. That could only mean that Cañizares had whisked her away as he had suggested he would. I knew I would have to make my move soon. I slugged half the Pimms and asked a question.

"Ces, if I'm going to pull this off I need a plan. How am I going to keep his woman's attention? She's bound to rumble me."

Cecil grinned and took a hit on the JD.

"Mate, it's simple with women, ain't it. You're either in or you're out. And this football geezer's in, on two counts. He's got his missus *and* his bit on the side. A geezer needs a bird that worships him. It's that or nothing, yeah?"

"I suppose, but how does that help me right now?"

"Listen, you're going in on the upside. I told'ya. His girlfriend's here, even though she knows he's married. That tells me she worships him and he can't do no wrong. You go over there with a bit of swagger. You're the daddy. Flash a bit of that cash, give it the old alpha male mumble, and it's a piece of piss. She'll probably wanna shag'ya by the last race."

I ignored Cecil's final remark. I downed the last of the Pimms and hoicked another off a passing tray.

"I'll give it a go, Ces. For you and the lads. But I don't feel right. I mean, what if I screw up? I know nothing about his wife. Suppose the girlfriend starts asking questions about the marriage. Like, has he told her he's leaving Chiara, for example? I messed up once already with that reporter. I told him I... Cañizares, was joining Man United and it turns out that's not happening. He's signed a new deal with Madrid. I'm operating in the dark. I could screw up both his relationships and his career if I say the wrong thing."

Cecil beckoned to Jasper, who was hovering close to a couple of girls who seemed in an exuberant mood. He held up four fingers and mouthed something that I took to mean 'shots.' He turned back to me.

"For fuck's sake, geezer. What's with the analysis paralysis stuff? You know the old saying, yeah? Careful where you put your dick and your signature. If matey boy's shagging around, that's his issue. You worrying about a multi-millionaire that earns enough in a week to feed and clothe a village in Africa for a frigging year? You can't do nothing that he ain't got an army of lawyers to sort out and make him come out smelling of roses. Trust me, as long as that nobhead can kick a bag of air into a fucking net and sell overpriced shirts to mug punters, he can do no wrong."

"Okay, okay. But remember I'm pretending, pretending to be him. Pretending to be something I'm not. It won't be easy to carry it off. And on top of that, he's got his own personal bodyguards here. They'll take some fooling. They must watch him all the time, know his every move."

"Ain't he told them what's going on?"

"No idea, Ces. He didn't say. Just that it wasn't a problem. It's the girlfriend I'm worried about though."

Cecil shrugged, his accompanying expression revealing a hint of frustration. "Look, you just told me, the man himself thinks you're him. If you convinced him, and trust me, you did 'cos he just give'ya five large, you ain't got no problem with the girlfriend. And as for his protection, don't worry about them goons. If he's got any sense he'll have tipped 'em off. Bottom line is they're paid to do as they're told and keep their mouths shut. They ain't gonna bother'ya. They'll just see what's in front of 'em and that's the geezer what pays their wages."

Jasper appeared with four shots of dark liquid. He handed us one each, and the four of us raised them into the air in a symbolic pyramid.

"Cheers." Jasper led the ritual.

"No... ¡salud!" Carlos said. "Our man here's meant to be Spanish."

By then I didn't care what nationality I was. The task was way out of my comfort zone, alien and unnatural. The shot hit the cement mixer, and it churned once more.

7

I straightened my jacket, thrust out my chest alpha male style, and braced myself for the walk across to Lorena. I had made four metres of floor space when I felt a tug on my left arm.

"Ciao, tesoro mio. Come stai? Felice di vederti. Sei sorpreso di vedermi?"

I turned and came face to face with Chiara Rustichelli.

My expression may have answered her question, but I had no way of knowing. She laughed, a fulsome, hearty sound that indicated a passion for life. Up close, she was beautiful, her cheekbones highlighted just enough to emphasise their prominence, her lips full, and a natural pout that added intrigue to her dark eyes.

The whole impact threw me.

"Err... hola. Hello! Uh, we speaka de... inglés," I said, dropping into a deeper tone, trying to follow Cañizares's advice about fooling his girlfriend and hoping the same would work on his wife. And then I remembered that his wife was Italian. I hardly understood a word of Spanish and I was way out of my depth with Italian. "Yes... I mean, sí... we speak the... err, English. When in England we must try. One day, I play here, maybe."

Chiara frowned. "That is no happening. Maybe Italia, no England." She smiled. "But I no mind we speak English. I practice in America. She hooked her right hand into the crook of my elbow and kissed my face. "Mmm... you smell good. I like. No your usual?"

"Uh, no. Err, I try new one."

Chiara laughed and said, "Okay, but I ask if you surprised to see me, sweetheart?"

"Err, sí … I know. Sí… yes, very surprised. I thought you were in…" I struggled to recall what Cañizares had said. "… in, err… Yorkshire."

"York sher?" A puzzled frown clouded her good looks. "New York. Where is this York sher?"

"Yes, I mean New York. Err, difficult sometimes with the language."

"You look surprised, but you are pleased I am here, yes?"

"Erm… yes, of course, Señorita… I mean, uh… darling."

"So no kiss for me, Ignacio?"

Kiss. A man who hasn't seen his wife for a while would kiss her. I had to try to be natural. I leaned forward to kiss her cheek as she had done mine, but she met me head on with a full pout and a long, sensual kiss on the lips, her lipstick leaving a lingering hint of soft summer berries. Momentarily flummoxed, I didn't resist the slight tug that pulled me in the direction of a small bar area on one side of the room. I cast a furtive glance towards Lorena and knew that any plans that Ignacio Cañizares had in mind, now had to be very fluid. Clearly, he had not found Chiara after we had parted company.

As we made our way into the bar, Chiara directed me towards a table where the woman I had seen her enter the room with, sat fiddling with the label on a bottle of Chianti that was positioned between two glasses.

Chiara went to speak, but I had the presence of mind to anticipate the outcome.

"No, we speak English. I have a big deal here maybe. Manchester United are interested."

Chiara unhooked her arm, a frown crossing her brow. "I said, no England. We are not going to Manchester. It rains. It always rains. You know this."

Her English was surprisingly fluent when she wanted it to be.

"Well, maybe Chelsea. It's... south. Sunnier. London. Err, great shopping."

"Shopping! I shop in Milano. I don't need London."

"Hey, you two. Arrête. No arguments." The woman at the table got to her feet. Her accent had a distinct French intonation. She looked into my eyes, her gaze quite startling.

"Bonjour, Ignacio. You surprised to see me?" She kissed me on either cheek.

I smiled at her, trying to feign recognition. She was an attractive woman too but in a more petite sort of way. Everything about her seemed delicate and refined. I wondered if she was the business manager that Cañizares had mentioned but she seemed too glamourous to be associated with anything as mundane. She had to be a model too.

"Uh, yeah. Err... nice to see... a nice surprise." I was trying to keep a grip. I was in the pool. Too late to back out. If there were sharks, I would have to deal with them.

Chiara reached for one of the glasses. "Sit down, relax, my darling," she said to me. She held the glass out. "We need more wine, Huguette."

I noted the name. To play this effectively, I would need to remember names.

Huguette poured two glasses of Chianti and with a flick of her slender fingers conjured up a third glass, which she filled. She passed it to me and raised hers. "Santé!"

I smiled and took a sip of the dark red liquid. As I placed the glass back on the table, I caught a glimpse of Ignacio Cañizares in my peripheral vision. Immediately I leaned forward to block Chiara's direct view behind. He hesitated as he crossed the room, taking in the scene to his left where I sat with his wife. I hoped that he didn't think I had screwed up. But his hesitation was only momentary. He could not afford to be spotted by Chiara, and his plan had to be fluid. He made his mind up, and I watched as he headed towards Lorena. After a brief exchange of words, they made their way towards an exit that led onto a balcony. And that meant I was stuck with his wife, the woman who probably knew him better than anyone. I still had the same role to play whether it was with the wife or the girlfriend, but somehow I figured that it would have to be more of a performance with the wife.

"Excuse me, ladies," I said. "A moment. My... my agent. A quick word."

I left the table and began to look for the lads. I found them by the main bar, each staring at a TV monitor that was churning out the odds on the first race. Cecil saw my approach.

"Mate, how's it going? I see you're with the missus then. And by the looks of that lipstick round your face you ain't doing bad."

I wiped my hand across my mouth.

"Thought you was s'posed to be blagging the girlfriend?" Cecil continued.

"I had no choice, Ces. She ambushed me. Cañizares has gone off with the girlfriend. The plan's changed." I nodded at Jasper. "Jas, I'm going to need a favour here, mate. Cañizares said he'd take his wife somewhere else on the course, but now I reckon he's taken the girlfriend there. He won't have left as he knows they both want the day out and he can't take either of them away without raising suspicions. I need you to keep tabs on him. I know it's a pain, but if I can get a swop round with him so I'm with the girlfriend then –"

"You wife swapping already, geezer," Cecil snorted.

"Look, if I'm going to do this right I got more chance with the girlfriend. That was what was supposed to happen. The wife's no mug. And she's with a friend who knows me... him, too."

Jasper patted me on the shoulder. "Done, Matt. I'll keep an eye out, do a bit of wandering about and if I see him, I'll have a word. No bad thing to have a wander. Plenty of nice chicks out there."

"Great, thanks, Jas. He went out the balcony door, the one to the right. Look, I'd better get back. Catch you bit later, boys."

"Hang on, mate. Before you go, you holding?" Cecil asked.

"Holding?"

"Yeah, moolah. First race starts in a minute and I ain't had a chance to get to a cashpoint. I need a monkey."

I let out a sharp breath. "Ces, I haven't been either. I was expecting to pick up two hundred and fifty quid from you for the ticket. I've got no cash either."

"Yeah you have. The footballer give'ya five large. I'm only after five hundred. I'll give it back later. And you kind of owe me, geezer."

"Owe you?"

"Yeah, for the ticket."

I scratched my head. "What, I owe *you* for the ticket? How come?"

"Well 'cos you didn't come through with any ticket, did'ya? And then you was trying to charge me two fifty for something you ain't got. I mean, mate, some people would call that extortion."

If I hadn't felt so stressed, I might have laughed at Cecil's logic. "Ces, I laid out for your ticket. Okay, I screwed up and got it wrong, but I don't understand how that means I have to give you the money when it hasn't cost you a red cent. And in any case, I got you in here, and now I'm having to perform like some undercover secret agent just to make sure we stay here. And as for the cash I do have, that's not mine. It belongs to Cañizares. I can't go giving it away. It's for bets."

"Kinda the same thing," Carlos cut in.

"Geezer, I'm only asking for a loan. I'll get to a cash point later on. First race is a dead cert."

I had lost the will to argue. I had to get back to Chiara. I really didn't want her wandering around looking for me and then running into her husband and his girlfriend. I reached into my pocket and pulled out the cash. Jasper let out a slow whistle. I peeled off ten fifty pound notes and handed them to Cecil.

"There you go, but I want it back. Okay?"

Cecil's response was a grin and a wink. I turned and headed back across the room where I found Chiara and Huguette deep in conversation. As I approached, Chiara reached out and took my hand.

"Darling, I was just telling Huguette about your tattoo. Why don't you –"

"My tattoo?" I pulled my hand away rather more abruptly than I'd intended.

A frown played across Chiara's forehead. "Yes, that you had done in Milano recently. Show Huguette. She want to see it."

Huguette nodded.

"Err... I can't."

"You can't? Non è una cosa di cui ci si debba vergognare."

"Sorry? English, please."

"I said, it's nothing to be ashamed of. You are just showing your love for me. It is why you have it."

"I'm not… not ashamed. No... it's the... the err... the dress code here. You can't take your trousers off in the bar."

"Your trousers?" Chiara laughed out loud. "Why you want to take your trousers off? You must mean jacket. Your English is not so good."

And at that moment I realised I had no idea where this tattoo was supposed to be.

"Err… yes, jacket. Yes, I mean jacket. No trousers. No-one should take their trousers off in the bar. I would definitely be thrown out for that."

"So, you take your jacket off and roll your sleeve up." She tugged at my jacket.

"What about the dress code?"

"You not be thrown out for taking your jacket off." Chiara was not to be deterred.

Other than fainting or setting fire to the bar, neither a credible option, I couldn't think of a get out. I took my jacket off and began to roll up my right sleeve while frantically scouring my brain for a reason why I had no tattoo.

"The other arm. What is wrong with you today?"

And then I caught a glimpse of a TV monitor showing racehorses parading back and forth behind the starting stalls as their handlers began the loading process.

"Wait." I grabbed my jacket. "The first race. It's going to start. I have to bet. I'll be back."

I paced across the room towards a row of betting desks in the corner. Cecil and Carlos were already there.

"What was that horse in the first?" I said to no one in particular.

"War Envoy," Cecil said. "You getting on it?"

"Yep, got to place some bets for the footballer's girlfriend."

"Thought you was with the missus?"

"I am, but I have to lose her right now and find the other girl. And I need a distraction. Where's Jasper?"

"He's outside somewhere. Said he was away to look for the footballer and the lassie, like you asked," Carlos said.

"Can I help you, sir?"

I turned to see the smiling face of one of the betting desk cashiers. Her name badge said 'Wendy.'

"Err, yes. A grand... I mean, a thousand on number four to win, please."

"You sticking a bag on it, geezer? Nice one," Cecil said.

Wendy took my money and ran a slip of paper through a machine. Then she handed the paper to me with a smile.

"Good luck, sir."

"Oh, thanks." I checked the slip and noted, War Envoy, one thousand pounds to win. I turned back to the lads. "Has he found them yet? Has Jas been back?"

"Not yet. What's the panic?" Cecil asked.

"The panic is the wife thinks I've got a tattoo. Seems the husband had something done in Milan, something special by the sound of it and she wants to show it off to her French friend."

"What's she like?"

"What's who like?"

"The French friend. I could come over there and give it the old mumble. Be your wingman. Let you concentrate on the missus."

I glared at Cecil. "I don't want to concentrate on the bloody missus. I'm not trying to get off with her, am I? And I don't want you over there making things more complicated than they already are. Are you not getting this, Ces? We're in here because I'm impersonating this woman's husband. I've done a deal with him to stop him getting in the shit and keep him from blowing our cover and messing up the whole day. Remember? And it's gone too far now to back out."

"All right, geezer. Chill."

"Chill? Easy for you to say that. The wife's expecting to see a tattoo on my arm and I haven't even got a tattoo, let alone the one she's expecting to see. So the whole things goes down the pan unless I can find matey boy and get him to roll up his sleeve."

Cecil flicked his hair back with a brush of his right hand. "Just blag it, mate."

"Blag it? How do you blag a frigging tattoo, Ces? You either have one or you don't. I can hardly tell her it must have faded and disappeared, can I?"

"Mate, you'll think of something." His eyes flicked towards a television screen. "Hang on, the race is off. Shut it for a minute. I wanna see this."

From my right, a loud cheer had gone up as the first race of the day started. All heads were focussed either directly on the course below the stand or the numerous television monitors around the room. In the distance, the horses tracked around a bend, grouped tightly in a pack. As they came out of the turn, the pack started to lengthen as the frontrunners stretched the field. Coming round into the straight, a clutch of six horses had put some daylight between themselves and the following group. The noise level in the stand rose in a wave of sound as punters, wide-eyed and anxious, focussed on where their money was going. In fifth place, I spotted the number four on a strongly galloping chestnut horse, his head bobbing with the effort as he made ground on the leaders. As the field approached the two furlong marker, I could see the distinctive white diamond marking, high on the horse's head and the white blaze on his nose that identified War Envoy. The noise level had now hit a phase where it was impossible to hear the race commentary. War Envoy cruised upside the leader. A furlong left to run and the two were neck and neck. With less than a hundred metres to go, War Envoy switched gears and started to ease past his rival, his jockey urging him on with the reins bouncing up and down in his hands. At the post, he was a full length winner.

The cacophony of noise subsided into a general hubbub of chatter.

Cecil slapped me on the back. "Geezer, you doubled your dough, ain't ya? He was two to one at the off. You made two grand, and you get your stake back as well. Right result. I had a ton on it too."

"What, a hundred quid? That was a bit risky."

"Nah, mate. Told'ya. Dead cert. Right, let's get another few glasses of that fizzy stuff. We got a bit of celebrating to do." He nudged Carlos. "Carlos, grab that geezer with the tray and get him over here with some drinks."

Carlos headed for the waiter.

"I can't hang around here drinking champagne, Ces," I said. "I have to go back or Chiara'll wonder where I've gone. I'm sure she didn't just turn up today out of the blue. She's suspicious of her husband and with good reason. She's not going to let him disappear for too long without coming looking. And I don't want her doing that in case she finds him with Lorena."

Cecil grinned. "Mate, you can have a quick glass with us, can't ya? I mean you're two bags up and that's gotta be worth a drink."

"It's not my money, is it? I won, but it was Cañizares's cash that made it happen. I have to give it back."

"Give it back? What's the matter with ya? He give it to'ya for gambling. And gambling means he's prepared to lose it. He didn't say nothing about what happens if you lose, did he? He ain't expecting to get it back. Lose it, you lose it. Win, and you get to keep the winnings. Mate, in any case, five grand is nothing to him. He won't even remember he give it'ya."

"Except that I'm supposed to be spending it on his girlfriend's day out. He might remember that."

"Yeah, but now you're spending it on his missus. All the same, ain't it?"

I didn't answer. Carlos came back with a waiter in tow, three glasses of champagne on a tray. We took one each, tapped them together and toasted our win.

"Right, I have to get back over there before the wife comes looking. Catch you later."

8

With my cement mixer stomach rolling, I headed back across the room, my mind focussed on how I could lose Chiara. She made me nervous. I figured that Lorena had to be a lot easier to handle. Lorena seemed more subservient. I had seen Cañizares pull her away abruptly when he had first spotted his wife. I couldn't imagine him getting away with that with Chiara.

And then I ran into Arabella.

"Oh, hello. You again," she said.

I stopped in my tracks.

"Hi." Nothing else came to mind.

"So did you win?"

My blank expression fuelled the need for Arabella to elaborate. "On the race. Did you have the winner?"

"The winner? No... I mean, yes... yes, I did."

"Oooooh, lucky you." A pout accompanied her next remark. "My horse ran like a dog." She lowered her glass and took a step closer. "My friends say you're a famous footballer. Is that right? I'm really sorry, I don't follow football. I'm a rugby girl. Much more Neanderthal." Her eyes widened, the blue becoming apparent from behind the dark lining.

"Well... uh... it's, erm... I'm just keeping a low profile to be honest... just a quiet day, bit of downtime."

"Oh, I so know what you mean."

"You do?"

"Of course. I'm a singer and actor. I get all sorts of people coming up to me, darling, especially when they're pissed." My lack of an articulate response spurred additional clarification. "I understand you're Spanish so you may not know me. Arabella Leslie. I do a lot of theatre work and some occasional TV."

"TV... err, I watch TV. What are you in?"

"All sorts, darling. Whatever comes my way. I do studio session work, tours, acting and singing. A group of us were given comp tickets for today by one of our theatrical agents, so we do get some perks. Neets is good like that."

"Sorry? Neets?"

"The agent."

"Oh, I see. Uh… well, that's a bonus. Pays to keep your contacts, I s'pose."

"It does. An actor can't afford to be choosy. I've got several agency contacts. I'm versatile. I've been doing some presenting work recently on the shopping channels, but unless you buy your own football boots, I don't suppose you watch that sort of thing." Arabella laughed and sipped her glass of Pimms.

"Uh… yeah, sounds interesting." I glanced around, nerves on edge and feeling exposed standing in the centre of the room. "I ought –"

"It can be. It's varied at least and I get to travel too. I have a tour of Europe coming up next week, starting in Milan. Then, coincidentally, I go to Madrid... Teatro Calderón. You know it?"

I gulped wondering why her tour didn't move on to Moscow or somewhere that I could have no possible knowledge of. "Erm… sort of. Everybody in Madrid knows the… the… err... the Teatro," I said, hoping it wasn't some small provincial amateur dramatic venue on the outskirts of the city, that nobody had ever heard of.

"I'm doing a series of musical dramas with a theatre company. As I say, Milan for a week, Madrid for three weeks and then Paris for two weeks. I'll be in Madrid from Sunday the seventh. Perhaps if you're around you might like to see the performance. I'm currently rehearsing and need to be off book by Monday."

"Off book?"

"Oh, sorry. Yes, no script. I have to know my part."

"Oh… of course. Makes sense."

Arabella smiled, reached out and flipped my tie. "You've changed your tie. Didn't you have a blue one earlier?"

The conversation was getting too involved, and I had no real inclination to engage in further discussion. I needed to keep that low profile I had referred to. Any choice I had in the matter was swiftly taken out of my hands.

"So there you are. This is your fancy woman. Puttana!"

I wheeled round at the last word, catching the snarl as Chiara hurled what sounded like an insult in Arabella's direction.

Arabella smiled, her composure intact. "Puttana? I think you have the wrong person, madam."

"Sì. Puttana... bitch."

"Chiara, wait." I stepped between the two women, a guiding hand pushing Chiara back in the direction she had come from. "It's, err, no how you think. She's just a... a rugby fan... I mean football. She just wanted an autograph."

The sceptical look in Chiara's eyes said she wasn't convinced, but the flashing anger had subsided.

"Look, let's go back to Hew... to Hug –"

"Huguette. Are you drunk?"

"Err... yes. I mean, no. We can have another drink."

"And you can show your tattoo, yes?"

I'd forgotten that bit. "Do we need to do that here?"

"Yes, it will make me happy and Huguette has no seen you since it was done. I tell her how you had it after the game against Italia."

Happy seemed a good state to strive for with Chiara. Having witnessed the spark of Italian temper, I knew I couldn't afford a scene. But with no tattoo, I had to think fast. She threw a final withering glance in Arabella's direction, beckoned me to follow and walked off.

When we reached the bar, Huguette held out a champagne glass and asked, "Did you win?"

"Uh, yes... yes I did."

"C'est bien! Well done!"

I took the glass and gulped down a full mouthful.

"Ignacio, show the tattoo now," Chiara said.

I looked at Huguette. "You don't want to see a tattoo, do you? You must have seen lots of them."

"I do."

"She does," Chiara confirmed.

I was cornered. My mind raced. Tattoos don't fade, and they sure don't disappear.

Chiara tugged at my jacket. "Hurry."

I slipped off the jacket and reached for the champagne.

"Quickly. Pull up your sleeve."

I undid the cufflink. Chiara grabbed my hand, spun it over palm up and pushed the shirtsleeve along my arm. I took a deep breath and stood motionless. As she stared at my bare arm, Chiara's eyes looked like they would eject themselves from their sockets at any second. Presumably, in trying to retain a connection with her eyeballs, she lost the ability to speak. It gave me an opening.

"I've been meaning to –"

As soon as I opened my mouth, Chiara regained her power of speech. "Che cosa hai fatto?"

"Err, sorry?"

"What have you done? Our beautiful tattoo with our names. Where is it?" Her eyes never left my arm.

"That's what... why I didn't want to show… "

Chiara raised her eyes and stared at me. In the depths of their watery luminescence, I could see the stirring of fire. "It's gone!"

"No... uh, no it's not... not gone. It's... "

There was no doubt it had gone as far as Chiara was concerned. I had no excuse. I had no idea why I had begun to dispute it. As I stared back into her eyes, I prepared for the outburst that I knew was coming. And I knew that if the sample I had seen unloaded at Arabella was anything to go by, I was about to be hit by an Italian tempest. And then the thought of Arabella gave me an idea.

"It's not gone. It's still there, but I've... err, covered it up with, what you call in English... one of these... a skin graft."

It was Huguette who reacted first. "A skin graft?"

"Yes... no, I mean a transplant thing... you know... uh, artificial skin, like they use in theatres and films… for make up." I was trying to hold on to my deeper foreign accent but struggling.

I felt Chiara's grip loosen on my hand. I pulled it away and slipped my sleeve down. As I did up the cuff, I heard the question, a question I had to answer with some plausible explanation.

"You covered up your tattoo. Why?"

"Well, err... it is because... because... err, sì... we have new medical team this season and I hear the doctor no like tattoos. He think they give you, erm… blood poisoning. You know, in athletes, because they sweat a lot more than... people, I mean ordinary... and the... the ink leaks through the pores and affects performance."

I could scarcely believe what I'd said, so I wasn't too surprised at Chiara's reaction.

"Questo è stupido. Dici al tuo dottore che è un idiota."

I raised my hand. "English." I took a wild guess at her choice of language. "You know my Italian is no good."

She barely took a breath. "That is stupid. You tell your new doctor that he is… un idiota. You tell that your tattoo is a symbol of your love for your wife and you want the whole world to see it. And if he has problem, then you will go to Manchester. Capisci?"

I dismissed the thought of highlighting Chiara's dislike of Manchester's weather. "Err, yeah... I cap... sí." I pulled on my jacket, relieved that somehow I had got away with my explanation. It was short lived relief.

"What are you doing? Take it off. Show your tattoo."

"Take it off?"

"Yes, take off this... this artificial skin."

"I... erm... I... can't. It has to be done by a... a specialist. One of my medical team."

"Then you must do it today."

"Today?"

"Yes, today."

"It's not that simple."

"Make it simple. You are a famous person. You know people. If you have not removed that... that stupid thing and show our tattoo then we are... finito. I will go back to Milano and we are... what do they say in English?"

"Over," Huguette chipped in.

"Yes, over."

I nodded and looked at Chiara. Her stare, the intense eyes, told me just how serious she was. I had to find Cañizares.

"Okay... okay."

I downed the remnants of the champagne and tried to focus on how I could get Ignacio Cañizares back to his wife. I put my glass on the bar and turned to find Cecil next to me.

"Got you a beer, geezer. Fuck all that bubbly shit. Get that down'ya."

I stared at him. The confusion around me needed a moment's breathing space. Cecil holding out a beer bottle provided that. Familiarity.

"I thought you liked champagne," was all I could say.

"Yeah, I do, but sometimes a geezer's gotta get back to basics. Northern European geezers do beer. It's in the genes, ain't it?" He thrust the bottle towards me again. "Drink up, mate."

I took the bottle and glanced at Chiara. Her expression had softened a little, the stern blazing eyes filled now with curiosity.

"And who is this man?" she asked.

"Err... this is –"

"Cecil Delaney, darlin'. You must be the missus." He held out a hand and took Chiara's, shaking it in a friendly greeting as if she was just another guest in the bar. His gaze then shifted to Huguette. "And what's your name, darlin'?"

Huguette smiled. "Je m'appelle Huguette."

"You French, then? Love the accent. Well sexy."

I kicked Cecil's foot to get his attention. He turned towards me. I frowned and shook my head. Chiara noticed.

"And how do you know my husband, Mister Cecil?" she said.

"We go back a long –"

"He's my nutritionist. One of the new medical team." I saw a glint in Chiara's eye and I realised what I had said.

"Are you this stupid doctor who says that my husband –"

"No, no. He isn't a doctor. He advises on diet and the things I can drink," I said, rolling the beer bottle in my hand and feeling a sudden need to conceal it.

Chiara shrugged. "But if you are with the medical team then you can talk to this doctor. Is he here now?"

Cecil ran a hand through his hair. I jumped in before he could say anything further.

"Chiara, wait. Let me talk with Cecil in private. I am sure we can sort this out. I'll be back a bit later." I pulled Cecil away and led him towards the alcove by the lavatories where we had talked earlier.

"What's all that about, mate? What's she on about a doctor for?" he said when we stopped.

"The tattoo. She's seen that I don't have one. She made me roll up my sleeve to show the frigging tattoo that I don't have."

"Thought I told'ya to blag that?"

"I did bloody blag it, Ces. I told her I had it covered with a theatrical skin graft and now she's told me to get it off."

Cecil laughed. "You did what?"

"I just told you."

"That ain't blagging, mate. Blagging is when you don't even roll your sleeve up. Blagging is not putting yourself in that situation, so you ain't blagged nothing. All you've done now is come up with some bollocks that she ain't gonna swallow unless you can prove it."

It wasn't what I wanted to hear but I knew Cecil was right. All I had done was bought time, and in that time I had to find her husband. "You're right. She's like a dog with a bone. I'm starting to feel sorry for the footballer. She's right on the case. She doesn't trust him."

"Sounds like she's got reason not to if he's here with his bit on the side. That's the trouble with women, ain't it?"

"What is?"

"They wanna mould'ya, don't they? They meet some geezer who's top of his game, bit of a flash git, loadsa top birds round him, and then try and turn him into what they want him to be, yeah. They wanna take off all the rough edges. A geezer likes going out, plenty of mates, you know the gig, and then they start the moulding thing. And you never wanted fucking moulding. All you ever said was she had a nice arse. And next thing you're marrying her and your life changes forever. But not the way you wanted it changed. No way, mate. It's their agenda."

A Cecil rant about women was the last thing I needed.

"Ces, listen. I don't care about any of that right now. I have to sort this out, or we all get rumbled and we're out of here. And it's gone too far now for me to tell his wife I'm not her husband. The minute I do that, she's going have it in for him *and* me." I glanced in Chiara's direction. She was deep in conversation with Huguette. I turned back to Cecil. "You seen Jas?"

"Nah, mate. Dunno where he went."

"He was supposed to be on the lookout for Cañizares. I bet he's got hooked up with some woman or something. You know what he's like."

"Mate, you can't expect him to come here and stand round doing your dirty work all day, can'ya? I mean the geezer's here to have a good time too."

"Dirty work? What d'you mean dirty work? Look, Ces…" I bit my tongue. There was no point in starting a debate I couldn't win. My situation was my own fault and I knew Cecil would point that out. "Forget it. I'll find him myself." I turned away.

"Where you going?"

"I told you. To find Cañizares."

"The next race is off in five."

"And? I got bigger things to worry about."

"Mate, got another blinding tip. King Boletc. Good price too, five to one."

I thrust a hand into my jacket and pulled out a wad of notes. "Stick a grand on the nose then."

Cecil took the money, flicked the notes through his hand and grinned. I recognised the look.

"Hang on. It goes straight on that horse… King…"

"Bolete. King Bolete."

"Yes. Nothing else. And I want to see the slip, right?"

"Course, mate."

9

I left Cecil and strolled across the room in the direction of the balcony door. I turned right along a crowded area that gave an excellent view towards the parade ring and the racecourse in general. I pushed my way through a crowd of people checking their race cards and sipping complimentary drinks, but kept my head down, one eye on the lookout for the footballer and the other searching for Jasper. And then I spotted Cañizares at the far end, deep in conversation with Lorena and a tall, dark haired man. My nerve deserted me. I couldn't approach in full public view, and I knew, if I did, it would unsettle Lorena. I turned back and went inside. To my right, I saw Arabella in conversation with two men, a glass of champagne in her hand.

"Excuse me interrupting but I need a word with the lady," I said and took her hand. I led her onto the balcony, through a different exit, taking care to turn to the left, away from Cañizares's location.

"Arabella. First of all my apologies for what happened earlier with… with that woman and –"

"That woman? Your wife, isn't she?"

"No, she's not my wife. It's a long story. And sorry too for grabbing you just now but I need some help."

Arabella smiled. She seemed used to dramas, and I realised, given her profession, there was no reason why real life ones should phase her. An actor could adapt to the circumstances.

"Help, darling? How can I help?" she said, her tone calm and even.

"Okay, listen. I'm not really that footballer you mentioned earlier. I'm kind of an actor too… a double."

"A double?"

"Err… yeah, you know… a lookalike. I'm a… a distraction, a distraction so that the real footballer doesn't get hassled. But there's been a massive cockup with something, and I can't be seen with him."

Arabella laughed. "You mean a massive cockup with his wife, by the sound of things?"

"Yeah, something like that. So, I wondered if you could do me a favour?"

"Of course. Anything to help a fellow actor."

"If you look over your shoulder, back there, the far end of the balcony, you can just make out a guy with his back to us, in a dark blue suit. That's the real footballer."

Arabella, turned and looked in the direction I had indicated.

"You see?"

"Not really. Too many people."

I led her back inside and along the glass façade that separated the balcony from the main room, until we reached the other door. I pointed through the glass, towards the end of the balcony. "There."

"Oh yes. I can see the resemblance."

"Exactly. That's him. And I need you to get a message to him."

"Okay, what's the message?"

"Ask him to meet me in the toilets in ten minutes."

A raised eyebrow and the hint of a smirk betrayed Arabella's amusement.

"We met there earlier. I can't be seen with him, so it's the safest place. Just tell him Matthew needs to see him urgently. He'll understand."

"Are you Matthew?"

"Yes. I am."

"Sounds intriguing. What's it worth?"

"Worth? You said anything for a fellow actor."

"I'm joking, but a drink together at least?"

"Uh, yeah. Of course."

"Okay, I'll do it. But, look, that woman, the wife, she's that model that pops up on adverts and magazine covers, Chiara, isn't she?"

"Yeah, apparently so. You know her?"

"I thought so. I know of her, but I don't move in that circle. She mentioned someone else though... Huguette. Not Huguette de Villiers by any chance, the singer?"

"Uh, I don't know, I just met her. I don't know her other name. I assumed she was a model too, not a singer. Why, do you know her?" I asked, hoping I hadn't just complicated my life by telling Arabella that I wasn't the footballer.

"I wouldn't say I know her. Neets, my agent, knows her, but I did some backing vocals on one of her studio albums about five years ago. I never met her properly at that point. I was just called in with a couple of other singers to do some chorus work after they'd recorded the main tracks. Then I was on her last tour a few years ago, just as a vocalist. She had a choir for a few of the songs. I was in that. I wasn't one of her main backing singers, unfortunately. As I said before, I'm versatile."

"Sounds like you are," I said, my focus back on getting Cañizares and not really on Arabella's career history, but she was in chatty mode.

"I did meet her a few times at the after show parties. She was a lot of fun, upbeat and in party mood most of the time. She had a lot of time for people, always interested in them, but I don't suppose she'd remember me. There were always a lot of performers and hangers on at those parties I can tell you, and they did get a little wild at times."

"I've no doubt. Anyway, would you mind going to –"

"If I get a chance I might try and say hello. You never know, might be more work in it."

"No… no, I wouldn't do that," I said, alarmed at complicating things. "I mean, not in front of Chiara… err, the wife. You saw how volatile she is. If she sees you anywhere near her husband or her friend, she might, you know, get the wrong idea again."

Arabella frowned. "But you just asked me to go and speak to him."

"Uh, yeah, I know, but I meant discreetly. Chiara's not there. You could just ask for an autograph or something and then tell him I need to see him."

She took a sip of champagne, smiled and winked at me. "Okay, Matthew. I guess I'd better not ask him to sign my cleavage then." She placed her glass on a nearby table and headed off towards Cañizares. I went back inside and ran into Jasper and Carlos.

"Where did you get to?" I said to Jasper.

"I was outside. I took the stairs from the balcony. Tried to find the bloke but I didn't see him and then I got talking to two girls."

"Aye, nice lookers too," Carlos said, a grin breaking across his face. "I think they like a bit of the ol' Latino style."

"Well you were mesmerising them with that Spanish lingo, I'll give you that," Jasper said. "How's it going your end, Matt?"

"It's not. Long story. Listen, Carlos, I need you to do me a quick favour. The footballer's out there on the balcony. I've sent Arabella to ask him to meet me in here and –"

"Who's Arabella?" Carlos asked.

"Never mind about that now. I'll tell you later. I need you to go outside and see that she gets Cañizares back in here. If the girlfriend is anything like his wife, she might throw a wobbly if she sees some good looking woman chatting to him. Just make it clear he has to come and see me. Tell Arabella I sent you because you speak the language. She'll understand."

"What's she look like?" Carlos asked.

"She's wearing a red dress with black bits on the sleeves, low cut and… great tits."

"I'll go," Jasper said.

"No, you had your chance. And I don't need you distracted by tits. I need you to go find Cecil. He's got a grand of my money to put on a horse. Make sure he does that… please."

"Okay. Cool."

"Right, Carlos, I'll be in the loos over there, okay."

I didn't wait for a reply. I made my way straight across the room, through the alcove and into the gents' lavatories. I stood in front of one of the sinks and pretended to wash my hands in case anyone else came in. I must have been there five or six minutes when Cañizares walked in, followed by Carlos.

"¿Qué está pasando?" Cañizares said.

"Sorry?"

"He asked, what's going on," Carlos cut in.

"Ignacio, I'm sorry about the mix up. It couldn't be helped. Chiara just grabbed me and now she's…" I beckoned to Carlos. "Carlos, it would be much easier if you translated."

"Nae problema, pal."

I ran through my tattoo story with Carlos, who translated the information for Cañizares. I made sure that he knew he had to get back to her and show her that he had uncovered the tattoo. When Carlos finished explaining, Cañizares turned to me and smiled.

"You go then, take care of Lorena. She with my man, you know, one of my business people. She no problem. You need more money?"

"Err, no. I'm good. But there is one thing."

"Okay, what is this?"

I turned to Carlos. "Ask him if I can see the tattoo."

Carlos nodded and slipped into Spanish mode. "Él quiere ver tu tatuaje."

"You want to see?" Cañizares said with a grin.

"Yes, I need as much information as possible. I need to be able to answer questions. Right now, I have nothing."

Carlos reinforced my message with a further string of Spanish words.

Cañizares winked at Carlos, took his jacket off and rolled up his left sleeve. Emblazoned across his inner forearm from elbow to wrist was the colourful image of a snake entwined around the thorny stem of a rose. Either side of the head of the rose were the names 'Chiara' and 'Ignacio.' My first thought was that such a design would take some covering up, and my second was curiosity about the symbolism, but I didn't ask.

"You like?"

"Err, yeah, of course."

"Good. I had it after we beat Italia in the match three weeks ago. It make Chiara happy," Cañizares said. He rolled his sleeve back down and put on his jacket. "Now I must go. Hasta luego."

"Hang on. Your bodyguards... did you tell them what's going on, uh... that your wife is here?"

Cañizares smiled. "Sí. I tell about Chiara. I say I can... how you say?" He glanced at Carlos. "Resolver esto?"

"Sort it out," Carlos said.

"Ah, sí. Sort it out. I tell that I have help."

"So they know about me?" I asked.

"No. I no say. It is too... complicado."

"I took a deep breath. "But I thought you said you'd tell them?"

Cañizares looked at Carlos and then back at me. "No, I tell to you they not a problem. They do what I say. I not tell them much so they not get... con... uh, confundido, you understand?"

"He doesn't want them getting confused," Carlos said.

"Sí. I say much, they make things wrong. I tell them ask no questions, you understand? So, is good and like a... a... prueba," Cañizares said and glanced at Carlos.

"A test. Proving things."

"They think you me, is good test, no?"

My initial thought was precisely that, 'no' indeed. The last thing I needed was a test, but I let it pass and just nodded. I looked at Carlos. "Tell him that if it gets tricky, he has to tell those guys.

It's hard enough dealing with his wife and his girlfriend let alone worrying about those two."

Carlos told Cañizares what I'd said and Cañizares nodded his understanding. He looked at me. "Is okay, mi amigo. Now I leave."

"Señor Cañizares," Carlos said. "Discúlpeme un momento."

Cañizares turned around. Carlos smiled and said something in Spanish. Then he put his hand in his pocket and pulled out what looked like business cards and handed them to Cañizares. Cañizares glanced at them briefly, turned one over, nodded and put them into his jacket pocket. He turned to leave again.

"Wait," I called out as he moved towards the door. "Your tie. You need it back."

Cañizares shot a look at Carlos. "Qué?"

I caught the puzzled expression and realised I had to spell it out.

"It looks better. Looks right. I had your tie on when I bumped into Chiara and –"

"Bummed Chiara? What is this bummed?"

"No, bumped. You know, err, like two people who run into… explain it to him, Carlos."

"Ah, I understand," Cañizares said when Carlos had finished.

"Good. So you need the tie. Trust me. Fewer questions." I pulled off the yellow tie and held it out.

"Gracias, mi amigo." He took it and with a few deft movements tied it around his neck. A final nod and he left.

I pulled my blue tie from my pocket, stood in front of the mirror and tied it in a neat knot. I turned to face Carlos, grateful that he'd been there to help.

"Thank you, Carlos. Thanks for that. I've got enough buzzing round in my head right now without having to explain things in detail to him."

Carlos shrugged. "Nae problem. Now you go back out there and sort this out, okay?"

"I will. Oh, and what was all that about? What did you give him?"

Carlos grinned. "Just a few promo cards for MacFadden's. You get two for one drinks when you hand one of them in."

I stared at Carlos for a moment, trying to comprehend what he was thinking when all around me there was chaos.

"Carlos, do you seriously think a major international footballer is going to show up at your bar in Kingston and, even if by some remote chance he did, expect to come looking for a two for one promotion? Are you mad?"

Carlos shrugged. "Maybe not, but I gave him a few for his friends. You never know. And don't forget, Mateo, it was you that said I need to keep advertising."

There was not much I could say and, even if I had thought of something, it was the wrong time to say it. Carlos was right. I had pushed him to market his bar when it was struggling for customers. I took a deep breath, opened the door and went to find Lorena. As I crossed the room, Cecil came up on one side.

"Mate, you won."

"Won?"

"Yeah, King Bolete. Five to one. That's five large, plus your stake back."

"Shit! That's... six thousand quid."

"Yeah, mate. Big time. I had another ton on that one too. You're on a roll, geezer. Your lucky day."

I smiled. "Lucky day? I wish it was. Not even my money. Talking of which, have you got it? The betting slip?"

He stuck a hand into his trouser pocket and pulled out a wad of cash.

"Cashed it for'ya. There's five and a half there."

"Five and a half? We just said six, with my stake."

"Yeah, but I bought a bottle of Cristal. Little celebration. Cost a monkey, didn't it."

"A monk... five hundred quid?"

"Cristal don't come cheap, mate. You pay for quality."

"But, I just said, it's not my cash, is it?"

Cecil rolled his eyes. "We've had that conversation, ain't we? What you worrying about? Nobody's checking what you won. You're well up and you still got the Spanish geezer's stake if he did come asking, which he ain't gonna. So who's counting?"

"Maybe, but you can't just go spending it on champagne."

"Mate, I gave you the tip. Bit of payback. Call it commission." He grinned and then said, "You changed your tie again? What's that about?"

"Nothing. Don't worry about it. I'm more worried about you spending..." I hesitated as I caught his eye. "Oh, forget it."

There was little point in arguing. I took the rest of the money, told him I would see him later and went off to find Lorena.

10

I found Lorena outside on the balcony talking with the dark haired man that I had seen her and Cañizares with earlier. Standing a little way behind them were Cañizares's bodyguards, both dressed in dark suits, crisp white shirts with black ties and dark shades. The taller of the two, well over six feet it seemed, had two or three day's stubble to go with his ponytail hairstyle. As I approached, he nodded to his colleague and both focussed their attention on me.

Seeing their sudden alert body language, Lorena turned in my direction, a broad smile lighting up her face. Up close, she was beautiful. Her hair, a shimmering blend of auburn and red highlights, fell loosely onto her shoulders and contrasted spectacularly against the deep blue of her tight fitting dress. She couldn't have been older than mid-twenties and certainly a few years younger than Chiara. My stomach churned as I contemplated having to pull off yet another deception, but I knew that there was no point in being timid. Cañizares was a confident guy. I had to look and play the part. And although I was nervous about the presence of a stranger, the businessman that Cañizares had referred to, and the proximity of the bodyguards, I had to carry it off. I took a deep breath, stuck out my chest and decided to go for it. But my positive attitude took an immediate knock.

"You have a new tie," Lorena said.

"A new tie?" I looked down at my chest as if I had no idea that I even had a tie. "Err, yes... sí... " A moment's confusion rendered me speechless as I remembered Cañizares's yellow tie. I cursed my blue tie error but knew I had to style it out. "A fan... sí, a fan... she wanted... I mean, he... he wanted to swap ties."

The businessman looked me up and down. I thought I detected something critical about his gaze, but I shrugged it off as just me being oversensitive. He was well dressed, probably in his early forties, a hint of arrogance and the affected air of an English gentleman. He made me uneasy and I had no idea why.

"Didn't you take your tie off earlier?" he said. He pulled a cigarette pack and a lighter from his jacket pocket. "You didn't have one on."

Lorena waved her glass in the direction of a table on which two jugs of Pimms had been placed. "David, my drink is finished," she said, looking at the businessman.

David put the cigarette pack and the lighter on the table and filled two fresh glasses. He handed one to Lorena and offered the other to me.

I took the glass, pleased that Lorena's intervention had diverted the focus away from my choice of ties. "Thanks," I said. "You not having one?"

"No, I'll stick to my vodka." His accent cultured, clipped English tones, but I detected a slight slurring. I sensed that he was probably not one of Ignacio's Spanish entourage but couldn't be sure. He reached behind one of the jugs and picked up a tall glass, its contents clear except for a slice of lemon. He held the glass out in a toast. "Mine's a large one. ¡Salud!"

I was slow on the uptake, my hesitancy caused by my nerves and the use of the Spanish word.

"Err… yes, ¡Salud!" I hoisted my drink to acknowledge the toast, but far too abruptly. The top of the glass caught David's hand, causing his drink to pitch towards him. A large slop of vodka splashed across his tie and the jacket lapel that held his race badge.

"Shit. Waste of good vodka," he said, stepping back in a reflex action but a little too late.

Lorena giggled. David looked irritated.

"I'm sorry… uh… amigo... David. Are you –?"

"It's okay. Don't worry." He placed the glass on the table and began to wipe his clothes with a rapid hand motion as if the speed would dry them instantaneously. As he brushed down the lapel, the metal bracelet on his watch snagged on his tie and the continued hand movement started to draw a thread of material out from one side.

I pointed it out. "Your tie... it's coming loose."

He looked at me and then back down at his tie. He pulled his watch away, but the snagged thread began to elongate even more.

"Bollocks," he said, and then I knew he was definitely English.

I stepped forward. "Hang on, you'll only make it worse if you keep pulling. Here."

I took the end of the thread that was nearest his watch, looped it around my finger and pulled. It snapped cleanly, disentangling it from the watch strap.

"Thanks... but look at my damn tie. I'm at a dinner tonight. Some particularly important clients I need to keep onside."

"Uh... it no look... err, how you say... too bad," I said. "It's fine, comprenda... uh... comprendo?" I stared at the tie. The damp patch was evident, and now a long dangling thread hung loosely in the air. David tugged at it again but only succeeded it making it unravel further.

"Don't pull it," I said, feeling guilty about disfiguring his attire. And then I remembered a tip. I grabbed the lighter from the table.

"Let me. I read that if you burn a thread, it melts it and seals the end."

I flicked the lighter button. It sparked into a bright blue flare. I held it to the bottom of the thread. The end seemed to shrivel as a tiny glowing ball of yellow light took hold. Then in a pink tinged flash, a tongue of flame shot up the thread consuming it in an instant. And suddenly one side of the tie ignited. David threw up his hands in shock as the front caught fire. The flame licked across his suit lapel, causing it to smoulder too. My reflexes kicked in. I grabbed the top of the tie just below the knot and yanked it in the direction of the table. Thrown off balance, David came with it as I plunged the flaming material into a full jug of Pimms. My enthusiastic tug brought his face down onto the rim, and my clenched hand hit the jug causing it to tip forward and deposit its contents over his suit trousers. He recoiled instinctively as my grasp on his tie loosened. But the suit lapel was still ablaze with a yellowish-blue flame, which had also caught the race badge. I grabbed Lorena's glass and flung the contents at the burning jacket, dousing the flare up instantly.

"What the fuck!" David shouted, his face a mix of horror and surprise.

"Lorena burst into a fit of laughter."

"It's not bloody funny," he said, holding out the charred remains of his tie. "My damn clothes are ruined. Look at my suit, my shirt. I only bought the damn thing at Harvey Nic's yesterday."

I stared at the shirt. The left side, that had been a pristine white, was now a shade of smoky grey. One side of his jacket was scorched up to the shoulder, his race badge blackened and barely legible. The jacket was also adorned with a sprig of mint and a slice of orange. My instinct was to leg it, but there was nowhere to go. The two security guys had taken a step closer but seemed uncertain about what they should do. I had to think how a famous footballer would react.

"Chill, amigo. You shouldn't wear them stupido polyester ties." I pulled the wad of cash from my pocket and peeled off twenty fifty pound notes. "Get yourself another suit. Them cheap ones are crapola. Oh, and if you need a tie, here." I pulled off my blue tie and held it out.

A mix of surprise and fury played across David's features. I felt a tug on my sleeve.

"Usted no debe hablar así, Ignacio," Lorena said, her eyes wide in surprise.

"English, bitchola."

"You no speak this way to David. It is rude. He is a good man. And you could lose your contract."

I hesitated. I didn't like the word 'lose.' I couldn't afford to lose anything for Ignacio Cañizares. And at that moment my attempt at a bigtime Spanish superstar persona faded into oblivion. I was pleased that the word 'bitchola' did not appear to be a familiar Spanish term.

"My contract? Who is he?"

"Are you drunk, Ignacio? You know who he is." My blank stare caused a frown to darken her green eyes. "David. David Anderson. He organised your cologne contract. You want to lose that?"

"Cologne? Not United? Or Chelsea?"

"Excuse me?"

"Oh, nothing. I was just –"

"You must apologise."

I turned towards David Anderson, who was still looking bemused in his blackened tie, burnt jacket and soaked trousers.

"Err, look... David. Sorry about that. Accidents happen, sí? I err... just joking... the cheap suit thing. Spanish humour, eh?"

His features darkened. "It's not a fucking cheap suit. I don't do cheap suits. I have clients, important people. Deals. Big deals. You think only famous footballers dress well?"

My expression and lack of reaction must have had an impact. He leaned forward, his face close to mine. "Look, it's okay. I know what's going on with Lorena and the wife. You're stressed. I'm sorry. Not your fault."

His change of tone took me by surprise. I wasn't sure what he meant by the comment about Lorena and Chiara but I thought it best to leave it in case I put my foot in it. I tried a smile but it didn't come easy. He lifted his tie and stared again at the damage. "It must have been the vodka."

"The vodka?"

"Yes, straight vodka. It's flammable."

If only he had been drinking Pimms. "Err… okay. Here, take this money, get another suit and I'll see you back here, and we can talk about… err, Cologne." I held out the cash again but he didn't take it. I turned to Lorena and pointed at the bodyguards. "Tell them to call our driver. He can drive David." It was a wild guess, but a famous footballer was unlikely to have arrived by train. Lorena beckoned to the bodyguards and said something in Spanish. The shorter of the guys nodded and pulled a mobile from his pocket.

"You okay, David?" I said. "Sorry again. Listen, take the money. It's only right I pay for the damage. We'll see you later when you get more clothes, sí?"

David shrugged, took the cash and undid his charred tie.

"Err… did you want this?" I said, holding my tie out again.

He took the tie, examined it and put it on the table. "No, don't worry. I'll get another one with the suit." He pulled the singed lapel badge off and slung it on top of the tie. "You can hardly read the damn thing. Luckily, I've got a ticket."

I looked at the bodyguard with the ponytail who was watching his companion make the call to the driver and saw an opportunity to get rid of them both and make my life less complicated.

"You two, you go with David, sí. You make sure he is good. You no worry about me. I am… uh… okay… err… " I searched my brain for the correct Spanish word. I felt it was needed for credibility with the security guys. "Err… I'm…uh… bono."

The two guys looked puzzled. Lorena glanced at me. "Estas bien?"

"Uh… sí. Is what I say, no?" I focused on the guy with the ponytail. "Bien. I'm… uh, bien. Now… you… go."

The bodyguard turned away. David Anderson nodded and followed him, the other bodyguard right behind him. I noticed that David had a slight limp as he walked. He'd been drinking, but it was a limp, not a stagger and it couldn't have been anything to do with setting light to his jacket and tie. I dismissed it.

When they had gone I grabbed the remaining jug of Pimms and topped up my glass and then did the same with Lorena's. She took a sip and asked a question.

"Are you okay? You seem not to be yourself."

I gulped hard and tried to keep up the persona. I was glad to have lost David Anderson and the protection team. It would be a lot simpler one to one.

"No, I am just… just pleased to be here with you today. A little too mucho of the champagne. Is good, no?"

She smiled, her eyes expectant. "It's good to be here, Ignacio. But can I say something?"

I nodded.

"I know I said I would not talk about it on this trip, but I keep thinking about it. I have to ask. Have you told her?"

"Told who about what?"

"Your wife. About the divorce."

"The divorce?"

"Yes, you said you would tell her. I must know." She hooked her arm around mine.

I said nothing. Chiara was not someone I wanted to discuss.

She pulled her arm away. "You haven't told her, have you?"

I had no clue. Had he told her? I hedged my bets.

"Sort of."

"Sort of? What does this mean?"

I was saved by Rob Black.

"Ignacio. I've filed the story." He stared at me for a moment. "You lost your tie?"

"Err… yes. I… I spilt something on it." I pointed to the discarded tie on the table.

"And what happened to that?" Rob Black said, pointing at the burnt lapel badge.

"Oh, uh…nothing… just an accident." I scooped up the tie and badge, shoved them in my pocket and shot a look at Lorena, but she was still considering the divorce issue and had missed the new version of my tie story. I focused again on Rob Black. "So why you come back here?"

"Story's filed so came back to enjoy the rest of the day." He waved his mobile at me. "Doesn't take long with the old internet. Headline tomorrow. Cañizares to Man U."

"Err, change of plan, Señor... Señor Black. I've signed for Cologne."

He screwed his eyes into a tight squint so that his eyebrows met in the middle.

"Cologne? FC Köln? In the Bundesliga?"

"Err, Cologne, Germany."

"You're joking me. Not United?."

"No, I've done a deal."

"You're going to have to brush up on your German then. FC Köln *is* Cologne." He glanced down at the racecourse and then turned back to face me, a frown playing across his forehead. "So when did this happen? I've filed the fucking story."

"You'll have to un-file it then. This afternoon."

"You better not be winding me, kid, or you and your little lady here are gonna be all over the front pages tomorrow. Your wife won't wanna be seeing that, will she?"

"No, look, it is, err... good story. I just speak with the... err... agent. It's confirmed."

Curiosity replaced Rob Black's irritation. "What's the deal? How much?"

"Err... still being, how you say... finalised. No details. A hundred and fifty, maybe... look, you better get that story changed before somebody else gets news of it. You no want to print a wrong story."

He paused for a moment, his mind assessing the damage that an incorrect story could do to his reputation. And then he turned abruptly and was gone.

I downed the remainder of the Pimms in one. Lorena stared at me, hands on hips.

I put the glass down. "What? What's wrong?"

"I think I am right. There is something funny going on. You drink too much today. Not like you. And why did you tell that man that you were going to Cologne?"

"Because... because he was going to write a story about me and United. And you told me, I mean, reminded me, about the Cologne contract so I thought if he's writing story, he must get it right. You must keep good relationship with journalists, sí?"

Lorena stared again and then said, "Aftershave."

"Aftershave? What about it?"

"The Attaque contract. Your deal with David Anderson's company, Chuchoter.

"What? Attaque?"

"Yes! The *aftershave* brand. What is wrong with you?"

And then I realised that Anderson had to be the business manager Cañizares had mentioned. "Of course... sí. I just... forget... sometimes... with the, uh... football."

Lorena's intense stare gave way to a dark frown. "You make fire to his tie and jacket, soak his trousers and insult him. And now you tell that journalist you are transferring to a German club. You are being very... how they say... en inglés ... odd. And what about your divorce?"

I pulled out my wad of cash and broke off five hundred pounds.

"Lenora... I mean, Lorena... I can explain but... I'll be back soon. Get a bottle of Cristal. Wait here."

"Where are you going?"

"I need to find the journalist."

A frown creased Lorena's face. "You keep going away and leaving me here. We are supposed to be having the day together. And now Sergio and Lucero have gone too, and I am alone with nobody that – "

"Who?"

Lorena waved in the general direction of the crowd beneath the balcony. "Sergio and Lucero... your men. What is wrong with you?"

"Yes... err, sí ... Sergio and Lucero. I know, I wasn't thinking. Look, I will be back. I have to find Señor Black."

I pulled Lorena towards me, kissed her on the cheek and left.

11

I ran down the staircase that led from the balcony, and in the direction I had seen Rob Black take. He was nowhere to be seen. I paced up and down a crowded walkway, but people were beginning to stare and point and I felt uncomfortable. The afternoon sun shone brightly from a clear sky, its heat adding to my discomfort. I retraced my steps, checked that Lorena was out of sight and went back into the hospitality area. I headed across to the betting desk where I found the lads.

"Where you bin, mate? Next race is nearly ready for the off and we got a tip," Cecil said.

"I'm not bothered about the next frigging race, Ces. I've got issues."

"We know that, geezer. Here, get a glass of this Cristal down'ya. Proper nectar." He hoisted the bottle from the ice bucket and in mid pour said, "What was that French girl's name... y'know, the wife's mate?"

"Huguette?"

"Yeah, that's it."

"What about her?"

"I just see her chatting to that big geezer with the ponytail. One of the footballer's minders, ain't he?"

"He is, yeah. I thought he'd gone by now. I just sent him away with one of Cañizares's contacts. I can't cope with all his people. What were they talking about?"

Cecil frowned. "How am I s'posed to know that? For a start they're foreign, and they were too far away. But tell'ya what I did see." He put the bottle back in the ice bucket. "He's slipped her something, y'know, bit like the old handshake mumble, and then she's gone off towards the women's toilets."

"Where did he go?" I asked, anxious to know that he was not still in the building.

"He just caught up with his mate who was with some other geezer. I didn't get a proper look at him. They were going somewhere in a hurry."

I felt relieved. I sipped the champagne. Cecil said, "You know what I reckon?"

"What?"

We were interrupted by Jasper and Carlos.

"Boys, they're loading 'em in the stalls. You done your bets?" Jasper asked.

"I have, but he ain't," Cecil said, nodding at me.

"I'm not that fussed, to be honest," I said. "Got enough to think about."

"Mate, what's the matter with ya? You're s'posed to be having a laugh with your mates, having a good time, not worrying about that playboy footballer. And I just told'ya. It's a right tip. Spanish Player, ten to one. It's an omen, ain't it? You gotta have a little tickle on that."

"Yeah, I'd go large," Jasper said.

"The boys say yer way ahead, Mateo. And yer havin' a tricky day," Carlos said. "So you may as well give it a wee go."

Tricky day. Too true.

"Yeah, you gotta go for it. If it comes in and you ain't on it, you're gonna be well pissed off," Cecil added.

They were right. It was the reason I had come to the course. To enjoy and watch top horse racing at a fantastic venue. And it would be a momentary distraction. I was ahead even if it wasn't my cash. I checked the race card.

"Spanish Player? You sure?"

"Mate, it's tight. He's a blinding tip at them odds. Jas was given it," Cecil said. He glanced at his watch. "You got three minutes before the offski. Get on it."

I scanned the race card again, my eyes drawn to the stakes. "Who gave it to you, Jas? Number three, Alcatara, is odds on favourite."

"Some actress. She said she knew one of the trainers. Reckons it's a live one."

"An actress?" I thought of Arabella.

"Yeah, got chatting at the bar. Might be that girl you mentioned. She had a red dress, fab tits."

67

"What was her –?"

Cecil slapped me on the shoulder. "Mate, you gonna get that bet on? They're loading up."

I nodded. I had nothing to lose. I approached the betting desk.

"Two thousand win, number nine, please, Wendy."

"Feeling lucky again, sir?" Wendy said, her smile filling me with positivity.

"Yep. In for a penny, in for a pound." I slapped the cash on the counter and waited for the slip. Cecil peered over my shoulder then turned to the boys. "He's only gone large, lads. Two bags on the nose. Get in."

A ripple of approval went up behind. I took the betting slip and stared at the TV screen. With a metallic crash, the stall gates flew open and nine powerful, majestic horses reacted to the impetus to run. A colourful wave emerged in unison, each animal straining to release itself from the confines of its temporary cage. Within half a furlong, the field had merged into an orderly queue, no more than three abreast as the leading horse began to dictate the pace. A thumping heart focussed me on the fact that fate had now taken control of the next few minutes. I stared at the screen searching for number nine, but in the early tussle for position, I couldn't locate Spanish Player.

"Where's nine?" I enquired of nobody in particular.

"Middle of the field," Cecil said, his gaze fixed on the action. "Blue cap."

I tried to focus on the commentary, but my attention was drawn to the lead horse who had started to open up a two length gap. *'Lunar Conquest gallops on into the lead, making the early running...'*

I stared, unblinking, at the screen, my heart thumping, a wall of noise around me. *'At the five furlong marker Lunar Conquest is two clear from Prairie Rain, going well in second...'*

The commentary was not so much informative as anxiety inducing. I searched the pack for number nine, but tension had stifled my ability to see detail. A blur of activity careered across the screen; the pit of my stomach telling me that my gamble was at risk. I stared straight ahead as the horses swallowed up the first half mile.

'... Alcatara in the middle of the pack as they pass halfway and run righthanded into the home bend...'

An elbow in the ribs broke my transfixed state. "Go on, son." Cecil's right fist clenched, his gaze direct and unwavering.

'*As they reach the three furlong marker, Spanish Player is travelling well...*' The commentator's voice suddenly had meaning.

Cecil yelled at the screen. "C'mon, get him outta there. Don't get him boxed in." Then, in a lower tone, "Here he comes, lads."

I focussed on the action. On the outside of the field, the blue cap was visible as they took the bend, the jockey's arms pumping at the reins, his legs tucked up high against the saddle, urging his mount forward.

"C'mon. Go on, son. Get in." Cecil was riding the race, his eyes wide with a desire to propel the horse forward. As if by some telepathic response, Spanish Player found a gear that took him past three of his rivals.

'*Two from home and Prairie Rain takes up the lead from Lunar Conquest...* ' The commentators tone, urgent, reflecting the excitement as the field careered down the home straight. '*... and here comes Spanish Player, in the blue cap, with a run on the outside...*'

One by one, Spanish Player cut down his rivals until he was alongside Prairie Run, their heads bobbing in a coordinated dance as they fought for position.

"He's got it, boys," Jasper shouted. "Go on, my son."

With just over a furlong to go, Spanish Player eased a short head in front of the leader, trying to get clear to take up a run on the rails.

"C'mon, c'mon you beauty." Cecil was practically driving the horse.

And then all four of us took a deep breath. The favourite, Alcatara, had hit his stride. The commentary increased to a breathless pace and pitch; the crowd roar intense and frenzied as the action unfolded.

'*And here comes the favourite, Alcatara, on the inside, pressing the leaders...*'

It was obvious Alcatara had the momentum as he swallowed up the field from three lengths back on the inside rail. With less than a furlong to go, he levelled with Spanish Player. In five or six strides, they took out Prairie Run and fought for the line. I looked away from the TV monitor and glanced through the window as the battling horses passed beneath the grandstand.

"Fuck it," Cecil cursed. "The favourite's gonna nick it."

My heart sank, that feeling of doom and helplessness that tells you that you have no control of the inevitable. I stared again at the screen, the action so much closer. Alcatara edged half a length in front, but Spanish Player was not giving up the fight. He attacked the leader gamely, a lung-bursting surge keeping him in touch and closing the gap. In an effort to get clear, Alcatara veered left, the pressure getting to him. Spanish Player momentarily checked his stride, his head coming up sharply as he readjusted his run. And in that instant I knew it was lost. Alcatara went clear and cruised past the post to take the race.

"Bollocks," Jasper said. "I was gonna do him. I looked at it this morning. Papers said he was dangerous. But odds on's no value."

"It's a lot more value than a ten to one loser," Carlos said. "I had a wee side bet on him ma'sel."

"And I've blown two grand," I said. "I've never had that kind of money on a horse."

"Good job it ain't your wedge then, geezer," Cecil said. "Let's get 'em in. Need a drink after all that excitement."

'*Stewards*' *enquiry. An objection by Spanish Player's jockey...* '

"You hear that? An enquiry," Jasper said.

"What's that mean?" Carlos asked.

"It's called when there's been some infringement of the rules."

"So what happens?"

"They look at the race and see if the result can stand."

Carlos seemed impressed by Jasper's racing knowledge. "And then what?"

Jasper was about to respond when Cecil pointed at the TV monitor. The closing stages of the race were being rerun in closeup. We stood transfixed by the different camera angle, this time head on. And then the action slowed and the screen shot zoomed further in on the front two horses.

'*Yes, there is*,' the commentator said, '*... there's a coming together.*'

I watched as Spanish Player's head reared up again, this time the slow motion exaggerating the movement, the head on shot showing Alcatara bumping Spanish Player.

'*Whether that's enough for the stewards to...*'

In the general hubbub that greeted the rerun the commentary was lost.

"To what?" I said to Jasper. "What's he saying?"

"To alter the result, I s'pose."

"Alter the result? How? Who wins then?"

"They disqualify the winner. It should go to our guy."

"You're joking?"

"No joke, mate. If they think Alcatara has impeded him, taken his line, they won't let the result stand."

I glanced at Cecil who was focussed on the TV screen and remarkably quiet for him. And then I realised the whole area around us had come to a standstill. It was clear that, at odds on, the favourite had a lot of money riding on it.

Carlos seemed the only one unperturbed. He topped up my glass and winked.

"I guess you win either way, Carlos," I said.

"Aye, a hundred on the favourite and twenty on the other fella. If the favourite wins I'm fifty up and if yours wins, it's two hundred and forty."

"Two forty?"

"Aye, just seen the odds. It was ten to one as they were going to the post but it started at twelve to one."

I dismissed the information. No sense on dwelling on it until the result was clear.

We waited a further ten minutes and then a wave of noise rolled from outside in the grandstand. It was picked up immediately in a deafening roar of excitement that spilled across the room. All around people were reacting, some with elation clear on their faces and some with their disappointment just as obvious.

I turned back to the screen to see the caption – *'Objection upheld. Winner: Spanish Player.'*

Cecil punched the air. "Get in, my son. Reeesult! You had two grand on that, didn't ya?"

"Uh… yeah, I did," was all I could say.

"That's twenty-four fucking grand. Twenty-four and your stake back. If this don't call for a celebration I dunno what the fuck does. Get that waiter over with another bottle of fizz." Cecil stretched out a hand in my direction. "Twenty-six thousand quid, mate. Twenty-six grand. Give us your ticket and I'll collect the wedge."

I stared at him for a moment. I heard the number. I heard Jasper repeat it. Carlos slapped me on the back. I wasn't prepared for a win like that. When Ignacio Cañizares had given me the original five thousand pounds, I hadn't thought about what would happen if I won. It was for spending. I hadn't expected to keep it, let alone turn it into a windfall. In a dreamlike state, I let the number sink in. All around me, the crowd became a blur of faces, my friends saying things to me that I wasn't hearing. In my head I replayed what Cañizares had said when he handed me the cash... *'Five thousand English pounds. No matter if you lose. You... how is it? Entertainment... entertain Lorena.'*

Twenty-six thousand pounds was a lot of entertainment.

12

Cecil returned from the cash desk with three envelopes bound together with two thick elastic bands. I checked the contents. Two of them contained ten thousand pounds each. The third had the balance of six thousand. I placed the two larger amounts in my jacket pockets and took out the cash from the remaining envelope. I peeled off twenty fifty pound notes and put them in my wallet. The remaining five thousand I split into two equal amounts, rolled them tight and double wrapped each roll with the elastic bands from the envelopes. I then slipped them into my trouser pockets, one on each side.

"Don't be flashing all that cash about, mate. What you doing with it anyway?"

"Splitting it. Different pockets, it's easier to manage. I've got the rest in my back pocket. But I wouldn't have thought any of the high rollers in here would be thinking about mugging me, would you?"

"Maybe not, but all the same, y'know."

The next fifteen minutes shot by in a blur of banter and champagne. But I went with it. It was the first time since I'd arrived at the racecourse that I had felt relaxed. Cecil poured the champagne freely. He even persuaded Wendy, the cashier, to indulge in a cheeky drop.

"Go on, darlin', you bin a lucky mascot. Every bet you took off us, we've won."

"I can't, sir. I'm on duty."

"Don't worry about that, love. Give us a teacup or something, let me top it up. Nobody's gonna know any different. Gotta keep the dream alive, ain't ya."

And then Cecil brought me back to the issue I had been battling with all day.

"You sorted them two yet?"

"Hardly, Ces. It's going tits up. The girlfriend's getting suspicious. The footballer is with the wife and her mate... oh, and talking of which, what were you going to say?"

"About what?"

"You know, before the race. You said you reckoned something, about Huguette?"

Cecil scratched his chin, pausing while he collected his thoughts. Carlos and Jasper stared at him intensely, waiting to hear what he had to say.

"Yeah, I reckon he's dealing."

"Who? Dealing? Dealing what?"

"The big geezer with the ponytail. The old Colombian marching powder."

"Eh?" Carlos said, frowning.

Cecil looked at Carlos. "Yeah, dealing. Coke. Co-fucking-caine."

"Ah, why didn't you say so in the first place, Cecil. I've nae heard it called that before... Colombian marching powder?"

"You're having a laugh, ain't ya? You must've heard it. Mate, most of it comes from your neck of the woods, don't it?"

"Hang on a wee second," Carlos said, sharply. "I'm half Peruvian, nothing to do with Colombia, so dinnae go tarrin' us all with the same brush. South America's a big place. And, besides, I have nae interest in drugs and gettin' people addicted."

Cecil grinned, enjoying winding Carlos up. "No interest in drugs? Yeah? You sell plenty of booze in that bar of yours and if that ain't getting people addicted, I dunno what the fuck is."

"That's nae the same, Cecil and you know it. For a start, booze is legal, and I don't push it. And, anyway, you spend enough on it yersel', ah'noticed."

"Yeah, mate, I'm keeping you in business." Cecil slugged the last of his champagne and banged the glass down on the table. "And, in case you didn't know, geezer, Peru shares a border with Colombia."

"Aye, it does, but what's that gottae do with anything? It disnae mean that –"

"Hey, you two, cut it out," Jasper interrupted. "Don't matter where the coke comes from. We're s'posed to be having a laugh, not worrying about what anyone else does. These people with money are all into that recreational drug stuff."

"The footballer won't be, will he? They get tested and all that," Cecil said.

"Yeah, but you said it was Huguette that was slipped something," I said.

"What did you say her name was?" Jasper asked.

"Huguette."

Jasper laughed. "I've just tumbled who she is. Makes sense now. Hugs."

"Hugs? What the fuck's that, Jas?" Cecil asked.

"Huguette De Villiers. She was big time, modelling, about five years ago. Then she started a singing career, trying to be a pop star. They called her 'Hugs.' She did all right in France but then faded out."

"Mate, I didn't know you was a fan of French pop music," Cecil said.

"I'm not. The girls at work have mentioned her, mostly 'cos of the modelling. She still does a bit."

I'd heard enough. It wasn't helping me get through the day. "Look, lad's, I don't really care who's doing what and whether models, footballers or anyone else is doing drugs right now and nor where it's coming from." I checked my watch. "All I know is, for what's left of this afternoon, I have to keep the wife and the girlfriend apart or –"

"Or what?"

"Or... or we all get thrown out of here, and that's the day ruined."

Cecil grinned and flicked his hair back. "Mate, it don't matter no more. I've told the guys the mumble. They know you fucked up with the tickets. It's cool."

"You told them?"

"Yeah, they're your mates. What happens to you is our problem too. In it together, geezer."

I stood speechless for a moment, embarrassed by my lack of trust. It was Jasper that cut through the moment.

"Chill, Matt. It's cool. You got us in here. It's been blinding. Couldn't have had a better laugh." He raised his glass. "Cheers."

"And it dinnae matter if we get thrown out, Matco. There's some good wee pubs down the road," Carlos said.

Cecil slapped Carlos on the back and said, "Nobody's getting thrown out." He looked at me, his brown eyes intent and focussed.

"You got wedge now, mate. You're holding, what... best part of thirty kay?"

"Thirty-three and a half to be precise."

Jasper whistled. Carlos puffed out his cheeks and then expelled the air slowly.

"Don't look so surprised, lads. I had one winner at two to one, one at five to one and then the biggie at twelves. I've spent a grand on Cristal –"

"When d'you get the other one? We've only had one bottle," Cecil said.

"I got one for Lerona… Lorena, I mean… the girlfriend. That was what the money was for after all. To look after her. And I spent another grand on a suit –"

"A suit? You bought a fucking suit? When d'you have time to do that? And what for?"

"It wasn't for me. For some other bloke."

"You bought a suit for some geezer? What, you a charity now? Why? You losing it?"

"It's a long story. I'll tell you later. And then there's the five hundred I lent you which you haven't given back."

"Well, you don't need it now, do'ya? And I give you the tips so you wouldn't be holding that kind of moolah if I hadn't."

I ignored Cecil's comment. He was right. He deserved something, even if he did have an odd way of getting it.

"Anyway, so, yeah, I have thirty-three and a half thousand pounds, including the five grand that the footballer gave me and my stake back for each winner."

Cecil frowned and then ran both hands through his hair, sweeping it back off his forehead. It was a mannerism I had become used to and something he did when he was thinking deeply or about to give his view of a problem.

"Right, so even if we did get thrown out, which we ain't, you can hardly say the day's ruined can'ya? Geezers who got money make things happen."

"But it's not my money."

"Yeah it is. The Spanish geezer give you five large to keep your mouth shut and do his dirty work. In return, he says he won't rumble'ya. But he don't give a fuck about you being in here. Makes no difference to him. He can still get all the VIP freebies and still buy his Cristal. He's pulling a fucking trade on'ya, geezer. He don't care about no five grand. I already told'ya that. Pocket money, mate. He don't even care if you spend it on his bit on the side either. And he ain't gonna worry if you blow the lot on the horses or not. He just wanted you running round keeping his arse out of trouble. A trade is about staying the course. It's poker, ain't it. And now you got moolah. Changes the deal, 'cos now it's *you* that don't give a fuck. You don't have to play his game now. Front the geezer up. He ain't got no fucking idea what you got."

"Got? I've got nothing. No tickets, and if he pushes it, it's not even my cash. I can give –"

"Shut the fuck up, geezer. We've bin through the cash thing. You got more than you started out with, so it's your money now. You turned his five kay into a lot more, so you earned it. And now it's time to sort him out. The geezer's some halfwit that made it out of a backstreet slum. So he could kick a football better than his other loser mates, and now he's billy fucking big bollocks. Yeah? Well listen, mate, you came in here with fuck all and guess what? Now *you're* billy big bollocks. Nobody can screw with'ya. You got wedge."

"But –"

"Ain't no buts, mate. If some nobhead wants to throw us outta here, you got enough wedge to go where the fuck you like. Mate, the minute you're standing holding a bottle of Cristal with hot chicks eyeing you up across the room, ain't no sucker gonna fuck with you. It's gravy, ain't it."

"Spot on, Ces", Jasper said. "Cheers, pal." He thrust his glass toward me.

My heart thumped like it was dealing with a mainline drug. I wanted an escape but escape required confrontation. Cecil locked onto my uncertainty.

"Mate, you're the man. Call the geezer's bluff. Ain't your problem if he's trying to juggle two women. None of us lads give a toss whether we stay in here or not now. We know how to party wherever we are."

"Really?" I took a sharp intake of breath and glared at Cecil. "So why didn't you say that earlier? Might have saved a load of bloody aggro."

Cecil grinned. "Didn't wanna spoil this little party. And you weren't wedged up then, were'ya?"

In an instant reaction, a burning burst of irritation coursed through me. Carlos saw it. He pulled at my shoulder, his enthusiasm dragging me to one side.

"Hey, Mateo. You cool, amigo. Comprende?"

I shrugged him off.

"Mateo. Chill. What's up? You know Cecil. You know what he's like. You cannae let him wind you up. Be cool. He's a player, you know that. He sees things different."

"I know but... I'm pissed off. Look, Carlos, I know I screwed up on the tickets thing, but I was just trying to fix it, that's all."

"Och, aye, I know but dinnae worry about it. Relax."

"Not that easy, is it. It's been a tense day. I can't quite square off this cash thing, and I don't know whether I'm coming or going, trying to play these two women. Talking of which, I nearly screwed up on the tie thing."

"How d'you mean?"

"Well, when Cañizares left the toilets I gave him back his yellow tie and then put mine on. Lorena noticed the difference."

Carlos cracked a grin, but it quickly turned to a frown.

"Hold on, Mateo. I remember now. He didn't have a tie. When he came into the toilets, he didn't have a tie on. Come to think of it, when I went to speak to him before that, he wasn't wearing a tie either."

"Yes, that's because I had it. When he went back to Lorena she probably just thought that he'd taken it off and nobody said anything because of who he is. But then I went to her, and I was wearing mine."

"So what happened?"

"I had to blag it. Easy to screw up though."

"Well, at least you got away with it. Where's the tie now."

"In my pocket."

"Relax then. Leave it off. Easier that way. Like Cecil just said, you got cash so just chill out and enjoy the rest of the day. Whatever happens, happens."

Easier said than done. The voice behind me stopped any thought of chilling out.

"What are you doing here? Who are these people?"

I turned to see Lorena, her face tense with confusion. Cecil felt the need to respond.

"S'all right, darlin'. We're friends. We –"

I cut Cecil off. "Let me handle this, Ces."

I took Lorena to one side, but before I could say anything, she launched into a tirade.

"There's something going on here. You behave very funny today. You disappear and leave me on my own. And you won't tell me what is happening with your wife. You no want to talk about this. You have something to hide, I think. And I think it funny with the aftershave too."

"The aftershave? That was just a joke," I said, trying to find an explanation for my error with David Anderson.

"No jokes. When we met this morning, you were wearing the cologne from your sponsor. But when you kissed me earlier, it is different perfume. I think something is wrong with you."

I hesitated. There was no suitable response. I thought that perhaps this was the time to come clean, to explain in detail what was going on. Cecil had given me a get out. I didn't need to continue the deception. I stared at Lorena, and as I did so, I noticed the moistness in her eyes. And at that moment I realised I couldn't say anything to hurt her. It was not my job to sort out Ignacio Cañizares's personal life. It was his mess and his problem.

"Err... it's... a new one. I'm trying it out. Dave... David gave it to me earlier and I... yes, I just put it on. Their newest cologne."

Lorena frowned. "Okay, so tell me about your wife. What is happening?"

Again I hesitated, this time because I had no idea what to say. As I was searching for a sensible response, Cecil stepped in.

"All okay, mate?"

"Uh... yeah, I was just –"

"Telling me about his wife," Lorena said.

I glanced at Cecil. "Yes, I was but –"

"He is supposed to be leaving her. You know this?"

Cecil frowned. "He don't talk to me about personal stuff, darlin'."

"He say he will leave her, but I don't believe him. He is making a fool of me. Every time I am with him, I see that tattoo. And it hurt me. You understand?"

Cecil winked at me. "He's had it removed, darlin'."

I grimaced. Not the tattoo. "Let's forget that." I shot Cecil a surreptitious wink, but Lorena had locked on to his statement.

"You have removed the tattoo? Why did you not say? You know how I hate it. You show me."

"Not in here, Lenor... Lorena. We could get thrown out for... taking our clothes off."

Lorena frowned. "We don't take our clothes off, Ignacio. Why would we take our clothes off? You just take your coat off and show me."

"Jacket."

"¿Perdón?"

"Not coat, jacket." I was trying to distract her, but she was not to be distracted.

"Your jacket then. Take it off."

"There's no need. You don't need me to prove how I feel about you. Let's just enjoy the day. Look, I won." I pulled out my cash-stuffed wallet and showed it to her.

Lorena didn't even look at it. "Put it away. I am no interested in your money. You know what I want. Show me your arm."

I knew that taking my jacket off to reveal my non-existent tattoo would not work. Next time she saw the real Cañizares, the tattoo would be evident. I really didn't want to complicate matters. I wanted Cañizares to sort out his own chaotic love life.

"Show me, and then I will believe that you care about me." Lorena's eyes were defiant.

Cecil saw it and decided to intervene. "Excuse me, darlin'. A quick word with your boyfriend." He pulled me aside. "Listen, geezer, you don't need all this palaver. It ain't your problem. Show her your arm and tell her to go away."

"Go away?"

"Yeah, tell her to go back home, or wherever it was they met up today and wait there. It gets her out of your hair and then she can sort it with the footballer. You show her you ain't got no tattoo, she'll do whatever you tell her. Then go sort out billy big bollocks."

"She must have seen it already, this morning, before they came if they were together."

"Don't sound like she did from what she's said. Maybe he only flew in today or something. Who knows? Just blag it, mate, then she's out the way."

The prospect of getting rid of Lorena had appeal. If it helped me loosen the grip Cañizares had on my day too, that would be a bonus. I slipped off my jacket, handed it to Cecil and turned towards her. I rolled up my left sleeve and displayed my forearm.

"See. Nothing there."

Lorena's eyes widened as she stared at my bare arm. As the realisation that there was no tattoo sank in, her surprise turned into a delighted smile. And then she leapt on me, arms outstretched grabbing my shoulders, pulling me to her in a smothering hug.

"Ignacio, I am so happy. We will be together now. Thank you. I love you."

It was too much. I felt like a cheat. I pulled myself free and held both of her hands in mine.

"Lorena, I want you to go back to where we met today and –"

"The airport?"

"Err, no… I mean, maybe, the… the hotel?"

"Sí, Claridge's, where I stay."

"Yes. Claridge's, that's it. Go back and wait for me there. I'll call you, or I'll come later. Okay?"

She nodded.

"And listen, don't always believe what you see. Don't always wait for others to do what you would like them to do. You are a lovely girl. You can get whatever you want. You don't have to have what belongs to someone else."

Her delight turned to a puzzled frown. "Ignacio, what do you mean? What is this?"

"It's nothing. I'll explain later. Just go now and wait for me." I hugged her. She smiled and walked away.

When Lorena had gone, Cecil slapped me on the shoulders. "Nice one, geezer. Well handled."

"Thanks." I let out a deep sigh. "It's not fair though, Ces. People shouldn't mess with one another. Not with emotions. It's not right. I feel sorry for her." And as I thought about fairness, I came to terms with my cash dilemma. I drained the contents of my glass.

"C'mon, let's go sort out Señor Cañizares."

13

It was their total surprise that put them on the back foot and gave me the upper hand. The only one who didn't seem too fazed was Huguette. She smiled as I approached, but Cañizares and Chiara remained open mouthed, clutching their race programmes.
"Señor Cañizares, I need a word," I said.
He glanced at his wife and then back at me. "Over there," he said, pointing towards the far side of the room.
"No, right here will do just fine."
Chiara stood up. "Who are you?"
"He's Ignacio Cañizares, darlin'," Cecil cut in.
She turned to her husband but addressed her question to Cecil. "So who is he?"
"He's Ignacio Cañizares too, darlin'."
Chiara sat back down, her face screwed up in bewilderment. Next to her, Huguette giggled.
I had no idea what Cecil was playing at, so I ignored him. Then he raised a hand in the air and beckoned across the room. I focussed on Cañizares and took him to one side, but before I could say anything, he asked, in a whisper, "Where is Lorena?"
"She's fine. Don't worry about her right now. I thought you were going somewhere else on the course with your wife?"
Cañizares shrugged. "She no want to. She want to stay here."
"Might have been better for you if you had." I reached into my back pocket and pulled out a roll of notes. I peeled off most of the wad. "First of all, here's the five thousand pounds you gave me earlier, every penny of it." I held it out towards him. "Take it."
"But we have deal, Señor Malarkey."
"No, no deal now. Take your money. I don't want it. I didn't ask for it, and it isn't mine." I thrust the cash into his hand and

stepped back. As I did, I saw Carlos and Jasper arrive at Cecil's side.

"You know I can get you out of here, amigo? I have my security. I say only one word and this happen," Cañizares said and drew his hand across his throat.

I smiled. "They're not here. They've left already. I sent them away."

For a fleeting moment, the arrogant attitude deserted him. But he recovered quickly, self-assurance his default position. "No matter. I know people. I get you and your compadres... what is it? A bandana."

"A bandana?"
"Yes, I can do this."
"You mean banned."
"Sí, ban... ed."
"No... banned."
"Banned. You no come back here ever."

I shook my head. "But you won't. Not unless you don't mind me calling Rob Black and telling him all about you and Lorona... err, Lorena. Or telling your wife about her and that you told her you were divorcing. And not unless you don't mind me calling David Anderson and telling him that his aftershave is shit and he dresses like a paraffin."

Cañizares's eyes flashed anger, but he seemed to realise he had to stay cool.

"David? How is this? Paraffin?"

I smiled. It felt good to have control. I played it.

"Don't forget, I am you. I know what you know. Oh, and a paraffin, it's somebody that doesn't dress well. A tramp. You understand?" I was sure he didn't. Cecil's grasp of cockney rhyming slang had rubbed off on me but perhaps hadn't translated to Europe yet. I smiled at Cañizares's confusion and continued. "As for the deal, we have no deal. You can't just take advantage of people just because you can buy it. Get someone else to do your dirty work. That's not me. I'm just looking out for my mates like people do when they care about each other. Do you care for your wife? Do you care for Lorena?"

There was no response.

"I thought so. You don't know what you care about. You are so used to people just falling over themselves for you that you don't even care what they think. Lorena is a nice lady. You need to sort that out. Let her go. You have a wife. Let her go too if you can't make her feel important."

I paused, surprised by my outburst.

"Where is Lorena? Where you put her?"

"She's okay. She's gone back to the hotel. She's waiting for you. Don't make her wait. Be truthful. Let her go. She doesn't deserve to be treated that way."

Cañizares reached into his trouser pocket and pulled out a mobile. He tapped the screen and put the phone to his ear. At the same time, he glanced at me. "You no worry about what I do. You need to be careful, Señor Malarkey. I find out about you. I –" Abruptly, he turned away. "Lucero, ¿dónde estás?" A stream of Spanish words followed whatever Lucero had said by way of reply. Cañizares killed the call and grinned at me. "My man, he come here now. He no go far when I am in público."

I shrugged. "Makes no difference to me. You still have your wife and Lorena to worry about. I'd focus on sorting that out if I were you... err, which, funny enough, I am today."

Cañizares frowned. He knew he had the immediate problem of his wife to deal with. He shot a look at Chiara, a look that seemed to galvanise her into action.

"Show me the tattoo." Chiara was on her feet, ignoring Cecil's attempts to stop her approaching. Cañizares saw a way of gaining back control. He pulled off his jacket and held it out in a manner that said he was used to having a minion at his beck and call. Carlos stepped forward and took it. The sudden activity threw me. I hesitated, unsure of how I should react.

Cecil intervened. "You too, geezer. Let's get it on."

I stared at him, my frown an attempt at getting a tacit understanding that this was a crap idea. I'd had enough of games.

He ignored it. "C'mon mate. Give it here." He tugged at my sleeve and I slipped off the jacket. He took it and handed it to Carlos.

Cañizares was eager. He rolled his left sleeve up and proudly displayed the distinct tattoo on his forearm. I had a feeling that there was little point in me competing but encouraged by the boys, I went with it. Chiara stared and, seeing my bare arm, practically spat out her response.

"Impostore! You try to make fun of me and my husband. You are a... phoney. You try to make –"

"Easy, darlin'. Don't get too excited," Cecil said. "It's a promo stunt, ain't it. Your old man's commercial team are doing a little advertising thing for his boot sponsors."

Chiara looked unimpressed. Her face raged, but Cecil ignored her and continued.

"Yeah, with Madrid doing the league and cup double last season, they decided they'd do a little mumble about some ordinary geezer dreaming about being a bigtime footie star. So they thought they'd get a lookalike, you know... a double. Saves 'em doing all that trick photography stuff too. And now they're on a live rehearsal, test thing. Thought if they can fool his missus, they can fool any mug. And it works."

Chiara still looked a long way off impressed.

Cañizares smirked. "You lose, my friend. You look out. Like I say, I know people."

Jasper stepped forward, fists clenched, anger in his eyes.

"Leave it. Jas," Cecil said. "Let's go get a drink. It ain't worth wasting good drinking time on this mug. Thinks he's the fucking daddy. Geezer got no soul." He turned to Carlos. "You got Matt's jacket, mate?"

Carlos nodded and handed me the jacket.

"You will need your jacket, amigo," Cañizares said, his eyes blazing. "You need it because you no here in next five minutes. You screw with me, I screw with you."

I ignored it. I had nothing left to worry about. If we got thrown out, we could go somewhere else. And I had money. If Cecil was right, cash would do the talking. I smiled as dismissively as I could at Cañizares and turned to walk away. I was stopped by Lucero.

"¿Adónde vas, inglés? Where you go, inglés?"

I gulped. Up close, he was huge, and his face bore the menacing frown of a man with bad intent. I was saved from confrontation by Huguette.

"Hey! Mes amis. What are you doing? You are in a civilised place. Behave." She raised her hands, gently parting the confrontational stance.

Lucero took a deep breath and glared at me. "I no forget your face."

Unlikely he would forget me, given I'd been impersonating his employer all day. I shrugged, trying to affect a nonchalant air. I said nothing and Lucero walked away. I turned to Huguette,

"Thank you. I think he's upset."

She smiled, a warm smile. "You are funny, monsieur. You know, I knew there is something different. And now I know. I think that you have kind eyes. Ignacio does not have this. I see this when you talk to us, but it confuse me. You are a good man."

"Thanks. Been a tough day. One I don't ever fancy doing again. I'll be glad when your friends are back in Madrid. I don't suppose I'll ever run into Ignacio again."

Huguette smiled. "Maybe, if you visit Madrid?" She noticed my frown. "No, I joke with you. Is a big city. You should visit."

"Who knows? Maybe I will. Ignacio said something about going there with my friends, but right now I've gone off the idea. Shame, it might have been fun."

"You should go. You don't have to worry about Ignacio. You are your own man. You prove that today."

I liked the compliment. "Well, you never know. Maybe in a few weeks. We'll see."

Huguette leaned forward and kissed me on either cheek. "Au revoir, monsieur." She turned and walked away. I slipped on my jacket and caught up with my friends.

"Sorry about that, boys. Bit of aggro with that bloke with the ponytail, Lucero, one of the bodyguards."

Cecil responded, his gaze scanning the room. "What's he done? Where is he?"

"Nothing. It's okay. Leave it, Ces," I said. "Just bad losers. It's sorted."

"You sure?"

"Yeah, I'm cool."

Cecil stared at me for a moment as if checking my 'coolness', then he said. "Yeah, mate. Fucking losers, the lot of 'em. But we're winners, mate, and I got a feeling you can afford another bottle of Cristal." He winked at Jasper. "Keep the dream alive, boys."

I pulled out the rest of the cash from my back pocket and peeled off five hundred pounds. A bottle was duly delivered, and four glasses filled. A celebratory toast was called, and then I had a question.

"Where did you get all that stuff about a football boot commercial and the double thing, Ces?"

"Jas's idea. He's your marketing man. Worked a treat too. Fooled his old lady enough to buy you some time."

I had to laugh. The boys were always tuned in, ready for backup or wingman mode. I glugged down a few mouthfuls of champagne, wondering why, with the amount I had already consumed, I felt so sober. Time to change that and have a chilled day. I let my shoulders drop out of their clenched grip and thought about a bet. Having missed one race due to sorting Cañizares, we scanned the penultimate race of the day. Our deliberations were cut short by a guy in uniform.

"Excuse me, sir. I'm from VIP security, and I have reason to believe that you have entered this area without authorisation and you do not have valid tickets. A customer has made a complaint."

My blank stare caused the uniformed guy to focus on his question. "May I see your VIP invitations?"

A wave of panic spiralled from the pit of my stomach. I felt the eruption and tried to stay ahead of it. If it got to my brain, there was no certainty of the outcome.

Money. Cecil had said it. 'Nobody can screw with you. You got wedge,' or something. But it was crunch time. How does somebody with 'wedge' behave? Bribery. Had to be. I reached into my back pocket and pulled out two grand in cash.

Cecil grabbed my arm. "What you doing, geezer? Show the man your tickets."

Tickets. I stared at Cecil, certain he had taken leave of his senses.

"Mate, sort it. There's a race going off in ten minutes."

I was dumbstruck

"Show him." Cecil's emphasis on the word 'show,' focussed me. Something was afoot. I glanced at Carlos and Jasper. Carlos nodded. I had no idea why, but a nod had to be positive.

The uniformed guy glared at me. He required a response. My hesitation prompted Carlos. He approached the security guy and held up a hand.

"Un momento, Señor." And then he turned to me. "Check your pockets."

With no other option, I reached into the inside jacket pocket, instinct rather than thought. To my surprise, I discovered what felt like a small book. I pulled it out and stared at it. Carlos grabbed it.

"His passport. He's a Spanish citizen." He opened it to reveal a photograph. "See, Ignacio Cañizares. You know him? You should do. Ballon D'Or winner in 2014, top scorer in La Liga. A proper VIP. Why are you asking questions?"

The uniformed guy cleared his throat, ruffled but determined to stay with his job programme. "I need to see your passes or your tickets. The passport is just ID."

Carlos nudged me. I delved into the right side jacket pocket and pulled out two pink lapel badges. Hiding my surprise, I held them out.

"There you are, Señor," Carlos said, "You cannae ask for more."

The guy blushed but tried to cover his embarrassment. "Thank you, but there are four of you. That is just two badges. I need to see all your race badges or your tickets."

There was an awkward silence. I realised the game was up. It had been a good day, and we had agreed that if we got thrown out, it wouldn't matter. It was just a shame we would have to leave the course.

I was about to come clean when I caught Carlos's eye. He nodded, a sign I took to mean that he knew something. I hesitated. He nodded again. I dropped a hand into the left jacket pocket, fumbled around and pulled out six MacFadden's business cards, but no badges. I stared at them, wondering what they were doing there and then stuffed them into my back trouser pocket. Then I went for my left trouser pocket but only found the tightly rolled cash bundle. In the other pocket I found the second cash roll, but also my blue tie. I pulled it out, and as I did, something dropped to the floor. Carlos retrieved it instantly – David Anderson's badly singed race badge. He handed it to the official. He stared intently at it, turning it in his hand. Only the top edge of the badge had any colour, the pink design for that day's racing.

"What happened to this, sir?" he said to me.

"Err... it got burnt," I said, a fact that was blindingly obvious.

"Burnt? How?"

"Uh... well, err... it's my birthday. I was... you know... I was..." I had no idea where I was going with my rationale. Why I mentioned a birthday, I wasn't sure, other than that the passport may have been a psychological trigger. Cecil picked up on my floundering and butted in.

"Yeah, he was leaning over blowing out the candles on his birthday cake earlier and the thing caught fire. Fucking fire hazard. Could've been a lot worse too. Health and safety thing if you ask me. And the other badge, mine, I chucked it. Can't be going round wearing anything that dangerous. But if you still need to see it, I know which bin I put it in if you wanna come with me."

The uniformed guy hesitated. Cecil saw it and kept going.

"I'm thinking of putting in a complaint, to be honest. Top footballer nearly severely burnt. Imagine the insurance pay out on that mumble. And the bad PR. Lucky we got it sorted." He ran a hand through his hair and then gestured towards us. "I mean, we give you enough proof ain't we that we're legit, but if you need to see my other badge follow me."

"My apologies, sir, but I have to do my job. I do understand." He turned to me. "It's just that somebody here is saying that he is you. He complained and we have to follow up any complaints."

Cecil cut in again. "We've had trouble with him before. Gate crashing parties and stuff. Thinks 'cos he looks like Ignacio here, he can live his life too. And, yeah, mate, I get you're only doing your job and a good job you do too, I have to say. Now, you gonna chuck this blagger out?"

"Yes, of course, sir. I will have to if he has no ticket."

"Trust me, he ain't. And don't be fooled by all that Spanish chat. He's got bullshit down to a fine art. Just let him know that if he starts any trouble, he's on CCTV. Won't do his lookalike career any favours if stuff like that ends up all over YouTube."

"Thank you, sir." He turned back to me. "Sorry about the fuss. Enjoy the rest of your afternoon. Oh, and err... I'll have a word about the badges."

I smiled, out of relief rather than any amusement at the guy's change of attitude.

"Err... Thanks. We all have a job to do," I said.

"Thank you. Oh, one other thing. Can I... can I ask you for an autograph?" He pulled a notepad from a back pocket and offered it to me along with a pen. I scribbled what I thought would pass as a signature and, with a polite smile, he went away.

I took a deep breath, followed closely by another slurp of champagne. The bubbles finally hit.

"What the fuck is going on? This is getting way too stressful."

I saw the quick interaction between the lads. Jasper spoke first. "There's nothing going on, Matt. We were just dealing with what was in front of us. We've seen you're getting stressed out with all this shit, so we're on the case."

"Okay, cool... but how come I had Cañizares's passport and his guest badges?"

Jasper laughed. "It was off the cuff, mate. Once I came up with the marketing bullshit, we were all on it. Carlos took the jackets, remember, and did a switch. They're identical."

"Yeah, we guessed he might have had tickets on him or something that would be legit," Cecil said.

I turned to Carlos. "But you seemed fairly sure. How did you know the badges would be in his pocket?"

"I didn't, Mateo. I thought, maybe we'd get lucky and find some tickets."

"And it gave us a chance to put one over on billy big bollocks," Jasper said.

"Yeah, and all blokes have some ID with 'em… wallet, credit card, something," Cecil said. "The geezer was so full-on with that tattoo bollocks he was never gonna notice a jacket switch. Carlos give me the nudge and we went for it. Took a gamble that he'd try to rumble'ya once you fronted him up. Bit of insurance, and better he gets fucked off out of it than us. Turned out all right. Geezer only got his passport on board too."

"You got lucky with that then, boys."

"Lucky? We're at the fucking races geezer. It's all a gamble, ain't it? You win some, yeah. And talking of getting lucky, what was all that bollocks about your birthday? Show me that passport, Carlos."

Carlos handed over the passport. Cecil flicked to the ID page. "Yeah, like I thought. The security bloke only had to look at the passport again to see your birthday ain't today. So you got lucky there, mate." He gave me the passport and I slipped it into my inside pocket.

Jasper laughed. "Yeah, but you blagged it big time, Ces. I thought the poor bloke was gonna have a breakdown. Nice one."

"Yeah. See that's proper blagging, ain't it."

I finished my champagne. "Boys, thanks. I was about to come clean to be honest."

"Nah, mate. Gotta rinse the blag as far as you can, ain't ya? I mean if he weren't buying it, yeah, we would've had to swallow it and fuck off. But he went for it. Poor geezer thinks his badges are dodge too and there ain't nothing wrong with 'em."

I laughed at Cecil's bold and brash attitude, something I was well aware of and secretly envious of too.

"Where did that burnt badge come from anyway, Matt?" Jasper asked. "Lucky you had that."

"I forgot I had it, to be honest. It belonged to one of Cañizares's sponsors. There was an accident. The badge got burnt. I picked it up with my tie. Long story."

"We got plenty of time," Cecil said.

"Uh... I set fire to his tie when –"

"You did what?"

"He spilt his drink on it and –"

"What, so you thought you'd set fire to it? How's that work?"

"It was an accident. He snagged his tie. I was trying to help and accidently set fire to it and burnt his jacket. He was the guy I told you I bought the suit for."

"You made a right impression on him then, mate."

I didn't wish to dwell on the incident. "It's all sorted. There'll be no comebacks." I raised my glass. Anyway, I got twenty-eight kay left so I'm sure we can stretch to another one of these. What do you think?"

There was no objection. I reached for my wallet and pulled out one I didn't recognise.

"Shit. I've got Cañizares's wallet too." I looked at the blue leather wallet that was filled with nothing more than credit cards. "He must have mine."

"He ain't got yours, geezer. We got Carlos to lift it before we switched jackets. We weren't gonna lose your wedge. You're cool." Cecil reached into his back pocket and pulled out my wallet. "It's got twenty fifties in there, mate. Where's the rest?"

I pulled the two rolls of notes that were wrapped in rubber bands from my trouser pockets."

"There's five grand there." I delved into my back pocket. "Two grand there... and the rest is..." I felt the blood drain from my face as I dipped a hand into the right side jacket pocket, "... in *my* jacket. Shit. I had two envelopes with the rest of the winnings." I turned to Carlos. "Did you not get them?"

Carlos shrugged. "No, I didnae. I had to be quick. I just went for your inside pocket. That's where most blokes keep their wallets. I didn't want your ID falling into Cañizares hands. Then I just switched jackets. I had no time to search through the other pockets. I didnae remember where you'd put yer money."

"But there was twenty frigging grand... Cañizares has got it! I didn't even think about it when that security bloke had me searching for the badges."

Cecil and Jasper reacted, pushing their way through the crowd in the direction of where we had last seen Cañizares. Carlos legged it after them. I remained rooted to the spot, contemplating my change of fortune.

14

My mind was a fog. Twenty thousand pounds lost in an instant. Easy come, easy go, they say. Even though I had been fortunate to have made that sort of money, it still hit hard. I stared at the remaining cash. Seven thousand pounds left plus the thousand in my wallet. That was still a good day and more than I had ever expected. But the loss of twenty thousand was difficult to dismiss.

A voice distracted me. "Hello." Arabella was standing next to me, a broad smile on her face. "I was hoping to bump into you again." Her smile faded to a frown. "You all right? You look miserable."

"I uh... I'm, err, yes... I just lost some money."

She stared at the cash in my hands and laughed. "Really? Doesn't look like you've done too badly."

"What?" I stuffed the money into my trouser pocket. "Oh that, no. I've lost some serious money."

"Everybody loses money at the races, darling. Get over it. Easy come, easy go."

I didn't really need to hear the phrase that had rattled through my head articulated. But Arabella had a point, and it reinforced the thought.

"I guess so. You said you were hoping to bump into me again. Why?"

A small frown creased Arabella's forehead. "Charming. You know how to make a girl feel wanted."

"No, I didn't mean it like –"

She placed her hand on my upper arm. "I'm only teasing. You intrigue me, that's all. It's not unusual to want to spend time with intriguing people, is it?"

"Err, no. I s'pose not."

"So, did you get to meet your footballer friend in the toilets?"

"Oh… uh, yeah. And thanks for helping with that. Sorry to get you involved."

She smiled. "My pleasure. Everyone needs someone's help from time to time. He seemed like a nice man. And then your friend came along and whisked him away. Uncanny likeness though, I must say." She glanced around the room and then turned back to me. "Anyway, I found this and thought it looked like yours." She held up a blue jacket. I hadn't noticed it dangling in her other hand. "But I see you've got yours. I'll hand it –"

"Hang on. Let me see. Where'd you find it?"

"It was on the back of a chair on the other side of the room. I was going to hand it in. Then I thought it looked like the one you'd been wearing, so I came to find you."

"It *is* mine," I said and reached out to take it.

Arabella snatched her hand away. "But you've got yours on, silly."

"Yes, but... no, this isn't mine. That one is. Look in the pockets. There should be some money."

She slipped her hand into the inside pocket.

"No, the side pockets. There should be an envelope in each."

She dipped into one of the pockets and pulled out a white envelope.

"That's it! That's the money I lost. I meant I'd actually lost it, not gambled it."

She searched the other pocket and found an identical envelope.

"There should be ten grand in each," I said.

Arabella's eyes widened. "Twenty thousand?"

"Yes. That's what I meant. You'd look miserable if you mislaid that amount of cash." I pulled off Ignacio Cañizares's jacket. "There was a… a thing with the footballer. I've got his wallet and passport. Here, check the inside pocket."

Arabella slid a hand inside the jacket and pulled out the passport. She flicked through the pages and then looked up. "Okay, I'm convinced," she said with a smile. "But he does look like you."

We were interrupted by the return of the lads. "Geezer's gone, ain't he," a breathless Cecil said.

"And yer jacket isnae where'a left it," Carlos said, his face tight with worry. "He musta took it."

"Chill, guys, it's okay. It's sorted. Arabella got my jacket. The money's all there."

"Do what? All there?" Cecil said, a confused look creasing his features. "And who's Arabella?"

"This lady here."

Jasper stepped forward. "We met earlier," he said, his smile giving away his pleasure at seeing Arabella again.

"Right result, darlin'. You better join us for a little celebration then," Cecil said. "Got any mates?"

"Of course I have, but they're both men and gay. And I'm not sure you're their type." She winked at me and then said, "But they are in the racing business."

Cecil grinned. He liked women with spirit.

"We saw the security man again," Carlos said. "He told me they'd asked yer man to leave. He went with no fuss. Probably the missus giving him grief too."

"Must've made a quick exit to forget about his jacket," I said.

Arabella laughed. "Maybe he just couldn't find it. I saw a group of people and security men in a huddle when I picked the jacket up. They were quite a way away from where I found it, so I didn't think it belonged to any of them. I just thought it looked like Matthew's."

"Aye, that's right. I left Mateo's jacket on the back of a chair," Carlos said. He turned to me. "When I switched the jackets and gave you Cañizares's jacket, I couldn't walk off with yours in my hand. One of his people might have noticed. So I stuck yours on a chair well away from the footballer. I meant to go back for it but that security fella turning up when he did distracted me."

"I reckon he forgot all about his jacket with all that aggro going on," Jasper said. "Probably got plenty of them and a big limo waiting for him."

"Maybe. Odd that he wouldn't think about his wallet and passport though," I said.

"Mate, he probably don't need to. He's got people who do his thinking for him. He don't have to worry 'bout the sort of stuff we do," Cecil said. He turned to Arabella. "Nice one, Arabella. We're all sorted. And these mates of yours, they got any tips? Two races to go, ain't there?"

Arabella flicked her hair from her face and pushed her impressive cleavage forward, more an intuitive action rather than any deliberate move. "I can ask, but I've done your friend enough favours already. He owes me a drink." She turned to me. "Remember? You promised."

"Erm… yeah, of course. Uh… what will it be?"

"Something large, darling," she said, a mischievous grin lighting her features.

Cecil laughed and elbowed me in the ribs. "Mate, you know the mumble. Don't keep a lady waiting when she needs a large one, yeah. Cristal's large enough for now if you get the drift?"

Sometimes Cecil didn't take much 'getting.' I made my way to the bar and ordered a bottle – and ran into Huguette.

"Monsieur! You are still here, I see."

"It's Matthew… uh, my name."

"Pleased to meet you, Matthew. I hope you had a good day after all."

"Uh… yeah, yes I did. You too."

"I did. It has been fun, and with a little drama." She moved slightly closer, a smile playing on her lips. "I know about Ignacio. He likes to play, more than just football, you understand?"

I nodded.

"In France, you know, sometimes we accept these little… how do you say this in English? Dalliances? Is that right?"

"Uh, yes. It is."

"But Italian women, they do not like. Ignacio was my friend too one time. I knew as he got famous he would have temptation." She shrugged. "C'est comme ça!"

I felt a moment's guilt at having helped Cañizares with his deception. Huguette saw it.

"Matthew, it is not your fault. These things happen around famous people."

I smiled, grateful that Huguette saw things the way they were. "Thank you. So… err… will you stay for a drink? My friends over there would like that, and I'm just getting some champagne."

Huguette glanced across in the direction I had indicated. "You have a lot of friends? They seem fun."

"Just a few but, yes, they are."

"I met your lady friend, we speak earlier. It is coincidence. She sings and says we have met before on my tour. I didn't recognise her. She has changed her hair, I think. Then I remember. You know how it is, you meet a lot of people in this business."

"I guess so. I only met her today, myself."

Huguette winked. "Ah, I see. She is a nice lady, very attractive, very chic. Maybe you two have fun, a little romance, peut-être?"

"Uh… err, no. We're just… I have someone." The barman placed an ice bucket on the bar and uncorked the champagne bottle. "Look, come and join us. If Ignacio and Chiara have gone, no point in being on your own."

"I'm sorry, monsieur Matthew. Another time." She smiled. "I have already called my driver. I go now."

"Oh, okay. No worries." I glanced behind, aware that my friends were waiting for me to sort the drinks but enjoying the calm after the day's dramas – Jasper giving Arabella his usual full-on delivery, his cheeky grin fully loaded, beaming his, 'I like you big time' message; Cecil, on the case too, waiting to strike the minute he saw an opening; Carlos patient, his Latin American side telling him that his time would come to impress. And I had a thought.

"Hey, err… maybe next time you're in London…" I pulled a few of Carlos's business cards from my pocket and handed them to Huguette. "… maybe you'd like to try somewhere different."

Huguette examined one of the cards and said, "MacFaddens's Bar? What is this?"

"It's my friend's place. Worth a try if you like a night out," I said, trying to dismiss the contrast between a provincial wine bar and the high octane social lives of Huguette's circle of 'catwalk' and musician friends. "Maybe give some to your contacts."

She slipped the cards into her handbag. "Merci, Matthew. I go now. Adieu. Bonne chance, mon ami."

I smiled as Huguette walked away. I liked her. She hadn't thought bad of me, and it made me feel better about things. My thoughts were interrupted by Cecil. "Geezer. Over here. C'mon. Group photo."

I looked round and saw Cecil had managed to persuade Wendy, the cashier, to take photos of the lads with Arabella. I picked up the champagne and went and joined them. We raised our glasses in celebration as we posed for the camera.

The day had turned out well.

15

I woke up with a hangover. I suppose I was entitled to. I'd paid enough for it. But it's hard to differentiate between an expensive hangover and a cheap one. The body still tells you that you've been a nobhead. I showered, dressed, and made a call to a bike courier firm. Next, I placed Ignacio Cañizares's wallet and passport in a Jiffy Bag and wrote his name and the word "Claridge's" on the front. When the courier arrived I gave him the envelope and the other jacket, and a twenty-pound tip to make sure he delivered the goods speedily.

I called a taxi and headed to MacFadden's for breakfast. Carlos was already behind the bar.

"Hola, Mateo. How's yer head?"

"So so, mate. Yours?"

"Och, I can handle my liquor. Coffee?"

"That's not what Ces says. No, get me a Bloody Mary."

"Ah, so you *are* suffering. And never mind Ces. He'll be down in half an hour. Texted me earlier."

Carlos busied himself mixing my drink and firing up the coffee machine for one of his favourite black coffees. I reached across to one side of the bar and picked up a newspaper from a stack that was still neatly folded as if just delivered. I scanned the front and then turned to the back page.

The headline caused me to sit upright. "You seen this, Carlos?"

"Seen what?" he replied over his shoulder as he poured a coffee.

"The papers."

"Nae time to read papers, Mateo. They're for my customers. I got a bar to run." He turned and placed a tall glass of Bloody Mary on the bar. "There you go."

"Look at this." I spun the paper round and watched Carlos crack a smile as he scanned the headline that said, '*CAÑIZARES IN SHOCK TRANSFER MOVE TO COLOGNE.*'

As he read it, I had to laugh. That would cause some confusion in the world of football. For a moment I felt sorry that it had come to this for Ignacio Cañizares. He would have the media attention to deal with, a relationship problem to sort out and an angry reporter on his case once the story was shown to be untrue. But my sympathy for his predicament passed just as quickly as it had arisen.

We were interrupted by Cecil's arrival.

"Hi, Ces. You're early."

"Yeah, mate. Fancied a bit'a breakfast. Give us one of them, Carlos," he said, pointing to my Bloody Mary. Carlos pushed two menus across the bar and then set about making another Bloody Mary.

"You seen the papers, Ces? Cañizares is all over the back page."

"And the rest." He pulled a rolled up newspaper from his back pocket. "Check page five."

I opened the paper and found the page. My eyes were drawn to the top right corner.

"Bloody hell."

"Yeah, you're looking good, mate. Fame at last eh?"

In full colour and sharp focus, a photographer had captured the moment on the balcony when I had kissed Lorena on the cheek. To emphasise the detail, it was accompanied by the headline, '*La Liga star in Ascot date with Spanish broadcaster.*' A smaller, library photograph in the middle of the article showed Cañizares with his wife, over a caption that said, '*Cañizares with model wife, Chiara Rustichelli.*' Yet another picture showed a headshot of Lorena with her full name underneath, '*Lorena Márquez.*'

"I wouldn't want to be in his shoes this morning. He's going to be glad I've sent back his passport."

"Did'ya? Well the wife's his problem right now, but he'll land on his feet."

Carlos handed Cecil the Bloody Mary.

"Cheers, boys," Cecil said and took a sip. His eyes screwed tight shut for a second as the spice hit home.

"So, where's Jas this morning? He coming down?" I asked.

Cecil laughed. "Maybe. Last I saw of him he was hitting on that Arabella, big time."

"Typical."

"Anyway, mate, what you gonna do with your winnings?"

"Good question, but I've been giving it some thought. Cañizares offered me an all-expenses paid trip to Madrid if I helped him out. No chance of that now." I reached for my drink, my brief chat with Huguette flashing through my mind. "But there's no reason why I can't treat my mates to a lads' trip to Madrid myself. We don't need some famous footballer to make that happen."

Cecil grinned. "I'm on that programme, geezer. Nice one. Keep the dream alive."

We clinked glasses. "Cheers, Ces."

He placed his Bloody Mary on the bar. "Weren't a bad day out after all, mate."

I nodded. Not a bad day at all.

16

I suppose I should have expected a twist of fate to rear its head since I was used to odd occurrences and coincidences happening in my life. So why should a trip to Madrid be any different? As I strolled through Heathrow Terminal 5, the 'odd occurrence' called my name.

"Matthew?"

I turned in the direction of the voice, my gaze scanning the immediate surroundings. And then I spotted her.

"Erin! Erin Farrell! Wow! Fancy seeing you."

Erin stood up and came towards me, arms outstretched, and embraced me in a warm, welcoming hug. Then she stepped back, her smile wide, and said, "How lovely to see you. I thought it was you as you walked in, although I had to do a doubletake. What's going on with the beard?"

I stroked the eight days' of stubble that adorned my chin. "Oh, that. Hardly a beard. Just a… you know, temporary thing."

"Let's hope they recognise you at the gate then," Erin said, and then, on seeing my frown, added, "I'm only teasing. You look fine. Where are you off to?"

"Madrid. Bit of a break… me and the lads."

"The lads? You mean, Cecil and the guys?"

I nodded. "Yep."

Erin laughed. "Oh dear, trouble ahead then! How are they doing?"

"They're all good. You can find out for yourself. They'll be here any minute. So, what you doing here? You on duty?"

"No, I'm on leave at the moment, couple of weeks. Popping down to Marbella to meet some friends who live there. Using one of my work freebies. I'll spend a few days there, then I'm driving up to Bilbao and taking the ferry to Portsmouth. Bit of a road trip, seeing the sites and where it takes me."

"Sounds fun. Perks of working for an airline, I s'pose. You do like to do things differently!"

"And why not? What time's your flight?"

"It's, uh… one-forty, I think. Yours?"

"Three." Erin smiled. "Glad we're not on the same flight. Remember last time?"

I thought back to my Ibiza trip and to what, in my mind, was a near death experience return flight. "How could I forget that? I'm glad I'm just a passenger this time."

"You did so well though. Love a man who can take control." Her green eyes twinkled.

"Not sure I had a choice, to be honest, seeing as how that lunatic was trying to kill us all." The face of that 'lunatic', Johnny Scalapino, was etched on my memory forever. I let the Ibiza diamond episode flash through my head and quickly dismissed it. "I'm done with drama, Erin. All I want is a quiet life now."

"Nothing wrong with a bit of excitement, Matthew. Keeps the pulse ticking."

Erin Farrell and I had crossed paths a few times and each time there was more 'excitement' than I ever needed. I knew she thrived on anything that killed the boredom of routine. Her good looks and thirst for adventure drew people to her, and things always seemed to happen around her. She brushed a wayward hair from her face and said, "Come on, let's get a drink. We've got plenty of time, and it would be good to see your friends again."

We made our way to the bar and ordered two gin and tonics, Erin choosing strawberry and black pepper gin, while I settled for a conventional one. She sipped hers, savouring it for a moment and then said, "So tell me, last time I saw you… what was it… oh, ages ago now, you'd just got engaged… to… erm…"

"Louise."

"Of course. Sorry. All still good?"

I smiled. "Absolutely. All going well."

"Oh, and speaking of your engagement, I saw Diana for lunch a couple of months ago."

"Diana? Diana Twist?" I only knew one Diana so it had to be her.

"Yes, we hit it off at your little get together in that wine bar… McDuff's or something."

"MacFadden's."

"That's the one. Yes, we had lunch in the City. We seem to have quite a bit in common."

I wasn't quite sure what Diana, a lawyer, and Erin, who sometimes sailed close to the wind where the law was concerned, might have in common, but on reflection, they were both spirited women with very clear ideas about where they were going in life, so perhaps it shouldn't have been a surprise.

"I suppose you do," I said.

"Yes, we do, including both having the hots for you."

I felt myself blush. "Err… well, I'm not sure about that…"

Erin smiled. "So when's the big day then?"

"The big day? Oh… uh, no date yet. Maybe a year or so. Louise is busy with work at the moment, and we're kind of saving up for it. No rush."

"Cool. Well don't go spending all your savings in Madrid."

"I won't. I had a bit of luck at Ascot a few weeks ago, so treating the lads. The rest gets stashed away."

"A stag do?"

"No, just Louise is on a training course for a few days, so we agreed it was a good time for the Madrid trip. I promised the boys after I'd had the win. Long story!"

Erin flashed a mischievous smile. "Cat's away, eh?"

"Uh… no… just a… bit of a… you know… a do."

Erin saw my moment's embarrassment. "I'm teasing, Matthew. I'm sure you, Cecil and the boys will all behave perfectly." She picked up her glass and then hesitated, distracted by something. "Talk of the devil. Look who's walking in like he's some feckin' rock star!"

I turned in the direction Erin had indicated to see Cecil striding towards us, followed closely by Jasper and Carlos. It didn't take long for Cecil to take in the situation.

"Mate, you don't waste any time, do'ya? Drink in your hand and chatting up some hot… " And then recognition kicked in. "Bloody hell… Erin… Erin Farrell. I never forget a face, 'specially a good looking one."

Erin laughed and stood up to hug Cecil. "Cecil Delaney. Still full of the old Irish blarney, aren't you? You don't change."

"You know how it is, darlin'. Got to be one step ahead, giving it large. How've you bin?"

With the greetings out of the way, we sat for another hour, indulging in a few drinks and teasing banter, spirits high, holiday mood kicking in. And then it was time for us to make our way to the departure gate.

Erin said, "Lovely to see you guys. How long are you in Madrid? I drive back that way. We could catch up if you're about?"

"Just over a week. We fly back next Saturday night."

"Cool. Keep in touch. You've got my number still?"

"I have."

"I haven't," Cecil cut in.

Erin laughed. "I'm sure Matthew will give it to you, Cecil."

17

The taxi cruised along a wide treelined carriageway, ahead, a clear blue sky, to the far left, an expanse of green open land that I took to be one of Madrid's many parks. Then we turned right into a narrow brick paved alley that sloped upwards between rows of tall yellowstone buildings, their balconies close enough to one another that it seemed the occupants might be able to shake hands across the street.

"Calle de Almadén," the driver said. "What you say is número?"

"Uh… five, número five, por favor," I replied, recognising the apartment street name. We'd arrived – and, at that moment, a wave of concern struck me causing me to reflect on the conversation I'd had with Cecil just a few days earlier in MacFadden's.

"So where we staying, mate?"

"Booked an apartment. AirBnB."

"An apartment? Not all that self-catering bollocks? Mate, you got the moolah. Why not some fully loaded five star gaff?"

"Ces, chill. It's cool. Four bed, top quality. Come and go as you please." I watched Cecil's expression, looking for some 'tells' that might say he was warming to the idea. Nothing. His frown remained fixed. I needed a gamechanger. "And the good thing about an apartment is no restrictions. You can party all night, invite back who you want. No concierge giving you the once over."

Cecil ran his hands through his hair, sat back and said, "Yeah, maybe. Maybe you got a point. You sure it ain't in the middle of nowhere? I ain't traipsing halfway round Madrid to get to a decent bar."

"You won't have to, Ces. It's pretty central, in the Barrio de las Letras."

"Mate, I ain't interested in where it is. All I need to know is it's close to the action, yeah?"

Action. I reflected on what 'action' might mean. In Cecil's mind, it was kicking bars, hot women, and the bright lights. Jasper had a bit of that going on too but more subtle, probably because his movie star looks meant that 'action' of one sort or another, could happen anywhere. Carlos was laid back. His 'action' was a lively crowd that he could engage with, creating some attention by being different, by intriguing people. His Peruvian Scottish mix gave him a head start there.

'Action' for me was simply enjoying the company of friends. Nothing more. No agenda. I was more settled than I had ever been. I had my relationship with Louise, a relationship that focussed me and gave me something positive and of value. But I still liked the 'edge' that hanging out with my friends added to life. Action? All relative.

And now, we'd arrived. A quiet, narrow residential street some way off the main 'action' it seemed. I paid the driver and got out of the taxi, avoiding Cecil's gaze. I knew if I caught his eye, there would be questions. I checked my mobile. The text said there was a padlocked box clamped to an iron window grille at pavement level and it contained the apartment key. I bent down and pushed in the code, and sure enough, the key was inside. As I stood up, Cecil started.

"Mate, I thought we'd have a reception at least but looks like it's gonna be self-service." He waved his arm in a sweeping arc. "And I tell'ya what, boys, by the looks of things we're well out the loop here."

"Gi'us a break, Cecil, man," Carlos said, "we only just got here. Let's wait and see. Mateo said it's a top quality apartamento and it cannae be more than a wee cab ride to the centre. Were you not looking out the taxi window, Cecil? We came right through the city."

"Yeah, chill, mate," Jasper chipped in. "It'll be fine. Carlos has a point. Let's see."

Relieved to have a bit of back up, I unlocked the front door. It opened into a tiled hallway that led to a flight of wooden stairs, each of its treads a solid piece of highly polished rustic timber, uneven and knotted. Three flights up and we were outside our apartment. I fumbled with the heavy metal lock, my focus on what I would find inside rather than on the job in hand.

"C'mon, mate. Stop fannying about," Cecil called out, which didn't help get the door open. The lock was stiff, its chunky design intended to make the door tamper proof and secure.

"Here, let me," Jasper said, stepping forward. He took the key and with a few turns, had the door open. He went in, Cecil in his wake.

"Wow, blinding!" Jasper said as he took in the view.

Cecil paced across the open-plan room that was split by three wooden pillars and stopped in front of one of two tall, floor to ceiling windows that overlooked the narrow street below. His gaze roamed across the high ceilings and exposed brick walls, some of which contained a variety of arty paintings, taking in the whiteness of the décor and light airy feel of the main room.

"Quality, geezer. Good choice." Satisfied by his first impression, he flopped down on one of two large, white cloth sofas. "I like it, mate."

Carlos said, "See, you just need to be a wee bit patient, Cecil. I knew Mateo would pick a good'un."

Cecil just grinned and didn't respond. his mood a bit more relaxed than when we'd arrived at the door. He stood up and wandered off down the hallway. Jasper crossed the room and undid one of the tall windows that opened onto a tiny balcony. He checked the view both right and left and said, "It's not bad at all, lads. You got the main drag just down the road there and I reckon if we explore a bit, it won't takes us long to get the layout."

Carlos had walked back through to the kitchen area and was busy exploring the cupboards. "Who fancies a coffee? It's all stocked up with the basics." He pulled open the fridge door. "Yep, milk as well. I'll get the kettle on."

Cecil came back into the room, a broad smile on his face. "Mate, top gaff. I'm liking that little en suite double bed mumble at the back there. Bit of me, ain't it."

Carlos flicked the switch on the kettle, turned to Cecil and said, "Hang on, pal. Before you go deciding you're having the best room, I think Mateo should get first pick. I mean, he's paying for the place after all."

I liked Carlos's sense of fairness and also that, of all of us, he was the one who tried to keep a check on Cecil. But I had no particular concern about which room I had. It was a great apartment, and all I needed was a place to sleep.

Cecil made his views known. "Fair enough, geezer, but since the bloke looks like a paraffin with that beard, maybe he don't care where he crashes."

Jasper laughed and shot a look at me.

"It's hardly a beard, Ces," I said, "I just didn't shave for a week or so, that's all." I hadn't told them that after the issue with Ignacio Cañizares, something in my subconscious felt the need for me to hide. As the Madrid trip grew closer, I had a nagging concern about running into him again or being mistaken for him. The unshaven look was an attempt at disguise, a need to deal with a sense of vulnerability. "Anyway," I continued, "I've got no issue about where I sleep. It's no big deal. They're all nice rooms. Sort it between yourselves."

"Done then," Cecil said and headed off in the direction of the master bedroom.

18

With the apartment arrangements sorted out and settled, we set off for something to eat. Carlos and I took a while to persuade Cecil that it was a good idea to eat before we explored any bars. The last food we'd had was on the flight. The promise of a livener or two after we'd eaten was enough for Cecil in the end, but he felt it necessary to add that we were not 'a bunch of tourists.'

We found a place on the corner of Calle de San Pedro and Calle del Gobernador, not far from the apartment, called Motteau. Outside it occupied the street level section of a large apartment building, all red stone above and grey, granite-like block at its base. Inside, it had the appearance of a farmhouse kitchen, open plan with a glass partition that let you see the staff making cakes and preparing the food. We sat at one of the heavy marble-topped tables and ordered coffee, croissants and pastries.

"S'all right here, ain't it?" Cecil said, through a stream of dough flakes as he stuffed a mouthful of croissant.

"Aye, no bad," Carlos replied, "but it isnae typical Spanish. More French bakery, I'd say."

"Doesn't matter what it is," I said. "I'm starving."

"Boys, we ain't here doing a restaurant tour," Cecil said. "When we're done, we got a bit of exploring to do."

"Cool," Jasper said. "They reckon the Royal Palace is worth a look and the –"

"Nah, you nob. Checking out the night life. Getting the lay of the land. Plenty of time for all that tourist shit. Dunno if you guys noticed but there's some blinding looking Spanish señoritas out there. I'm clocking it, boys, don't you worry about that."

Jasper grinned. "I'm with you, Ces. I'm on that programme."

"Good. Here's the plan then. We check out a few bars this afternoon, get the old mumble on what's cool, then tonight we go large, yeah?"

Carlos winked at me and then said, "I think we should stay in tonight, Cecil. First night, we need to rest up a bit. The jet lag and all that. Then we'll be fresh for tomorrow."

"You having a giraffe, geezer? Jet lag? What fucking jet lag? We got a plane from London, not Vegas! Mate, if you ain't up for it, then you stay in. You guys are up for a party, ain't ya?"

The three of us stayed quiet for a moment, Jasper catching on that Carlos was on a windup. Then Carlos banged the table with his fist and burst out laughing. "I had you going there, cucaracha!"

Cecil grimaced. "All right, geezer. Calm down. I knew you was taking the piss. But, mate, if you can't hack it... "

"Cut it out you two," I said. "Let's get the bill and go check the place out."

We spent the afternoon wandering around the city. Madrid was like any major capital city, a mix of hustle, bustle, car horns, traffic and people but despite that, it had a relaxed vibe. Perhaps it was the sunshine. It's easy to get stressed in a busy city when you have to carry an umbrella or wrap up in several layers of clothing. Whatever it was, I was glad I had booked the trip.

We slipped into the 'no rush' vibe, stopping at pavement cafes trying a beer or two, enjoying the afternoon sun. For once, Cecil seemed quite chilled. A cold beer and *'the sun on the back of my neck'*, seemed give him a relaxed demeanour but, at the same time, the prospect of the night ahead was never far from his thoughts. He made sure that Carlos, with his command of the language, got as much detail as he could on the social scene. I knew that, later, the laid back demeanour of the day would give way to a strategic attack on the city's night life.

I woke at 9.30 a.m. No-one else was up. The night before had gone on until 4 a.m. The city didn't come alive until gone ten, so that had dictated the pattern of the evening. I headed for the kitchen, grabbed a bottle of water from the fridge and switched on the kettle. Ten minutes later, Carlos emerged from his room.

"Hola, Mateo. You okay?"

"Bit of a thick head, to be honest."

"Aye, a few too many cervezas and then all that wine. Cecil was hitting the Rioja like it was juice. He's an animal!"

I laughed. "You knew that already, Carlos. Just because Madrid is cool and laid back don't mean Ces is going to change. Coffee?"

"Aye, laddie. And five sugars." Carlos pulled out a chair and sat at the table. He examined the TV remote control for a moment and then pushed it to one side. "He don't like that queuing up, does he? He was getting a wee bit moody with some of them bouncers."

"I know. His 'how are ya' doesn't seem to cut it here." Cecil never liked queuing and never queued to get in anywhere in London. His *'how are ya'* handshake with a ten pound note concealed in his hand for the doorman usually took care of the queues, but it hadn't worked the night before, even with twenty euros a time. "I kept telling him to chill but he wouldn't have it. I wouldn't mind, but the worst queue was only a ten, fifteen minute wait."

"I know. I dinnae know what he expects. "

Carlos and I were on our second coffee when Cecil surfaced, his hand adjusting the front of his boxer shorts, his hair dishevelled and the effects of a late night evident in his eyes.

"Mate, gimme one of them," he said, pointing at my cup.

I poured a coffee and pushed the mug towards him. He grabbed it, took a couple of slurps, and ran his hand through his hair. He scanned the room as if familiarising himself with his surroundings and said, "Lads, we gotta think about this."

Carlos shot me a look and rolled his eyes.

"Think about what?" I said.

"This whole mumble. Them bars. I ain't doing that fucking queuing. Nah, mate. I don't queue. We gotta sort that out."

"Whatever you say," Carlos said. He picked up the remote, pointed it at the TV and walked over to the sofa. He had no interest in a Cecil rant at that time of the day.

"It wasn't that bad, Ces," I said. "We only queued around ten minutes or so at a couple of bars. I can handle that."

"Yeah? Well, what you're missing, is once you're in there, the bars are mobbed. Four fucking deep, and in my book that's another queue. I ain't got time for that shit. We're s'posed to be partying, not waiting round like some dumb arsed tourists."

"We got served in the end. What's the problem?"

Cecil stared at me for a moment, then said, "In the end? That's the problem. I don't wanna be served 'in the end.' I need to be served in the beginning... bit of priority, mate. I mean we're spending top dollar so I want... you know what I'm saying. No queuing to get in, no pushing and shoving to get served."

I ignored the fact that most of the 'top dollar' we were spending was coming from my racing winnings and just shrugged. Best to leave Cecil to his own devices when he was in post night out mood. He stood up and walked over to where Carlos had spread himself on the sofa, two cushions behind his head, absent-mindedly watching some Spanish sports programme. Cecil stared at the TV for a moment. Suddenly, he shouted at Carlos. "Wind that back, geezer."

"Wind what back?"

"That... the telly."

"Eh?"

"Gimme that remote, Carlos. It's SKY, ain't it? They do live pause."

Carlos threw the remote to Cecil who caught it and pointed it at the TV. He fiddled with the buttons and the programme scrolled back through its previous images. He let it roll until he saw a football clip and then played it in normal time. The screen showed footballers at a training ground, a reporter saying something in Spanish as the clip progressed. Then he paused it, the camera focussed on three players as they played 'keepy-uppy' between themselves. A broad grin crept across Cecil's face.

"That's it, boys. Sorted."

Carlos rubbed his eyes, trying to wipe away the sleep mode that his prone sofa position had induced.

I walked across to where Cecil stood and said, "What's sorted?"

Cecil laughed. "Mate, you know who that is?"

I stared at the image on the screen. Three footballers, a full length shot slightly blurred by the pause. I didn't get time to respond.

"It's him. Cañizares, ain't it. They're training, preseason."

I stared harder at the screen. "So?"

Before Cecil could answer, Jasper came into the room, a towel wrapped around his waist, his hair wet from the shower.

"What's happening, lads?" he asked.

"Mate, I got an idea," Cecil said.

"An idea? About what?"

"To stop all that queuing, Jas, like we was doing last night." Cecil turned to me, his expression intense, enough to cause me some trepidation. And then it dawned on me.

"No. No. That's not happening, Ces."

"Mate, it ain't gonna do no harm. We can't be queuing up like muppets then getting the knockback 'cos some fuckwit doorman don't like the look of us."

"No, Ces… no." I turned away and walked back to the kitchen area.

"What's going on?" Jasper asked. "What's not happening?"

Cecil smiled and pointed towards the TV screen. "It's simple, geezer. We just need Matt to use the fact he looks like that footballer and get us a bit of priority."

Jasper laughed. "Yeah, that'd work. Fast track us in, maybe a bit of the old VIP treatment. I like it, Ces." He picked up a cup and poured a coffee.

Cecil turned to me. "See, mate. It ain't difficult. It's a blag, ain't it."

"No, I'm not, Ces. No way. You forgotten all that aggro we had at Ascot? It's not worth it. We don't need to go clubbing. There's plenty of cool bars here."

"Mate, what's wrong with ya? Nothing happens here before midnight. Clubs are where it's going on. And that's where all the hot chicks are."

"Yeah, but I –"

"Listen, none of that bollocks is gonna happen again. You ain't gonna run into that footballer. Madrid's a big fucking place, geezer. What're the chances? And you're here with the boys, bit of moolah in your pocket. Might as well go for it."

"I don't know, Ces. It just doesn't feel –"

"What about Jas and Carlos?"

"What about them?"

"Well, you pull off this little mumble, open a few doors and that, you'd be taking one for the team. Don't forget, these boys got your back when any shit happens."

"Well, I –"

"And nobody's asking you to pretend you actually *are* the geezer. It ain't like that bollocks at Ascot. Just let the mugs think it, yeah? A few days, mate. You don't have to give it large. Just get us in a few places, jump the queues, bit of VIP treatment... you know the swerve."

I let out a deep sigh and walked across to the sofa. Carlos had fallen into a deep sleep, oblivious to what was going on. There was no point in waking him to ask his opinion. I turned to face Cecil.

"Okay, all right, but just to get us in. That's it. I'm not playing the game after that. Once we're in, I'm just being myself. If there's any problem, we walk away, right?"

"Cool. That's all we need, ain't it? Now, let's get started."

"Started? What d'you mean started?"

"Well you gotta get that fucking beard off for a start."

19

The evening came too soon, and with it, an increase in my trepidation levels. Cecil's first remark as I emerged from my room did nothing to alleviate that.

"You ain't going out like that, are'ya?"

"Like what?"

"Like that. T-shirt, trainers."

"Well, yeah, I was. Relaxed look."

Cecil shook his head. "Nah, mate. That ain't gonna cut it. If you're gonna pull off this mumble, you gotta look the part."

"Look the part? Ces, we said it's just a bit of a blag to get past the queues, right? I'm not playing a part."

Cecil stood up, went to the fridge and pulled out two beers. He topped them and handed one to me. "Listen, mate, nobody's expecting you to play a part but you gotta look it, y'know... create the image so the mugs draw their own conclusions."

"What, don't play the part, just look it? How am I s'posed to do that?"

Cecil ran a hand through his hair, a frown playing across his features.

"There's a difference. You don't have to give it some full-on impersonation shit, but you need to look realistic. No player earning the wedge that Cañizares geezer's on, is gonna go out looking like that. If he does, you can bet his threads cost him more than you earn in a year. So for a start, stick a jacket on and a –"

"A jacket! It's roasting out there."

Cecil laughed. "It's appearances, ain't it. Cañizares is Spanish. He's used to the heat. You can take it off once we're in. And you got them cool Oakley shades. Stick them on and a proper shirt."

"But it'll be dark by the time we get to any late bars." I glugged down two large mouthfuls of beer, hoping a quick hit would make Cecil's scenario more acceptable.

"Mate, what's wrong with ya? You know what these celebs are like. They ain't wearing sunglasses to keep the sun out their eyes. Told'ya, it's an image thing – look at me people, ain't I fucking cool."

Just as Cecil finished his sentence, Jasper walked into the room, white shirt, tight black jeans, sharp shoes, his toothy smile gleaming against the early stage tan he had acquired. Cecil pointed at him. "That's more like it. If Jas looked like the footballer, he'd be right on the programme." He turned to Jasper. "Mate, you might have to take one for the team and lend him your shirt and jeans. You're both about the same size."

Jasper nodded, but I could only laugh. "You're joking, Ces? I'm not gonna get in those jeans. You can see how tight they are."

Cecil rubbed his chin. "Yeah, you got a point. The shirt's good though. Yeah, that shirt, your jacket, and the shades. And another thing, the geezer's got a tatt, so keep the sleeves down in case some smart arse wants to get clever, yeah?"

"I'm not going to forget that."

"You got a decent pair of jeans, ain't ya?"

"Yeah, I have but –"

"But what?"

"I'm not sure I can pull this off."

"Fuck's sake, you pulled it off at the races, mate, when you had to. No reason you can't do it here."

The evening went better than expected. The shades and jacket along with Carlos's Spanish, Jasper's style, Cecil's directness and the fact I was stopped for numerous selfies outside several bars, seemed to create the right image. Without ever making a direct claim to be anyone, we were fast-tracked past queues and straight to the best tables. Girls, attention and first class service. Cecil's plan seemed to work, much to his satisfaction.

By the next evening, I had almost grown into the role. It became second nature. I relaxed. I made no claims to be the footballer and no questions were asked by those who just wanted to get close to what they thought was a celeb. It wasn't my fault if they saw what they wanted to. Cecil, it seemed, had been right when he'd said, '*create the image so the mugs draw their own conclusions.*' That was happening. Even the door staff were taken in, mainly because, when I arrived at a venue, it only took one observant fan to jump to the conclusion that I was Cañizares and it created some sort of hysteria in the queue outside. That focussed the security guys on dealing with the situation. Their objective was to keep order, remove the cause of any disorder and get me in off the street. The hustle and bustle of the fans, calling out and pointing their phones to get a picture, took care of any fine scrutiny of my credentials. In any case, had we been turned away for any reason, it was only a matter of moving on to the next place. But we were never turned away and things went remarkably smoothly.

It was the next evening that things took a turn.

20

Circulo de Bellas Artes was busy. There was a queue outside, apparently a nightly occurrence, punters waiting patiently to gain access to the venue's rooftop terrace, but once again we were fast tracked in, guided to the lift, and escorted to one of the best tables. The terrace bar area afforded a spectacular view of the city – the Edificio Metrópolis, immediately opposite, with its black slate dome, accentuated by golden decorative inlays, and Winged Victory statue, catching the eye straight away.

Carlos wanted a group selfie against the skyline backdrop. Having become accustomed to the attention that our table was getting and adapting to my part in the plan, I said that it wouldn't look cool. Anyone who takes a selfie in a venue is not used to being there, so it would undermine the image. Carlos's response was direct.

"Mateo, dinnae get carried away wi'this bullshite, pal. We done the blag, we're in. It disnae matter what the punters think now. C'mon."

Cecil grinned and stood up. I sensed that he didn't care too much once the main objective had been achieved and our table had an ice bucket with a bottle of champagne in it – for which I was paying. I placed my jacket on the back of the chair and followed the lads to the roof edge. It didn't take any effort to get a willing photographer to capture the four of us on Jasper's phone. The only downside, away from the VIP section I spent the best part of fifteen minutes accommodating selfie requests with football fans. Carlos eventually stopped the melee with a stream of Spanish that sounded suitably assertive. He guided me back to our table.

I drained my champagne glass and sat back. "It does get a bit full on, doesn't it. Not sure I'm cut out for that celeb thing."

Jasper grinned. "Only for a week, Matt. I reckon it's blinding." He spun his phone around to show us the pictures. "Not bad, eh? We look like rock stars."

Carlos frowned. "And the same goes for you, Jas. You cannae get carried away with all that celeb thing either, pal. Remember, these people are only hanging around 'cos they think Mateo here's big time."

"Yeah, I know that, Carlos, but we might as well rinse it while we get the chance. I mean, I got propositioned twice already and got three phone numbers, not to mention that little looker last night who was coming on strong, and I ain't even the footballer! I reckon you could rinse it properly, Matt, if you wanted."

I shrugged and thought of Louise.

"Yeah, too right he could," Cecil said, "but that's up to him, ain't it. Point is, it's game on for all of us. People wanna get connected and some of them birds don't mind dropping the white ones if it gets them on a celeb party."

"The attention level's gone stratospheric," Jasper said. "I gotta get famous."

"You don't do too bad with the ladies as it is," Carlos said. "But if you'd let me teach you how to rumba, you'd up yer game big time. The ladies love a wee bit of Latino groovin'."

I smiled at the thought of Carlos's dance moves. His unique style certainly attracted attention, most of it from women who were fascinated by his mix of Latin styles and his own added flair that often left me wondering if he was attempting to drill himself through the floor.

Cecil grinned. "You call that dancing, geezer? I reckon you're only pulling them weird moves 'cos you ain't got the chat, so it's the only way you get noticed. And all that groping's gonna get you arrested one day."

Carlos sipped his champagne and then said, "Yer a bit jel, pal, 'cos you cannae dance. And dinnae worry, I got plenty of chat. Once the lassies get up close and moving, they like a bit of banter. And as for groping, yer missing the point. Latino is about body contact, it's all about chemistry and body heat."

Cecil was about to reply but I jumped in first. "Cut it out you two. Everybody's got their way of doing things. There's no right or wrong."

"Chill, mate. Just having a bit of chat with the geezer," Cecil said.

I raised a glass. "I know. Anyway, cheers, lads. Here's to a fun trip. And... uh, I have to say, Ces's idea... you know, the footballer thing... seems to work. Well, so far, although I worry a bit we might run into him in a bar."

"No chance of that," Jasper said. "He's on preseason training. You saw on TV. No way he's gonna be hanging out in bars now."

"Makes you wonder what the punters in here think though if I'm... he's supposed to be training. Not my problem, I s'pose. So, apart from the selfie thing, there's no real issue." I turned to Carlos. "And thanks, mate, for keeping it under control. No idea what you're saying to them but it works. Cheers."

Carlos nodded.

"Like I told ya," Cecil said. "Piece of cake. We're just taking advantage of a situation. It's up to them mugs what they wanna see. Now, whose round is it? Oh yeah, Matt's?"

The sun dipped slowly behind the Madrid skyline, a spectacular sight from the rooftop. We were three bottles of champagne down and Cecil was itching to find the nightlife. In fairness, each of us had that early alcohol buzz that said, 'let's party', the buzz that looks no further than the moment. My earlier apprehension had given way to a 'devil may care' attitude and I felt relaxed and ready for a full-on night out.

We finished our champagne. The bar security escorted us again to the lift. On the ground floor, we walked through the spacious marble floored lobby, out through the entrance and down the steps. As I turned left towards the busy Calle de Alcalá, I was stopped by two police officers.

"Buenas noches, Señor," one of the officers said to me. He followed it up with several sentences that I didn't understand. I turned to Carlos.

"What do they want?"

Carlos didn't reply. Instead, he got involved in an animated discussion with both police. I tugged at his arm. "What's going on?"

Carlos turned around. "They want to search you, amigo."

"Search me? What for?"

"They say they have reason to believe you're carrying drugs."

"What? Fuck's sake, Carlos, tell them they've got the wrong person. What's all that about?"

Carlos turned back to the two police officers and unloaded a stream of Spanish, but they didn't seem persuaded by whatever he had said. Cecil approached and tried to intervene. Carlos pushed him away and turned back to me. "They insist on searching you, Mateo."

"Can they do that?"

"I don't know but –"

"Forget it. I haven't done anything. No problem. Let's do it and get out of here."

Carlos nodded at the two police. I was taken to one side, under the covered entrance next to the Circulo de Bellas Artes doorway. One of the officers patted me down from shoulders to ankles, then said, "Quítese la chaqueta, Señor."

I turned to Carlos, a quizzical look telling him that I needed help.

"They want you to take off your jacket."

I shrugged, removed the jacket and handed it to one of the police. He moved away from me and patted the jacket down. Then he began to focus on one side. A minute later, he beckoned his colleague over. They huddled together for a moment, and then the second officer came over to me. "Venga aquí, Señor."

Carlos tugged my arm and led me over to the police officer who had my jacket. The officer held out his hands and showed me several polythene resealable packets that contained a white powder.

I stared at it uncomprehendingly as he said something in Spanish.

Carlos cut in. "Mateo, he's arresting you for possession of cocaine."

I stared at Carlos, trying to absorb what he'd said. "What?" I looked at the two policemen. "What? What are you on about?" There was no response. "Carlos? Mate... what the fuck? What's going on?"

"I don't know, Mateo. They reckon they've found the packets in your jacket. There's ten grams of cocaine there and they're arresting you for dealing."

"In my jacket? Dealing? I... what? Tell them it's a mistake. Nothing to do with... I don't ... cocaine?"

It was the last thing I said. I was arrested and taken away.

21

The office building was modern, bright lighting and a maze of open plan workstations. I was led along a corridor that ran parallel to the work areas and taken to a small room that had four chairs lined up along one wall. After twenty minutes, one of the two police officers that had arrested me came back and led me to a large private office. Inside, a man in plain clothes stood, leaning against the edge of a desk. He had the distinguished look of the mature man, dark hair cut short, greying at the temples and a neatly trimmed goatee beard flecked with grey. As I entered, he straightened up and indicated for me to sit in a chair next to the desk. He walked around to the other side and sat down. Next, he opened a drawer and pulled out a brown paper folder and my wallet, which had been in my jacket. He opened the folder and stared at a piece of A4 paper that had several lines of text on it.

"Señor Matthew Malarkey," he said. "I am Ricardo Armendarez, Director Adjunto Operativo... Assistant Director of Operations... for the Spanish National Narcotics Agency." His English was good with only the slightest hint of a Spanish accent. He looked back down at his notes. "You know why you are here, Señor Malarkey?"

"Uh, no, not really," I said, "except that your police officers are trying to say I'm dealing drugs, which I'm not."

Ricardo Armendarez looked up from his notes. "You were found in possession of ten grams of cocaine, Señor Malarkey. That is enough to suggest you are selling... dealing. Are you saying that it was not yours?"

"Of course it wasn't mine. I'm just a tourist. Why would I be going round dealing drugs in Madrid? I only got here on Saturday. Even if I wanted to deal drugs, which I don't, I wouldn't know where to begin. I don't know anyone."

Armendarez shrugged. "It's not difficult. If you go to the clubs, it is not difficult to find people to sell to. So, the cocaine was for your own use? That is a lot of coke, maybe eighty to a hundred lines."

"No... for my use? No, I didn't say that. I don't do drugs. Look, I have no idea how it came to be in my jacket."

"It was hidden in the lining at the back. The sort of thing a dealer would do. How do you think it got there?"

I leaned across the desk. "I just told you, I don't know. You said it was in the lining. I don't understand."

"A small cut... how do you say in English? A small... oh yes... slit. You made this slit in the lining just enough to slide in the packets? Just enough to hide them and easy to get when you need?" He reached below the desk, pulled on a drawer and took out my jacket. "It is your jacket, si?"

"Yes, yes it is, but I don't know how... where's the slit?"

Armendarez spread the jacket out and opened it so that the lining was exposed. He pointed to the right, just to one side of the single vent at the back.

"See? There. This is where we found your drugs."

A neat cut, about six inches long ran horizontally across the lining. It meant the lining could be parted enough to slide in a slim envelope or small packet which could then sit inside the jacket. Next, he took a brown envelope from the drawer and a photograph. He pushed the photograph towards me, turning it so I could see the image the right way up. I stared at what seemed to be a picture of the brown envelope that he had just placed on the desk. The picture showed the envelope held open with a number of small polythene grip seal bags inside, each filled with powder.

I looked up, about to say something but Armendarez pointed to the envelope on the desk. "This was in your jacket. There were ten packets inside, each with one gram of cocaine." He reached out and picked up the wallet. He flipped it open and made a point of staring at the contents for a moment. "You have a thousand euros here, Señor Malarkey. That's a lot of money to carry on the street. You know the street value of ten grams of cocaine?"

"No, I don't. It's not my –"

"It sells for one hundred to one hundred and ten euros a gram, so, por casualidad... uh, by chance... this is also about one thousand euros. Maybe you sell some before this?"

I felt a wave of panic begin to rise from the pit of my stomach as I heard the association that Armendarez was making with the amount of cash I was carrying and the quantities of cocaine. I did my best to quell the panic and try to think clearly.

"Wait, yes, I had a lot of cash but that was because I was treating my friends to the trip to Madrid. I won a lot of money at horse racing in England so I promised them a break and –"

"A break?"

"Yeah, a holiday. I don't know the Spanish… a vacation."

"Ah, sí… vacaciones."

"Yes. So as I was paying for everything, I had a lot of cash with me."

Armendarez frowned and stared at the cash in the wallet. Then he looked up and said, "Señor Malarkey, why you not use a credit card like other tourists? Why you risk carrying so much money in a big city like Madrid?"

I shrugged, unsure of how to answer. "I didn't think about any risk. I just thought it was easier for me to have euros in cash so I didn't have to touch my bank account. I budgeted about two-fifty a day and brought two thousand with me. And I have already spent almost seven hundred."

"I don't think you understand, Señor. You cannot explain why we have found cocaine in the jacket that you agree is yours, and you have large amounts of money, also in the jacket. It is like we find with most drug dealers. Always a lot of euros." He closed the wallet and put it back in the drawer. "I must send this money to our laboratorio to test for traces of drugs."

I didn't need the Spanish term translated and, at that moment, I knew things were stacking up against me. I couldn't explain why cocaine had been found in my jacket, and even though I knew I was innocent of any wrongdoing, I realised it was going to be hard to convince Armendarez of that.

"I want a lawyer," I said.

Armendarez leaned forward, his elbows on the desk. "Señor Malarkey, you do not know Spanish law, no?" He didn't wait for an answer. "You are suspected of a serious criminal offence and my department can hold you here for seventy-two hours for questioning if we feel it is necessary. After that, you can get a lawyer. Until then, no lawyer."

I swallowed hard. "Seventy-two hours? I can't stay here for seventy-two hours. I'm only in Madrid until Saturday as it is. And surely everyone can have a lawyer, can't they?"

Armendarez smiled and looked away for a moment. "No possible, Señor. You must follow the law here in Spain, you understand?"

I nodded.

"So, now I let you go tonight, but you must report tomorrow to the Comisaría de Policía Centro at Calle de Leganitos and bring your passport for me."

"My passport? Why?"

"Señor, it is, uh... standard... standard procedure for foreign national who is arrested on serious crime. You know, you try to leave the country then you have bigger problem. We do not want this. You bring your passport in... uh... un paquete... a packet and –"

"Packet? An envelope, you mean?"

"Sí, an envelope. You write my name. I will keep your wallet until I have results from the laboratorio and I can decide how we must proceed."

"Can I have my bank and credit cards?"

"No possible, your cards must be tested too. They may have been used to cut the cocaine. Now I need some details of your address, and then you are free to leave for now."

22

It was 2.30 in the morning when I got back to the apartment. The boys were sitting around the table, a bottle of red wine open with most of the contents drunk. I stumbled in, a state of shock still wrenching at my system. I said nothing as I met the gaze of my four friends. It was Cecil who broke the silence.

"Mate, where'ya bin? We was worried about'ya."

"Yeah, we went to three police stations in Madrid and they'd nae heard of you," Carlos said.

I pulled out a chair and sat down. "I'm fine. I'm not sure which one they took me to. I was in some sort of special unit, I think."

Cecil emptied the remaining contents of the wine bottle into a glass and shoved it across the table. "So what the fuck were you doing with all that gear? You never said nothing."

"You *are* joking, aren't you, Ces? You think it was mine?"

Cecil didn't answer.

I took a sip of the wine, let it slip down and followed it quickly with a bigger gulp. As I put the glass down, I saw the expectant look on each of my friends' faces. They needed an explanation, but I didn't have one.

"I've no frigging idea how the coke was in my jacket. It wasn't even in one of the pockets. Turns out it was hidden inside the lining."

"It was planted then. Stands to reason," Cecil said. "You bin stitched, mate. What did the cops say?"

I told them the story of how I was taken to an office and questioned by Ricardo Armendarez and that he'd kept my wallet with the thousand euros.

"What, the geezer took a thousand euros off'ya? D'you get a receipt?"

I pulled the sheet of paper from my back pocket. "Yeah, I did. Look."

Cecil examined the slip of paper which had been pulled from a standard receipt book and had a police logo stamped on it. Armendarez had scribbled a signature across the logo.

"Hang on," said Carlos. "They didn't let you have a lawyer? That cannae be right. I'm no expert on Spanish law but that disnae sound right, amigo."

Jasper picked up his mobile from the table. "What did you say the copper's name was? I'll look him up."

"Ricardo Armendarez."

Jasper thumbed through his mobile and then said, "Yeah, Matt, he's legit. A Police Chief. Don't say anything about the drug squad though." He shoved the phone across the table. The screen showed a picture of the officer I had sat across the desk from earlier.

"Yeah, that's him." I browsed through the text, noting his credentials. "The Spanish National Narcotics Agency thing must be an undercover role or something." I slid the phone back across the table to Jasper. "All I know is that somehow I'm in the shit."

Jasper picked up the phone. "Look, Matt, we all know they weren't your drugs, right, and the fact they were hidden in the lining of your jacket must mean something." He frowned and looked across the room. Then he turned back, gesticulating as if he had hit on the answer. "What if somebody knew there'd be cops outside, a dealer maybe? Had some sort of tipoff, realised he had to unload the stash quick so he wouldn't get rumbled, and used you."

I nodded. "Maybe."

"Yeah, but why wouldn't they just drop the packets in his jacket pocket? A lot easier," Carlos said.

"Nah, that don't work," Cecil replied. "That amount of gear's got a lot of street value. They don't wanna lose it. Any straight geezer sticks his hands in his pockets and finds something that shouldn't be there's gonna report it and hand it in. They can't risk that. So they plant it on some mug who ain't gonna get searched 'cos he looks like he's a tourist, and then once he's outta the place, they follow him and get it back. That way, if they think they're gonna get pulled, they're clean. Simple. It can only go wrong if the tourist is searched."

I sipped my wine and dismissed being categorised as a 'mug.' Cecil's rationale made sense. I'd just been in the wrong place at the wrong time, or the right place as far as any dealers were concerned. "Well, I *did* get searched. You could be right, Ces, but how am I s'posed to sort it? The police think I'm a dealer. How do I prove I'm just a mug… I mean, a tourist?"

"Mate, I dunno right now."

Jasper said, "Show us the jacket. You reckon they slit the lining?"

"Yeah, they did. The cops kept it. Said it was needed for forensics."

"So what happens next?"

"I don't know. I'm stuck here. I have to give them my passport and –"

"What, your passport?" Cecil said.

"Yep. Armendarez said I need to hand it in tomorrow."

"Yeah, but we're s'posed to be going home Saturday."

"I know, and he knows that now. That's why he wants the passport. Doesn't want me trying to leave until he's done his investigation."

"What about your wedge? When d'you get that back?"

"I don't know that either. He told me he's sending it to a laboratory to test for traces of drugs."

Cecil frowned and scratched his stubbled chin. "Fuck's sake, mate, that ain't gonna turn out well, is it?"

"Why not?"

"Don't be a nob. It's well known that if a wad of notes is tested, there's gonna be a percentage that's bin used for the old marching powder. You had a thousand euros, what… tens, twenties, the odd fifty?"

"Pretty much."

"That's a lot of notes, mate. Chances are, one or two have bin in some punter's nose somewhere down the line."

Carlos leaned across the table. "Hang on, you been charged? Charged with possession?"

I scratched my head as I recalled the interview. "Not yet. He took the cash, asked for my address and told me to bring in the passport. That's it."

Carlos frowned and looked at Jasper and Cecil. "Don't make sense. They take him to a special unit, take cash off him, want his passport and there's no official charge. I don't get it."

"Well not yet there isn't," Jasper said. "Look, we don't know how Spanish law works. Maybe 'cos he's a UK citizen they don't need the hassle. Maybe they'll just confiscate his drugs, keep the cash and make sure he's on the plane home on Saturday."

"Nah, that's bollocks," Cecil said. "He'll be hearing from 'em, trust me. They find any traces of drugs on them notes and, what with his jacket being fully loaded and carrying all that cash, they're gonna make a case."

I took a slurp of wine and looked at Jasper. "Just for the record, Jas, they're not *my* drugs." I sat back in the chair. "Ces is probably right. I reckon they'll charge me. What else have they got? They find ten packets of coke in my jacket, nobody else involved. It don't look good. Any ideas?"

Jasper got up and took another bottle of red from the rack in the kitchen. He uncorked it and topped up each glass, making sure it was distributed fairly. When he had done, he raised his glass in a toast.

"Cheers, lads. We've got out of scrapes before. No reason we can't sort this one."

Cheers indeed, Jas, I thought. That wasn't the answer I was looking for.

23

I couldn't sleep. The previous night's incident rattled around in my head, no matter how I tried to replace it. I got up and went to the kitchen. It was seven o'clock, and I was tired. I made a cup of tea and took it back to bed. When I'd finished it, I laid down and managed to doze fitfully. An hour and a half of tossing and turning later, I decided there was no point in staying in bed. I got up. No sign of life from the others. No point in trying to wake them either. I made another cup of tea and sat on the sofa. I checked my phone. A WhatsApp message from Louise asking how I was and if I was enjoying myself. What could I say? I texted back, a reassuring 'yes' and told her I missed her – no sense in worrying her about my situation. I finished my tea and stretched out on the sofa with two cushions propped behind my head in the hope that this new location might induce some much needed sleep. Forty minutes later, I gave up. Sleep wasn't going to come. I stood up and opened the tall balcony doors, the fresh air welcome. It cleared my head of the immediate need for sleep. I decided a long walk may help me relax and take my mind off things.

 I showered and dressed, a t-shirt, shorts and trainers. I put fifty euros in my pocket and collected my passport from my room. Better to get that done sooner rather than later. I checked the police station address on my mobile and found that it was only a couple of kilometres away at Calle de Leganitos. I could do with the walk.

 Outside it was already warm, the sky a strip of blue between the tall buildings that stretched the length of Calle de Almadén. From the apartment I turned right and walked to the junction at the end of the road and turned right again. The grey bricked street stretched into the distance, a single corridor that divided rows of shops, tapas bars and apartments. It was still quiet, a few people moving about, getting their day started, the odd van dropping off deliveries to the bars. I kept walking, feeling a sense of relief that I was on my own for a moment with time to think.

Ahead, the street crossed a number of junctions, side streets similar to the one I was on. I continued to the next junction where I spotted a tapas bar that was just opening up, Cervecería El Diario, on the corner of Calle de Jesús and Calle de las Huertas. I fancied a coffee and went in. I took a seat in a corner, near the entrance, at the end of a long bar that had a glass display cabinet filled with a variety of tapas dishes. To my right, a large bronze statue of what appeared to be two nymphs, entwined in an embrace as one of them poured water from a jug, took centre stage. The bar had an authentic feel so I decided to stop there for a while. A waiter brought coffee and some tapas – ham, bread and olives. I didn't feel hungry but I knew it was a good idea to eat.

On a ledge by the window, I spotted some maps of Madrid that were on display for tourists. I picked one up, spread it across the table, and as I drank my coffee, focussed on where I might go after I had been to the Comisaría de Policía. The Royal Palace caught my eye. It wasn't far, a few minutes' walk from the police station, and looked like it was worth a visit, a bit of a distraction until I could come up with a way of dealing with the police incident.

Twenty minutes after finishing my coffee, I found myself outside Comisaría de Policía Nacional Distrito Madrid-Centro. Hesitantly, I approached the entrance and went in. As my eyes adjusted from the brightness of daylight, I took in my surroundings. On the left side of the doorway, there was an airport style scanner and on the right an office. A police officer in a dark navy uniform and a flat-topped baseball style hat stepped forward. After asking me if he could help, he led me to a desk where another officer was stationed. I told the desk officer who I was and that I had been asked to deliver my passport to Ricardo Armendarez. The officer gave me an envelope and asked me to put the passport inside. Then he sealed the envelope, wrote Armendarez's name on the front and gave me a receipt. I had expected to see Armendarez so I could give him the passport personally, but I was relieved that the whole process had taken only a matter of minutes.

I left the police station intent on finding the Royal Palace. I followed a maze of narrow avenues that cut through residential areas and eventually arrived at the Plaza de Isabel II, an open square surrounded by tall buildings, with a Metro tube station at one end and, right in front of me, a magnificent stone structure, the Teatro Real – the Madrid Opera House. And suddenly, I remembered Arabella, from Ascot, and her tour.

I walked across the square towards the building where posters displayed the details of current and future performances. I scanned each one looking for her name, Arabella Leslie, but it wasn't there. There was a chance that she was operating under a different name but that seemed unlikely. I realised that I couldn't recall the name of the theatre that Arabella had mentioned, but it didn't seem to be the Teatro Real. I smiled as I thought back to the meeting at the racecourse and how cool Arabella had been. And then my reminiscence was interrupted.

"Matthew."

I turned in the direction of the voice. A woman I'd never seen before. Blonde shoulder length hair, early forties, she was dressed as if going to an office and wearing a pair of sunglasses with huge dark lenses, that seemed to be more for disguise than for the sun.

"Err… yeah. Do I know you?"

She smiled. "No, you don't." She nodded towards the back of the plaza. "Have you time for a coffee? There's a nice café bar just along there."

I hesitated, unsure of what was happening but my curiosity aroused. "I'm sorry. Who are you? How do you know my name?"

She took a step closer. "Put it this way, I know about your predicament."

"My predicament?"

"Yes, with the police."

I felt the blood drain from my face. "Look, who are you? What's this about?"

"I'm trying to help you, Matthew. You want that coffee or not?"

"Not unless you tell me who you are and what this is all about."

She shrugged. "Okay. You know what? That's up to you. If you don't want my help, that's fine." She turned and began to walk away.

My instinct was to run. A strange woman approaching me who knew my name and also knew that I had a problem with the police. It unnerved me, but the prospect of help caused me to hesitate.

"Wait."

The woman turned round. I walked towards her.

"Okay… okay. Let's talk but tell me who you are first."

She smiled, a broad smile that crinkled her eyes and gave her a gentle look. "Just call me Anita."

"That your real name?"

She flicked a strand of hair away from her face and said, "It doesn't matter. What matters is how we can help each other."

"Help each other? You just said you were trying to help me. What do you –"

She reached out and placed her hand on my arm. "Stop asking questions. Let's sit and talk." She led the way back across the plaza to a one of the streets that adjoined it. In my sudden state of alert I noted the name, Calle del Arenal. A short distance in, she stopped at a café that had a row of four tables stationed outside. She pulled out a seat at an end table and sat down. I followed and took the seat opposite. A waiter, who had been serving at an adjacent table, turned in our direction.

"What are you having, Matthew?" Anita said.

"Uh... I don't know... erm, un café con leche por favor," I said, directing my attention to the waiter.

The waiter nodded.

"I think I'll have a glass of wine," Anita said to no one in particular and then, removing her glasses she focussed on me. "Fancy one?"

Her question took me by surprise as did the way she stared at me, intense and questioning. She had warm, kind eyes and I was taken aback. I had no idea who this woman was and yet, at that moment, she seemed like a friend.

"Err... yeah, okay." My anxiety about her approach hadn't subsided and I hoped a drink might help me relax.

"Tráeme una botella de Rioja Blanco," she said to the waiter.

The words rolled off her tongue quite naturally, yet when she spoke to me her accent was articulate standard English.

"You no want café now, Señor?" the waiter asked.

I shook my head. "No, gracias."

Anita smiled and I began to wonder how I had ended up about to share a bottle of wine with a stranger. She stared out across the colourfully tiled walkway, its geometrical patterns weaving a path between rows of tall buildings, their lower levels each containing a shop, a boutique or a café, and said, "What a lovely day. Fabulous for people watching."

People watching. Maybe, on any other day, it would be 'fabulous' to sit in the sunshine with a chilled glass of wine and watch people stroll by, but that wasn't why I had agreed to a drink.

I leaned forward. "Can we get to the point. How do you know me? What way do you think you can help me?"

"Relax, Matthew. As I said, I can help you out of your predicament. You interested?"

Of course I was interested, although I felt that even if I said 'no', this woman wouldn't let it drop. A stranger doesn't approach you, knowing your name and that you have a problem without having some angle themselves. So I said, "Yes."

"Good. So let me explain. I know all about your problem with the police, and you know how?"

I shook my head.

She smiled again and shot a glance to her right. It seemed like a mannerism rather than any watchfulness, almost as if she were seeking clarity of thought before saying anything meaningful. At that moment, the waiter returned, a silver ice bucket that contained a wine bottle in one hand and two glasses cupped in the other. He placed the glasses on the table and then the bucket, and with deft casualness, uncorked the bottle. He poured a small amount into one of the glasses and stopped, but with a flick of her hand Anita indicated that he should continue pouring. Good idea, I thought. I was hardly in the mood for wine tasting. The waiter nodded, topped up both glasses and disappeared. Anita picked hers up, took a sip, squinted slightly as the flavour hit her taste buds and said, "Now where were we?"

"You were about to explain how you know about my police problem and how you could help me." I grabbed my glass and took a couple of large gulps.

Anita looked over the top of her raised glass. "Nice?"

I nodded and put the glass on the table. "So...?"

"Okay. I work with some people who are looking to supply a service to some of the holiday resorts along the coast –"

"A service? What kind of service?"

"Yes, a service. A recreational service."

"A recrea... what sort of service is that?"

Anita raised an eyebrow, pursed her lips for a moment and then said, "Matthew, stop being so bloody naive. Coke... Charlie, powder."

"Powder?"

"Yes. Do I need to spell it out for you? Cocaine."

She stared at me as I sat open mouthed, absorbing what she'd said. My brain began to tumble the data into some sort of coherent pattern, making a link to my arrest.

"You don't think it's a coincidence that the police are charging you with possession, do you? You were set up."

Anita's words seared into my brain, connecting the link firmly and irrevocably. Set up meant that somebody wanted something from their target. I felt a shiver course through my body despite the midday heat. "Set up? Why? How?"

"The 'how' was easy. It's the 'why' we need to deal with." She sipped her wine and stared at me for a moment. "How? You left your jacket on the back of the seat in the rooftop bar when you and your friends went to look at the view of the city. A small slit was made in the lining, just enough to slip an envelope inside. That way you wouldn't have discovered it. In your pocket, you might have found it before you left."

I was speechless. I grabbed the wine glass and necked the contents. Anita slid the bottle across the table. "Looks like you need more."

"But who... who would... ?" The rush of the wine hit kicked in, temporarily fogging my thoughts.

"Who? Don't worry about that right now. As I said, it's the 'why.' I told you, you were set up. It was no coincidence that those police officers were outside the bar as you left. All part of the deal. So's the police chief you saw last night. He –"

"What? Ricardo Armendarez?"

"Yes, Ricardo organised the search."

"But that's... that's corruption!"

"You might call it that but some would say it's just supplementing his income. Look, the people I represent are aiming to pull off a major transaction that will make everybody a lot of money. But we need credibility, either payment up front or a cast iron guarantee. That's where you come in."

"Me?"

"Yes... you."

I shuffled in my seat and reached for my glass. "Me? I haven't got money and I have no idea what I could do that would guarantee anything."

Anita laughed. "You don't need money, Matthew, but I need *you*. You're key to this deal."

I said nothing. I didn't need to. My expression must have told Anita that I was not only baffled but also panic stricken. She reacted.

"Okay, I'll cut to the chase. We're closing a deal that could be worth several million euros. We're looking to be sole distributors for all the cocaine that comes through this part of the mainland and gets channelled to all the resorts along the Costa Blanca, Costa Brava and out to the islands. It's a huge market and the consortium behind it knows this. It's up for grabs right now as the suppliers' original business associate got busted big time. Now all the trade routes have changed and it needs fresh thinking and new blood. That's where we come in. We're pitching for it. The suppliers will provide any quantity we want, but they have a minimum order and that's big bucks. Unless we take fifteen kilos a time, they won't do business with us. We can put money up front but not enough for that quantity as a first time shipment. And that's the amount we need to gain exclusivity. So unless we give guarantees that we can handle it, we won't get in. And the only guarantee we have right now is you."

I sat in silence, mesmerised by how Anita had made a criminal activity seem like a legitimate business deal, and still baffled how I was her passport to achieving that deal. Her next statement confused matters even more.

"We need your face, your image."

I reached for my wine and took another large gulp. Anita made it sound like I was to be the poster 'boy' for a brand launch. "What the fuck you talking about, Anita?" was all I could say.

"Calm down. All you have to do is play a part."

"A part? Like what?"

Anita glanced away and then smiled. "Like you were doing the other night."

"What?"

"Don't play the innocent with me, Matthew. You were using your resemblance to the footballer, Ignacio Cañizares, to get your friends some advantage in clubs and bars over the last two nights. We've been watching you. We know you were seen in a number of places around Madrid, but we knew that Cañizares was elsewhere. And it seems you have history?"

"History?"

"Yes, according to my contacts you did the same thing in England."

"In England? No... uh, yes... I mean... not the same thing. That wasn't my fault. It was just that –"

"Matthew, I'm not interested. I couldn't care less what you did in England. The point is, it works and I need you to do it again."

My mind tried to process what I was hearing – the footballer, guarantees, image. "Hang on... no... no. That's not happening. I'm not... no way. I –"

"... don't have any choice. You're already on the hook. If you don't cooperate, you'll have charges pressed for possession of a Class A drug with intent to distribute, and that carries a serious penalty here in Spain. So if you want to get off that hook, you really should think long and hard about what you do next."

I felt my throat constrict, my mouth dry up, a cold sweat break out on my brow. I grabbed the wine bottle and topped up my glass. Anita simply stared at me as I took a long swig. I put the glass back on the table and sat back, allowing the wine to hit the spot. The midday sun warmed my face as I stared up at the clear sky, my thoughts now focussing on a double predicament. Whatever Anita wanted me to do was associated with criminal activity. But I was already involved in a criminal act as far as the police were concerned, and if one of them was a bent copper, he was likely to extract the maximum penalty if I didn't cooperate. Anita was right, I had no choice. I had to at least listen to what she had to say.

"Okay, what is it you want me to do?"

"It's nothing too complicated. All you need to do is come to a meeting, pretend to be Ignacio Cañizares and do as we tell you."

"Really? Not complicated? But why? What has the footballer got to do with your... your... business?"

"Nothing directly, but he has money. Fifteen kilos of coke is going to cost us over half a million euros. But we can double that, and more once we get it to the distribution network. We want to be part of that supply chain."

"Yes, but what has Ignacio Cañizares's money got to do with anything? He's hardly going to provide you with cash for drugs."

Anita laughed. "No, of course not, but if it looks like he's guaranteeing the payment, that he's part of the deal, it gives us credibility. Right now we can put half that amount up as a down payment. Cañizares earns that in a week. Once we trade our first shipment, the profits cover the next one and we don't need any more guarantees. Then we're looking to do twenty kilos a month to start. That's over seven hundred thousand euros but with a return of almost two million on the street. Once it's established, we intend to expand to supply the Côte d'Azur too. And we know we'll shift it. It's banging flake."

"It's what?"

Anita smiled and brushed her hair back with her hand. "Top quality product, Matthew."

I stared at her for a moment, the detail of her grand scheme sinking in, but more importantly, trying to come to terms with her assessment that my part was 'nothing too complicated.' My thoughts were interrupted by the waiter who picked up the bottle and poured the last dregs of wine equally between Anita's glass and mine. Around me, tourists and Madrid locals ambled by, their smiling, relaxed faces focussed only on their surroundings, oblivious to the gravity of the conversation that was taking place just yards away. I drained the last of the wine and said, "You keep saying 'us' and 'we.' Who else is involved? How do I know I'll be let off your hook if I go along with this?"

"You will, Matthew. We just need you for this one thing. You don't have the balls for anything illegal, I can tell. You'd be a liability once the pressure was on, and I can't have you behaving like a dickweed. This is a means to an end." She glanced around again and then let out a short sigh. "You know two of my associates already... Lucero Garrido and Sergio Colas."

I took a deep breath as the names hit home. "What... Cañizares's security? You mean... ?"

"I do. Another good reason why this works. They're well known, often seen in media shots and TV with him. I told you... credibility. Now, you going to cooperate?"

Two choices and no choice. "Okay, so how's this supposed to work?"

"Well, first of all we go shopping."

24

I got back to the apartment at 2.40 p.m. The lads were there, Cecil spreadeagled on the sofa in his boxers and a t-shirt, Jasper browsing his mobile and Carlos sipping coffee at the wooden table. As I walked in, Cecil was the first to speak.
"Where you bin, mate? And what you got in them bags?"
"Nothing, just shopping. I went for a walk. Lot on my mind."
"Yeah, bit of ag with them cops last night but we'll get it sorted," Cecil said, as he scratched his crotch through his boxers.
"Won't be that easy. Things have just gone tits up."
Carlos put his coffee cup on the table and said, "What's happened, Mateo? I thought you looked a wee bit stressed."
I pulled out a chair and sat down, elbows on the table, head in my hands, fingers kneading my temples trying to massage away the throbbing headache that had settled in. I let out a deep sigh and looked up. Cecil went to the fridge. He opened the door and pulled out four bottles of beer, two in each hand. Grabbing an opener from a drawer, he topped all four in quick succession and placed them on the table.
"Get one of them down'ya, geezer. You look like shit."
I sighed and reached for one of the bottles. "Look like shit? I feel like shit!"
"What's going on?" Jasper asked.
I gulped several mouthfuls of beer, placed the bottle back on the table and began my story. When I had finished, there was a moment of silence which I took to be the result of initial disbelief. Carlos broke it.
"I cannae see how that'll work, Mateo. There nae gonna believe you're the footballer, even if you do look like him. For one thing you dinnae speak Spanish and if you trying to pull some deal, they're gonna want a wee chat."

"Yeah, and mate, why would a footballer on the sort of wedge he's on each week wanna get involved in drug deals or even need to?" Cecil said. "Players are tested all the time… random dope tests, y'know. Your drug dealers ain't gonna swallow that bollocks."

"Yeah, he's right," Jasper said. "And if they think you're trying a blag, they won't be happy. These people don't mess about if they think you're scamming them."

I stood up. "Hang on. Chill a minute. Do you not think I've asked all this stuff? Look, I don't know how you think I'm going to get out of this drug thing with the police, especially when one of them's bent as fuck and in on the deal. Got any ideas?" I turned to Cecil. "Well, have you? You said we'll get it sorted. How?"

Cecil shrugged and swigged his beer. "All right, chill, mate. I dunno yet, but –"

"Thought not. That's what I mean. I have no choice."

"You could take a chance and tell the polis," Carlos said. "They'd be very interested in closing down a drug ring."

"Of course I can't, you dick." I sat down again and necked half the beer. The combination of the earlier wine and now the beer, coupled with the stress of the situation, had made me reckless and angry.

"All right, Mateo. Be cool. I was only saying."

I took a deep breath and suddenly felt remorseful for shouting at Carlos. "I'm sorry, Carlos. I didn't mean that. It's just… if I go to the police and make accusations about one of their own, especially a senior guy, it's going to look like I'm just trying to find a way out. And it sounds like he has the two cops in on it that pulled me the other night as well."

"Aye, that's if they're real polis," Carlos said.

"Well, whatever, the police are not going to believe me and even if somebody did, it's only going to end up on Armendarez's desk anyway and then I'm well in the shit. And on top of that he's then going to do me for possession."

Carlos nodded and clinked his beer bottle against mine. "It's okay, pal. I know you're stressed."

"So what else is there?" Jasper asked. "It's well risky getting involved with these people, Matt."

"I know that, but that's all I have. Listen, once I came round to the idea that this might be my only way out, I asked the same questions you're asking me. Yeah, I can't speak Spanish. So this woman... Anita, says it's not a problem. They've got all angles covered. They've told the suppliers that I can't risk being recorded, so I'm not prepared to say anything." I glanced at Carlos. "I asked if you could be with me as back up, so I know there's nothing dodgy going on."

"Me? But they'll be suspicious of me, won't they? You said they'll know who the other two security boys are but –"

I raised a hand. "I'll come to that, mate. And, yeah, the other big thing, why would a footballer want or need to get involved? You know how they've covered that?" I saw three expectant faces waiting for a reply. "His wife... what's her name?"

"Chiara," Jasper said."

"Yep, Chiara. They've told them that Chiara has a coke problem... you know, on the party scene with all her model friends, A-list celebs, rock stars... and Cañizares can't take the risk that any coke getting to her, anywhere from Marbella to Madrid, or even in Cannes and St Tropez, is not from a top quality source. So the only way he can do that is to make sure he has an interest in what's being supplied, make sure it's high grade stuff with no impurities."

"But, if they're looking to do that much stuff a month he'd be putting up a lot of money every time," Carlos said. "Why would they think he's gonna do that just because his wife wants to party now and then? She could buy what she needs for a lot less."

"I just told you. Their blag is, he wants to keep control. And as a spinoff, once they trade it, Cañizares will get his cash back, with interest, through a bogus company, straight into an offshore account."

"But what about the taxman and his accountant? If he's spending that amount every month, it's going to look well dodge," Jasper said.

"What? Jas, I just said. It's a blag. They're creating a scenario to make it sound credible. He knows nothing about it. I'm the mug who's on the line here."

"Yeah, I know that. I'm just trying to think of things that might make them suspicious in case you get asked stuff," Jasper replied.

I shoved an empty beer bottle to one side and said, "These people, the suppliers, I don't suppose they're that interested in the fine detail. I reckon what Anita's people are relying on is, if they see a famous face that's good enough. They'll know where to find him if something goes wrong."

Cecil took another four beers from the fridge and handed them round. "Yeah, but why wouldn't they think, if he's so worried about his missus, he'd not try and get her in rehab or some shit like that?"

I laughed. "Funny enough I asked Anita the same question. She said it was simple enough. The story is Chiara doesn't think she has a problem. She likes to party and the two of them are a 'brand' with their business interests outside their careers, so they don't want any negative press either."

"Fuck's sake, who is this Anita bint? She's taking some risk spinning them all that bollocks," Cecil said.

"I don't know, Ces. All I know is they intend it to be a one off to finance the initial deal. Once they get a partnership going and they're paying up front for the gear, there'll be no problem, and their suppliers won't care about how they're getting paid or whether Cañizares is involved or not. With Cañizares... err, me... at this next meeting, along with Sergio and Lucero, they're banking on that being their guarantee, like I said. It's a major blag but they seem to have all questions covered."

"Hang on a wee minute," Carlos said. "What about me? You said you'd come to that, Mateo. How do I fit in?"

"I already said why I want you there but as far as the suppliers are concerned, they'll be told that you're the link for Chiara's parties and social scene, her husband's man, to make sure there are no cockups with the stuff and she gets it from the source he's expecting."

Cecil took a swig of beer, ran his hands through his hair and then said, "Mate, I'm coming with'ya. You can't go there without back up."

"That's not happening, Ces. I've got to play this by the book like I agreed with Anita."

"So when's this meeting?" Jasper asked.

"Tonight. That's what the shopping's for."

25

Carlos and I were picked up at eight o'clock that evening. A black Mercedes was waiting outside the apartment, its engine humming gently. Anita stepped out of the passenger side as we emerged from the entrance doorway.

"Very stylish, Matthew," she said, her gaze taking in my appearance.

Very stylish indeed and so I should be given that Anita had spent almost three thousand euros on improving my sartorial image that afternoon. "You need to look the part", she'd said and I wondered again when would everyone stop saying that. As I stepped into the warmth of the early evening, I didn't feel comfortable, my anxiety causing me to perspire, something not helped either by my brand new designer outfit: black leather Balenciaga shoes, Givenchy slim leg trousers, a Giorgio Armani monk-collared white cotton shirt and a Paul Smith single breasted houndstooth blazer. The whole ensemble was topped off by a pair of Moscot sunglasses and a diamond earring on my left ear.

Anita opened the back door and indicated that we should get in. Carlos climbed in first and I got in behind the driver. When she was back in the car, Anita turned to me and said, "I think you two already know one another." She nodded in the direction of the driver. "My colleague, Lucero Garrido."

The driver turned around, a smile playing on his lips. "I know him." A menacing glare replaced the smile. "I told you, amigo, I no forget your face."

I glanced at Carlos who frowned, aware of the tension and then I spoke to Anita.

"Look, Anita, this is not going to work too well if he's going to have that attitude all the time. You better explain to him that I'm supposed to be on his side. If he wants this to work, he'd better forget any grudge he has with me and focus on the job. Remind him that he's supposed to be protecting Cañizares and if I'm playing a part, he'd better get his part right too."

Anita nodded. "Okay, okay. Chill. I'll speak to him."

The car headed off down Calle de Almadén until it reached the junction with Paseo del Prado where it turned right and joined four lanes of Madrid traffic. As we weaved through the congestion I had plenty of time to think. What would happen to me if I was rumbled straight off? Trying to con hardcase villains would not be taken lightly. Was my look good enough, the clothes, the style? My mind shot back to Cecil and the conversation before I'd left.

"Mate, what you doing with that fucking earring? She got you to pierce your ear as well?"

I laughed. "No, it's not real. It's a false one. Here… look." I removed the earring and held it out in the palm of my hand. "See, it's got a small magnet that sits behind the ear and keeps it in place."

Cecil examined the earring and the magnet. "Didn't know they had them. It ain't no diamond though, is it. Looks right cheap up close."

"No, it's not. It's crystal rhinestone, according to Anita. Apparently Cañizares has started wearing different diamonds in his ear so we've had to do something."

"Yeah? Didn't notice it on the telly the other day, nor at Ascot. Footballer with too much money."

"I don't think they wear them when playing or training." I put the earring back on.

"Maybe not," Cecil said, scratching his chin. "But one thing's missing, mate."

"What's that?"

"A decent watch. Every footballer's got a decent watch... a Patek, a Tag or something."

"She was hardly going to spend five or six grand on a watch, was she?"

"And the rest! So what you gonna do?"

"About what?"

"The watch."

"That's the least of my worries, Ces. If you think it's that big a deal, I'll just wear my own and make sure I keep the shirtsleeve over it."

"Yeah, all you can do, I s'pose. They probably won't notice. You look the part in all that clobber. First impression is what counts. Make sure you style it out. Walk in there like you own the place, yeah?"

"Easier said than done. I'll give it a shot."

"Good man. Now listen to me. If you or Carlos get a chance, you text me. I need to know what's going on in case you need back up."

"Cheers, but only if things get weird. I can't have you showing up there and interfering. This has got to look real, no cockups."

And now, as I sat in the car thinking about that conversation, I realised it was reality time. Either I would get away with it, or it *would* get weird. I had to dismiss the latter thought.

After driving for about ten minutes, we pulled up outside Casa de Suecia, a tall grey-stone building with four huge glass windows dominating the lower floor. Lucero drove off, and Anita led us through the main entrance. She turned left into a long bar that ran parallel to the street and had rows of tall plants lining the four windows. The bar itself was well lit, a soft yellow glow giving it a warm, welcoming feel. Immediately above it ran a balcony seating area. Anita led us to a table at one end, away from other customers some of whom had stared at our group as we entered, a look of curiosity on their faces.

"Let's get some drinks while we wait," Anita said.

"Wait for what?" I asked.

"My contacts. We have to wait here until I get the meeting location."

I glanced at Carlos. He shrugged, his hands splayed as if to say, 'we have no choice, do we?'

I looked at Anita. "I could do with a drink. I'll have a large Jack and coke."

Anita smiled, her eyes flickering with mild amusement. "No you won't. It's water for you."

"Water?"

"Yes, water. As far as I'm concerned, they could be watching. They told me to come here and wait. These people don't like taking chances where their business is concerned."

"But what's that got to do with having a quick drink?"

"Look, no footballer who's in preseason training will be seen drinking alcohol. Got it? These people leave nothing to chance, and if you're supposed to be a pro who's about to start the season, you won't be knocking back large JDs, will you? So, still or sparkling?"

"I'll have a whiskey," Carlos said and winked at me. I scowled at him.

Anita ordered drinks and then came back to the table.

"So, if I'm meant to be in preseason training, what am I doing dressed up like this? Bit over the top for a meeting with drug dealers?" I said, still irritated about being told what I could drink.

Anita looked away, her gaze scanning the bar. Then she leaned towards me. "Matthew, shut up about drug dealers. Discretion, please. Listen, I don't want this meeting going on all night. I want to get in there, get the business done and get out. The only reason we're here is for you to put in an appearance as our guarantor, okay? So I told them you are going out to dinner tonight with one of your sponsors and you're on a deadline."

I took a deep breath. Anita seemed to have all the answers. The drinks were delivered, Carlos's whiskey and a small glass of white wine for Anita. I sipped my water, trying to stay as calm and relaxed as I could in the circumstances. I knew that if I could pull this off, then the threat of prosecution by Ricardo Armendarez would be removed. It was in my interest not to let my nerves get the better of me.

Fifteen minutes later Lucero walked in, followed closely by Sergio. Lucero bent down and whispered to Anita. She nodded then looked at me.

"Okay, it's on. Remember, you say nothing. The fact that you're here should be enough. Remember, I've said you wouldn't risk being recorded." She turned to Carlos. "You'll answer any questions they ask, okay?"

Carlos nodded.

Anita stood up, leaving the rest of her wine. Carlos gulped his whiskey down in one hit and stood up too. Lucero and Sergio led the way with Anita just behind. We followed them up a short wooden staircase to the reception area and then to the lifts that were situated at the far side of the reception desk. Sergio pressed the lift call button and we waited. Once the lift arrived, he swiped a keycard across a reader, then selected the fifth floor and the doors closed. I glanced at Carlos. He'd noticed the fact that you couldn't go up in the lift without a keycard. I hoped that the same did not apply to get back down again.

The doors pinged open at floor five. Just before we exited Anita said, "Remember, Matthew, you say nothing." We turned right and headed down the corridor. Halfway down, Lucero stopped outside one of the rooms and knocked on the door. After a moment, the door was opened by a guy in a dark suit, his head shaved, a bushy black beard compensating for any lack of head hair. He led us into a spacious suite. As I walked in, I remembered Cecil's advice to 'own the place' and paced in as tall and confidently as I could. The suite consisted of a spacious sitting room with the bedroom separate from the main area. At the far end of the room, three guys in sharp suits stood with their backs to a window and a doorway that led out to a terraced area. Two of them were tall and dark, Mediterranean in appearance. The other one was shorter around five-ten, balding and middle aged, his suit grey check, a contrast to the black ones of his colleagues. It was apparent by their positions and body language that he was in charge. He spoke first, his Spanish heavy with East European tones.

"Señor Cañizares, gusto de conocerlo." He held out his hand. I made a point of looking round the room and up at the ceiling as if looking for hidden bugs, my subconscious suggesting this would emphasise my desire not to speak. I then shook his hand as firmly as I could despite my stomach telling me I should be in flight mode.

I leaned towards Carlos and whispered. "What did he say?"

"Just that it's nice to meet you," he said under his breath.

"Tell him, likewise."

I saw Anita frown, a frown that said, 'keep your mouth shut.'

"El Señor Cañizares dice que también es un placer conocerte," Carlos said.

I nodded acknowledgement at the older man and hoped that my whispered comment would further emphasise my desire to remain silent.

"No hablo español muy bien," the older man said, "Uh... El inglés es mejor para mí. Uh, my English it is better. Is okay?"

He glanced at Anita who nodded. "English is fine."

Carlos had noticed Anita's earlier concern and said something long and rambling in Spanish to me. When he had finished, I nodded and gave a thumbs up sign.

The older guy smiled and then indicated the terrace door. "Please. Let's go outside. It is nice evening." He led the way onto a balconied terrace area that followed the angles of the building and afforded spectacular views across the city. A white table with four chairs around it stood on an artificial grass base just outside the room. On the far side of the door, the grass led to a raised decking area where four low planters enhanced the ambience with an array of colourful shrubs. The guy nodded towards the table, pulled out one of the chairs and indicated that we sit down. I pulled out the chair opposite, and Anita and Carlos sat either side of me. I noticed the two 'dark suits' take up a standing position close to the balcony wall. Sergio and Lucero had stayed in the suite.

The older guy looked at me and said, "My name is Kreshnik. I run the business of importing all product into this... uh... this part of Spain."

I smiled and nodded, resisting the urge to respond. Carlos leaned over and said something in Spanish, which I took to be a translation of Kreshnik's sentence given that the last word was 'España.'

Anita held a hand up and said, "We can brief Señor Cañizares afterwards. He hasn't got time for everything to be translated tonight."

There followed a monologue from Kreshnik in his heavily accented English, that covered his cocaine import business, his expectations and his willingness to work with a new distributor that he could trust. But then he cut to the chase and I saw the shock on Anita's face.

"This is very important market for us and big opportunity for you," he said, addressing Anita directly. "But you must know that, in this business, you can trust nobody. Our business is about clean transaction, cash. We supply, you pay." He stared at me and then looked at Carlos. "It is an honour for me to work with famous international football player and I respect that he is come tonight to meet." He focussed again on Anita. "But, as I tell you, I trust nobody, not even your famous football player. You tell me that Señor Cañizares is here to protect his... uh, wife, and be sure that product is good. But I know Señor Cañizares is wealthy man so I not understand why he expect only to give part time payment and –"

"Part payment," Anita corrected.

"Yes... part payment," Kreshnik repeated. He waved his hand in a sweeping gesture. "If we work with you as new partner to distribute product you must proof that you are serious."

"Prove," Anita corrected again. "Prove, how? We are serious."

"You prove by making full payment for product."

"That wasn't the arrangement that we discussed before with your representatives. The deal was fifty percent up front and then the final payment two weeks after delivery. That is why Señor Cañizares is here tonight, to guarantee payment, otherwise we would not ask him to come."

Kreshnik shrugged. "Things change. It's good you have a rich man to guarantee but, as I say, it is not possible to trust in this business." He smoothed down the lapels of his jacket, then looked at Anita, a fixed uncompromising stare. "If you want this deal and the opportunity to supply your distribution network and work with us, I want full payment for the product. You take or leave it."

I glanced at Anita. Her eyes flashed annoyance but her voice was calm as she replied. "I'm not happy but I will talk with Señor Cañizares. He is a partner here. We need some time alone."

Kreshnik smiled, his arms splayed in an open gesture. "Okay. How you say? Uh... up to you, but I need your decision tonight. You have twenty minutes or deal off."

Anita frowned and stood up. Carlos and I stood too, unsure of what to do next. Anita nodded in Kreshnik's direction and walked back into the suite. Carlos and I followed. Once inside, Anita beckoned to Sergio and Lucero who were both sitting on a cream sofa that lined one wall. They got up and followed her to the entrance door.

Carlos looked at me and shrugged, his gaze then shifting towards the door. I didn't need a second invitation. I was anxious to get out. We left the room and made our way to the lift.

26

We stood in silence for a moment as Lucero selected the 'ground' button, zero. The lift doors slid to a close. My mind raced. Things had gone badly for Anita and her syndicate, and I wondered what that meant for me. I needed to find out.

"Looks like your deal's off," I said to Anita, "but that's not my fault. I did what you asked me to do. So can you call off your bent cop and leave me alone now."

Lucero glared at me. Anita stared straight ahead. "It's not over yet. You think we give up that easily? You know how much money's at stake here?"

"Yeah, you told me, but you heard that Kreshnik bloke. Unless you stump up the cash your deal's going nowhere."

"He's right," Carlos added. "It's nae happening."

"You can't come up with the money. Simple as that. You heard what he wants and you can't do it. So I want out. That was our deal."

"Matthew, listen to –" Anita's reply was interrupted by the ping of the lift door as we reached the ground floor. We walked back to the bar and sat at the table we had occupied before. Sergio went to the bar for a jug of water and five glasses.

"I need a proper drink," I said to Carlos.

Anita slapped her hand hard down on the table. "Matthew! Stop being a dickweed. We've no time for drinks. I have to sort this out." She stood up, took her mobile from her bag, walked away from the table and made a call. I watched as Anita spoke, her face tense, her free hand gesticulating to emphasise her words. After a few minutes, she put the mobile back in her bag and came back to the table. She sat down and said, "I think he's bluffing."

"Bluffing?" Carlos said.

"Yes, bluffing," Anita replied. She sat up straight and looked at me, her eyes fixed and determined. "Okay, here's what we do. We still have you as our trump card. They know that Cañizares has money. Kreshnik even mentioned it. They're only in this business for hard cash. Kreshnik never said anything about anyone else when he gave us his ultimatum. He just –"

"Anyone else? What d'you mean?" Carlos asked.

Anita smiled. "When he said he needs a decision tonight, he didn't say anything like, you know, there are other syndicates after this deal. That's why I think he's bluffing, trying to force our hand to get cash up front because there's nobody else who has that kind of money right now. So we bluff him back."

"How?" I said, Anita's determination evaporating my optimism that, even if the deal fell through, she would call off Armendarez.

"Simple. We go back in there and tell him you're not prepared to put money up front until the product is delivered, quality tested, and you know it's a fair deal. Once delivered and tested, you're prepared to commit finance. Don't forget, until tonight they had nothing concrete to go on, and then you show up, and they realise we mean business and our proposal is plausible."

"Wait a minute. There's a hole in your bluff," I said.

Anita checked her watch. "A hole? What hole?"

"You said the reason you gave them for Cañizares involvement was to protect his wife and protect their brand. Keep her safe, the brand safe. If he's prepared to walk away, that destroys that reason. There's no other point in him getting involved with drug dealers."

"Maybe they'll think he's more concerned about the brand than his wife's welfare. You know how much they make from 'Brand Cañizares?'" She didn't wait for an answer. "Look, they'll know he wants to keep the status quo. Chiara is big time at the minute, and together they rake it in. But maybe they'll think that he could walk away and look for another option if he had to. And everyone knows he's got an eye for the ladies. Something goes wrong for his wife, he'd have another model on the go pretty damn quick and the whole circus moves on again. So don't you worry about any of that. If I have to pull out another argument, I will. Now let's go. We've got six minutes."

I thought back to my first encounter with Cañizares at Ascot and his relationship with Lorena Márquez, the newswoman.

We left the table and walked to the lift. Sergio pressed the 'call' button and we waited. As the doors opened, Anita tapped me on the shoulder.

"You screw this up for us and I'll make sure Armendarez throws the book at you."

Back in the room Kreshnik was pacing the floor as we entered. Nobody said anything until we had sat down, this time inside the suite, Carlos and me on the sofa and Kreshnik in a red armchair positioned on one side of a low coffee table. Anita stood.

Kreshnik crossed his legs and brushed down the lapels of his suit. "Have you come to a decision, my friends?"

Anita flicked a stray hair from her face and then looked at Kreshnik. She paused for a moment, but her eyes said it was for effect, not hesitation.

"Yes, we have. I'm afraid Señor Cañizares is not prepared to enter into this arrangement on the terms you have set out. If you recall our initial discussions when we first expressed an interest, you mentioned guarantees. Señor Cañizares is our guarantee that you will be paid. However, he is not prepared to commit large sums of money or risk his career without some good faith from you. You said earlier you needed a decision tonight, so that is our decision." She moved towards Kreshnik. "If you can't deliver the arrangement we were promised, it shows *you* can't be trusted. So, yes, you're right, there is no trust in this business. It seems that I've wasted my time." She beckoned to Sergio and Lucero, turned and began to walk away.

Carlos tugged at my arm to get up. I had expected Anita to bluff her way through as she had indicated earlier, not play hardball. I looked at Kreshnik. His face was ashen, but his eyes had narrowed with bad intent and were focussed on me. And I realised where he was placing the blame for any failure of the deal.

Without altering his stare, he called out, "Wait!"

From the corner of my eye I saw Anita turn around. It was only then that Kreshnik shifted his gaze.

"I like you. I like your... how is it... uh, business face. You talk straight, like me. I like." He stood up and began to pace again. "So I tell you what I do. I like to do deal with you, but I need... uh, to be ensured, you know?"

"Ensured?" Anita said. "You mean, you need assurance... insurance?"

"Yes, something that mean if this go wrong I have some comeback."

"Insurance then," Anita said.

I wondered why, in the middle of this deal, Anita felt the need to correct Kreshnik's English.

"Yes, insurance. I tell you there is no trust in this business, so I need more than guarantee from your famous player here," Kreshnik said, waving a hand in my direction.

"Okay. What do you want?"

Kreshnik nodded towards the bearded guy with the shaved head who then went into the bedroom. From where I was seated, I could see him opening the wardrobe. Then he opened a drawer and took something out. I couldn't see what it was. He came out of the bedroom and handed whatever he had removed to Kreshnik. Kreshnik held his hand out to reveal a small polythene grip bag that contained a white powder, identical to the items shown to me by the police outside Circulo de Bellas Artes.

"This is my product." He sat down and tipped the contents onto the coffee table that stood between the sofa and the armchair. Next, he reached inside his jacket, took out his wallet and then removed a credit card. With several deft strokes he used the edge of the card like a razor blade to cut off a thick line of powder, moving it away from the rest of the package contents. Then he flicked the card edge back and forth through the powder to form a longer line before cutting that, dragging a portion to one side and, with several more deft swipes of the card, forming two separate thin lines. When he was satisfied, he looked up, opened his wallet and took out a twenty euro note. Next, he rolled it from one corner to form a tight straw-like shape and held it out in my direction.

Straight away I knew what he wanted and I reacted. "No! No!"

Anita glared at me and I remembered her words, 'You screw this up for me and I will make sure Armendarez throws the book at you.'

Kreshnik waved the 'straw' in front of me and spoke to Carlos. "You tell Señor Cañizares, this is my insurance. He has to do these lines. My friend will record."

I caught a glimpse of the bearded guy with his mobile poised.

"If he do as I ask, I deliver the shipment," Kreshnik said, looking at Anita. "You pay fifty per cent in front and in two weeks you pay the other fifty per cent. If this does not happen, or you fuck our deal, the video goes to newspaper and television people and our friend's career is over. Your choice."

I looked at Carlos. His expression conveyed precisely what I was thinking. If I didn't do it, I would be shafted by the bent cop. I looked across at Anita, who was tight lipped and tense.

Carlos broke the tension.

"Mister... err, Kreshnik. Señor Cañizares is a professional athlete. He is tested regularly. If he gets called to a random drug test and it's positive, his career is over anyway."

I realised it was a final attempt by Carlos to save me from doing what he knew I didn't want to do.

"It is his problem, my friend, not my problem. This is my insurance, yes? Do this, we have deal," Kreshnik said. He winked at his colleagues. "And this way, he understand what his woman like to put up her nose."

"Okay. He'll do it," Anita said, without so much as a glance at me.

"Good," said Kreshnik. He pointed at Carlos. "You tell Señor Cañizares that he must snort both lines up... uh, complete, one in each nose, no mistakes. Tell him to squeeze one... nose side shut when he snorts in the other. If he not get it right, we make him do it again. We have plenty this stuff."

Carlos went through the motions, a stream of Spanish, no doubt passing on Kreshnik's instructions. I knew I had no choice. I reasoned that surely it couldn't hurt. It was a one-off, a means to an end, a step in freeing me from the set up in which Anita's syndicate had trapped me. For the sake of credibility, I feigned protest and a series of anguished expressions. Then I shrugged, reached out and took the twenty euro 'straw' from Kreshnik. My mind flashed back to Las Vegas where I'd encountered the drug before but had managed to avoid the experience more through accident than design. I dismissed that thought and focussed on what I had to do. There seemed to be no way out this time, deliberate or accidental.

I knelt on the floor to get myself lower to the coffee table. With one end of the note positioned at the end of the line of powder and the other end inserted in my left nostril, I pressed my right index finger against the right side of my nose. My stomach churned, my hands shook, and in my anxious state, I let out a deep breath that blew one line of powder off the table.

Kreshnik picked up his credit card and cut another line from the remaining powder. Again he shaped it into a thin strip and said, "You try more, Señor Cañizares." He nodded at the bearded guy who raised his mobile and pointed it in my direction.

I positioned the rolled up 'straw' at the end of one of the lines, as I had done before, pressed the right side of my nose and inserted the note in my left nostril again. And I sniffed, hard, running the note up the line as the powder disappeared. Without waiting for any reaction, I quickly transferred the 'straw' to my right nostril and did the same thing. I sat back on my heels, my head tilted, waiting for something.

And then I felt it.

The coke dribbling down my throat, my nose numbing, almost cold, chilling my tongue, anaesthetising it; the taste, bitter, cool, edgy as the hit captured my brain. I hadn't expected the liquid sensation in my throat. Then I focussed on the faces staring at me, all seemingly intense. To my left, the guy with the mobile was checking what he had filmed. Then he showed it to Kreshnik. I saw him smile.

My mind began to race. I tried to keep a grip. I saw Anita stand and I heard her say something to Kreshnik. They shook hands.

27

We left the room and entered the lift. My head was buzzing. My mouth felt strange, like I needed to lick my lips all the time. I was hot, as much from the tension of the meeting as the clothes I wore. I ran my hands over my face, trying to clear my head. Then I felt a strange euphoria envelop me, a confidence that said things are going to be fine, and my situation was not as bad as it seemed. It would all work out.

It was Anita that focussed me again. "Well done, Matthew. You did well."

"Didn't have much choice, did I?" I wiped the sweat from my face and brow and undid a couple of buttons on my shirt. "Now, you lot going to call off your bent cop? I've done my bit. Your deal's on. I want out of this. I want to go back to enjoying the trip with my mates that you lot screwed up. And you should be compensating us. It's costing –"

"Hey, slow down, Matthew. All in good time. Once we receive the shipment we'll tell Armendarez to shred your file and you'll be in the clear."

"When's that? The shipment due?" Carlos asked.

The lift came to a halt and the doors opened. Anita walked straight towards the lobby exit. Then she turned around.

"Two, three days, maximum. Then we'll be in touch." She turned to walk away.

"Hang on," I said. "Two or three days? We're due to leave here on Saturday. I need my passport back by then, and my bank cards. Three days is Friday now, isn't it? Suppose it's late? What then?"

"I'll be in touch," was all she said and turned and walked out, followed by Sergio and Lucero.

Carlos looked at me. "I dinnae know about you, pal, but I need a drink."

"Large Jack for me, but not here. Down the road."

We found a discreet table at Circulo de Bellas Artes. Once we had ordered two drinks, Carlos said he would call Cecil. I caught one side of the conversation.

"It's fine, Cecil... no, he's okay... yeah, they've gone... at Circulo de Bellas Artes... I'll tell you when you get here... aye, see you both then."

Half an hour after the meeting Cecil and Jasper arrived at the bar.

Cecil stared at me. "Mate, what the fuck's going on? And what's happening with your face?"

"My face?"

Yeah, you keep licking your lips and opening your mouth like you're some sort of fucking horse. You okay?"

"Uh... I didn't realise. They made me do two lines of coke. My head's buzzing and I –"

"What? Made you? How? What for."

Carlos cut in and told Cecil and Jasper how the evening had unfolded.

Cecil laughed. "Mate, you have taken one for the team. And where's that stoopid earring you had on?"

I felt my ear. "Uh, dunno. Must have come off. Don't matter. Don't need it now."

"So once they get their shipment of coke, you're in the clear?" Jasper asked.

"Should be, yeah."

"Until then we just lay low," Carlos added.

"Lay low? Fuck that," Cecil said, his eyes defiant. "We ain't done nothing wrong, have we? We came here to party and that ain't changing. It's down to them geezers to sort their drug shit out." He pointed at me. "And I tell you what, once that's done, if I run into either of them two mugs again what set you up, I'm gonna make sure they get what's coming to 'em."

I nodded. It was the wrong time to point out that they might be dangerous.

Cecil carried on. "And right now, that bit of Charlie you did ain't gonna do'ya no harm. In fact it's gonna make you party a bit harder."

Jasper laughed. "Right, boys, what you having?"

The next day, I felt rough. I hadn't gone to sleep until almost seven in the morning. My head throbbed with the impact of the combination of the cocaine, several beers, numerous shots and no rest. I'd also spent most of my remaining cash apart from about ten euros in coins, and without my cards, I couldn't get any more.

I checked my watch. It was twelve-thirty. I needed fresh air, coffee and some food. I felt too jaded to make coffee in the apartment, so I threw on a t-shirt, a pair of shorts and some trainers. There was no-one else up, so I decided to head to the restaurant that I'd been to before, Cervecería El Diario on Calle de Jesús.

It was busier than the last time, the bar counter stools fully occupied mostly by men drinking coffee and eating tapas. The table I had sat at before was free. I pulled out a chair and sat down. I ordered coffee, ham, cheese and bread and hoped my head would clear when I'd eaten. A waiter brought the coffee almost straight away. I asked for a glass of water.

As I sipped the coffee, I reflected on the night before. I had a sense of relief that the meeting with Anita's suppliers was over and done with, and some optimism that I would be free of the charge that Armendarez had hanging over me. That optimism, together with the cocaine hit, had driven me to party just as hard as Cecil and Jasper and to ignore Carlos's advice that I should slow down a bit. And now I was paying the price, a throbbing head, a demanding thirst and a severe need for sleep.

My thinking was interrupted by the waiter placing a glass and a bottle of water on the table. As he moved away, I caught sight of Anita standing in the doorway. She'd spotted me immediately and crossed to my table.

"Buenos días, Matthew," she said, her smile warm. She flicked her hair back from her face and said, "May I join you?"

My surprise at seeing her was replaced quickly by annoyance. "Doesn't look like I have any choice. You following me?"

She sat down opposite. "Nice to see you too! I'm not following you, but we need to know where you are until the shipment is delivered."

"Why?"

"Well, we don't want you or any of your friends doing anything silly that might jeopardise our deal, which brings me to why I'm here."

I poured a glass of water and said, "Go on. I'm listening." I raised the glass and drained most of it in one slug.

Anita looked to her right, a brief survey of the bar area and then said, "Have you seen the news this morning?"

"No, why?"

"Ignacio Cañizares left with the team for a preseason tour in the UK. They're playing two friendly games, one in London and another in Manchester. It was in the breakfast news sports section... the team boarding the coach for the airport early this morning. He even said a few words to camera."

"So what?"

Before Anita could answer we were interrupted by the waiter with my food. He placed it on the table, turned to Anita and asked if she wanted anything.

"Un café con leche por favor," she said. Then she focussed on me. "The point is, if he's out of the country we can't risk you being seen in Madrid."

"How's that work then? You expect me to spend my time sitting in my apartment?" I said as I bit into a piece of bread and ham.

Anita nodded. "Yes."

"You are joking, aren't you? How long's he away?"

"A week. Back next Tuesday night."

I couldn't help but laugh although there was nothing to laugh at. "You do realise I go home on Saturday, don't you? Well, if I get my bloody passport back from your crooked cop."

"You do?"

"Yes, I told you last night."

"That's no problem. I'm sure Saturday will be fine, but for the rest of the time you're here I need you to lay low. We've done the hard bit so just need to be patient. And it's only three days. Once we get the shipment, we start distributing and then you can do what you like."

"Three days is the rest of my trip... Wednesday, Thursday, Friday."

"Look, if you want to get the all clear, I need you to keep an extremely low profile. So no bars or partying. We can't risk wannabe girls posting selfies with you or mobile pictures on their Facebook and Instagram accounts. If that sort of thing gets reported back to Kreshnik, he's going to get suspicious. Cañizares out of the country on a team tour will make the news over here every day. We can't risk anything jeopardising our deal when we're this close."

I finished the glass of water and poured another.

"You should have thought of that before, shouldn't you? You've got those two goons, Sergio and Lucero, working with you. They're Cañizares's personal protection, and you mean to say they didn't think to say anything? They're obviously even more stupid than they look."

Anita frowned. "Hang on a minute. They knew about the tour, but Cañizares strained an ankle in training over a week ago. He was only doing light training and wasn't expected to go. The physio gave him the all clear late yesterday afternoon. Sergio and Lucero found out early this morning when they were told to stand down as they weren't needed. The club takes its own security on tours. Apparently he decided late last night that he'd travel. So nobody's being bloody stupid here, Matthew, except you."

I sat back and let out a deep sigh. My head still hurt. The last thing I needed was confrontation. But I felt defiant and also recalled Anita's willingness to bluff.

"Look, Anita, like I said last night, I carried out my side of the agreement and did exactly as you asked. It wasn't easy, and it's probably criminal too because I'm assisting you with a drug deal. So the way I see it right now, you can do what you like with your bent cop and your threat, because if I'm going to get stitched up for drugs, it might be better to get done for ten grams than fifteen kilos! And on top of all that, you've completely fucked up my break in Madrid with the lads, so I'm not hiding in my apartment just to save your deal."

Anita laughed. "Oooh, the real Matthew Malarkey shows his face. Fine time now to turn alpha on me. Okay, have it your way." She pulled her mobile from her bag, checked the screen and then thumbed in a text. When she'd finished, she put the mobile back and stared at me for a moment.

"Good luck, Matthew. Safe journey home." She got up from the table and left.

I watched until she disappeared from view. I finished my coffee and poured the last of the water. The waiter brought Anita's coffee and placed it on the table. I pushed the remaining food to one side. My stomach had begun to churn, and I couldn't eat any more. I reached for my mobile and noticed my hands were shaking. My moment's bravado seemed to have disappeared along with my appetite. There was a text from Carlos.

'*Where are you? You OK?*'

I replied saying I'd just gone for something to eat and I'd be back in around half an hour or so. I reached for Anita's coffee and began to sip it. No sense in wasting it and I needed the caffeine boost.

Twenty minutes later, having paid the bill with my last ten euros, I was walking along the narrow Calle de Fúcar, not far from the apartment, and had just reached the junction with Calle del Gobernador, when I heard a car coming down the slope to my right. I stepped to one side to let it pass, but it pulled to a stop right in front of me. As I attempted to go around it, the rear door opened. A guy in a black t-shirt, black jeans and dark glasses leapt out and lunged at me. I had no time to react. He grabbed my right arm and pulled me towards the open door. At the same time someone came out of the driver's front door and pushed me hard in the back, throwing me onto the rear seat. A hand came from behind and pressed a cloth firmly against my mouth.

The last thing I sensed was the smell of chemicals.

28

I came to, slowly, my head swimming, my vision blurred. I was aware of movement, fast movement. And then I realised I was in the back seat of a car, my hands tied behind my back. In front, I saw the back of the driver's head. He had dark hair and a ponytail. Lucero Garrido. To my right, I became aware of a passenger. I tried to focus on his features but I didn't recognise him. He caught my look and reached out and pulled me towards him. In my groggy state, I was unable to react. He pushed my face down hard against the leather seat and tied a piece of dark cloth around my head so that it covered my eyes. I felt it knot tightly at the back of my head. Then I was pulled back up to a seated position. Not a word was spoken. I said nothing either.

The car sped on for what seemed like another hour or so, its speed changing little. I concluded that we must be on a motorway, or similar, to be able to maintain such a consistent pace for so long. Then it slowed and I felt a slight change of direction. Maybe a motorway exit? Then what felt like a roundabout, followed by a much slower speed. After that, the ride became less smooth, the speed erratic, the turns numerous. With my vision obscured, I became disorientated. About half an hour later, the car took a slow left turn and pulled to a halt. The driver switched off the engine. The passenger moved towards me and I felt the knot on the blindfold loosen. The driver, Lucero, turned round.

"No funny stuff, amigo. We untie... uh, las manos. You good?" He indicated my back seat companion. "He have gun. ¿Me comprendes?"

"Err, sorry?"

"You understand?"

I nodded. I understood gun.

The guy in the back seat produced a switchblade knife from the pocket of his jeans. He flicked the blade out and began to cut through the tape that bound my wrists. Once my hands were free, I shook them to help the circulation and relieve the tension of being bound.

I heard the car door locks click. The two men got out. Lucero opened the back door. The other guy came round and pulled me out onto a dusty strip of ground. I stood up straight, my head still not clear of the previous night's partying and whatever chemical had rendered me comatose during the journey. I glanced at my watch. Twenty past six. That meant I'd been in the car for almost five hours.

Around me, I could see a number of properties but no sign of any activity. The car had pulled up next to a high whitewashed wall that had a wooden double doorway, painted lilac, in its centre. I noticed the purple bougainvillaea spilling over the entire length of the wall, but I had no time to observe much more. Lucero grabbed my arm and led me towards the entrance. He inserted a key in the lock and a single door opened within the double frame. We stepped through into a long courtyard. To my right lay an open expanse of ground planted with cacti and fruit trees. To my left, a low wall topped by a wood trellis, bordered a walkway that led to a whitewashed villa. Through the trellis I could see a wide space dominated by a swimming pool. At the far end of the wall, an arch with a metal gate formed an entrance to a patio area that stretched the length of the villa. An extension at the front of the building jutted out at a right angle towards the poolside. Lucero led me through the gate and across the patio to the property entrance.

Once inside, Lucero directed me across a tiled hallway into a spacious reception room. A large mirror dominated one wall and a sofa backed up against another. On the far side of the room, I could see two doors. Lucero directed me towards one of them. He opened the door and, with a nod, indicated that I should go in.

"Why am I here?" I asked.
"You stay here," Lucero replied.
"How long? Where is this?"
Lucero scowled, my questions irritating him. "You no need to know."
"But... can I get food? Why am I –?"
"There is... uh, keep houser."
"What? Oh, housekeeper."

"Sí. Now you go in."

There was no further point in discussion. I was aware that the other guy might be close by and that he had a gun as well as an aggressive looking switchblade. I didn't fancy getting acquainted with either, so I did as Lucero asked. Once I was inside, he closed the door. I was relieved to hear that he hadn't locked it. My relief was short-lived. That could only mean they were confident that I wouldn't be able to get out of the premises, or that it was in such a remote location that it was not an option to try to escape.

The room was box-shaped, three walls painted white and one painted light blue. A window looked out onto the courtyard. Above the doorway, a large air conditioning unit hummed as it dispensed cool air. The only furniture was a single bed, a wardrobe and a plain, wooden bedside cabinet with a small lamp on it. Opposite the bed, a door led into a small bathroom that had a shower cubicle, a sink and a toilet.

I checked my pockets. No mobile phone. They must have taken it. I sat on the bed and considered my situation.

I was a prisoner and the box room emphasised that feeling.

29

Surprisingly, I slept well. Exhaustion perhaps, and the result of a series of late nights having taken their toll. I checked my watch – 7.53 a.m. I rolled out of bed, showered and dressed in the only clothes I had, my shorts, t-shirt and trainers. I paced the room and reflected on my situation. I realised that Anita was responsible for my abduction and, once she knew I wasn't going to keep a low profile, she'd decided to get me out of the city. A remote and secure location some distance away made sense, so travelling for nearly five hours meant I could be anywhere between two or three hundred miles north, south, east or west of Madrid.

I stood up and pushed open the window and looked outside. All I could see was the courtyard and the expanse of ground with the plants and cacti. Beyond that the high perimeter wall enclosed the whole area. There was nothing that gave me any clue as to where I might be.

My thoughts were interrupted by a knock on the door. Before I could reach it, the door was flung open. A slight woman, her hair greying and cut short, walked in holding a tray with a cup and a plate on it. She placed it on the bedside cabinet. The plate contained a couple of slices of ham and a bread roll.

The woman smiled but said nothing. Her smile gave me some encouragement. I attempted a conversation. "Uh… Señora. Buenos días. Err… you… you hablo… uh, English… inglés?"

She shook her head.

I looked at the cup. A black coffee. "Uh… you have water… agua, por favor?"

She nodded and left the room. I was aware that she made no attempt to close the door, which suggested to me again that my abductors knew it was not possible to get out.

Anita's decision meant that I was likely to be kept captive for two or even three days, until she received the cocaine shipment. After that, there was no reason to hold me. Even if Cañizares was not back from the tour it wouldn't matter once they had their shipment.

I sat on the bed, sipped the coffee and ate some of the ham and the roll. The woman returned with a glass of water and then left again without saying anything. I reasoned that, although my situation was not ideal, they intended to treat me well and I would be freed once the deal was done.

When I'd finished the coffee, I took a tentative peek outside the room. There was nobody around. I walked across the reception area towards a large window that looked out onto the poolside. To my left there was a water cooler, a jug and some glasses. I poured a glass of water and decided I would risk exploring further. The front door was open. Outside it was already warm, the sky clear blue, the only immediate shade from four tall palm trees that lined one side of the house and bordered the pool. I stood for a moment, tense with an expectation that Lucero, or the guy with the gun, would appear and drag me back inside. But it was eerily silent, with only the occasional bark of a dog from somewhere in the distance. I made my way to the metal gate that led to the courtyard. It was unlocked. I stared at the lilac doorway to my right that broke the expanse of perimeter wall. With adrenaline coursing through me all of a sudden, I placed the glass of water on the ground and walked briskly towards the doorway. A glance over my shoulder told me there was still nobody around. I grabbed the door handle and tried to open it. I yanked it up and down but it wouldn't open. I pushed against it, but it was firmly locked.

My surge of adrenaline crashed, replaced by a wave of frustration. There was no way out. I turned and walked back towards the pool. Just as I walked through the metal gate, the gun guy came out of the house.

He grinned, but it didn't hide the menace in his eyes. "You go somewhere, Señor Malakee?"

"Malarkey. Uh... no... I, err, was just... err... just –"

He moved towards me, a finger stabbing at my chest. "You stay... aquí... here. You no go. You no try go." He waved an arm to indicate the pool area. "You go here, in swim... is no problema." He pointed at the lilac doorway. "But you no go aquí...

here. Is big problema. ¿Me comprendes?" He opened his jacket to reveal the gun holstered on his left side.

I nodded. I understood.

For the rest of the day I hung around the pool. There was nothing else to do. I found some sunscreen in the bathroom cabinet and dozed in the heat on one of the two white, plastic sun loungers that occupied one end of the poolside. The only highlight in my day was when the housekeeper brought food, more bread and ham at lunchtime but with cheese, olives and gherkins, and paella in the evening. I caught the odd glimpse of the guy that had put me right about where I could and couldn't go, but he never spoke to me and mostly he remained in the house. I felt sure that he was simply reminding me of his presence. That night I went to bed as soon as it got dark but slept fitfully this time. Boredom and concern continually playing with my thoughts.

On Friday, things changed.

30

Lucero turned up at the villa on Friday morning. I was outside sitting by the pool, but he ignored me and went straight inside. After lunch, the weather changed and turned cloudy. I went back to my room and laid down on the bed. The air seemed heavy, the room claustrophobic. I opened the window and got back on the bed intending to have a rest, mostly to kill time but also because I was tired after my poor night's sleep. A few minutes later, I had slipped into a half-conscious pre-sleep state, when the sound of voices brought me back to full alertness. The sound seemed to be coming from outside. I got up and went to the window.

Lucero and his gun toting sidekick.

Despite the conversation being in Spanish, I decided to listen and try to pick up anything I could. The chat was interrupted by the ring of a mobile. I heard Lucero answer with, "Hola, Anita." The rest of what he said was just too quick for me to interpret any of the words. I could only hear one side of the conversation, in any case, and it was clear by Lucero's intermittent murmurs that Anita was doing most of the talking. When the call finished I heard him speak to other guy.

"Está bien, Vincente, el hombre del teatro viene a hacer el tatuaje."

"¿Cuándo viene?"

"Mañana"

"¿Para él?"

"Si... uh, Matthew?"

"¿A qué hora ?"

"Las diez de la mañana."

It was all I heard. The two men began to move away, the conversation fading as they got further from the building.

When they had gone, I began to focus on what I'd heard. I tried to recall each word to see which ones I could translate, but with my limited Spanish, most of them were just sounds and said too fast to focus on. I sat down on the bed and concentrated on picking out whatever I could. I'd heard my name, so I knew they were talking about me. I was familiar with the word 'mañana' – tomorrow. So something was happening tomorrow, Saturday. That was the day I was due to return home. I'd heard the word, 'hombre', which meant 'man.' Now I had, 'Matthew, tomorrow and man.' I juggled the words around to see if some connection would appear. 'Tomorrow, Matthew, man... man, tomorrow, Matthew.' No matter which way I arranged them, there were only three to work with and therefore minimal interpretation. It had to be 'a man coming tomorrow for Matthew.' Perhaps they were taking me back to Madrid so I could leave the country. I focussed on that. My thoughts were interrupted by the door opening. Lucero entered and held his mobile out towards me.

"Llamada telefónica."

I took the mobile and said, "Hello?"

"*Matthew, it's Anita. You okay?*"

"Of course I'm not frigging okay. What's going on? Where am I?"

"*Calm down. You're safe. You –*"

"Safe? I'm not bloody safe. I've been abducted, almost poisoned on the way here and there's a lunatic running around with a knife and a gun. What's safe about any of that?"

"*Stop being so melodramatic. They're looking after you, aren't they?*"

I stood up and paced in circles, Lucero blocking the doorway. "Well, if you call getting three small meals a day and a tiny box room in a place I don't want to be, looked after, then yeah, perhaps I am! But I'm here against my will and I'm not –"

"*You gave me no choice. I asked for your cooperation in keeping a low profile, but you wouldn't agree so we had to have a backup plan. I told you, we have to protect our interests. There's a lot of money at stake here.*"

I sat back down on the bed. "So what happens next? How long you going to keep me here? I'm supposed to go home tomorrow. You coming for me?"

I heard the hesitation and then Anita said, "*I'm afraid not, Matthew. There's a complication.*"

"What?"

"*A complication. Kreshnik wants to see you again. There's some uncertainty.*"

"What uncertainty? What do you mean?"

"*One of his men found your false earring in the lift after he left the room. It was obvious it was a cheap imitation, especially as he found the magnet too. It's caused Kreshnik some concern.*"

"Shit." I remembered Cecil mentioning it the night before and realised it had fallen off – in the wrong place. "Uh, must've come off. What did you tell him? Couldn't you bluff it?"

"*I tried. I gave him some story about you not wanting to go into a meeting with his guys with an expensive diamond earring, but he wasn't having that. He said you could have taken it off if you were concerned. Now he needs you to prove you're actually the footballer.*"

"Prove I'm the footballer? How am I supposed to do that? Do some 'keepy-uppy' in a hotel room? Demonstrate my ball juggling skills? How's that going to work? And when am I supposed to be meeting him again?" I stood up and began to pace.

"*Leave the proof to me. As for when, it can't happen until Cañizares gets back to Spain on Tuesday night. The team are doing press and media engagements on Wednesday, so the earliest I can get a meeting is Wednesday evening. I've arranged to meet Kreshnik then.*"

"Wednesday! You are joking. I'm not staying here to Wednesday."

"*I don't think you have any choice, Matthew. I'll be in touch.*" The call went dead.

I was stunned, confused, angry and worried. Lucero snatched the mobile from my hand and walked out, banging the door behind him.

I laid down on the bed, my fingers massaging my forehead as I tried to think straight. Whatever plan Anita had to convince Kreshnik I was the footballer wouldn't happen until Wednesday night. Then they still had to get the shipment of cocaine. Even if things went well, I was unlikely to get out of Spain for another week at least. The lads would be wondering what had happened to me, but I knew they wouldn't leave on Saturday without me. As I lay on the bed, I felt the need to sleep, perhaps a subconscious desire to cut off the negative thoughts that were racing through my head.

It was an hour and a half before I woke again. The room seemed dark. I checked my watch. It was still only three-thirty. I crossed to the window. Outside it was raining. I sat on the edge of the bed and thought about the call with Anita and the fact I was going nowhere for several days. Then my mind flashed back to the earlier conversation I'd overheard between Lucero and Vincente and the three words I'd picked up. 'Matthew, tomorrow and man.' Now my interpretation didn't make sense. After what Anita had said, there was no 'man coming tomorrow for Matthew.' I tried to recall the rest of what I had heard and realised that a couple of other words sounded familiar – 'teatro' and 'tatuaje.' I'd been to the Teatro Real, so it must be a reference to a theatre, although I didn't understand the relevance to my situation. The other word was just a sound – 'tah-twah-heh' – but I was sure I'd heard it somewhere before. I repeated it over and over out loud, slowly and distinctly, trying to see if I could make any sense of it.

"Tah-twah-heh... tah-twah-heh... tah-twah-heh."

And then another word jumped out at me. 'Proof.' *'Leave the proof to me.'* Anita's words. In an instant, my mind shot back to Ascot, and a vivid picture formed in my head.

The snake entwined around the thorny stem of a rose, with the names 'Chiara' and 'Ignacio.'

31

I sat for a while contemplating the scenario that lay before me. Surely Anita and her syndicate wouldn't go as far as having my arm tattooed just to convince Kreshnik that I was the footballer? But then again they were criminals, engaged in criminal activity. While Anita didn't look or sound like a criminal, she was part of a plot to build a cocaine business that supplied numerous major holiday resorts. As she had said, the deal was worth 'several million euros.' That was probably enough to kill for, let alone leave someone's arm scarred for life.

I got up and went out to the reception area. All was quiet. I went to the window and saw that the rain had got heavier, the water bouncing off the pool surface in a multitude of ripples. I walked over to a sofa positioned against one of the walls and sat down. Maybe I was overthinking things. Maybe I'd got the translation of 'tatuaje' wrong. And then something made me realise I hadn't. I remembered where I'd heard the word. Carlos asking Cañizares, in Spanish, to show me the tattoo, in the lavatories at Ascot. 'Tatuaje.' That was the word he had used. The same one.

I tried to be rational. I'd never had a tattoo and knew little about the process, but a tattoo had to take longer than a week to heal, so maybe that wasn't the plan. But, on the other hand, Anita's syndicate might be getting desperate, fearful that their deal was unravelling, and if so, perhaps they would try anything to save it. My mind raced with the possibilities, but I knew that if there was the slightest chance that I was right and there was a tattooist coming tomorrow, I was in trouble. I went back to my room and tried to think of a solution. There wasn't one.

My evening meal arrived at eight o'clock, more paella. I finished it and showered, ready for bed. I checked outside through the bedroom window. The sky was black and angry, the rain heavier than before. I went to bed hoping that sleep would come quickly and that tomorrow would come slowly.

I was woken in the early hours by the sound of thunder and the rush of flowing water. I switched on the bedside lamp and checked my watch – 3.50 a.m. I got out of bed and opened the window. The rain was relentless, crashing down in heavy sheets of water across the courtyard. Flashes of lightning, almost continuous, like strobe lighting, illuminated the wet tiles, followed quickly by the deep, angry rumble of thunder. Water cascaded off the roof and pooled up against the walls. I watched and listened for a moment as the raging storm warned off the world, nature asserting its dominance. In the distance, a dog barked its concern at the noise of the night sky. This was not a time for man or beast to be outside. And then a wild thought occurred to me – it was the perfect time to attempt an escape.

I pulled on my t-shirt and shorts and went over to the bedroom door, the wild thought acquiring some logic as I moved. The sound of rain beating hard on the roof and thunder rolling across the sky would cover any sounds I might make trying to get out. It was worth the risk. I eased the brass handle down slowly until it would go no more and then pulled. The door was tight against the frame and creaked as it opened. The silence in the house emphasised the sound. Outside, a light glowed dimly in the reception room but enough to illuminate the area. I waited, watching for movement. There was none. At four in the morning, anyone in the house had to be asleep, although I knew the sound of the storm was enough to wake the sleeping. After a moment, I realised the light was no more than a night light.

I picked up my trainers, closed the bedroom door and tiptoed across the floor space, my bare feet making no sound on the tiles. As I reached the far side of the lobby, a flash of lightning illuminated the room, followed immediately by a fierce bang of thunder that crashed across the roof. Instantly the light in the lobby cut out. I stopped, frozen by the impact, listening for movement. Nothing. I made my way towards the window. Outside, the pool light had gone off and the whole courtyard was in darkness. The power had gone down. Perfect.

On my right there was a door that I knew led to the entrance hall and the exit to the terrace and poolside. It opened easily. I approached the exit door only to find it was locked. I turned back to the lobby area and inched my way along the wall back to the window. I tried the handle. It moved. I opened the window and eased my way through. The rain lashed against my face and torso, soaking me straightaway.

Once outside, I knew that crossing the poolside to the perimeter wall would put me in full view of the property windows. I couldn't risk it. I moved to my right and stayed tight to the side. The route along the pool narrowed as it ran parallel to the villa extension. The palm trees and plants that lined the building afforded me some screening. I made my way to the corner at the top end of the pool. At that angle, I was less likely to be seen should anyone wake up.

The rain continued to pour down. A flash of lightning lit the area momentarily. It picked out the two lounge chairs that I might not otherwise have seen in the dark. I eased my way around them. At that point I stopped, unsure of what the escape plan was. My earlier enthusiasm had not considered that an escape meant getting over the perimeter wall. I scanned the area as best I could and realised the wall to my immediate right was too steep to attempt to climb. I would have to try on the far side of the pool.

My eyes began to adjust to the darkness, but I still had to feel my way around, careful not to trip on anything and make noise. I stayed tight to the wall as I crossed the poolside. I reached the corner and could feel the point where the bougainvillaea grew in a thick mass of vines and flowers, up and over the wall. It might give me something to grip onto if I could get a footing. I put my trainers on my wet feet and grabbed hold of the thickest vine. I tugged on it to see how secure it was. It seemed sturdy. I got a foothold on a low concrete ledge that formed the base of the wall, gripped the vine and hoisted myself up. I raised my free leg and pushed my foot through the plant looking for another foothold. I found a crevice in the blockwork mortar line. Using the plant like a rope and by pushing my weight onto the crevice, I managed to hoist myself up further.

I was about five feet above the ground but I had to get higher to get a grip on top of the wall. I paused, searching for the edge. Wet leaves brushed my head and dripped their excess water down my t-shirt; rainwater battered my face, blurring my vision but adrenaline drove me on. I raised my leg, and my foot found another groove in the mortar. I tugged on the bougainvillaea in one last effort to get close to the top. But my weight was too much. I felt the plant shift slightly, moving away from the wall. Then, with a rustling and tearing sound, it began to rip away completely. I had no choice but to jump or risk ending up on my back on the poolside. I flung my body away as a huge swathe of the plant tore off the wall. I twisted in the air but landed awkwardly on the wet tiles. My left foot slid across a puddle causing me to stumble backwards. I struggled to keep my balance, but my heel caught the edge of the pool and pitched me headfirst into the water.

    A muffled rush of noise rang in my ears as my body hit the water and I sank below the surface. I wondered if they'd heard the splash in the villa. For a moment, I wanted to stay under, a misguided thought that I could remain hidden from view, but survival instinct drove me back up. As my face broke the surface, I shook the water from my hair and face and turned to look at the villa. All was silent, no movement, no lights. And then I remembered the power had gone down. I moved to the side of the pool next to the building and waited, my head just above the surface but concealed from view by the pool edge. I waited and watched, watching for torchlight, listening for sound. Nothing. I waited for a further five, maybe ten, minutes, my pulse pounding. If anyone had heard anything, they would have come out. The noise of rain and thunder must have covered any splash my fall had made. There was no point staying in the pool. If anyone did come out, it would only be a matter of time before I was discovered. I might as well be caught attempting to get over the wall as hiding in the water. An early morning swim wouldn't cut it as an excuse for being outside in a storm.

    I made my way towards one of the steel pool ladders, grabbed the sides and pulled myself out. There was no time to worry about my soaking wet clothes. I had nothing else anyway. I edged my way back round the pool, past the sun loungers, to the corner. I stepped through the broken bougainvillaea that lay spread across the tiles and continued further along the far side. As I eased forward I tripped on something. I crouched down and realised that it was a slatted wood platform, about two inches high, positioned under a pool shower. I continued on, looking for a place where I might be able to climb, but there wasn't one. The wall was too high and even where the bougainvillaea was less dense, it did not seem possible to climb, especially in dark and wet conditions. My captors had not had the courtesy to leave a ladder lying around. Desperation and despair began to take hold.

And then I had an idea.

I went back the way I had come, to where the sun loungers were. I picked one up and carried it back around the pool to the wall. I straightened it out so that the backrest was in the flat 'lying down' position. Next, I lifted the wood shower platform and repositioned it so that one end was tight against the raised pool edge. Then I leaned one end of the lounger, seating side face down, against the wall with the other end jammed against the platform. This put the lounger at roughly a forty-five degree angle. I pushed down on the hard plastic to make sure it was secure. With the base side facing up, the grooves that ran the length of the lounger made ideal footholds.

I turned and looked across the poolside at the villa. It was still in darkness, no sign of activity. Rain bounced off the tiled roof; lightning illuminated the courtyard casting fleeting, ghostly shadows as it picked out cacti and trees. At that moment, I felt a surge of confidence. Nobody would be crazy enough to leave the house.

I pushed down on the edges of the lounger, one final test of its robustness. Then I placed a foot at the bottom end, gripped the sides firmly and began to climb. There was no time for hesitation. The middle section flexed and creaked as it took my weight. As I stepped onto the end section and made a grab for the top of the wall I heard a crack, but the lounger remained sturdy. With one hand on the edge of the wall, I pulled my weight forward and swung my other arm up so that I could get a two handed grip. Without hesitating, I used my momentum to pull myself up and clamber forward so that my waist draped over the top of the wall. Then I swung my right leg up, pushing down with my hands so that my centre of balance was poised on the wall edge. It was then only a matter of twisting around and lowering myself down by my arms and hands until I was in a position to let go and jump. I landed in a strip of gravel that lay between the wall and the tarmac. As my feet hit the ground another flash of lightning lit the area. Directly opposite stood an orangey yellow property. Ahead, the road met a wider section at a junction and then got narrower as it ran between two other properties.

There was no time for thinking. I started to run.

32

The narrow road turned sharply right and led between two whitewashed properties into a clearing that looked like a village square. There was no actual village, just a few scattered buildings. The area was too open for me to delay in, even under cover of darkness. The sound of dogs barking, alarmed by the storm, could wake someone. I had to get away, somewhere less exposed.

I turned left and chose the narrower of two roads that lay ahead. A few metres further on the road split into two, the left hand side nothing more than a single strip of tarmac. Further on still, a dirt track veered off to the left. I took that option. It seemed less accessible to cars. I followed it for roughly quarter of a mile, my pace slowed to a cautious walk by the limited visibility and the rain lashing into my face. Underfoot, the ground became more pitted and rougher, loose rocks causing me to tread more carefully. My feet were soaking wet where my trainers had found puddles deep enough to cover them. None of that bothered me. My focus was on putting distance between me and my captors. A thumping heart and sheer adrenaline drove me on.

As I ploughed on into the darkness, the terrain became more difficult. I had stumbled twice, my hands finding wet, soggy trenches in the soil. My progress was slower, my direction aimless. I began to worry about the possibility of ending up back near the house from where I had just escaped. I stopped and tried to take stock, my breathing heavy, my state of mind bordering on panic. A flash of lightning lit up the landscape ahead, and I caught a glimpse of several rows of small trees that I took to be almond or olive groves. I decided that if I could shelter there until dawn approached, I had a good chance of finding a better route.

I made my way forward until I found the first tree and then, using touch and the limited vision I had in the dark, I was able to track a path through the grove until I was in a more sheltered spot. I sat down on the soggy ground, my back against the short trunk of one of the trees and tried to rest. There was no risk of falling asleep. Tiredness had long since been driven from my body by adrenalin. My mind raced with conflicting thoughts. Had I got it wrong? Should I have stayed where I was? An escape would tell the syndicate that their deal was in jeopardy, and that would change things. Had I become an even bigger target?

The thought only served to reinforce the need for me to get away.

I took a deep breath and tried to ignore the fact that I was shivering in my wet clothes. If I could wait until the first signs of dawn, I would have a better chance of finding a way to gain distance. But daylight would mean I would be more exposed. I tried to think rationally. The house didn't see any real activity until around seven-thirty when dawn broke. Breakfast was usually an hour or so later. It was likely then that I wouldn't be noticed missing until at least eight-thirty. If I could make use of first light as dawn began to break, I had a minimum of an hour and perhaps a bit more to get ahead. My only concern was that someone might notice the torn bougainvillaea on the poolside before that. I checked my watch. Almost five-fifteen. Two and a quarter hours until daylight but perhaps only an hour and a half to the first signs of dawn emerging.

It was six o'clock when the rain eased up. My sheltered position had helped reduce my exposure, and the storm was moving on. It was still dark, low-level cloud keeping visibility limited. Half an hour later, I could just make out a ribbon of dark blue sky struggling against black thunder clouds on the horizon.

I got to my feet and tried to get my bearings. The sun rises in the east. If I headed in that direction it would take me back to where I'd come from. I needed to keep going in the direction I had done earlier. I waited a while longer. By six forty-five the darkness was fading, although there was low visibility with the sun still not above the horizon, and the remaining cloud. My eyes adjusted quickly to the change and I scanned my surroundings. On one side I could see the path I had taken earlier before I veered off into the grove. Ahead lay an open expanse of wet soil and more trees, but in the distance, I could just see a high embankment at the top of which there appeared to be a raised roadway. A roadway meant escape. It rolled away in a curve from the east, heading south. That was good enough for me. It took me away from my captors.

I walked to the edge of the grove and checked in both directions. There was no sign of life. I turned to my right and followed the track that led towards the embankment. I picked my way through the puddles and wet soil until I could see the raised roadway ahead. At the top, a crash barrier lined the edge of the elevated section. I clambered up the embankment until I was behind the barrier. Daylight was emerging slowly and I could see the roadway clearly. I checked to my right and left. There were no vehicles.

I stepped over the barrier onto the tarmac and headed in the southerly direction. The road continued to rise until it reached its highest elevation where it crossed a motorway. A motorway was a fast exit out of the area if I could get a lift, but I knew that it was illegal to wander along the carriageway. I would probably get picked up by the police who would run a check and very quickly tie me to Armendarez's drug bust. In my present state I would look like a vagrant, a runaway. I had to keep moving.

The road over the motorway was my only option but crossing it would put me at my most vulnerable. There was no hiding place on top of a raised roadway. I had to take the chance. I ran, anxious to get across to the other side where the ground was flat and lined with shrubbery and almond groves. As I came down the far side, I heard a vehicle engine somewhere behind. I stepped off the tarmac onto the soil and laid flat behind a row of shrubs. With the road deserted and in an open landscape, it was easy to hear the sound of an engine some way off, and that gave me time to hide. A few moments later, a car passed. It never altered its speed, and I had no reason to think it was anything other than someone just going about their business. When it was out of sight, I stood up and went back to the road. On the horizon, I could see the outline of a range of mountains. Behind me, the land was flatter and I knew that somewhere in the small outcrop of buildings that I could just make out, was the house I had escaped from. I had to put more distance between me and that location.

The sun was rising and my clothes were beginning to dry out as a result. There was a gentle breeze too, but I knew that would disappear once the morning wore on. I was tired, dirty and anxious, but I had to stay focussed. I heard another vehicle, this time coming from the other direction. It was less likely to be a concern coming towards me, but I took no chances. Again I got off the road and hid behind the almond trees. I let it pass and disappear into the distance before I returned to the road and walked on.

Half mile further on I saw a road sign. Stop – 150m. That had to mean a junction. A junction meant choices. Maybe I'd get lucky and be able to get a lift somewhere. I followed the curve of the tarmac and came to a main road, a T-junction, marked N-332. Right in front of me, a sign displayed the choices. To the right Cuesta Blanca, one kilometre and Mazarrón, twenty-eight kilometres; to the left, Molinas Marfagones, four kilometres and Cartagena, nine kilometres. One kilometre and four kilometres seemed too close to where I'd escaped from. Twenty-eight kilometres, too far to travel if I was unable to get a lift. I'd be exposed on the roadside for too long. Nine kilometres seemed reasonable, close enough to travel to, but far enough not to be local. I turned left.

I crossed to the right side of the road so that I would be on the same side as the traffic heading in the direction of Cartagena. On my right, a farmhouse bordered the carriageway. I walked past it, aware that if I stood too near seeking out a lift, I would arouse suspicion should any of the occupants see me. Further along, there was a clearing that sat back off the road. I made my way towards it. It was an entrance to an industrial site. On one side, the area contained a yard for construction materials, and on the other, a unit for the manufacture of metal products. It was an ideal location, far enough back from the road to hide should I need to and the perfect spot to view both the junction I had just come from and the road further along. The location had another benefit – a large display sign that contained the name of one of the businesses, fixed into the ground close to the roadside. A row of heavy stone blocks formed a rectangle at its base. If I stood back far enough, it screened off the view of the carriageway and would take me out of the line of sight too.

The N-332 was busier than the road I had walked along earlier, which meant I had more chance of getting a lift, but it also heightened my sense of fear. I decided I had to choose carefully and not try to flag down any random vehicle. My best option was a truck or a van. A commercial vehicle would have drivers going about their daily work routine. Cars could have people looking for me.

I stood a little way back into the entrance but in a position where I could scan the road to my left. A car approached from the junction and stopped at the carriageway. I hopped over the stone blocks and ducked behind the sign. By lying flat, I could see under its base and keep track of the car's movement. The vehicle's indicator said it was turning onto the carriageway in my direction. It pulled out slowly and then began to speed up. As it passed, I could see the driver, an elderly man, and a female passenger. I watched as it disappeared into the distance, relieved that it was merely someone just going about their morning routine.

I let several cars pass, and then I spotted a box van approaching. I took a deep breath and stepped out from my concealment. I stuck out my arm and 'thumbed' at the driver. The vehicle began to slow and then, a few metres past my position, came to a halt, its red brake lights on. I had a moment's doubt about my choice, but there was no perfect choice if I wanted to get out of the area.

Too late to change my mind. The driver had seen me.

33

The van was white, slightly battered in places and with red lettering on the side that said, 'Mugga Transport.' Underneath that, there was the place name, 'Mazarrón', and a telephone number. With the sun in my face, I walked towards the cab door and then realised the driver was on the far side. I moved around the front of the vehicle to the driver's side. As I did the window came down and I was greeted by a dark-skinned man with a wide, toothy smile.

I spoke first. "Err... no hablo Español, Señor. Uh... can you give me –"

"It's not a problem, my friend. You English?"

"Yes... yes, I am."

"I speak English, no problem. You need a ride?"

"Please, yes, I do. Err... you go to... Cart... uh, Carta –"

"Cartagena? Sure. Jump in."

I walked round to the passenger side and opened the door. The cab was basic but neat and tidy. The driver wore navy-blue work trousers and a yellow t-shirt. A denim jacket hung on a hook at the back of his seat. His hair was dark and curly and he had a rugged unshaven face. His most striking feature though was his ready smile, white teeth gleaming, a smile that lit up his eyes.

I pulled the cab door closed. The driver checked his mirror and then pulled off. As he did so, I felt a sudden relief, the first time in days that I had experienced any sort of security.

"Thank you," I said.

"It's no problem, my friend. You look like you have trouble. I like to help." He held out his hand. "My name is Muggabusca. My friends, they call me Mugga."

I shook his hand. "Uh... hi, err... Mugga." I was unsure, nervous about my situation and revealing my name, but instinctively I trusted Muggabusca's face. In any case, he was a random stranger who had happened along in a van, and he was unlikely to be connected with any of my pursuers. "I'm Matthew. Good to meet you."

"Good to meet you too, Matthew. So what you do here on the road? You look like you been in the storm last night."

"Uh... yeah, I was. I didn't know it rains that much in Spain."

"Not usual this time of year. September, maybe, but not like that in summer. Maybe freak... freak storm. If you were outside, then you must have trouble."

I hesitated, wondering whether I should come up with an alternative story but realised that my dishevelled state confirmed the 'trouble' Muggabusca had referred to. "You're right. I do. I've been... uh... yeah... it's a long story..."

"It's okay. I listen good."

"Look... err... Mugga, before that I just need to know some things. I'll explain the rest in a minute."

"Okay, my friend. As I say, no problem. I like if I can help you."

"Appreciate it, Mugga. Thank you." I needed help, no question of that. "So where exactly are we?"

He laughed and shot a glance at me. "You don't know? Murcia. Is a big area of Southern Spain."

"*Southern* Spain?"

"Yes. We are heading to Cartagena. I go every day. I deliver to markets, supermercado, shops. Today tomatoes, other days vegetables, sweet potato... from the farms, you know."

I nodded. "Cartagena, is it big? And where is it?"

Mugga laughed again. He had a deep, rumbling laugh, the kind that told you he loved life. "Big enough to hide in. You need to hide? You look like you run away from some place, no?"

I hesitated. There was no doubt I looked like a vagrant with my dirty t-shirt and shorts, dust covered legs and arms. "Sort of. So where is Cartagena, you didn't say?"

Muggabusca slowed for a roundabout and then said, "By the sea. A port. You have Alicante to north-east and Almeria south-west."

"Almeria? I don't know it, but Alicante I do, because of the airport."

"Okay. You know Malaga? Bit further south west."

"Uh, yeah." I tried to visualise my location, but a proper understanding would be more forthcoming if I could see a map. I realised though, that my captors had taken me some distance south of Madrid.

The road narrowed as we approached a small residential area. We drove across a number of junctions and then Muggabusca slowed the van and pulled into the kerb next to rows of shops that lined both sides of the street.

"I have delivery here." He pointed across the road. "Spar supermercado. Tomatoes."

"Where are we?"

"Molinas Marfagones. I will be quick." He opened the door and jumped out of the cab. I pulled down the sun visor and slid down in the seat, my head bowed.

Muggabusca was no more than ten minutes. He got back in the cab, started the engine and said, "Okay, my friend, let's go. Next stop, Cartagena." He eased into the traffic and once clear of the village he said, "So, you like to tell me your trouble? Maybe I can help."

I needed to tell someone, and it was clear that Muggabusca was an ordinary guy going about his business. His demeanour had made me feel safe.

"Okay. Yes, I'm running but I've done nothing wrong. I have some bad people after me who took me here just because they want something from me. They took my money, my cards and my phone. It's complicated, but I have to get back to Madrid."

"Madrid? My friend, that is more than four hundred and fifty kilometres from here. A long way with no money!"

"Four hundred and fifty kilometres? Is it? My friends are there. I have to get in touch with them. They're my only hope of sorting things out."

We cleared a roundabout and, without warning, Muggabusca pulled the van off the road and came to a halt on a piece of waste ground next to the carriageway. He cut the engine and pulled out a mobile phone from his pocket.

"Here, you call your friends." He handed me the phone.

I took it and then realised that I didn't know any of the boys' numbers. Nobody stores numbers in their heads. It's all on screen, in the phone's memory. I didn't even know Louise's number, although even if I did, this was not the time to alarm her.

"It's no good. I don't know any numbers."

Muggabusca frowned, his expression almost pained. He reached behind his seat and slipped a hand into his jacket. He pulled out his wallet and removed a twenty euro note.

"You take this, my friend. I only have thirty euros today and I need to keep some for diesel." He waved the note at me.

"No... no, I can't take your money. It's very... really good of you, Mugga, but I can't."

"Why not? I try to help you. You get some food and water. Not much money but it helps." He waved the note at me again. "You know something? I come to Spain five years ago from Morocco. I have nothing. Nothing, no money. I sleep in the street. One day, an old lady, she see me sitting on a bench, my clothes dirty and she give me twenty euros. She ask no questions, just smile and give me money. My heart, it warms. So I go to get food because I have not eaten for two days. I buy cheap burger and water, and when I'm there, I meet a man who need people to dig holes for pipes to his house. Cheap pay, but I take job. Money give me food and somewhere to live. No big palace like king, but a place I sleep. Then people see I am good worker and honest man. I get more jobs and now I have this one. I buy the van with money I save and make small business. It is old van so hard to keep going, but I work every day. Make some money. Soon, maybe I have enough to go back to Morocco. So, my friend, twenty euros is small money, but maybe it make you free like me."

I was speechless. Muggabusca waved the note at me again. This time I took it. I muttered a 'thank you.' There was nothing else to say. He started the engine and moved off.

In the next fifteen minutes, the landscape changed significantly. The countryside gave way to a myriad of interconnecting streets and rows of buildings as we entered the outskirts of Cartagena. I stared through the passenger side window at people going about their daily lives, seemingly with no stress and no issues. It was called normality and I wanted it back.

The van picked up the flow of the early morning traffic, switching lanes, trying to beat the lights. Muggabusca was evidently in a hurry, and I realised that he had a job to do and my drama had held him up. We turned sharp right at another roundabout and sped along a dual carriageway. At the next set of traffic lights we took another right and Muggabusca pulled over on the left side of the road, stopping in a marked parking space. He pointed ahead where the road narrowed between rows of buildings and shops.

"I have to do my job now, my friend. Lot of deliveries. I cannot be late... the restaurants... you know?"

I checked my watch. 8.41 a.m. "Hey, I do. No worries. It's fine. Thank you, Mugga. You've been... so kind. I appreciate it." I reached over and shook his hand. "Thank you so much." I opened the door and stepped out of the cab and realised we had stopped right in front of a hotel – Los Habaneros.

I heard Muggabusca rev the engine as he selected reverse. The van moved back slowly, careful of the oncoming traffic. Just as he'd manoeuvred the vehicle back onto the road, I thought of something. I ran into the street straight in front of the van, my hands waving to attract his attention. He wound down the window.

"Mugga. Sorry. I need your phone again."

He handed it through the lowered glass.

I checked the screen. "Sorry, can you unlock it."

Once Muggabusca had keyed in his pin, I took the phone and ran into the hotel. There was a man behind the reception desk. I asked him for the hotel telephone number. He handed me a card. I checked the phone's screen and selected 'Settings.' The screen showed the available wi-fi options, one of which was the hotel.

"Señor, do you have a code… err, for the wi-fi, por favor?"

The man on reception nodded, took the card from me and wrote down the code on the back. Once I had a connection, I typed in 'MacFadden's Bar, Kingston.' A website came up – www.macfaddens.uk. I scrolled down and found the phone number. I checked my watch again – 8.47 a.m. Somebody had to be there, stocking up, getting ready for the day. I dialled the number.

It was Hanka that picked up the call. I told her that she needed to contact her boss, Carlos MacFadden, as a matter of urgency. I gave her the hotel number and asked her to tell Carlos that he must phone and ask for me as soon as he gets her message. I made her promise to get in touch with him immediately. I finished the call and went back to the reception desk.

"Señor, por favor… mi amigo, he is going to call you and speak to you. He speaks, uh… español. He will call soon, I think, okay?"

The reception guy nodded but I noticed the slight concern on his face. I was a strange sight, dishevelled, unkempt and smelly. Not the usual clientele, I suspected, but not something I could do anything about right at that moment.

I went back outside where Muggabusca was waiting in his truck, the engine idling.

"Thank you so much, Mugga. Sorry to make you wait." I gave him his phone.

"You will be okay, my friend?"

"I think so. Look, I have no idea if I'll ever see you again to give you back your money, but if you – "

He smiled. "It's no problem. I like that I can help you. Now, I must go. I am late. You take good care. Adiós, my friend." He shook my hand, revved the engine and drove off.

34

The hotel foyer was narrow and long, spacious, with the reception desk just inside the glass-doored entrance and the lifts opposite the desk. On the left of the doorway a corridor led to the bar and restaurant area. It seemed calm and peaceful after the hectic hours I had spent on edge and anxious.

The guy on reception eyed me cautiously as I paced up and down, but it gave me time to think and try to come up with some sort of plan as I waited on the call. To the right of the desk a wall rack held some local maps and general tourist information. I took one of the maps and spread it out so I could get an idea of my exact location. On one side, there was a detailed view of Cartagena with local places of interest highlighted. I flipped it over. The other side had a more general view of the south-east region of Spain, from Valencia on the east coast to Gibraltar on the southern coast. I studied it in some detail and realised that Madrid was too far north to be included. I found Cartagena on the south-eastern coastline, with Alicante north of it and Almeria and Malaga further south, precisely as Muggabusca had said. And then one other familiar place name caught my eye, just as the reception phone rang.

Instantly, I focussed on the desk. The guy answered it, said a few words in Spanish and then beckoned to me. "Señor, your friend is on the phone. He wants to speak to you." He handed me the receiver.

"*Mateo?*"

"Carlos, yeah, it's me. Listen, I'm –"

"*You okay, pal? Hanka asked me to call you. Where are you? We've been worried. We couldnae go to the polis.*"

"Carlos, listen. I'm in a place called Cartagena and I –"

"*Cartagena? How the hell did you get there?*"

"Lucero and some guy called Vincente. They hijacked me on the street and took me here."

"*Bloody hell, Mateo. How you gonnae get back?*"

"That's what I wanted to talk to you about. I had an idea. You remember Erin, who we saw at the airport?"

"*Aye, I do.*"

"I need you to contact her. She was down in Marbella and she should have a car. I know it's a long shot, she might have left now, but she's my best bet to get out of here. I need you to see if she can come and get me as soon –"

"*In a car?*"

"Yeah. Look, Carlos, I haven't got all day. I need to sort this –"

"*¡Vaya! ¿Estás loco? Are y'aff yer rocker, pal? She cannae drive to Colombia!*"

"Colombia? What? What you on about?"

"*Cartagena, you're in Colombia?*"

I let out a gasp of exasperation. "No, you dick. Cartagena, Murcia... Southern Spain. They drove me here. I'm at a hotel, uh... Los Habaneros."

I heard Carlos laugh. "*Why didn't you say that? I thought you meant Colombia 'cos of the coke thing. The Cartagena I know is in Colombia, South America so I –*"

"Carlos, shut it for a second. I haven't got time for a frigging geography lesson. I'm in trouble and I need to get out of here and back to Madrid."

"*Can'ya no get a train?*"

"No, I've got no money... apart from twenty euros, and even if I did, I couldn't risk it in case they're watching the station."

"*We'll come and get you, me and the boys.*"

"No... no, you can't. Once they realise I've escaped, they'll be watching you lot to see –"

"*Escaped? Escaped from what?*"

As quickly as I could, I gave Carlos the short version of how I had been held in the villa and ended up in Cartagena. Then I said, "So, I need you to make a call to Erin and ask if she'll come here and take me back to Madrid."

"*How far is it?*"

I thought back to my discussion with Muggabusca in his van. "About four hundred and fifty kilometres south of Madrid. What's that, about three hundred miles?"

"*Aye, something like that. Still a long way, whichever way you dice it. And Marbella must be a wee bit of a trek from you too. What makes you think the lassie'll do it?*"

I thought of Erin and how well I knew her and remembered her words at the airport. '*Nothing wrong with a bit of excitement, Matthew. Keeps the pulse ticking.*' "If she's still there, Carlos, she'll do it. I have no other option. Nobody knows she has any connection with us. I just need to get back and sort this mess out."

"*Okay, pal. I'm on it. Gimme Erin's number.*"

"I don't have it, mate. They took my phone. I've got no phone, no money, no cards."

"*Yer right in the shit, then, Mateo.*"

"I know that!" My mind buzzed, searching for inspiration. "Wait. I've got an idea. You remember Diana… Diana Twist, the lawyer?"

"*I do, yeah.*"

"Good. Give her London office a ring at Twist, Swivel and Spinn, she should have Erin's number. They kept in touch. Just tell her I need it. Don't give her too much info about why. I don't want her worrying."

"*Nae problem, Mateo. I'll get on it now and call you back soon as I know anything.*"

"Thanks, mate. One other thing. You guys are supposed to be leaving today, going home, so I guess you're checking out and heading back later."

"*Do me a favour, pal. We're nae leaving Madrid without you. I'm cancelling the flight and we'll find somewhere to stay too.*"

My mind began to race. If Lucero and his crew could be watching the station, they could also be watching the airport, and Anita knew we were due home that weekend. "Carlos, wait. Okay, but don't cancel yet. You guys need to travel to the airport at the normal time as if you're getting the flight home."

"*We do?*"

"Yes. It's got to look like you're leaving. That way they won't be looking for you, thinking you know where I am."

"*That's a wee bit of a palaver isn't it?*"

"Trust me, Carlos, these guys are looking for me. As far as they're concerned, I'm about to screw their multi-million euro deal, so one way of finding me will be keeping tabs on you. We have to stay one step ahead if we can."

Okay. Makes sense. What about the flight?"

"Just go to the airport and cancel when you get there. Leave it as late as you can. You don't want them calling you to board on the PA system, so not too late. Then hang around a while until after the flight has gone. Chances are, if anyone's watching the airport they'll see you show up and just assume you're going back home. Okay?"

"*Don't worry about it. I'll sort it. And listen, if you have nae money how you paying for the hotel?*"

"I'm not. I'm not staying here. I blagged a lift and it's where I got dropped off."

Carlos paused and then said, "*What's the name of the place again? I'll need to let the lassie have a pickup address.*"

"Hotel Los Habaneros. Uh, hang on." I took the hotel card from my pocket. "It's on... Calle San Diego, Cartagena, Murcia."

"*I'll look it up. Speak later.*"

"Hey, Carlos, make sure you tell Cecil not to get impatient. This needs calm. Give me a ring as soon as you know anything." I handed the receiver back to the reception guy and thanked him. I folded up the map, put it in my pocket and went and sat down to wait.

During the next hour I watched as guests checked out, listened intently as the desk phone rang a number of times and paced up and down in order to relieve my stress. I bought a coffee and some toast and jam with Muggabusca's twenty euros and went outside for some air, careful not to stray too far from the hotel front and grateful that a large section of it was screened from the street by a terraced area filled with tables and large awnings.

It was at 10.28 that Carlos called back. I had just walked back inside when the desk phone rang again. The reception guy picked up the call. He spent several minutes chatting before indicating that I should come to the desk. He said nothing as he gave me the phone.

"Carlos?"

"*Aye, it's me, Mateo. You okay?*"

"Yeah... yeah. I'm fine. Any news."

"*Aye, good news... erm, and bad news.*"

"Bad news? What bad news?" I'd had enough bad news. I wanted to get that out of the way first.

"*It's nae that bad, Mateo. I spoke to the lawyer but she wouldn't give me any information until I told her what was wrong.*"

Typical of Diana, but then again she was a lawyer. "So, what did you tell her?"

"*I didnae tell her much, only that you were in Spain and had a wee problem. She insisted that I tell her where you were otherwise she wouldn't give me Erin's number. And that's the good news. I got hold of Erin. She's up for it, but she cannae get there until tomorrow night.*"

"Fine by me. As long as I get out of here." The good news was better than Carlos's idea of bad news. I'd worry about Diana later. "She give a time?"

"*It's a four and a half hour drive up from Marbella, pal, so just expect her when she gets there.*"

"That's no problem. I'll lay low until then."

"*Lay low? What you gonnae do, Mateo? Sleep on the street? Listen, I've sorted out some credit for you with the hotel. You can have a single room. I said you got no ID and no passport because you lost them, but someone's coming to get you. They're cool with that. Any hotel expenses go on my card.*"

I felt a sense of relief. I had somewhere I could hole up safely until I could get picked up. "Thanks, mate. I'm really grateful. I'll get you the money once I sort this out."

"*There's nae rush, Mateo. One other thing, I'm guessing you have nae other clothes if you were kidnapped, so I'll get you a hundred euros cashback so you can buy some stuff and have a wee bit left for food. Just hand me back to reception and I'll give my card details.*"

"I appreciate it, Carlos. Thanks. Can you do me one more favour please? Get Cecil to message or ring Louise. She's expecting me back tonight and I've not been in touch. Tell him to say I've lost my mobile… which I have, but I'll be in touch. I'm sure he'll think of something."

"*Nae bother, will do. Call you tomorrow, about four-ish. I'll get your room number from the desk.*"

Ten minutes later I was checked in, in the lift and headed to a room on the second floor. I washed my t-shirt and shorts, cleaned up my trainers and took a hot shower. Then I fell into a deep sleep on the bed.

35

I woke up at just after 4.15 p.m. slightly delirious, unsure of where I was for a moment. As I became used to my surroundings, I realised that I had slept for almost five hours. I swung my legs off the bed and sat upright. The room was compact but comfortable. The wall at the end of the bed had a small desk against it. A window faced into the centre of the hotel block. My t-shirt and shorts lay over the sill where I had left them to dry, and luckily they hadn't fallen off.

I sat for a moment trying to make some sense of my situation now that I'd escaped my captors. With a multi-million euro drug deal at stake, it was clear they would not stop looking for me; and they had to find me before the meeting with Kreshnik. That meant, realistically, I had just three full days left to solve my situation. There was a chance too that Kreshnik's mob would go after Ignacio Cañizares if the deal collapsed and Cañizares, who was innocent of any wrongdoing, would have his career ruined. If I didn't find a solution, my best case scenario seemed to be arrest by Ricardo Armendarez for drug dealing.

My immediate problem then was Anita's syndicate. I had to second guess their movements. I thought back to my escape from the villa. Where would they think I would go? The obvious answer to that was Madrid. I remembered the signpost at the junction where Muggabusca had picked me up. I went to the desk and picked up the map that I had found in reception. I spread it out on the bed. I looked for the place names that I had seen on the signpost – Cuesta Blanca, Mazarrón, Molinas Marfagones and Cartagena. Each one was a long way south of Madrid. There was no straightforward route north other than the motorway. I studied the map more closely. Cuesta Blanca and Molinas Marfagones were just two small villages, and Mazarrón was twenty-eight kilometres west according to the sign. The most obvious starting point for Madrid was from Cartagena, heading north to Murcia, the region's main city. That information focussed me. My captors would be thinking the same thing.

My thoughts were interrupted by the bedside phone. I picked up.

"Hello."

"*Matthew? It's Diana. Diana Twist.*"

"Diana. Oh… hello. How are you?"

"*I wouldn't worry about that, Matthew. More to the point, how are you? Are you in some sort of trouble?*"

"Trouble... no, err... not proper trouble, I just need to –"

"*Proper trouble? What do you mean? Trouble is trouble in my book.*"

"I, uh... don't know... I mean... I lost my passport and –"

"*Your passport? Carlos said you'd lost your mobile. What's happened?*"

There was no way I wanted to get Diana's legal mind involved. I knew how sharp she was and had experienced it, in a social capacity when we first met on a date, and in her professional capacity when she had represented me. I also didn't want to worry her with any of the details. So, what happened indeed?

"Erm... yeah, I did… a long story but I need to get to Madrid."

"*I understand you're in a hotel in Cartagena, right now?*"

"Err, yeah. As I said, long story. I thought as Erin is fairly close, I could get a lift to –"

"*Erin. Close? Where is she? Carlos never said.*"

"Marbella."

"*Marbella! That's miles away, isn't it? Why don't you get a train?*"

Good question. I took a deep breath in the hope that my response would sound reasonable and calm. "Look, Diana, it's okay. I saw Erin at the airport on the way out and she said she might come to Madrid, so I just thought it would be nice to catch up."

"*Okay, but are you sure you're not in trouble? I know you, don't forget.*"

I let Diana's last comment slide. "I'm fine. It's cool."

"*The passport's a problem, surely? You know you can apply for an emergency travel document if you're abroad and your passport has been lost or stolen?*"

I wanted to say, 'how about if the police have confiscated it,' but I didn't. "Can you? How long does it take?"

"*I think it's about two working days. You should be able to get one through the British Consulate in Madrid. Costs about a hundred pounds.*"

A hundred pounds. Even if an emergency document was an option, I'd have to wait until I got back to Madrid to get one of the lads to pay. I also had a feeling that I would need to clear my name of any criminal activity before I attempted to travel home. If Armendarez got the nod to pursue me for drug dealing, my name would be circulated very quickly to ports and airports.

"Uh... okay, thanks, Diana. That's helpful. I'll look into it when I get to Madrid."

"*Okey dokey, but if anything gets complicated make sure you let me know. I have contacts.*"

"Of course. And thanks for sorting out Erin's number." I finished the call and put the phone down.

It was nice to know I had support, but I wasn't sure it was enough against the people that were out to get me.

36

I got dressed and went down to the restaurant to eat. Then I went to reception to collect the one hundred euros cashback that Carlos had organised. I needed to get some clothes. Apart from the fact that fresh clothes would make me feel more comfortable, getting rid of the shorts and t-shirt I had been wearing would make me feel less conspicuous. Mindful of the fact that my pursuers could be looking for me in Cartagena, I decided I would risk leaving the hotel rather than sit staring at the four walls of my room.

I checked the map for local information and planned my route to the central area. The location around the hotel seemed busy with activity and traffic, and I assumed that the main centre would be even busier. I turned left out of the hotel and followed Calle San Diego down through rows of tall buildings, most of which seemed to be residential with a sprinkling of convenience stores and businesses situated on the lower floors. When I reached Calle Duque, the street narrowed until it was a single strip of roadway. I continued walking until I reached a T-junction. There, I turned left and then first right, and continued walking until the street turned into a busy pedestrianised area. A few hundred metres further on, I found myself in Plaza Ayuntamiento, with its magnificent town hall building, the Palacio Consistorial, on my left and the impressive architecture that stretched away to my right.

I turned right, checking the street name as I did so – Calle Mayor – and followed the colourfully tiled pedestrianised pavement that led through an avenue of shops and bars. The whole area buzzed with activity, a hustle and bustle of tourists wandering in and out of shops, locals sitting outside café bars enjoying coffee and drinks, a hubbub of noise and chatter. In the enclosed space created by the surrounding buildings and the density of people, the early evening heat was oppressive, the warm air all-enveloping.

I mingled with the crowd, just another tourist, safety in numbers but I was conscious that I needed a change of clothes and some dark glasses. Almost four days without shaving had created an unkempt image, but I was still aware of my resemblance to the footballer and the possibility someone might pick up on that. I hoped that if I did cross paths with any football fans they would know that Ignacio Cañizares was on a preseason tour and my resemblance was just coincidence.

After picking my way through the throng of people for a few minutes, I found a clothes store named Inside. A browse in the window showed it had a variety of men's clothes. I bought two shirts, a pair of light trousers, a pack of underwear and a pack of assorted socks. I changed out of my t-shirt right there in the shop. Further along the street I found another shop that sold cheap sunglasses. I bought a pair and put them on.

With my new purchases in hand I felt a sense that things were changing for the better. I had escaped the villa, made it to a busy city where I would have some chance of anonymity, had made contact with the boys and had someone coming for me. But I knew I couldn't afford to get complacent. It was over twelve hours since I'd made a run for it and although I was still within ten miles of my prison, the more time that passed the more likely my captors would think I was some distance away. The first four or five hours had to be a critical time opportunity for them. After that, I could be anywhere. That thought, along with the density of people, comforted me. I checked my watch – 6.40 p.m. Darkness was still a couple of hours away. I needed to head back to the security of the hotel but the ability to move around freely was appealing. My waking hours had been one continuous adrenaline surge since I had escaped. I needed some downtime.

I turned left off Calle Mayor and followed a maze of streets that eventually led to Plaza de San Francisco, a wide, open square surrounded by shops and bars. The bars seemed busy but relaxed, rows of tables placed outside, people chilling with a coffee or something stronger. I could risk stopping for a beer. I needed a simple, chilled moment.

On one side of the square, a glass fronted bar in front of the main walkway caught my eye. I found an unoccupied table and ordered a beer. It was cold, delicious and tasted of normality. As I savoured it, I scanned the area, my mind still on alert mode. But there was nothing to worry about. I allowed myself the luxury of taking my time but I knew it could only be for a brief moment. I finished the beer and returned to the hotel.

I woke at 8.45 the following morning. I showered and dressed in my new clothes, my only concern that I realised I had selected a pack of briefs instead of boxer shorts. To say they were snug was an understatement. After breakfast I returned to the room. Even after my venture into town, daylight presented too many worries and I decided to kill time around the hotel and await Carlos's update call that afternoon. I was dozing on the bed when his call came through at four o'clock, just as he had said. I grabbed the bedside phone.

"*Hola, Mateo. You okay, pal? Still in one piece?*"

"Hi, Carlos. Yeah, I'm good. Looking forward to getting out of here. Did Ces get hold of Louise?"

"*Uh... aye, he did... yesterday.*"

"And? What did she say?"

"*Well... uh, Cecil said you wouldn't be back today...*"

I was beginning to worry about Carlos's hesitation. "Spit it out, mate. What did he tell her?"

"*He said we're enjoying the partying so we're staying a few more days.*"

I sat upright. "He did what? What did he say that for? What's he trying to do? End my relationship? He's a lunatic. That's the worst possible thing he could've said. He should know that. Couldn't he have come up with something more –"

"*Hang on, Mateo. Don't blame me. Not my fault. You know Cecil. He told me there was nothing else he could think of and, anyhow, it was more believable because you're with him. He did tell her you'd lost your phone, though, so you cannae get in touch.*"

"Great! So now Louise thinks I'm out partying, having such a great time that I can't be arsed to come home, and so off my face I've lost my phone. Created a good image there, hasn't he!"

"*Mateo, calm down, amigo. You told me to tell him to say you'd lost your phone. Remember?*"

"I did, yes, but not coupled with some bollocks about partying that makes it look really bad. So what did she say?"

"*She asked if she could speak to you but he said you'd gone out... to sort your phone or something.*"

"Or something? I mean, couldn't he have… forget it, Carlos. I'll speak to Cecil when I get back."

"*Yeah, it'll get sorted,*" Carlos said. I could hear the frustration in his tone. "*You got other things to worry about first. Louise'll understand once she knows what's happened.*"

I hoped he was right. "Okay… okay. Sorry for having a go at you. What about the airport, did you sort that? And where are you staying?"

"*We went to the airport like you said, but when we got there the flight was cancelled. The storm on Friday night was one of the worst Spain's had in a long time. Closed airports in Alicante and Murcia. Nobody was expecting it this time of year. Loads of flights cancelled and it's had a knock on affect here in Madrid. They said they could get us on a flight back later today but we refused it.*"

I thought about what Carlos had said, and then something occurred to me. "Wait a minute. If the airline cancelled the flight, that means everyone knows about it. That's different from you cancelling. And that means, if Anita's checking on your movements, her guys will know too. That's a problem, Carlos. You might have been followed."

"*Stop yer panicking, pal. Look, we went to the airport. If they were watching us, it looks like we intended to go home and without you. That could only mean we don't know where you are. We hung around for a while too… had a couple of beers to make it look real. Then we got a taxi back to Madrid a couple of hours later. Nobody'll have watched us that long.*"

"I wouldn't be so sure, mate. These guys have a lot at stake here. You still need to be careful. Where you staying?"

"*Casa de Suecia. The hotel where you had the meeting.*"

"What? That same hotel? You're fucking nuts! That's the worst… that's where Kreshnik and his… why did you think that was a good idea?"

"*Listen, Mateo. We had to go somewhere. And it's the last place they'll look if they think we're still in Madrid. And anyway, villains move around. They don't like to be seen in the same place all the time.*"

"Really? Whose theory's that then? No, let me guess… Cecil's. Well, I hope he's right." Carlos's lack of reply confirmed my thoughts. I changed the subject. "Did you hear any more from Louise?"

"*No, nothing, pal, but dinnae worry. We'll sort it.*"

"So why didn't Ces just tell her the flight was cancelled instead of giving her all that bollocks about partying?"

"*He didn't know that then, did he. He spoke to her before the airport.*" I heard Carlos take a deep breath, clearly wanting to change the subject. "*Anyway, listen. Erin messaged. All's good. She's leaving around six-ish tonight. You can expect her about half-ten, eleven.*"

Positive news, finally. "Good. I'll see you guys tomorrow sometime then. And look, try and lay low. We don't need any more complications."

"*Nae problem, pal. Oh, and Jasper has called work for you. Said you wouldn't be in tomorrow.*"

Work. I hadn't given it a thought. "Cheers, thanks, Carlos."

"*See you tomorrow.*"

I put the phone down and stood up. I checked my watch – 4.18 p.m. I rang room service and ordered a sandwich and a large bottle of water. I had another six or so hours to kill before Erin arrived.

By nine o'clock I was going stir crazy. I looked out the window. Dusk had settled, broken only by a few squares of light from the other hotel rooms. I thought back to my excursion into town the previous day and how good it had been to sit for a moment with a cold beer. I made a decision. It wouldn't hurt to slip out for an hour or so, a couple of beers and then back to the hotel before Erin arrived.

I changed my shirt, left the room and took the lift down to the lobby. Outside the air was still warm, light from the hotel lobby illuminating the area next to the entrance. I checked the immediate surroundings. Nothing unusual, no-one hanging around that might give me cause for concern. Satisfied that all was well, I turned left and set off, retracing my steps from the day before along Calle San Diego and Calle Duque. As I reached the next junction, a small plaza that linked five street options, I spotted Bar Sol. It looked busy and it afforded a good view of each of the streets in its vicinity.

Inside it was a hub of activity, waiting and service staff in continuous chatter with one another as they went about the business of dealing with their customers. I ordered a beer and took it back outside to where a row of tables hugged the exterior wall. None were free, so I stood near the door where I could 'people watch' and still enjoy the ambience. No-one took any notice of me, other than the occasional glance from people sitting at the tables as they took in the activity around them.

    I felt safe.

37

He must have been lurking in the shadows. I wasn't thinking about my surroundings as I walked back to the hotel. My thoughts were elsewhere, dwelling on how nice it had been to go out and have a beer and how desperately I wanted things to return to normal. As I crossed the narrow, steep side turning that was Calle Montanaro, I felt someone grab my right arm and pull me off the street. I had no time to react. My attacker pushed me face first against the rear of a black car. I felt the cold touch of an object pressed against my neck. My auto response was to stick both hands in the air, cowboy style. Bizarrely, in the nanosecond it took me to raise my hands, it crossed my mind that the reason cowboys did that was to show that they were not going for their guns given that their attacker had the drop on them. As I was carrying no weaponry whatsoever, it served no purpose other than surrender. It was the sensible choice, as the next words I heard were, "Make noise, amigo, and it last noise you make."

I said nothing. I felt the prod of the gun barrel as my assailant urged me to move round to the side of the car. I saw his hand reach forward for the door handle.

And then another voice. "Let him go… ahora!"

I felt the pressure of the gun against my neck ease.

"Put that gun down or they'll be cleaning the contents of your carotid artery off these shop windows in the morning." It was the Irish lilt that gave me hope.

"Matthew, turn round. Get the gun."

I turned. The first thing that caught my eye was the steel blade pressed across the throat of Vincente, the guy from the villa who had held me there at gunpoint too. Then I saw Erin Farrell, her green eyes focused, the knife gripped firmly, the pressure of the blade creasing the skin on Vincente's neck so that he realised one sudden move would be a wrong choice. His eyes bulged, his head held rigid, the gun hanging limply in his hand.

"Get the feckin' gun, Matthew." Erin's command pulled me out of my transfixed state.

I reached out and pulled the gun away by the barrel.

"Don't just stand there. Point the feckin' thing at him," Erin shouted.

I took a step back. I swivelled the gun around. My hand shook. The fight or flight mode sent surges of adrenalin through me. Erin still had the knife at Vincente's throat. I had to get control. My hand slipped around the gun handle, my finger seeking the trigger. I glanced at Erin. I saw the urgency on her face.

It was the lack of familiarity with firearms, it had to be. As I raised the gun, my finger squeezed the trigger. The bullet hit the brick paving, ricocheted through Vincente's right thigh and smashed into the rear passenger window of the parked car.

Erin threw herself to one side, an instinctive response to the gunfire. Vincente's screams were obliterated by the screech of the car alarm. He hit the ground in a heap, clutching his leg, his face contorted in agony.

I dropped the gun. Erin cursed loudly. I stood mesmerised, the realisation that I had shot someone hitting home. A hard slap on my jaw brought me back to reality.

"For feck's sake, Matthew, get a feckin' grip. Check his pockets."

"His pockets? What for?"

"A phone. He must have a phone."

"Why?"

"Just do it. I can't use my phone. We've no time to be fannying about."

I searched Vincente's jacket, side pockets and inside pocket, trying to ignore his moans and the patch of blood that was slowly colouring his jeans. I found his mobile in his back pocket.

"Give it to me," Erin said.

I handed her the phone. She shoved it into the small shoulder bag she was carrying and then bent down next to Vincente. She pulled the right side of his jacket away from his shoulder and eased his arm out so that the jacket was half off. Next, with the knife, she cut off a full section of shirt sleeve, wrapped the material above Vincente's wound, twisted the ends into a tourniquet and knotted it tightly.

When she'd finished she looked at me. "It'll have to do. We can't let the fecker bleed to death." She took Vincente's mobile from her bag, picked up the discarded gun and pointed it at Vincente's head.

"I need your pin, amigo... your code, the... pin del teléfono. ¿Me entiendes?"

He looked at her, appeal in his eyes but Erin's stare was cold, matter of fact, 'I mean business.' She pressed the gun hard against Vincente's head. "Pin del teléfono, amigo, or you die here. You understand. ¿Me comprendes?" She thrust the phone towards him.

He took the phone, his fingers trembling as he punched in four digits. Erin took the phone back and dialled a number.

"What are you doing?" I said, my anxiety at ballistic level as I looked at the blood from Vincente's thigh.

"Getting emergency services. I told you, he can't bleed to death. If he does, life gets a lot more complicated."

More complicated? It had already got more complicated. "I know, but what are we going to –"

"Hola." Erin focussed on the phone. I heard what she said but I didn't understand it. Her Spanish was good enough, it seemed, to deal with an emergency. When she'd finished, she said, "We need to get out of here." She bent down to Vincente. "Someone's coming for you, now… una ambulancia viene por ti." She nodded at me.

"Erin, we need to go, we need to get the fuck out of here. This is not good. That alarm's going to get –"

"I know that. We will. Just wait a second. We can't leave a feckin' mess behind." Erin searched through her bag again. She took out a small black case, opened it and pulled out a safety pin. She released the pointed end from the clasp and, with Vincente's mobile in her left hand, inserted the point into the side of the phone. The mini sim card popped out. She removed it and put the phone back in her bag. Then she took the card and after a quick scan along the street, dropped it into the drainage grid that ran cross the entrance to the turning where it joined the main road.

"What are you doing? We haven't got time for this. If you've called the emergen –"

"I'm getting rid of the sim card. I don't want us tracked. I'll dump the phone somewhere else." She pointed at the ground. "Get that, Matthew."

"Get what?"

"The feckin' shell cartridge. I'm not leaving that lying around."
I looked at where Erin was pointing. A small cylindrical object lay against the building wall. I picked it up and put it in my pocket. And then I had a thought. "But what about the rest of it, the bullet?"

"Forget it. We can't touch the car. Fingerprints. Now let's go."

We hurried along Calle Duque, through Plaza de la Merced and onto Calle San Diego. Erin never spoke as we walked. There was an urgency about her pace. We reached the hotel. I went straight for the lifts, avoiding eye contact with reception staff. Erin followed. My nerves were dangling on the edge of meltdown. I had the drug bust and Anita's thugs to deal with, and now a shooting. I pressed the call button, and as we waited, I said, "How did you find me?"

Erin flicked her hair back. There were beads of sweat on her brow. Her tone was breathless, adrenaline still fuelling her thoughts. "I came straight to the hotel. I got here about half-hour ago. The receptionist said you'd gone out earlier, probably into town. She said most visitors go left. I knew you'd be coming back here to meet me but I thought I'd take a walk, stretch my legs. It was just coincidence that I ran into you. I saw you walking towards me, or at least I thought it was you. And then you disappeared. I got suspicious. I knew –"

The lift pinged open.

"Wait," Erin said. "My bag." She went over to the reception desk and said something to the receptionist who then retrieved a bag from behind the desk. Erin returned to the lift. "My overnight bag."

I pressed the lift button again just as the doors started to close. They opened and we walked in. I selected floor two. As the doors shut, I turned to Erin. "Thanks for tonight and for coming to get me. I appreciate it."

"Well, if I'd known you were going to shoot at me I might have had second thoughts."

I looked at her. "It was an accident. I didn't mean the gun to –"

Erin laughed. "I know, Matthew. I could see you were jittery."

"Well, you would be too if you'd gone through what I have. Look, I need to get back to Madrid, and quickly."

"I know. Carlos told me you had a problem but that was it. So what's going –"

"I'll tell you the whole story later, but we need to get out of Cartagena. The fact that that guy... uh, Vincente, found me, means they know I'm here."

"They?"

"Yes, the people after me. We need to leave... now."

"Matthew, I've just driven nearly five hours from Marbella. I need some rest."

"I could drive."

"No. That's risky if we got stopped. You never know on a journey like that and late at night. Bored cops looking for something to do. You're not insured."

Insurance wasn't my concern, but cops were. I nodded.

The lift stopped at the second floor and the doors slid open. Erin followed me along the corridor. We reached my room door. I swiped the keycard.

"We'll get some sleep and leave at four in the morning," Erin said. "That way we can be in Madrid around half-eight, nine."

"Yeah, but what if Vincente talks?"

"That guy's not worrying about you right now. And nor is he able to contact anybody tonight with no phone. He won't want to be answering any questions in the hospital either. So just chill, okay. Stop fretting. Let's get some sleep."

Chill seemed a tad out of place given the situations that were closing in on me, but Erin's demeanour seemed relaxed. And then I focussed on 'get some sleep.' It was a single room, and maybe the bed had enough room for two, but I felt I had to deal with it.

"Sleep?"

Erin smiled. "Yeah, sleep. Why, what else did you want to do?"

"Uh, nothing. I meant, I only have the one... the one, err... this bed."

"I can see that. I wasn't expecting a suite. Anyway, it's nearly eleven. I'm going to freshen up, then we need to sleep."

She headed off to the bathroom. I sat on the bed. Erin was right. No sense in worrying. We'd be on our way out of Cartagena in no more than five hours.

I took off my t-shirt and trousers and hesitated. I remembered Erin's attempt to seduce me in Las Vegas. I was never really sure if she meant it or was just pushing her naughty streak to see how far it could go. And now there was only one bed. I sat there, in my pants, unsure. To get into bed would be accepting the fact that there was nowhere else to sleep and we had to sleep together. I thought of Louise. This was just practical, a means to an end, a stage in my escape from my pursuers.

And then Erin walked out of the bathroom.

I knew that she couldn't sleep in her street clothes, nobody does but I was unprepared for her appearance. Her dress had gone and so had her bra. I stood up, no idea why. I tried to look at her face, but such was my surprise my eyes were drawn to her body.

Erin Farrell was beautiful. I had always recognised that. A mature woman, early thirties, confident and alluring. Her breasts, firm, bold, almost a statement that said, 'look at me.' And I did.

Erin smiled and then pointed. "What on earth are you wearing? I have to say I'm impressed."

"What?" And then I remembered the briefs and was instantly embarrassed. "Uh… they… err… they're not my usual… I had to get some underwear. I must have picked up the wrong… they do them in packs of three. I thought they were –"

Erin burst out laughing. "You've gone red, Matthew. Don't be shy. I like a man who knows how to emphasise his attributes." She took a step closer. I stepped back. My legs hit the bed and I fell into a seated position.

Erin put her hands on her hips, her green eyes twinkling. Despite myself, I took in the full vision in front of me as she stood there in nothing more than lacy black knickers. My eyes returned to her breasts, her nipples firm and erect. I thought of the horrendous few days I had been through. A moment's light relief would be okay, in the circumstances. I had seen Erin naked once before and resisted. Tonight my resistance was low. I gulped as I thought about what it would be like to reach out and touch her. Erin stared at me, her gaze focussed, as if she could read my mind. She moved closer, her perfume hitting my senses.

The shrill tone of the bedside phone made us both react. Erin stepped back. I swallowed hard, tried to clear my throat and picked up the receiver.

"Hola."

"*Hola, Mateo. It's Carlos.*"

"Uh… yeah… err, hi, Carlos. You okay?"

"*I'm good, pal. You okay? You sound odd.*"

"No… no, I'm fine… err, sleepy. What's up?"

"*Just checking if Erin got there okay.*"

"Yeah… yeah, she did. She's here now." I looked at Erin. She smiled and walked away to the bathroom. "Yes, all good. We're leaving around four o'clock so should be in Madrid between eight-ish... nine, I think. Everything okay there? No problems?"

"*Aye, all good here, Mateo. Safe journey. See you tomorrow.*"

I put the phone down and crossed to the desk. I poured a glass of water and drained the contents in one long pull.

Erin came out of the bathroom, her bra on this time.

"Let's get some sleep, Matthew." She pulled the bed cover back and laid down. "Come on, get in. Sleep time." She moved to one side.

I climbed in and turned off the light. The moment darkness hit, my mind shifted into full gear. What would I have done if the phone hadn't rung? I was tempted by Erin, I realised that, but I had Louise at home. My hesitation, even when faced with Erin's allure, made me feel that I would have resisted. But I wasn't sure. And now she was in the same bed, close to me. Temptation was normal. It happened to people. But I hadn't done anything. There was nothing to feel guilty about. Many guys would have given in. I hadn't. I had resisted, but the phone call nagged at me. If it hadn't come at the time it did, what would have happened? I had to dismiss the thought and go to sleep. And then another thought occurred.

"Erin. You asleep?"

"No, and I won't be if you start chatting. Go to sleep."

"I can't. It's hard. I... "

I heard the giggle. "Is it? You want some help with it?"

"Help? With what?" I felt Erin's hair trail across my shoulder. Then her hand on my chest.

"Whatever it is that's hard." Her hand moved slowly, her fingers gently tracing down to my stomach. And then I realised.

I grabbed her hand. "No, I meant, it's hard to get to sleep. Not... " I turned onto my side to face her. "Erin, this is difficult for me. I've told you before, I find you extremely attractive and... well, in other circumstances... but I'm engaged... to Louise. It wouldn't be fair. You know that."

I heard the laugh but I couldn't see her expression. "I know, Matthew. It's fine. You're very teaseable. You bring out my naughty streak. I can't help it. You make me see how far I can go."

"You're just teasing then? You wouldn't actually... "

"Oh, I would! I like you and I'm attracted to you too, but I respect your values. It doesn't mean I won't try again though. You're a challenge."

There was no point in debating any conflict between respecting my values and trying again. Erin's naughty side would always make her push the boundaries. And now I was in bed with her, the warmth of her body close, her perfume intoxicating.

"Anyway, what did you want?"

"What do you mean?"

"You asked if I was asleep."

"Oh, yeah. I was just thinking about the knife you had. Where'd you get it? You didn't seem worried about using it?"

She rolled onto her back and said, "I'm not. I'm a woman travelling on my own. You never know what might happen. I bought it in Marbella. It's a switchblade. Lucky for you I had it."

"But would you have used it? I mean, you had it right up against that guy's throat."

"I don't know. I might have. He did have a gun at your head. Was I supposed to second guess whether he would use it? I don't think so."

I thought about it. Who knows what anyone might do in the heat of a tense moment? I admired Erin's courage.

"We better get some sleep, Matthew. We've got a long day ahead."

38

At 3.30 a.m. the alarm on my mobile played an annoying little jingle that woke me abruptly. I reached across to the bedside cabinet, fumbling for the phone. I tapped the alarm message killing the tone and then switched on the lamp. I looked to my left. Erin had stirred but was still asleep. I eased out of bed and headed for the bathroom. She could have another few minutes while I showered.

The warm water invigorated me, woke me up and focussed me on the day ahead. I stepped out of the shower and caught my image in the mirror as I went to brush my teeth. Five days without shaving had turned stubble into the beginnings of a beard, enough to make a distinct difference between my appearance and that of Ignacio Cañizares, who, in all the pictures I'd seen, was usually clean shaven.

When I finished in the bathroom I went back out to the bedroom. Erin was up and wearing the t-shirt I'd been wandering around in before I bought my new clothes.

"Morning," she said.

"Morning. Sleep okay?"

"Yeah, but not long enough." She brushed a hand through her hair and then rubbed her eyes. "I need to wake up. You done in the shower?"

"Uh, yeah. Help yourself."

Erin disappeared into the bathroom. I put on one of the new shirts and my shorts. I needed to be comfortable in the car. Then I put the other bits in the carrier bag I had from the shop and waited for Erin. She came out of the bathroom ten minutes later wrapped in a towel, her hair damp and dangling loosely onto her shoulders. She handed me the t-shirt.

"I feel almost human. Give me a few minutes and we'll be out of here."

I sat on the bed. Erin rummaged through her bag and pulled out a white cotton dress and a pair of flip-flops. She put the dress on the bed, threw the flip-flops onto the floor and went through the bag again.

I checked my watch. 4.06 a.m. "Erin, we need to get going."

"I know. Just looking for fresh knickers." She continued to rummage and then pulled out the gun that we had taken from Vincente. "Here, Matthew. Check that."

"Sorry, check?"

"Yeah, we might need it. How many rounds?"

"Rounds?"

"Yes, rounds... bullets."

I took the gun. I stared at it for a moment. It had 'Glock 19 Gen5, Austria 9x19' inscribed on the side and 'Glock' inscribed at the base of the handle. I had no idea how to check for bullets.

"Where do I look?"

"There should be a release button on the side somewhere. It pops out the magazine from the handle." Erin looked up from her bag search. "And don't point it in my direction." She saw my concern. "It should be fine. It's got a trigger safety mechanism. That little bit on the front of the trigger. Stops it going off accidently. You have to give it quite a pull to cock it and fire, but it's just safe practice never to point a gun unless you're going to use it."

"So how come it fired last night?"

"You were pumped up with adrenaline, I guess and must have squeezed the trigger hard."

I thought about what had happened. "I was just trying to hold it like I thought you're supposed to hold a gun, after you told me to point it at him." I looked at Erin. "Anyway, how do you know this stuff?"

She turned towards me. "I've been around guns, you know that. Remember Vegas?"

I nodded as I thought back to Erin in the Vegas desert and her handling of a weapon.

"And I've been to firing ranges. My dad had shotguns back in Ireland. They're just tools. Here, give it to me." She reached out and I gave her the gun. "It's a Glock. Look, like most handguns there's a release button... here." She pointed to a small button on the left side of the gun. She pressed it and the magazine popped out from the handle. Next, she slid the top of the weapon back to open the chamber. "Yep, there's one ready to go."

"What do you mean?"

"There's a bullet ready to fire." She fiddled with the magazine. "Thirteen rounds left including the one in the chamber. Two used, the one you fired, and the guy must've used one at some point."

I didn't reply. I realised just how close I'd come to ending up in a bad way. Vincente had held the gun against my neck. I'd never know if he would have used it.

Erin pushed the magazine back into the gun and put it in her bag. "I'll hang on to it, just in case." Then she stood up, dropped the towel and put the white cotton dress on. She returned to her bag, found the fresh underwear and finished dressing. She shook out her damp hair and gave it a vigorous rub with the towel to get rid of the excess moisture. When she'd finished she said, "Right, let's get going."

I paid my bill at the reception desk with Carlos's card information and checked out. It was dark outside and there was little sign of activity. Erin had a hire car, a small red Seat Ibiza, parked in an underground car park close to the hotel. She paid the parking fee at one of the pay stations and led the way to the car. With the satnav, she plotted the route to Madrid and drove off, the tyres screeching against the smooth concrete surface as we pulled away. At the exit, Erin popped the ticket into the machine and the barrier lifted. The car headlights picked out the roundabout ahead as we made our way up the ramp. Erin glanced to her left. There was no traffic at all. She hit the accelerator and we were on our way out of Cartagena, headed for the A30.

The journey was uneventful. We stopped once only, for coffee, a snack and fuel, just north of the city of Murcia. In the services area, Erin ditched the mobile phone she'd taken from Vincente.

As we drove, I told Erin the full detail of my predicament and how I had ended up in Cartagena. Carlos had told her that I was in trouble but he'd kept it to a rough outline. Erin listened intently to my story, her only reaction the occasional expression of surprise. In the moments of silence that occurred on the journey, my thoughts turned to Vincente and the fact that hospital staff might report a gunshot wound to the police. Erin seemed unconcerned and dismissed my worries saying that if Vincente was linked to a bent cop, somewhere along the line the incident would be suppressed.

By 9.45 a.m. we were on the outskirts of Madrid. Using Erin's mobile I called Carlos to get an update. The lads were in the Casa de Suecia hotel as Carlos had said. I finished the call and asked Erin if she could take me there.

"Sure," she said.

"What's your plans after that?"

"No big agenda. I'm heading to Bilbao eventually but I don't have to be back home until Sunday, so I might stick around in Madrid for a while. What's the hotel like?"

"What, the Suecia?"

"Yes."

"Great, what I saw of it. Seemed like a nice place."

"Good. I'll see if they have any rooms. I did say I might catch you in Madrid and with all the stuff you have going on, it sounds exciting."

The 'stuff' I had going on may have seemed exciting to Erin, but I just wanted rid of it. However, as I thought back to her timely intervention in Cartagena, I considered that it might not be a bad thing to have her around.

Twenty minutes later, Erin dropped me outside the hotel. She drove off to find somewhere to park. I went straight in and found Carlos waiting near the entrance.

"Mateo, good to see you," he said as he approached me. He grabbed me in a bear hug. "You look rough, pal, tired too and that beard disnae do you any favours."

"It's not a beard, Carlos. Anyway, don't worry about how I look. I'm just glad to be back. Where are the lads?"

"Upstairs. We've booked four rooms. It's all good, Mateo. We'll get this sorted."

I had no idea how we'd get it sorted and as I walked with Carlos towards the lifts, I felt a twinge of apprehension as the memory of my meeting with Kreshnik resurfaced. Carlos sensed my edginess.

"Dinnae worry, amigo. C'mon. Let's go up."

39

The rooms were on the fourth floor. We exited the lift and headed along the corridor. Carlos stopped at one of the doors and swiped his key card. Inside, I found Cecil and Jasper sitting drinking coffee. The minute I entered they both jumped up and came towards me. Cecil got there first.

"Geezer! Good to see'ya."

Cecil's bear hug was almost like a wrestler's grip, and I was taken by surprise. Cecil was never afraid to show his true feelings with people he liked, and I could tell by his reaction that he had been genuinely concerned about me. As he stepped back, he said, "So what the fuck happened? Carlos reckons you were kidnapped?"

I didn't get an opportunity to answer. Jasper gripped me in a back slapping hug and said. "We were worried about you, Matt. We couldn't go to the cops. Didn't know what to do. It was a relief when you got in touch."

"It's okay, Jas. I realise you couldn't do anything. I didn't know what was happening or where they were taking me. Anita must've followed me when I went out that morning. She turned up in the place where I was having breakfast. Right after that, they just lifted me off the street."

Carlos popped a coffee pod in the Espresso machine. "Mateo, come and sit down. I'll do you a wee coffee."

I sat in an armchair and waited for the coffee. "Plush rooms," I said, taking in the décor and layout of the hotel room with its king sized bed, seating area and mini bar.

"Yeah, blinding. We booked us one each. Makes sense to have a bit of your own space. It's all on your Madrid budget still, ain't it?" Cecil said, with a smile.

I nodded. Well it would be once I got my wallet and cards back. Then I realised I still owed Carlos money.

Carlos saw my expression. "I gave them my card. We can square it up once you're sorted."

"And we didn't push the boat out, mate. They're standard rooms. I mean, we could've had a suite each," Cecil added.

I ignored it, grateful that Cecil had shown some restraint. Carlos handed me the coffee, and for the next fifteen minutes I filled them in on the detail of my kidnapping, Erin's intervention and my worries about what might happen next.

"Mate, that's some story. These people are fucking serious," Cecil said.

"I know that, and what's worrying me right now is that you guys have booked the very hotel that Kreshnik and his crew used." I thought back to Carlos's explanation about second guessing the crooks.

"Mate, don't panic. It's perfect. They ain't gonna think you got the balls to go back to a place that you know they used, yeah. They're gonna be thinking you're staying well clear of Madrid and doing a runner. And anyway, it ain't that Kreshnik geezer you gotta worry about. His beef's with Anita and her crew, not you. It's them they're doing the deal with. Your problem is with her?"

I finished the coffee and stared at my empty cup for a moment. Cecil was right. Whatever Kreshnik's next move was, it would be against Anita, more than likely pulling the deal and finding someone else. My problem was staying clear of Anita's crew, solving the drug bust hanging over me and getting my passport back. I knew I had to address that issue urgently.

Carlos made another coffee. I sipped it and said, "So, how am I going to sort this out? Carlos keeps saying that 'we'll sort it', but so far I have no idea how we can do that unless you guys have come up with something."

Cecil ran a hand through his hair. "We gotta go back to basics, think about every angle. What's the main thing happening here? What do they want? What's the connections?"

"It's coke, isn't it?" Jasper said. "And the money."

"Yeah, we know that. But who's behind it? Who's the key player that's driving it? I don't reckon it's that Anita. She sounds too hands on. The key player always keeps a distance. They don't wanna get their hands dirty."

215

I thought for a moment. "I remember when Anita first found me she used the word 'people'. She said she worked with 'people... the 'people I represent.' Maybe you're right, Ces."

Cecil grinned. "Yeah, so think. Who do we know that's connected? You got Anita, the footballer's bodyguards... uh... "

"Lucero Garrido and Sergio Colas."

"Yeah, and then, you got his missus, Chiara. Then you got the bent cop, Armendarez. Who else?"

"There's Vincente," I said.

"Who's he?" Jasper asked.

"The one I said got shot in Cartagena. He was one of the guards in the villa."

"Mate, he's nobody," Cecil said. "He's just one of the backup guys, ain't he. Nah, I'm thinking who could be the brains of the operation."

Carlos said. "You don't think the footballer could be involved, do you?"

"Nah, mate, I think we can rule him right out the equation. Like I said before, the geezer don't need the money and if he was involved, they wouldn't need Matt to do his double act, would they?"

"Talking of Cañizares, what about the girlfriend he had at Ascot, Matt?" Jasper said.

"Who, Lorena?"

Jasper nodded. "Yeah, can't rule anybody out. You never know, she could be in it to stitch him up for ditching her."

"I doubt it. I just don't think she'd be involved in drugs. I mean, she was hook line and sinker into Cañizares at the races. She was hardly scheming against him at that stage. Whoever came up with the plan to use me was already involved in drug dealing and looking at a way to expand, looking at a possible partnership with Kreshnik. Then they saw an opportunity to pull off the deal and took it. Think about it. It couldn't all have happened from scratch just three weeks ago."

"S'pose not. Yeah, she's probably just thinking she's well shot of him if he's not leaving his wife."

Cecil stood up and paced towards the window. Then he turned around, a frown creasing his forehead. "What about the French bird, the wife's mate? We ain't mentioned her."

"Who Hugs?" Jasper said.

"Yeah, her. Huguette or whatever she's called. There's something dodge about her."

"What?"

Cecil scratched his jaw, feeling the stubble. "Think back. You know about women, don't ya?" he said, looking at Jasper. "When do they ever go to the toilet on their own? They don't. They don't do it. The only reason a woman out partying with her mate, goes on her own, is if she's hiding something. And here's the swerve. It has to be something fucking serious to hide it, 'cos they tell each other all sorts of shit." He looked at me. "You ask your woman, mate. She'll tell'ya."

I stayed silent. Not a discussion I needed to raise with Louise, given my extended stay in Spain. But my silence didn't deter Cecil. He was on a roll.

"Ask yourselves, what's gotta be serious enough for a bird to hide it from her mate?"

I looked at Carlos and then at Jasper. Carlos shrugged. Jasper stayed focussed on Cecil.

"Fuck me, boys, you got no clue about women, have'ya? And I thought you was on it!"

Evidently none of us had a clue, nor were we 'on it', as there was no response.

Cecil continued. "Let me enlighten'ya, then. Women talk about everything. They even talk about shagging their blokes, all that personal stuff, good or bad, makes no difference. I mean, some poor nob's sitting there on a couples night out in a pub, and the wife's best friend knows exactly how shite her mate's husband is in the sack. And the geezer's got no fucking clue what his missus has said about him."

Carlos interrupted. "Can you nae get to the point, laddie. What's that gottae do with the French lassie?"

Cecil ran both hands through his hair and sat down. Then he said, "Think about it. Only two reasons birds fuck off to the toilet on their own. Either they bin shagging their best mate's bloke and they're texting him, or they got some other issue that they know their mate ain't gonna like."

"Like what?" Jasper asked.

"Like a fucking drug issue, geezer," Cecil said, leaning across the table. "I see that mumble at the races. That fuktard with the ponytail, what's his name? Lucero… he's passing the French bird the gear. Okay, can't say I knew for definite what it was at the time, but you remember I said it looked like he was dealing, yeah? Now we know he's involved in the coke game, it makes sense. When he gives her the gear she fucks off to the toilet on her own. Stands to reason she knows more than we think."

"Hang on. You think Huguette's using coke?" I asked.

"Could be, but I don't reckon she is and you know why?" There was no response. "Think about it. The times we saw her after, there was nothing odd about how she was behaving. She seemed quiet, chilled all the time. That ain't the way a cokehead behaves, is it?" Cecil looked at me.

"What you looking at me for? I'm not –"

Cecil laughed out loud. "I'm not saying you are, mate. But you did them lines. And you was drinking. Makes you buzzed up, yeah?"

I nodded.

"Huguette was drinking too but she never behaved like she was on something, she always took a back seat, all quiet, low key?"

Carlos scratched his head and looked at Jasper and then me, perhaps hoping we would unravel where Cecil was going. "I'm confused, Cecil," he said. "If she's not doing coke in the toilets but you reckon the security fella is supplying her with coke, what's going on then?"

"Not sure yet, mate, but there's something weird about it. What I do know is there ain't no truth in Anita's thing about the footballers wife being on it."

"No, that's just a blag, Ces, to make Kreshnik believe that's why Cañizares is getting involved," I said.

"Yeah, I know. You said, but there might have bin something in it, her being in the old modelling game, mixing with them celeb party goers and that. If there was, she'd have bin on it at the races, especially if her husband's bodyguard's supplying and giving her mate the gear. She'd have bin straight in them toilets with her."

"Okay, I get that. Let's assume you're right and Lucero was giving her the stuff, where's that leave us?"

"Course I'm right. What d'you think he was doing? Slipping her a tip for the next race. Nah, there's definitely something dodge going on with her." Cecil turned to Jasper. "Jas, look her up online, mate, see what you can see."

Jasper thumbed through his mobile and typed in the word 'Hugs.' His brow furrowed as he scrolled through the data that came up, then a smile crossed his face. "Here we go. Huguette De Villiers, model, singer. Nice pictures."

"Don't worry about the pictures. We know what she looks like. What else's it saying?"

"Uh... let's have a look. Career... model... discovered at twenty-one... old for a model, I reckon... later life... singer... a few minor hits, last one four years ago..."

"We know about the celeb stuff. What else is there?"

"Okay, let's see... early life... born in le ves... vesi... uh, Le Vésinet, a suburb of Paris. Currently thirty-eight years old. Studied medical science at... Sorb.... Sorbonne Université... uni... in Paris." Jasper looked up from his phone. "Bit of a clever one, boys." He looked back at the screen. "Uh... dropped out to pursue career... was signed up by French fashion house –"

"Hang on a minute, mate. Hold it there," Cecil said. "She studied medical science?"

"Yeah, that's what it says."

Cecil ran both hands through his hair, his eyes closed for a moment. "What if she's the one that's behind it all... the syndicate?"

"How's that then?" Jasper asked.

"Look at it this way. Whatsername what's set Matt up... Anita... she's connected to the two bodyguards. So, let's assume that one of 'em, geezer with the ponytail, is passing gear to the French bird at the races. It'd be obvious she knows he's dealing, but like I just said, she ain't using."

Carlos drummed his fingers on the table. "So what's her part then?"

"Mate, it wouldn't take too much working out to think she might be the brains of the outfit. The one who set it up, and that Lucero geezer was giving her a sample. She ain't going to the toilets to do the coke. She's doing a... I dunno, a taste test, checking the quality. Maybe she's got a set up at home that can check what's in the gear... quality control. I mean, Jas just said she knows a bit about science and that."

I checked Carlos and Jasper for a reaction. Their expressions suggested they thought Cecil had a point. "That might explain Anita's thing about 'people'."

"Think about it. The two bodyguards are just the muscle. Their job is to lean on people, give it the old heavy stuff on the street, handle the product. Anita's probably the one who makes things happen on the ground, like she's doing with that Kreshnik geezer. She ain't getting her hands that dirty either. So, like I said, somebody's gotta be the brains and my guess it's the French singer. And I'll tell you something else, lads. She'll keep well out the way, keep her distance. She's got a name, bit of status, and she can't have her cover blown getting too close to the coal face. She'll have other people as well."

I thought about Cecil's theory for a moment. With nothing else to go on it seemed plausible.

"Okay, let's assume, again, that you're right, Ces. What doesn't make sense is how they knew I'd be in Madrid. Anita said they'd been watching me, but the set up with the police happened after I'd been here just four days. We only got here on the Friday. They can't have planned their approach to a deal with Kreshnik in that time. And, if you think about it, the selfies and all that stuff that Anita mentioned, only happened *after* you'd persuaded me to do the footballer thing, which was on our second night out. I was busted on the Monday night, so that would've given them, what… about forty-eight hours max to plan it and set up a meeting with Kreshnik? It can't have been *that* off the cuff."

"Aye, yer right, Mateo. Nae possible," Carlos said. "Did you tell anyone you were coming here?"

"Only Louise and people at work, that's all."

"I posted something on Facebook before I came," Jasper said. "And some selfies and a couple of shots of us lot since we been here, but only my friends would have seen that."

"Well, mate, unless you got that Anita, Huguette and them two fuktard bodyguards as your FB buddies, then that ain't gonna be it," Cecil said.

"Trust me, Ces" Jasper laughed. "I haven't, although I wouldn't mind having Hugs as a friend. Bit of a looker."

Cecil grinned. "Time for a beer I reckon. He went to the mini bar and pulled out four bottles. As Cecil handed them round, I stared at Jasper, thinking about what he'd said about Facebook.

"You've never met Anita, have you?"

"No."

"And the only time you've seen Huguette was at Ascot, right?"

"Yeah."

"And you never spoke to her? On your own, I mean?"

"No."

"What you thinking, Mateo?" Carlos asked.

I hesitated as a single thought swirled around in my head. I raised the beer bottle, took a long glug and said, "I mentioned something."

Cecil looked at me. "Yeah? 'Bout what?"

"I chatted to Huguette at the races, after all that stuff with Cañizares was sorted. I mentioned that we might go to Madrid."

"Ach, that's nae enough, Mateo," Carlos said. "Might go, and telling her that yer definitely going and when, are two different things. Unless she was having you followed, she'd never know what yer up to. And even that wouldnae make sense as you might not go for a month, six months, a year."

"I think I said, maybe in a few weeks."

Cecil frowned and said, "Still a long shot, but think. You tell her anything else?"

I thought back to the races at Ascot and my chat with Huguette. And then I remembered something. "I gave her some of Carlos's cards."

"What cards?" Cecil asked.

"His business cards for Fads." I turned to Carlos. "You gave some to Cañizares, remember? In the toilets that time."

Carlos nodded.

"And when I had his jacket on, I found them. I remember sticking them in my trouser pocket when I was looking for badges for that security... steward guy. Then when I was talking to Huguette, I gave her, I dunno, two or three of them, said she should visit."

"Good man, Mateo. I like it," Carlos said, a grin spreading across his face.

Cecil cut the moment, banging his fist on the table. "What's the matter with you two nobs? You think a big time footballer and his celeb friends are gonna come down to Fads?"

"Hang on, Ces, I did say that to Carlos at the time."

"So why'd you give his cards to Huguette then?"

"I... uh... I was just relieved that we'd sorted that shit out with the footballer and thought it'd do no harm."

"Do no harm? Geezer, we're in the social fucking media age. When somebody takes so much as a piss they post it online. Everybody knows everything about'ya these days." He pointed at Carlos. "Your bar, betcha got it online, yeah?"

"Aye, I got a website… macfaddens dot uk."

"And a Facebook page?"

"Aye, but I dinnae use it. Ma wee bar lassies, Hanka and Yanka, update it. They stick stuff up on that photograph one as well."

"Instagram," Jasper said. "I follow it."

"And you follow Fad's Facebook page too, I bet," Cecil said.

"Well, yeah."

"That's it then, ain't it?"

"What is?" Jasper said.

"Your Facebook's linked to his bar page. So you ain't hard to find by anybody following Fad's. And I bet you ain't set up the privacy stuff either, which means any punter out there can see what you post. You post stuff about going to Madrid, and then stuff when you're out here and it's game over. Everybody connected to you or following Fad's, knows when you're going, who you're going with and where you are. And I bet you got photos up there of us in Fad's as well as what you posted out here."

"Yeah… yeah I have and to be honest, I did the check-in thing on FB too."

"What's that?" Carlos asked.

"You can tell people where you are, if you're in a bar or someplace," Jasper replied. He scratched his head, frowning as he thought about what he was saying. "Look, guys, I didn't think, did I. There was no reason too. I post stuff at home like that so I just thought it was cool, you know, when you're away and that."

 Cecil blew out his cheeks in a deep sigh. "That explains it then, don't it. Anybody keeping tabs on us, knows exactly where we are."

I thought back to my meeting with Anita, just before I was kidnapped and her comment, *'we can't risk wannabe girls posting selfies with you or mobile pictures on their Facebook and Instagram accounts.'*

"They knew when we were going to Madrid," Cecil continued. "They knew where we were staying, and they know where we are any time we go out. So if they wanted to stitch Matt up, he was easy to track. It ain't rocket science, boys."

The three of us sat in silence for a moment, absorbing what we had just heard. The silence was broken by Cecil.

"Looks like I'm right. The French bird's running the operation. Question is, what we gonna do about it?"

40

My room was a welcome haven after the ordeal of the preceding days. Carlos had booked four rooms on the same floor. I was in 415. I took a long shower to freshen up after the early start and the car journey. As I stood underneath the hot water, my thoughts focussed on the conversation I'd just had with the lads. Cecil's view that Huguette might be the brains behind the operation was one thing, but even if he was right, I had no idea how that information would get me off the hook.

I thought about the meeting with Kreshnik, scheduled for Wednesday. I wouldn't be there unless Anita and her gang found me and forced me to show up. And if they did, how were they going to prove that I was the footballer? The tattoo had been the obvious option but with just two and a half days to go, that was no longer feasible. Nobody could create a replica tattoo in that time that would look normal. But the syndicate's financial credibility was based on Cañizares's involvement. So they had to have a backup plan, and that meant they wouldn't give up looking for me.

I turned off the water, stepped out of the shower and picked up a towel. As I dried off, I caught sight of my image in the mirror. The unshaven appearance made me look scruffy but I didn't care too much. Louise wasn't keen on beards and I resolved to be cleanshaven for my return home, whenever that might be. And then I remembered that I needed to call her, but I didn't have her number.

I grabbed the complimentary bathrobe and went out to the bedroom. I called Carlos's room and asked if I could borrow his mobile. He brought it round straightaway. Louise picked up within a couple of rings.

"*Matthew? You okay? What on earth's going on? I've been worried about you. Cecil said you'd lost your phone and you weren't coming home. And you don't even call to speak to me.*"

I hesitated. I didn't want to worry Louise by telling her the full detail of my predicament. On a personal level it didn't make sense to alarm her, and in her professional role as a detective, I knew she'd get involved in some way.

"I know... I know. I'm sorry. Louise, you're going to have to trust me and be patient. Something has happened here that I need to sort out and –"

"*What? What's happened?*"

"I can't say much at the moment but –"

"*What d'you mean you can't say much? I'm your partner. What's the big secret? You in trouble?*"

"Louise, listen. No... well, yes... a bit, but I'm safe. I'm with the boys. We're all safe. I can't get back just yet... my passport... I, uh –"

"*You've lost your passport?*"

It was partly true. I grabbed the get out. "Err, yeah. Yes, I have but I'm sorting it out."

"*You know you can go to the consulate?*"

"Yes. Listen, don't worry. It's under control. We're on it. Anyway, how are –"

"*So how come you've lost your phone and your passport? What were you doing?*"

Good question, I thought. I didn't get a chance to answer.

"*Partying with Cecil, no doubt.*"

Probably had a lot of truth in it given the shenanigans at Ascot and now in Madrid. "Louise, can you stop interrupting me for a minute. Look, it's a long story and I know I'm not explaining it very well, but basically, I need to get my passport back so I can get home. Give me a couple of days. I'll explain when I know more. It's all under control. I'll get it sorted. Okay?"

"*Okay. But I know what you're like, Matthew. If anything isn't right, call me... let me know.*"

"Of course. I'll call you Tuesday."

"*Just make sure you do. Let me know what's happening and when you'll be home. Look, I have to go. I'm working. Be good.*"

"I will."

"*Love you. Bye.*" And she was gone.

I gave the mobile back to Carlos.

"All good, amigo?" he asked as he took the phone.

"Yeah, good. Yeah... you know. Women."

We were interrupted by a knock on the door. Carlos opened it. Erin Farrell walked in.

"Hi, Carlos." She turned in my direction. "Reception said you were here. I'm all booked. Four nights. That should be enough time to sort this."

I admired Erin's optimism but I didn't share it. There was a gleam in her eye, an indication of her excitement at being part of an adventure and a determination to meet the challenge my predicament presented. "Any chance of a coffee?" she said.

Carlos grabbed a coffee pod and fired up the Espresso machine.

Erin looked at me and winked. "Nice bathrobe."

I needed to get dressed. Carlos had brought my luggage from the apartment to the hotel. It was good to have a choice of clothes again. I picked out some underwear, shorts and a t-shirt, headed back into the bathroom and dressed. When I came back out Erin was standing by the window sipping coffee. "Where's those other two reprobates you hang out with, Matthew?"

I looked at Carlos. "Down the hall," he said. "In their rooms, I s'pose."

"Get them in here. We need a plan of action."

Carlos called Cecil's room. Five minutes later, Cecil banged on the door.

"How'ya doing, gorgeous?" he said to Erin as soon as he was in the room.

Erin smiled. "I'm good, Cecil, but we haven't got time for your blarney today. We need to deal with Matthew's problem." She sat down on the bed.

"Okay, darlin'. So how we gonna do that?"

"Well, first of all we need to look at who we're dealing with and what their next move might be. Then we need to work out the best way to get that drug charge wiped."

Cecil sat down, looked at his watch and then said, "Give us one of them coffees, Carlos, mate." He then told Erin his theory about Huguette.

Erin listened intently, her green eyes focussed on Cecil as he spoke. When he'd finished, she stood up and walked towards the window. She stared out at the view for a moment and then turned round. "You might be right, Cecil, but we don't seem to have any way of proving anything. We have all these connections... the bent copper, that woman who contacted Matthew... what was her name?"

"Anita," I said.

"Yes, Anita and the two body guards and possibly Hugs. That's five people. According to what Matthew said, he's seen Anita and the bodyguards together but none of the others. So, not only do we have no proof of anything, we can't put them all together in one place or even connect them all up."

"The bodyguards, Sergio and Lucero, were at Ascot, so was Hugs," Jasper said.

Erin shrugged. "Yes, but the bent copper wasn't there and nor was Anita, was she?"

"No," I said.

"What about the girlfriend you mentioned?"

"Lorena? She turned up with Cañizares. Hugs showed up with his wife Chiara, after that."

Erin brushed her hair away from her face, a frown playing over her features. "We need to think about this. I'll try and find out more, see if there's any links between them other than what we've got. Do you know Anita's surname, Matthew?"

"No, I don't. I don't even know if Anita's her real name."

"You're forgetting one other problem," Cecil said.

"What's that?"

"If that Kreshnik geezer don't meet with the footballer on Wednesday night, he's gonna release that clip he took of Matt doing the old Charlie, ain't he. And if he does that, the shit hits the fan big time. Cañizares is gonna be onto his lawyers. They're gonna deny everything and say it's a set up. Then Anita and her crew are gonna realise their deal's dead in the water and what d'you think happens then?"

Cecil's question met total silence.

"I'll tell'ya. That bent cop's gonna give Matt's name to the press. Then he'll tell 'em he's wanted for drug dealing, and that he's bin impersonating the footballer to get into VIP areas so he can sell more gear. These people lose their deal, they ain't gonna be happy. For starters, they not only lose the chance to make shed loads of cash, but they know that no suppliers are ever gonna take 'em seriously again, not after Kreshnik puts the word out." Cecil looked in my direction. "So they're gonna stitch you up big time, geezer, and I wouldn't be surprised, once your name's out there and they arrest you, if Cañizares don't sue your arse off too. Remember, he's got a score to settle as it is."

I glanced round the room, checking the reaction of the others. They all seemed to be trying to absorb Cecil's take on my situation. I focussed on just one thing, it seemed the simplest.

"What score's he got to settle, Ces?"

"Mate, don't be stupid. You made him look a prick at Ascot, and you screwed up his little mumble with his bit on the side. Now he's gonna think your trying to take him down completely. He can't let that go. It's ego, ain't it."

I stood up and paced around the room, focussed now on a situation that had no way out and was totally out of my control. "Ces, this is down to you. If you hadn't asked me to –"

"Hang on, geezer. I ain't the one who stitched you up here. How am I s'posed to know there's villains on your case? Mate, if you guys weren't so lightweight with your social media shit maybe my –"

Carlos stepped in. "Boys, cut it out. There's nae sense in fighting amongst ourselves. We have to find a way out of this."

I turned to Carlos. "Like what? Turn up to a meeting and pretend I'm the footballer again so I can get their deal back on? Kreshnik's concerned now anyway, you know that. Even if I could get away with it, how am I supposed to find Anita, and what are they going to do this time to convince him I'm legit? That's why I ran away from that place in Cartagena. I thought they were going to tattoo me just to prove their point."

"That's not an option now, Matt," Jasper said. "They're proper villains. If they think you're scamming them, they won't think twice about getting rid of you."

"Cheers, Jas. You know how to reassure a bloke."

"Boys," Erin cut in. "For feck's sake calm it. We need clear heads here. Cecil has a point. If there's any heat coming your way, it'll be from Anita's lot first. We need time to think things through, one step at a time. I'm going to my room in a minute and I'm going to see what I can find out online about any of this lot."

"You could go to the press, I s'pose, Mateo," Carlos said.

"That's not going to work, Carlos. I can't prove anything. If I could prove that cop was bent, that'd be a start, but I've got nothing. Erin's right. We need to think."

Cecil stood up. "I do my best thinking in a nice chilled out bar with a cold one. Going fucking stir crazy in that room all day. Who's up for it?"

"I'm in," Jasper said. "I could do with a beer."

"Good man, then check out a couple of other places bit later," Cecil replied. He looked at me. "You look like you could do with some chill time, mate. Fancy one?"

"You're joking, Ces, aren't you? I can't go anywhere in Madrid. If I'm spotted... you know."

"You can't stay in here all the time," Erin said. "Look, I've got an idea. First of all, you need to shave but leave the moustache, okay. I'll pop out and get a couple of bits to sort you out. Come to my room in half an hour or so, 418."

Cecil winked at me. "Me and Jas'll be up on the terrace roof bar. We'll wait for you there. You coming, Carlos?"

Carlos nodded. The boys left the room.

Erin checked her watch. "It's twelve-twenty now. See you at, let's say, one o'clock."

41

At one o'clock I knocked on Erin's door. There was no answer. I knocked again and waited. Still no answer. I turned to walk away and heard the ping of the lift doors. A few seconds later, Erin came into view, a shopping bag in her hand. She greeted me and we walked towards her room. Once inside, she put the bag on the table and then inserted a pod in the coffee machine.

"Coffee?"

"Yes please."

As Erin waited for the machine to complete the cycle, she said, "Let's have a look at you." She stared at me for a few seconds, her head tilted to one side. "Okay, I think I can do something"

I sat on the edge of the bed. "Not sure what you've got in mind, but I'm not keen on the moustache thing. Makes me look like some seventies hippie."

Erin laughed. "It's only temporary. Get over it. I'm sure you don't want to be hiding in your room, do you?" She turned away, finished making one coffee and then put another pod in the machine.

"Right, what we need to do is make you look less like the footballer."

"What, a disguise?"

"Not exactly. Just alter your image a bit." The Espresso gurgled out the last of its contents. Erin collected the cup, picked up her bag and sat down on the bed next to me. She reached into the bag and pulled out a pair of black glasses. "I got you these. They're cheap, low strength, plain enough not to draw attention. Here, try them on."

I took the glasses, put them on and then turned to face Erin.

"Perfect. We're getting there."

"Maybe, but they make everything a bit blurred."

"You'll get used to them. Your eyes'll adjust." She delved into the bag again and pulled out a red container and waved it in front of me. "Talcum powder."

"Talcum powder? Do I smell?"

Erin laughed. "No, it's for your hair. I'm going to sprinkle it through your hair and a bit on that moustache. It'll make it look slightly grey, which makes you look a bit older."

"Will it?"

"Yes, it will. What we're trying to do is create a subtle effect that'll stop people doing that doubletake thing. At the moment, if they see you, they look twice thinking you might be the footballer. Their subconscious gets triggered and they make the association, enough for them to focus on you. The glasses, moustache and grey hair will stop that. Understand?"

It seemed to make sense. "I suppose so, but I'll feel awkward and self-conscious. I won't be relaxed."

"Matthew, I'm trying to help here. Get feckin' used to it then, and quickly. Drink your coffee and let's try it."

I drank the coffee and Erin led me to the bathroom. She told me to take off my t-shirt and lean over the bath. Then she sprinkled the talcum powder onto my hair and fluffed it through with her hand. When she was happy, she told me to stand up. She stood back and stared at my head. A few more flicks and she seemed satisfied. I turned to look in the mirror.

"No. Put the glasses on first. I want you to see what other people will see."

I did as she said and then turned towards the mirror. "It looks like me with greying hair and a moustache."

"But that's the point. It looks like you and less like Cañizares. People won't stare at you."

As I looked at my image I realised that Erin probably had a point. "Fair enough, but how does this change anything? How does it solve my problem?"

"Matthew, start thinking a bit more positively instead of looking on the downside all the time. Okay, it doesn't solve your problem and get you back home, but I'll tell you what it does do. It means you can leave the hotel and go out; it means that you're less likely to be spotted by any of Anita's gang. And trust me, if that deal is worth what you say it is, they'll keep looking for you. Remember, they know you can't leave Spain without your passport. And it also means you get time to think without being bothered by anyone."

Erin's upbeat attitude began to instil some confidence in me.

"Now, dab a bit of this talc on that moustache, then go find your friends and see what they think. I'm going to stay here and see what I can find on the internet."

I did as Erin said and then made my way to find the lads.

A glass fronted lift located close to the restaurant area took me up to the Terraza roof bar. I stepped out into a covered, open plan area but couldn't see the lads. The barman told me that the terrace was above us, up a short flight of stairs on one side of the bar. I bought a beer and made my way up. The boys were seated in the far corner, their drinks on a low round table. Cecil was sitting on a sofa, his back to two tall palm trees that stood in giant terracotta plant pots. Jasper and Carlos were sitting on two round, solid-piece stools, one pink, one blue that seemed to be a feature of the area. I crossed the timber floor towards them. Cecil was the first to react.

"Geezer, what the fuck? You look like some Woodstock throwback. What you done?"

I sat down on the sofa next to Cecil but before I could say anything he said, "And, mate, you smell like a fucking baby. What you bin up to?"

"Nothing, Ces. It's an image thing, trying to look… different. The smell's just talcum powder."

"It's worked then. Can you see out them bins?"

I fiddled with the spectacles. "Yeah, just about. They're low strength. It's Erin's idea. Makes me look different from the footballer. Means I can relax a bit more. What do you think?"

"It certainly makes you look different," Jasper said. "You look like your pushing fifty at least."

Pushing fifty didn't matter. In fact it was a good thing. "Doesn't bother me, Jas. That just makes it better. I don't want to look like me."

"Aye, yer looking like my daddy, pal," Carlos chipped in to roars of laughter.

"I wouldn't go that far," Cecil said. "He'd have to look like a right fucking Neanderthal to get away with being *your* daddy, Carlos."

Carlos scowled and said nothing.

Jasper pointed at my beer bottle. "Same again? May as well enjoy the extended holiday."

I ignored Jasper's last comment. My image adjustment had lessened my nervousness but 'enjoyment' still seemed a long way off. "Yeah, go for it."

Jasper ordered more beer. The boys raised their bottles in a salute. "Geezer, no matter what happens," Cecil said, "we're all in this together, yeah?"

"Cheers. Appreciate it, guys. We just need something to go right though."

"Been thinking," Carlos said. "You know I mentioned the press? I know you can't prove anything, but what about Cañizares's girlfriend… Lorena. How about going to her? She's in the media and –"

"Ex-girlfriend," Jasper said.

"That doesnae matter. My point is she knows Cañizares, and she'd be interested in a story. You'd be ahead of anything that gangster does with his video."

"Yeah, worth a try," Cecil said. "No TV station's gonna broadcast stuff without some background checks and talking to their lawyers. And they'll have crime researchers as well. Could have the old mumble on Kreshnik, or that cop, or even Anita. Might be a way in."

I swigged some beer and considered what I'd heard. "Okay. I've got no other options and nothing to lose, I s'pose. Worth a try. How can I get hold of her?"

Jasper fiddled with his phone and then said. "The TV station she's based at is here in Madrid. According to this, she does the six o'clock evening news now, Monday to Friday. That's got to mean she's there today. We should go down there and ask to see her."

"Wait. We can't all go," I said. "It won't look right, four blokes showing up. And we'll need an appointment, won't we?"

Cecil laughed. "Geezer, get a grip. An appointment? Mate, you could be a week waiting for an appointment. Nah, you ain't got that kinda time. You need to get down there and put some pressure on. If you're standing in front of 'em, in their reception or whatever they got, it gets their attention, don't it."

"Just checked Google Maps," Jasper said. "It's only about four kilometres from here, about fifteen minutes in a taxi."

"Okay. Let's do it. But just me and Ces." I turned to Cecil. "You spoke to her at the races. If I need back up, she at least knows you."

"Cool. I'm on it, geezer."

"Hang on," Carlos said. "You forgotten? You're in Madrid, Mateo. You dinnae speak Spanish."

"Lorena speaks good English."

"She may well do, laddie, but she's nae gonna be sitting in reception waiting for you. S'pose you have to speak to security or the reception staff, what then? It's a television station. They're nae gonna just let you in and let you start chatting to the presenters. You need me there, amigo."

"He's got a point," Jasper said.

I looked at Cecil.

"Yeah, he's right," Cecil said. "It's no biggie. I don't need to go. You gotta get this right, mate. You two go, and let us know what happens, yeah."

The afternoon traffic was light and the taxi took just twelve minutes to reach our destination. We pulled up outside large sprawling premises that had the name of the TV station emblazoned on its perimeter wall. The entrance gate had a barrier and a security office that controlled access, inside of which a uniformed guard was monitoring cars and pedestrians.

"Good job I came with you, Mateo," Carlos said. "This might be tricky."

I nodded. We walked towards the security office. The guard stepped out to meet us. Carlos approached him and said something in Spanish. The only bit I caught was the name 'Lorena Márquez.' The guard stared at us for a moment, his default position not to entertain random callers asking about presenters. Carlos rattled off another stream of words and, after some hesitation, the guard beckoned us to follow him into the security office.

Once inside, I said, "Do you speak English?"

"Sí, Señor. Your friend say that you want to speak to Lorena Márquez. How can I help you?"

"Uh, yes… yes, I do."

"Do you have an appointment with Señorita Márquez?"

"No, I don't but I… err, I know her and I need to speak to her."

"Señor, we have a lot of people, they come here and want to speak to our presenters, and they say they know them just because they see them on television."

"But I *do* know her. We met at Ascot in England. She was with Ignacio Cañizares."

The guard frowned, no doubt aware of Lorena's past association with Cañizares. "And your name is?"

"Matthew Malarkey… and I have some information that could be a big story involving Señor Cañizares."

"Just a moment, Señor Matthew Malarkey," the guard said. He picked up a desk telephone and pressed a button, his eyes fixed on me.

Carlos stepped closer and whispered, "Mateo, does Lorena know who you are? I mean, you were pretending you were the footballer when you met."

I didn't reply. I realised that the only way Lorena would know my name was if Cañizares had told her when he met up with her at Claridge's after the races. I dismissed the thought and focussed on the security guard who was speaking into the phone handset. I heard my name and the footballer's name. I glanced at Carlos.

"He's telling someone you're here and you've got a story," Carlos whispered.

There was a further exchange between the security guard and whoever was on the other end of the line. Then he covered the mouthpiece and said to me, "Señorita Márquez doesn't recognise your name, Señor. She asks what is this story you have?"

I hid the disappointment about my name and focussed on the question. "I can't say anything here. I need to speak to Lorena… err, Señorita Márquez, in person. When she sees me, she'll know who I am. It's important I talk to her."

The guard nodded and spoke into the handset again. Then he placed it on the desk and said, "Señor, we take security very seriously here. I need to show who you are to Señorita Márquez. Por favor, I take a picture and send it. Okay?"

"Uh, sure. No problem."

"Vale. Just a moment." He reached for a mobile phone, looked at the screen and selected the camera app. Then he pointed it at me and took a picture. "Gracias, Señor. One more moment." He tapped on the mobile phone's screen a number of times and then put it down on the desk. Next, he picked up the desk phone and waited. After a few moments he focussed on the handset, listening to whatever was being said at the other end, nodding in response but saying nothing. Finally, he put it down. "I'm sorry, Señor, I have spoke with Señorita Márquez and she say she does not know you and has never seen you before."

I stepped forward and placed both hands on the desk. "That can't be… look, we met… in England." I took off the glasses and leaned forward. "Can you take another picture? Maybe she'll recognise –"

"I'm sorry, Señor. She doesn't know you and will not see you. I have tried for you."

I felt Carlos tugging at my shirt. I brushed him aside and focussed on the guard. "But the story… it's big time and a major problem for Ignacio Cañizares. You have to listen. It could… it could end his career. He'll never play for Madrid again if this gets out. You need to hear this."

"Señor, we already know about the injury. We broadcast it on the news today. I'm sorry."

"The injury?" I glanced at Carlos.

"Yes, Cañizares has torn ankle ligaments very bad. He will not play for three or four months maybe, but not end his career like you say. He come back here early from England… uh… esta mañana."

"This morning," Carlos said.

"What? He's back in Madrid?"

"Sí. You do not watch our news? You do not read news on website?"

I didn't get a chance to answer. Carlos pulled me to one side. "Leave it, Mateo. He's not having it. You're not going to get to see Lorena. We need to rethink this."

From the corner of my eye I caught sight of another security guard approaching, who seemed to be taking an interest in our activity. I walked away from the desk and went back outside. "I can't believe Lorena wouldn't see me."

Carlos shrugged. "I'm not surprised, amigo. Nos follamos hacia arriba."

"What? What's that?"

"I said, we fucked up. Jasper was right."

"Right? About what?"

"You do look like your pushing fifty!"

42

It was mid-afternoon by the time we arrived back at the hotel. We went straight up to the Terraza bar where we found Cecil and Jasper deep in conversation. There were several other hotel guests seated around, enjoying the spectacular view of the Madrid cityscape and the warmth of the sun.

Cecil looked up as we came in. "How'd it go, boys? All sorted."

"No. She wouldn't see me."

"Why not?" Jasper asked.

I explained what had happened with Lorena and about the photograph. There wasn't a great deal of sympathy.

"Mate, you gotta say, with that 'tache, the grey barnet and the bins, she ain't gonna recognise you, is she?" Cecil said, a grin on his face.

"Really! So why didn't anyone mention that before I went there?"

"How we supposed to know you're gonna get your photo done, geezer? Yeah, you look different but if you'd got to speak to her face to face, would've bin a different mumble." Cecil drained the last of his beer and put the bottle down on the table. "You having one? Jas's shout."

"Go on then." I thought back for a moment to my discussion at the TV station. "You know what I don't understand, I gave them my name and mentioned Ascot but that still didn't do any good. Why wouldn't she be curious at least?"

"You know the score, mate. Famous footballer out for the day, he's gonna get loads of people hanging about. His bird's used to it. She ain't gonna take much notice. And I bet the geezer never even told her your name when they come to sorting it. He's gonna blag it all, make out it's some wannabe trying to scam him. He's gotta save face, ain't he?"

"I suppose so and now I'm no closer to solving anything. *And* he's back in Madrid. Came back a day early, injured apparently."

"What's happened to him?"

"Ankle ligaments or something. Anita said he had a dodgy ankle and nearly didn't go on the tour." I sat down on one of the pink stools. "Any news from Erin?"

"Nah, mate. We bin here since you left. She's still in her room, I think."

Jasper returned to the table with four bottles of beer. We spent another half hour or so chatting. Cecil was up for calling in another round. I stopped him.

"Not for me, Ces. I need to check on Erin, see if she's got anything. And I need to get some food too. I'm starving."

Back downstairs I knocked on Erin's room. She had just come out of the shower, dressed in one of the hotel robes, a towel wrapped tightly around her head. I told her about my attempt to meet with Lorena but didn't want to dwell on my failure. I was more interested in hearing if she'd found anything. Her smile suggested that her afternoon had been more productive than mine. She beckoned me towards a laptop that stood, screen open, on a coffee table. We sat down. Erin played with the touchpad until the screen came to life. I tried to focus but was momentarily distracted as one side of Erin's robe fell away, revealing an expanse of tanned thigh. She didn't seem to notice.

"Okay. So I've been searching the main people to see what I can find. There's obviously loads online about the footballer; the usual stuff, photos of his career, trophies he's won, clubs he's been at, none of it very enlightening, except for one thing. Look."

Erin clicked on a link that said, 'career history' and then on a menu item that said 'clubs.' The page was categorised by year with the most recent at the top. She scrolled down to the end. It seemed that Ignacio Cañizares's career had started when he signed as a professional at just sixteen, having been spotted by Spanish scouts while still at school. He played reserve football for a couple of seasons in the Segunda División of La Liga before going out on loan to Montpellier, then in Ligue 2 in the French football league. A year later, when he was nineteen, he moved to Paris, in what was a record transfer for a teenager, and played in the French first division, Ligue 1. Then he returned to Spain to play in La Liga and four years later, at twenty-eight, made a big money move to Madrid where he has played for the last six years

Erin minimised the screen and looked at me. "There's the interesting bit. Ignacio Cañizares spent roughly five years playing his football in France, almost four of them in Paris. And guess who else was in Paris at that time?"

I hesitated for a moment and then it occurred to me. "Huguette?"

"Spot on. So, I looked at all the gossip stuff about Cañizares and what do I find? He had a two year affair with Huguette de Villiers when he played in France."

"Wow. Affair? Was he married to Chiara back then?"

"No, he met Chiara through Huguette. I say 'affair'... fling, dalliance... whatever you want to call it. He didn't get involved romantically with Chiara until after he'd split with Huguette."

"Two years is a long dalliance. More like a relationship. Why did they split?"

"Don't know. Any one of the usual celeb reasons, I expect. She's five years older than him."

"Yeah, but that wouldn't make any difference, especially in France. They love the older woman relationship thing. Experience and all that."

Erin smiled. "True. How about you, Matthew? That you're thing? The older woman?"

"Uh... no... I... I was just saying, you know."

"I saw you looking at my thigh a moment ago. You really should focus."

"I... I wasn't... not looking. I couldn't help... and you're not an older woman in any case."

"I'm teasing. You're so easy to tease. You make me laugh." Erin brushed her hair away from her face and then pulled the robe across to cover her bare thigh. "Anyway, what else have I got? Let's see."

"Hang on, I need to get the others in here first. The more minds focussed on this, the more likely we are to find the connections."

Erin laughed. "What's the matter? You think I'm going to seduce you?"

"No... no... I didn't mean that. I was being serious. It would make –"

"Matthew, I'm only playing. Don't panic. Your resistance is impressive though. Sure, give the guys a shout."

I left the room and made my way back up to the Terraza Bar. A few minutes later, all four of us were staring at Erin's laptop.

Erin pulled up a Google page on which she had typed Huguette's name. She clicked on the tab marked 'Images' and a series of pictures of Huguette appeared on the page. Many of them showed her on the catwalk. Just as many showed her on stage, singing. Several showed her with Chiara Rustichelli, some in professional pose and others more informal. Erin scrolled through the page. Further down there were two pictures of Huguette with a youthful Ignacio Cañizares. Erin clicked on one of them and it linked to a news site that showed the couple in a number of shots – film premieres, leaving a night club and at an awards dinner.

"Well, that proves they had a thing going on," Erin said. She clicked on one of the pictures and the caption became clearer. *'Cañizares se sépare de sa petite amie, Huguette de Villiers.'* "My French is so-so, but pretty obvious what that says. Looks like he broke it off."

"Yeah, and it gives her good reason to have the hump with his missus too," Cecil said.

"How d'you mean?" Jasper asked.

"You know the rules, geezer. You don't go out with your friend's ex. Even if they've split up. Don't matter how much you fancy 'em. It shouldn't happen. And you don't go out with your mates' sisters either. Never get in the way of relationships."

"Whose rules are they, Cecil? Yours?" Erin asked.

"Nah, ain't mine. It's life. It's like a code you should live by, ain't it. Stands to reason. You go out with a mate's ex, your mate's gonna be thinking stuff all the time. Like, is she doing with him what she used to do with me? Is she saying the same stuff? Taking him the same places? Is he better in the sack? Too close to home. Same with women. Huguette had to be thinking all that shit about the footballer and her Italian mate." Cecil looked at me. "I mean, how'd you like it if you and Louise split up and then she started going out with me?"

I didn't have an answer but it reminded me that I'd promised Louise I'd call her.

Cecil continued. "You wouldn't, would'ya? It'd affect your friendship with me for a start, stands to reason. So, what I'm saying, that might be a motive for the French bird to stitch up the footballer for ditching her and then, not only getting involved with her mate, but then marrying her."

"Aye, but there's a problem there, Ces," Carlos said. "If your wee theory about Huguette being behind the drug deal's right, why would she stitch up the footballer? She'll want the deal to go through. Makes her money. And why would she still be friends with his wife?"

Cecil ran his hands through his hair. "I don't know yet, mate. I'm speculating, ain't I. You never know how a woman's mind works. All right, she might not have set out to stitch him up, but I bet she's never got over what he did. So she sees an opportunity that benefits her and if it means putting him on the line, she don't really care. She's got a foot in both camps. If the drug mumble goes right, she's quids in. It goes wrong, he's stitched up and nobody knows she's fucked his career for screwing with her. I mean, she might even *want* it to go wrong so he gets shafted. Who knows?"

Erin raised a hand just as a debate was about to break out around her. "Hold it, guys. Cecil might not be clear on how a woman's mind works but it's a good job mine does. We need to focus on this stuff until we have something that makes some sense. No point in just speculating." She tapped the keyboard again and returned to the general Google images of Huguette. None jumped out that showed more than an insight into Huguette's professional career in both its guises, that of international model and, more laterally, pop star.

"Nothing much on there about her medical science career," Jasper said, chuckling at the contrast between Huguette's celebrity and the life of an academic.

"Mate, nobody's bothered about that, are they. They'd all sooner watch people baking fucking cakes on TV. They're only interested in celebs, not people who can think."

Erin ignored Cecil's remark and continued to scroll down the page. When she reached the bottom she clicked on a link that said, '*Show More Results.*' Another raft of pictures appeared, only this time there were fewer photos of Huguette's professional life on stage and the catwalk, and more of the informal variety – backstage shots, parties and charity events.

And then things took a turn.

43

Erin got up to make coffee. She pulled the towel from her head and shook her hair loose so that it tumbled in damp strands around her face. I dragged the laptop around so that it was in front of me and started to examine the pictures. I scrolled down the screen, my mind beginning to numb at what I was seeing. Nothing jumped out, nothing that gave me any hope that I was going to find something useful. The lad's had begun to lose interest too. I could tell by their increasing restlessness. Cecil had gone to help Erin make the coffee although his intentions were probably more focussed on Erin than in being of any great assistance.

As I reached the end of the array of pictures, I let out a deep sigh. "I reckon this is a wild goose chase. We're not getting anywhere."

"There must be something," Carlos said. "We need to persevere."

"Try the video link," Jasper said. "Might be a bit more entertaining at least."

"Where? What video link?"

Jasper pointed at the screen. "There. On the menu bar. Videos."

"Oh yeah." I pointed the cursor where Jasper had indicated. The screen switched to a list of video icons with titles above them. For no reason at all other than it was first in the list, I clicked on the top one. The image changed to YouTube's site with the video I had selected displayed prominently in the centre of the page and a list of smaller video clips to the right, all relating to Huguette de Villiers.

The video began to play an advert intro. I clicked the 'Skip Ads' icon and the screen switched to what turned out to be a music awards event. The camera focussed on the event compere who was speaking in French from behind a lectern on a stage. When he had finished, he picked up an envelope and, with some theatrical deliberation, opened it. He pulled out a card and stared at it for a moment. Then he looked up and said, "Huguette de Villiers."

Another camera panned across an audience of people seated at several round dining tables. In a single uninterrupted shot, it zoomed in on one specific table and picked out the smiling face of Huguette. The camera lingered on her as she stood up and began to walk towards the stage. The clip finished with Huguette accepting an award from the compere and making a thank you speech. I paused the action and was about to click on another one from the selection on the right, when Carlos tapped me on the shoulder.

"Let's hear what she has to say, Mateo. We've been looking at pictures all the time and getting no information. You never know."

"But she's French, Carlos. None of us speak French."

"Erin said she knows a bit," Jasper said.

Erin turned round. "I told you, it's so-so. I can get by as long as they're not gabbling on."

"That'll do. Matt's got a clip of Hugs doing a speech at some music awards thing. Have a listen."

Erin came back to the laptop. I hit the play button. The clip continued, Huguette smiling and making her speech. And then she switched to English.

"She's just repeating what I just heard," Erin said. "Mostly thank you stuff, the usual guff these performers come out with. She's doing it in English too because the UK and American music markets are the biggest out there. Got to be onside with them. If they think you're just a European artist, you're going nowhere. Look at ABBA. Swedish band, all their major hits in English."

Erin's comments focussed me. I dragged the timeline back on the video and pressed 'play' again. Huguette was just coming to the end of her speech in French. As she began in English, I listened more intently.

"*.... award is a big surprise. I am so honoured. There are many people to say thank you to. Where can I begin? I must thank my band members... you all know those guys but this record cannot be made without excellent musicians. Et aussi... sorry... and also, it need people behind the scene. It is a team effort, and I would like to say... merci, thank you, to Marcel, my producer, who worked so hard with us to get this single finished; Augustin, our sound engineer and his team and, erm... everyone at the Cyrex record label, too many to say, but... I love you all. Oh, and special big* *thanks to Neets for all her work. Every artist needs a good agent and she is wonderful. And finally, merci to everyone out there who bought this record. You make it a big success. Thank you."*

The clip ended. I looked at the others. "You heard of any of these people?"

There was no response, other than a few dismissive shrugs.

"It was a few years back according to the clip title," Jasper said. "And her singing career took a nosedive a couple of years later from what I read. I don't reckon many people know Hugs these days, never mind heard of them others. You know what the music industry's like. One minute you're hot, then you're not. Simple."

I was about to select the next clip when Cecil came over, a coffee in his hand. "Heard of who?" he asked.

"Just some people Huguette mentioned on YouTube, Ces."

"I didn't see it, did I."

"It doesn't matter. There's loads of clips of her... singing, modelling..."

"Let's have a look. I'm clued up about the old music biz, ain't I. I might know stuff."

I caught Cecil's wink at Erin and wondered if he was trying his usual blag.

"Okay, go ahead." Better to pander to Cecil with a four-minute video clip than to spend three times as long debating the merits of his 'music biz' knowledge. I hit the 'back' button and said, "There you go. I'm getting a coffee."

"All right. Got it."

I made myself a coffee and came back to the laptop just as the camera was zooming in on Huguette. It may have been because I was now less focussed on specifics, having seen the clip already, but something caught my eye.

"Hang on, Ces. Pause it a minute."

Cecil stopped the clip. "What's up?"

"Roll it back a bit."

"Where to?"

"Just the bit where the camera's zooming towards the table."

Cecil did as I asked. I leaned over his shoulder, my gaze focused on the screen. "Stop! Hold it there." He clicked on the pause button. The screen froze, with Huguette and a section of her table guests centre frame.

"Take it back a bit… uh, a few seconds."

Cecil held the cursor on the red timeline and dragged it back until Huguette's full table was in shot.

"That's it. Pause it."

"What's it?"

I didn't answer. I stared at the image, my brain trying to make sense of what I thought I'd seen.

"What you looking at, mate?"

I knew what I was looking at, but I was still trying to understand it. The screen shot showed the full table, seven people sitting around it, Huguette, the focus of the screen zoom, in the top of the shot facing the camera. Next to her, on her left, sat a man, and further round the table clockwise, a woman. On Huguette's right, following the table seating plan anticlockwise, there was another man and to his right, a woman. Next to her, sat another man and on his right, at the lower end of the table, a third woman.

It was the woman on the left side of the screen, two places from Huguette anticlockwise, that had caught my eye. She was looking in Huguette's direction and the camera had captured her side profile, but it was partially obscured by the man sitting on her right as he leaned forward to speak to Huguette. But the image was enough to make me stop and think.

"I can't believe it. I think that's her."

"Who is?" Cecil asked.

"That woman there." I pointed at the left side of the screen. "I think that's Anita."

Cecil stared at the image. "You sure?"

I didn't answer. I just stared at the image. It wasn't the clearest. The man leaning forward had blocked most of the view, but the side of her face and her blonde shoulder length hair was visible, enough for me to make the connection.

"Yeah, as sure as I can be. I know none of you guys have met her, but I've seen enough of her to know it's got to be her. And if it is, you know what this means?"

"Yeah, mate. She's connected to Huguette," Cecil said. "And we know Anita's involved with the old Colombian marching powder, so it don't make my theory about the French bird too far wrong then, does it?"

Cecil had a point. It was the first breakthrough we'd had.

"Cecil, go forward, near the end," Erin said. "She mentions names in her speech. I want to hear the names again."

Cecil located the part of the clip that Erin had asked for. We listened intently. Marcel. Augustin. Male names. And then... Neets.

"Neets? What kinda name's that?" Carlos asked.

I scratched my head. "Rings a bell. I'm sure I've heard it somewhere before."

Erin clapped her hands. "That's it, isn't it? It's got to be a nickname for Anita. A-neet-a. Neets. Makes sense?"

Cecil and I exchanged looks. It did make sense, though I could tell from Cecil's expression he was just as unfamiliar with such a nickname. I turned to Erin. "Her agent? So Anita could be her agent?"

"Worth checking out."

"Too right," I said, feeling a surge of optimism at discovering something, even if I had no idea how it would help. "Jas, could you check that? Just anything you can find on any agent that Huguette might have had called Anita. I've just thought of something I need to look up."

"No worries, Matt. On it."

I typed in 'Ignacio Cañizares' into the search engine. A whole raft of results fired up, the most recent about his injury. *'Cañizares set to miss half the season'. 'Cañizares to miss vital Euro qualifying games.'* I clicked on one of the links and read through the detail. It reported that Ignacio Cañizares had played the second half of a friendly match in London against Arsenal on Thursday. Then he had started the match against Manchester United on Sunday, but was injured after twenty minutes, sustaining torn ankle ligaments in his right leg and an unspecified injury to his left arm. At the end of the article, there was a link that took me back to YouTube.

There were two videos at the top of the page that reported Cañizares's injury. I clicked on the first one. It opened to show brief highlight of Madrid's game at Old Trafford, Manchester. The focal point was the injury to Cañizares. As a high cross came into the penalty area, Cañizares ran forward and jumped to meet the ball. United's centre back went to intercept it, getting there just before the Madrid player. Cañizares's momentum caused him to crash into the United defender. They both went down, Cañizares landing awkwardly on his right foot and pitching heavily to his left, where the United player landed on his arm. The centre back was back on his feet immediately, but Cañizares stayed motionless on the ground. Medical staff came on to treat him but it was clear he could not carry on. After several minutes of medical attention, he was stretchered from the pitch.

The next video loaded automatically. It was short and to the point – a news clip of Cañizares walking through Madrid airport, his right leg encased in an Aircast support boot and his left arm wrapped in a sports compression brace that stretched from the top of his bicep down to his wrist. He used crutches to support his weight.

I watched both videos again and I had an idea.

"I'm going back to my room for a bit," I said. "I need to think some things through and get some food. Where you going to be?"

"We'll be in the bar up top. We'll get a table," Cecil said. "There'll be a crowd there later doing the old sundown thing. Best get there early."

"Okay. See you there later."

44

At six o'clock I made my way back up to the Terraza bar. It was busy, a buzz of people all keen to be in position to view the sun setting across the Madrid skyline as early evening approached. Carlos and Cecil were already there, a bottle of red wine placed on the table. I sat down opposite them. Carlos went to the bar and brought back another glass. Cecil poured some of the wine and I took a sip.

"Where's Erin and Jasper?" I asked as I put the glass down.

"We left 'em downstairs, mate. They were still going through the internet looking for stuff," Cecil said.

"Okay. Anyway, listen, I've had an idea that might get this sorted."

"Yeah, what's that then?"

I was about to explain but was interrupted by the arrival of Erin and Jasper. Erin had brought her laptop.

"Matt, we think we've found out who Anita is," Jasper said, his face giving away his excitement.

"Yeah? Who?"

Erin set the laptop on the table, flipped it open and said, "Take a look."

I stared at the screen, taking in the information. Erin had opened a webpage that showed someone called Anita Eliades. It said that she was a showbusiness and theatrical agent and had what appeared to be a professionally shot profile picture of the woman I knew only as Anita.

"That's her," I said. "That's definitely her."

"Okay," Erin said. "Now click on that other tab."

I did as Erin had said and pulled up a page that had details of a theatrical agency based in the UK called, 'Eliades Elite.' I scrolled through the text. There were a number of testimonials, one of which was attributed to Huguette de Villiers.

"Well that confirms the connection."

"It does, no question. I called the agency number that's on there, but it comes up as unobtainable. Then I realised that the webpage hadn't been updated for some years. So I checked the record on the Companies House website and found that her business went into liquidation three years ago, and Anita Eliades filed for bankruptcy."

"So what you saying?" Cecil asked. "Her agency's gone tits up and she's skint?"

"Yes, pretty much."

"And that's got to be why she's involved in the drugs thing," Jasper said. "Probably had a load of personal and business debts."

"Maybe, but none of this is helping me find her."

Jasper stared at me. "You want to find her? I thought you were trying to avoid her?"

"I was, yeah, but I've had an idea. A long shot, but it's the only thing I can think of that might get me out of this and back home. We have to make Anita's deal happen."

My statement met four quizzical expressions. I took a deep breath and began to lay out my plan. When I'd finished, I asked, "What do you think?"

"It's risky," Erin said, "but looks to me like the only choice you have."

"Yeah, I gotta say it's worth a go, geezer. We ain't got much else," Cecil added.

Jasper and Carlos nodded their agreement.

"Okay. So first thing I need to do is find Anita. That website and the info's no help if her company's gone bust, but I've already thought of how to get hold of her, and I'm going to need you for that, Carlos."

"I'm in, Mateo. What d'you need?"

"Cool. I'll come to that. First of all, I'm going to need someone to buy a mobile phone… what're they called… something cheap?"

"A burner," Cecil said.

Erin laughed. "I don't think that's what they're called officially. You mean one you can ditch when you've done with it?"

"Yes. And three prepaid sim cards."

"What do you want three cards for?" Carlos asked.

"Not sure yet, but one for my use, another to give to Anita and one as backup. You never know."

"I'll get the phone," Erin said.

"Great. So, Carlos, when Erin's got the phone, I need you to go to the police station and ask for Ricardo Armendarez. You're the –"

"What, the bent polis?"

"Yeah, him. You're the only one who speaks fluent Spanish. You need to get a message to him, and it has to be face to face. You tell him that Anita needs to contact me and you give him one of the burner numbers that I give you."

"Which police station?"

"Uh… the one I took my passport to, I suppose. That's where he told me to go. On Calle de Leg… something or other. I'll look it up. He must be based there."

"And if he's not?"

"If he's not, your just going to have to find out which one he *is* at."

"And what if the bastard arrests me? I'd nae trust him, Mateo."

"He's not going to arrest you, is he? You've not done anything. Look, it's in his interest too that this deal happens. You need to make it clear that this is the only opportunity they'll get. If Anita doesn't cooperate, then there'll be no further contact."

"Yeah, but he'll know you're still in the country and can't leave. He still has your passport."

"Forget that. We have to make him… and Anita… think that we have some options, that we're in control again."

"Yeah, mate, blag it," Cecil added. "You need any back up, I'll come with ya."

"Ces, no. Carlos just needs to be direct, keep it simple. He's delivering a message." I turned to Carlos. "And remember, it needs to be face to face… with Armendarez. Nobody else. You just tell whoever's on the desk to tell him it's connected to me and it's urgent."

"Aye, okay. Then what?"

"We wait. And one other thing. Before you get to the police station, buy yourself a Madrid Bus Tour ticket. Then, once you've finished, you get on the bus and spend a couple of hours or so going round Madrid before you come back here."

"What for?"

"I'm just being careful in case he thinks it's an idea to have you followed. I doubt he'll do that, but it just confuses things while I wait for Anita to call me. You can check in with Cecil or Jasper to see what's going on."

"Sounds like a plan," Erin said. "I'll go and buy the phone now."

"Thanks, Erin." I turned back to the lads. "Okay, nothing much else we can do until we hear from Anita... *if* we hear, that is."

"You will, mate," Cecil said. "Another drink?"

"One more only, Ces, and then I'm going to bed. I'm knackered. I've been up since half three this morning."

The early night revived me. The following morning I was up at 7.30. I showered and got dressed, remembering to run some more talcum powder through my hair. Carlos called my room and said he had coffee on the go and wanted to run over the details again before he left.

I called Erin and found that she'd managed to buy a cheap mobile and three sim cards. She told me which numbered sim she'd loaded in the phone and gave me the other two telephone numbers for each card. I wrote them down on the room notepad, in the order I intended to use them, tore off the sheet of paper and put it in my pocket. Then I went to Carlos's room, and over coffee I briefed him again on the message he had to deliver and gave him the mobile number to give to Armendarez.

At just after 8.30 a.m. Carlos left the hotel and headed for the police station on Calle de Leganitos. Then I went to Erin's room to collect the burner phone. Erin had put the other two sim cards into a small envelope. I put the envelope in my pocket along with the sheet of paper and then went back to my room to wait.

Just over one hour later, there was a knock on the door. I opened it to find Jasper outside, mobile in hand.

"It's Carlos, Matt."

I took the phone and beckoned Jasper to come in.

"Carlos?"

Carlos answered. His message was brief. *"Mission accomplished, Mateo. I spoke to the man himself. I'll call later to check on things. Got a bus to get."*

"Great. Well done. Did he say... hello... Carlos... you there?"

The call went dead. I handed the mobile back to Jasper. "Thanks, Jas."

"All okay, mate?"

"Yeah... yeah. He just rang off. Where's Cecil?"

"In the shower I think. We're going out to get some breakfast. You coming?"

"No, I'll order room service. I don't want any distractions if Anita decides to call. Carlos delivered the message so I can only wait. Let me know when you're back."

I didn't have to wait long. Twenty minutes or so after Jasper had gone, the burner phone rang. With shaking hands, I picked it up.

"Hello."

"*Matthew, our little runaway.*" I recognised Anita's voice straight away. "*Where did you get to?*"

"I don't think you need to worry about that. You and I need to talk."

"*I'm all ears.*"

"I don't mean here. Face to face. We need to meet."

"*Why would you do that? I thought you were avoiding us.*"

"Look, if you want your deal to go ahead, you need to meet with me and hear what I have to say. And I mean *you*, and you only. Any '*us*' and it's no go. If I get a sniff of any of your goons around, I'm out. Understand?"

I heard the giggle. "*Very alpha, Matthew. So, where and when?*"

"Where we met the first time, same café. This morning." I looked at my watch. "Ten-thirty."

"*So you're in Madrid?*"

"What?"

"*If you can meet that soon you must be close.*"

I felt a wave of anxiety at the question. "Uh… it's an hour and a half. I could be... err, anywhere. Look, we both want this sorted. It's urgent, so don't be worrying about where I am. I'll wait fifteen minutes, no more. If you don't show, I'm gone." I didn't wait for Anita's reply. I killed the call. I put the phone in my pocket and went to Erin's room.

"Just heard from her… Anita."

"And?"

"I've set up a meeting, me and her. Half ten this morning and I –"

"Isn't that risky? You can't trust her. She did have you kidnapped."

"It's a public space… a shopping area, cafés. I've been there before. Lots of people around. But I need your help. You're the only one of my friends that they don't know about and haven't seen."

"What do you want me to do?"

"I just need you to be at the café. Sit there with a coffee, like a tourist. Just keep an eye on things. If anything looks dodgy, just create a scene or something."

"I can do that. Where is it?"

"It's just up from the Opera House, on the corner of, erm… bloody hell, I can't remember the name."

Erin powered up her laptop and typed 'Google maps' in the search engine. In the search bar she then typed 'Madrid Opera House.' An overview map of the area appeared along with the names 'Teatro Real' and 'Lotus Opera House.' The first one caught my eye. "That's it."

Erin clicked on the link and a picture of the façade of the Teatro Real appeared. A prominent red marker picked out its location on the map. She moved the laptop nearer to me. "Here, you know where you are."

With a few clicks of the mousepad I minimised the side panel information and zoomed in on the red marker's location. Then I positioned the 'orange man' icon on one of the streets near the marker. Immediately the screen changed to a 'street view' image of the Teatro Real. I ran my finger over the mousepad and turned the view away from the theatre and across the Plaza de Isabel II. Then, with a few more clicks, I moved the image from the plaza to Calle del Arenal until I found the café.

"There, that's it. On that corner, where the Calle del Arenal joins with Costanilla de los Ángeles. See?"

"Got it. Okay. I'll be there."

"Great. Thanks, Erin. Oh, and one more thing. It would be good if you could follow Anita discreetly after the meeting. There might be no point but you never know. You might see something."

"Good thinking. I will." She reached into the drawer by her bed, pulled out the gun that she'd taken from Vicente, and put it in her bag. "I might need this after all."

I hoped not.

45

I arrived at the café bar at 10.25. I spotted Erin straight away. Wearing a plain, white cotton dress, dark glasses, flip flops, her hair tied back in a ponytail, she was sitting at a table close to the entrance. A folded copy of the Spanish newspaper El Mundo lay next to a coffee cup with a still unwrapped biscuit in the saucer. Like many lone diners she seemed focussed on her mobile phone. If I hadn't known her, I would have taken her for just another tourist or even one of the native *Madrileños*. She didn't acknowledge me and I tried not to look at her.

I scanned the area, partly to see if Anita was around but also looking for any of her associates that I knew by sight. There were a few customers around enjoying early morning coffee but no sign of Anita or anyone else familiar. I picked a table two away from Erin and sat down. A waiter approached and asked what I would like. I told him I was waiting for someone and I'd order then. I sat back and tried to relax.

The morning sun warmed the café area, the far side of the street shaded by rows of tall buildings. Already there were numerous shoppers and tourists ambling past, checking shop windows or heading to the open space of the plaza, nobody appearing to be in any particular hurry. I was glad the location was busy and very public. It gave me a sense of security. And then I heard a voice to my left.

"Matthew?"

I turned quickly. "Yeah. Anita."

She smiled. "A makeover, I see. I hope your experience hasn't aged you that much."

I ignored the comment. I was getting used to the image and had forgotten about my 'talced' hair and moustache and the glasses. "Sit down. We need to talk."

The waiter appeared. Anita pulled out a chair and sat. "What're you having?"

"Uh... coffee, I think."

"Okay, wine it is." Anita ordered a bottle of house white and then looked at me. "What?"

"It's only just gone ten-thirty in the morning."

"And?"

I shrugged.

"Look, if I'm going to sit here arguing with you, Matthew Malarkey, I at least want to enjoy it."

"Nobody's going to argue. We can be civilised about this."

"Really? So why did you run away? We had this under control."

I leaned across the table. "Well, first of all, I object to being bundled into a car, taken against my will to another part of the country and then locked up in the middle of nowhere. And secondly, I have a major problem with being disfigured for no reason other than your greed."

"Disfigured?"

"Yeah. I overheard the conversation about a tattoo artist, and I knew what you were up to. You had to prove I was Cañizares so you were prepared to create his tattoo on my arm, and you didn't care if I was stuck with it for the rest of my life."

Anita burst out laughing. "If you believe that then you're more stupid than you look right now, Matthew, and let me tell you, that's mega stupid. We weren't going to tattoo you! We had a theatrical makeup artist coming to replicate the image, sure, but even if we'd wanted to do a full blown tattoo, it wouldn't have settled in time. That wasn't an option. I've got contacts and I was confident the person I know would have done a convincing job."

The waiter arrived with the wine. Anita brushed aside his attempts to serve it with any finesse and told him to pour it. I was still absorbing what she'd said about the tattoo. She sipped the wine, placed the glass on the table and said, "Maybe you'd do well to improve your Spanish if you're going to eavesdrop on other people's conversations."

I waved a hand dismissively. "Look, it doesn't really matter whether I got that wrong or right. The point is you shouldn't have kidnapped me. That's the wrong bit."

"But I asked you to cooperate, stay out of sight. You wouldn't, so I had no choice. Anyway, we are where we are, and you've asked to meet me. What's your plan?"

I took a long hit on the wine. I had to keep control of things, not allow Anita any inroads. I glanced in Erin's direction. She was drinking her coffee, her demeanour indicating no interest in anything around her. I stared at Anita for a moment, meeting her gaze, looking for a 'tell' that might indicate her state of mind. There was nothing. Time to step it up.

"You still want to do this deal with Kreshnik, and I'm guessing you haven't cancelled tomorrow's meeting or you wouldn't be here, right?"

Anita nodded.

"And I'm assuming you've seen the news... the news about Cañizares?"

Again, Anita nodded. "I heard it from Lucero yesterday afternoon." She sipped her wine and then glanced to her left. I'd seen it before, a mannerism that gave her a nanosecond of extra thinking time.

"Look, you disappearing like that called for a rethink. I didn't cancel the meeting because I thought we might find you. But if we didn't, I was hoping we could come up with some other way of saving the deal. Cañizares's mishap complicates things, but then I thought it might be an excuse for him not being able to come to a meeting. Maybe buy me some time. And that might put some time pressure on Kreshnik; might make him take a chance and just go with the deal." She reached for her glass again. "Fuck! This should be done by now. You screwed it last time. The only reason we're in this position is because of that stupid earring."

"Not my fault. You chose the earring. Anyway, I'm prepared to do it... the meeting, but on my terms. You can't rely on a tattoo for proof now, but there is another way."

"Okay. I'm listening."

"You've seen the extent of Cañizares's injuries?"

"Yes."

"So, it's our one chance to pull this off. You want to close your deal, and I want to get rid of this frigging nightmare and go home. Kreshnik only needs to see something that reflects the here and now."

Anita's brow furrowed into a deep frown. "Go on."

"I don't care how you do this. It's your problem. You find me one of those air boots that Cañizares is wearing right now, crutches and the arm bandage thing, and I'll show up at tomorrow's meeting looking the part."

Anita hesitated, taking in my proposal. "Hmm... not bad, might just work. It's all we've got." She took another mouthful of wine, stared at the glass for a moment and then said, "It won't be that simple getting the stuff. I'll need to do a bit of research."

"Not my problem. It's the only chance you got to convince him who he's dealing with. Doesn't sound like you've come up with any other option." I paused, checking Anita's reaction and then continued. "The meeting's tomorrow night. I need those things by tomorrow afternoon or it's off. You've got until then. Once you have them, you call me on the number I gave you."

"Okay."

"I have another condition."

"What's that?"

"Your bent cop, Ricardo Armendarez, needs to be at the meeting venue with my wallet and passport and a document that shows all drug charges against me are dropped. If he's not there, I walk away. Once the meeting's done, he gives me back the passport and the wallet. If you don't agree to that, say so now. No agreement, the meeting's off."

"That's a ridiculous request, Matthew. He'll never agree. He can't risk being seen with anyone associated with this business. He's a cop. It only works because he keeps a distance."

"Again, not my problem. I need my passport and wallet back. Tell him to give them to you if it's such a big issue."

"He won't do that. As long as he has your stuff and the drug charge, he feels in control. I told you before, once we've met with Kreshnik and agreed the deal, you'll get everything back."

"Then we're on the same programme except that I want everything back immediately we leave any meeting room. No delays."

Anita looked around, then focussed back on me. "I'll see what I can do. And there's no need for any document. He hasn't pursued charges against you yet. Get this meeting done and there's no charge to answer."

"My rules, Anita. I don't trust him. I want a document signed by him and I want that before I go into the meeting."

"Okay. Leave it with me, but if you screw up and Kreshnik pulls our deal, then you'll get nothing and charges will be pressed."

"No, that's not how this works. Like I said, my terms. I don't intend to screw anything up. My job is just to go there and convince Kreshnik that Cañizares is bankrolling your operation. It's no concern of mine whether he does business with you or not. I'm not responsible for that. That was our original deal. So, win or lose, I'm off the hook, okay? If you can't give me that assurance right now, I'm out."

Anita took another sip of wine and sat back. "I wouldn't get too cocky with your demands, Matthew. Just to be clear, you're not dealing with amateurs here. This is serious stuff with a lot of money at stake. So you play by our rules too. You turn up, you do what's needed, you keep your mouth shut and do as you're asked. We'll decide whether you've cooperated or not."

I took a deep breath. I knew I had to keep some control. "Look, I've already said I'll cooperate. It was me who contacted you, don't forget. I just want this done, but if Ricardo Armendarez is not there tomorrow with my passport, wallet and the document I asked for, I'm out. I don't care about his drug charge. Let him do what he has to do. I'll take my chances. I'll get home somehow."

Anita reached for the bottle and topped up her glass. "You can't do that, can you? Without a passport you're stuck here in Spain."

"I'll go to the consulate, if I have to, and get another one." I pushed the thought of Armendarez circulating my name to customs controls, with information that I was wanted by the police on a drug charge, to the back of my mind.

"Okay. I'll talk to Armendarez, but I know him. If he thinks you're playing him or you're trying to implicate him in this deal, he'll press the drug charge. It'll be hard for you to come back from that. You'll be tied up in all sorts of shit for a long time. I doubt you'll get a replacement passport too easily." Anita's eyes took on a hard, cold stare. She gulped down a large mouthful of wine and stood up to go.

"Anita, wait... where's the meeting?"

"I can't give you that information yet. You'll be picked up at a prearranged location. Oh, and one more thing. The earring. You need to sort that this time. No more cockups. Enjoy your wine."

I nodded. "Don't worry. I will."

Anita headed off in the direction of the Plaza de Isabel II. The Ópera Metro station was situated there, in the centre of the Plaza, opposite the opera house. I assumed she was going to catch a train somewhere. When she'd gone just a few metres, I saw Erin get up and start to follow. I finished my wine and waited until they'd disappeared from view. Then I paid the bill and left.

46

I had two calls to make, the first to Carlos to tell him that the meeting with Anita had happened and that he could make his way back; the second to Louise as I'd promised her I would call her on Tuesday, and there was no way I could put it off any longer. Lifted by the thought of Anita getting my passport, I realised I could be back home in a couple of days. There was no need to worry Louise about the extent of my situation and complicate things as a result.

I called. Louise seemed reassured by my confidence that I might home soon and simply asked me to let her know when I'd booked my flight. As I ended the call I felt bad that I hadn't confided in her, but if I could get things resolved I could fill her in on the details later. I shoved the thought to the back of my mind and went to find Cecil and Jasper. Neither of them were in their rooms. I went downstairs to the Lobby Bar and found them at a window table at the far end.

"We're getting something to eat," Jasper said, handing me a menu. "How d'you get on?"

"Tell you in a minute." I browsed the menu. We ordered pasta, three coffees and a jug of water.

"So, what happened, mate? You meet her?" Cecil asked.

I was about to reply but was interrupted by Jasper. "There's Erin."

I turned and spotted Erin making her way towards the steps that led to reception. Jasper jumped up, strode across the bar area and intercepted her.

"Good timing," I said, when she got to the table. "I was just about to tell the boys about my meeting but you first. How'd it go?"

Erin sat down, poured some water from the jug and said, "So, yes, I followed Anita when she left you at the cafe. She went into the Teatro Real, the opera house. There's an artists and personnel door at the back. I waited across the square. She came out about ten minutes later holding what looked like a programme. I assume she went in because she's an agent and doing her day job. Who knows?"

"Yeah, but if her agency's gone bust, what's she up to?" Cecil asked.

"I don't know. She might still have a few clients for herself. Anyway, after that she got on the Metro. I followed as discreetly as I could. She got off at Antón Martín and made a call once she was back on the street. Then she walked up to the Teatro Calderón, another theatre. When she got there she went into the hotel next door, Hotel Cortezo. I had to keep some distance... the streets around there are quite narrow... but it looked like she went straight into reception and went up the stairs. She was there about fifteen minutes. Then she came out, walked back up to the plaza in front of the theatre and hailed a taxi. I lost her after that."

"That's great, Erin. Thanks. Appreciate you doing that." I said.

Erin smiled. "Not sure what it tells us other than it looks like she might still be active in the show business world."

"Yeah, but blinding cover for the old dealing swerve," Cecil said. "She goes about her day job as normal. Nobody's gonna tumble she's got something else going on. I mean, how much more straitlaced does it get than that theatre stuff?"

"Never judge a book by its cover, Cecil," Erin said, "especially a woman."

Cecil laughed. "Spot on, darlin'. I mean, look at you."

Erin winked but didn't reply. Instead she focussed on me. "Your meeting went smoothly enough from what I could see. What happened?"

I explained the gist of my conversation with Anita and said that the second meeting with Kreshnik was on for tomorrow night. I told them how I'd asked Anita to get the medical boot and the arm strapping and that I'd demanded that Ricardo Armendarez shows up at the venue. "It should be straightforward. I'm already halfway there because I look like Cañizares and once they connect the injury thing, that should be enough."

"Mate, you might look more like him once you get that stupid moustache off, sort your hair out and ditch the glasses," Cecil said.

"Well, yeah, I know that, Ces. Oh, and I just remembered one other thing. The earring. Cañizares's got that earring and after last time, I reckon they'll pick up on that. I can't afford any more cockups. Any ideas?"

"Well, short of getting your ear pierced, mate, no."

"There is a way," Erin said.

"Yeah? What's that?"

"Tell you later."

I had no idea what Erin's solution might be. I left it and focussed on the outcome I wanted. "Once we get this done, I get my passport and wallet back, we're out of here. I don't care what happens with Anita's deal after that. Not my problem."

"Wouldn't be so sure, geezer. I wouldn't trust any of 'em. They got an agenda. Bottom line, mate, you're dispensable."

"Cecil's right," Erin said. "We need a backup plan."

"Yeah, I'm coming with ya this time."

"No, Ces. We need to keep this as normal as possible. It'll be me and Carlos, like before. That's what they know. Plus he's supposed to be my interpreter."

"Yeah, but if that copper show's up, we gotta make sure you get your stuff back. Who's to say he don't screw you right after the meeting?"

"Leave that to me," Erin said. "None of them know me, do they? They know the rest of you, so apart from Carlos, you can't be seen. But I can. Once we find out where the venue is, I'll keep an eye on him."

"What you got in mind?" Jasper asked.

"Don't worry about that. Let's wait to hear where the meet is. It's bound to be a public place like last time."

I smiled at Erin's self-assurance. Her upbeat approach gave me the confidence that she'd have my back no matter what the situation.

Our pasta arrived. Erin stood up. "I'm going upstairs to have a shower, then I'm popping out." She put a hand on my shoulder. "I'll give you a shout when I'm back. In the meantime, when you've had your lunch, I suggest you go up on the terrace and have a couple of stiff drinks."

I shot Erin a bemused look, but before I could say anything, Cecil jumped on her suggestion.

"I'm up for that, lads."

"I'll find you when I get back," Erin said. "Have fun."

47

Stiff drinks, Erin had said. I took her at her word and had a couple of large Bulleit whiskeys with coke. I knew she was up to something but I wasn't sure what. The whiskey along with the afternoon sun, had a soothing effect, just what I needed to counteract the wave of anxiety I felt every time I contemplated the prospect of what I needed to do to get off the hook. It was one thing calling for the meeting and another to pull it off.

I was on a second drink when Carlos showed up.

Cecil asked, "Where'ya bin, geezer?"

"Out and about. Thought I might do the full bus circuit once I was on it. You can jump off and check out different places, then get on another bus and carry on. Seen a fair bit of the city."

"Proper tourist, ain't ya," Cecil said, laughing.

"Aye, maybe, pal, but there's a wee bit more to visiting a place than seeing the inside of bars."

"Each to his own, mate. We're s'posed to be on a break in case any of you boys forgot that. We didn't come here to play fucking Cluedo, did we?"

"Hang on, Ces," I said, irritably. "That's not on. Not my fault we're in this mess. If anything it's yours. *You* got me on the footballer thing."

Cecil put his beer glass down, a frown spreading across his brow. "Mate, you was happy enough when it was working, if I remember. No queuing, top service, hot women hanging out, even the freebies we got. Yeah, nobody was complaining then, were they? And if we're gonna point fingers, let's have a look at you geezers giving out business cards, Facebook info, Instagram stuff, to total strangers. That mumble, yeah. What about all that then?" He sat back, picked up his drink and continued. "And you know what makes me laugh? If we hadn't had them cops pull him, you'd all be going on about what a blinding fucking trip it is and how we blagged it big time. Yeah?"

It was Jasper who cut through the moment. "Ces, I don't think Matt meant anything. You're right, yeah, everybody's in it. We take the rough with the smooth."

"Jas's right, Ces," I said. "I didn't mean… you know. I'm just stressed by the whole thing, this meeting tomorrow night." I grabbed my glass. "Let's just enjoy the moment. You guys always have my back. Cheers."

"Hey, what about me? I havenae got a drink, ya'bastards," Carlos said.

Cecil laughed. "Get that tourist geezer a drink, Jas. Can't have him whinging all afternoon."

Jasper went to the bar. I turned to Carlos. "So what happened with Armendarez? How'd it go?"

"Not a lot. He never said much. I had a wee bit'a trouble with the polis in the station. But I said it was a serious matter connected to a Matthew Malarkey and I'd only speak with Ricardo Armendarez. In the end they called him. They took me through to a room. I was in there five minutes, just me and him. I got straight to the point. I said you can either take it or leave it, pal, and give him the number. A'didnae fuck about."

"Good man, Carlos. It worked. I met up with Anita soon after and it's all on for tomorrow night."

We were interrupted by Erin who walked in carrying a shopping bag. "Come on, you. Drink up. We have things to do," she said, nodding in my direction.

"Oh yeah? His luck's in then is it?" Cecil said, a broad grin on his face.

Erin winked. "Matthew's luck's always in as far as I'm concerned."

I slugged down the whiskey, trying to ignore the catcalls from the others and followed Erin. She led me up to her room and told me to sit down. She put the bag on the bed and began to rummage through the contents.

"What's going on?"

"I'm going to sort that earring for you. You had a couple of stiff drinks?"

"Yeah… bourbon, why?"

She pulled out a plastic container from the bag. "Well, along with this ice, the drinks should desensitise you a bit."

"Desensitise?"

"Yep. I'm going to pierce your ear. I've bought a decent, but cheap, diamond stud and I can –"

"Hang on, no!" I stood up. "I'm not having my ear pierced, 'specially not a hotel room bodge job and then walking round for the rest of my life with a bloody hole in my ear. No way."

Erin looked up from organising the contents of the bag. "Stop being a feckin' wimp, Matthew. It's a five minute job. You'll hardly feel it. And it'll heal up for feck's sake. Anybody'd think I was going to mutilate you forever. How else are you going to sort it?"

I hesitated, unsure of an answer. "What if it… if it, I dunno, goes septic?"

Erin laughed. "Then your ear falls off and you can never wear them glasses again." She saw my surprised expression. "I'm winding you up. I'll sterilise the needle and then treat your ear after." She held up a bottle. "Good old TCP antiseptic. You'll be fine. Now sit down. Let's get this done."

I realised I had no choice. The earring had proved my undoing last time. Something small and insignificant had led to a whole lot more trouble than I needed. It was all about detail. If we'd taken care of that one detail properly, I might have been back home by now. I knew it had to get sorted.

"Okay. Let's get on with it. What do you need me to do?"

Erin went to the minibar. She took out a small whiskey bottle, picked up a glass and handed both to me. "Here, get that down you. It'll calm your nerves."

As I sipped the whiskey, I watched Erin go about her task. She tipped the contents of the shopping bag onto the bed – a packet of sewing needles, cotton wool, a cigarette lighter and a small potato. From her handbag she took out the switchblade knife she carried and a small package. She opened the package.

"There you go. That's your new piece of jewellery. Nobody would know it's a cheap one unless they had a trained eye."

I looked at it. It meant nothing other than it looked like a diamond stud. "What's the potato for?"

"Don't worry about that. You leave it to me. Right, I need you in the bathroom by the sink. Take off your shirt."

I did as Erin asked and then went into the bathroom. She opened the plastic container and handed me two large cubes of ice.

"Hold these either side of your ear. Which one has Cañizares got the earring in?"

"The left one, if I remember."

"Correct. I already checked. Don't want any cockups with the wrong ear, do we?"

The question didn't need answering. I thought about detail again. An earring in my right ear instead of the left one, a small detail but one that would blow the whole charade.

I crouched over the sink and held the two ice cubes in position, one either side of my left ear. As the cold began to bite the soft flesh of my earlobe it felt almost painful, a strange sensation that then began to give way to numbness. Behind me, Erin was busy with her preparation. I watched in the mirror as she sliced off the end of the potato with the knife. Then, she took one of the sewing needles from the packet, picked up the cigarette lighter and began to heat the end of the needle. I was glad the whiskey had calmed my system. I felt trickles of water running down my fingers onto my neck as the ice melted, but my ear had started to numb.

"How's your ear feel?"

"Uh... cold."

"Good. Another minute. Use some fresh ice, then we go for it."

I picked out two more pieces of ice and held them in place.

"Okay. Drop the ice, turn round and hold still."

Erin stood on my left side. In her right hand she held the small piece of potato and in her left, the sewing needle. Her movements were quick. She put the potato behind my earlobe and almost simultaneously pushed the needle through the flesh from the front. It happened too fast for any reaction. I felt a sharp prod and a stinging sensation, nothing else. She withdrew the needle and grabbed a piece of cotton wool which she dabbed against my ear. I saw a small trace of blood smeared on the white material as she dropped it into the bin. Then she poured some TCP onto another piece of cotton wool and cleaned around my ear lobe.

"Okay. Stay still now. I'm going to pop this stud in." I felt Erin's fingers positioning the earring. When it was done she stood back. "There you go. Take a look."

I turned to the mirror. It looked perfect, although my ear was redder than I expected.

"Wasn't so bad, was it?"

"Uh... no. No, it was okay."

"Good. It will feel sore for a while, and you'll need to turn it regularly just to let it settle. I'll give it another little clean now and we'll keep an eye on it. Looks the part though."

Erin dabbed at my ear again with cotton wool and TCP. Then she wiped my neck and shoulders with her hand. "You've got melted ice on you." Her fingers lingered on my chest. Her expression took on a more intense look. She leaned towards me, her hair brushing across my shoulder. I felt her hand flatten and then stroke gently downwards. "You know the boys think we're up to something right now, Matthew. Shame to disappoint them."

Her touch was soft, my mind contrasting it with how efficient she had been with the needle. I felt her lips brush my neck. I gulped as I reacted to her touch. Her perfume and the smell of her hair overwhelmed my senses. My mind reeled, my resistance bombarded by the heady mix of whiskey and Erin's sensuous presence. And she sensed my weakness.

"That's good, Matthew. Let go, be yourself. Plenty of time to be the actor." Her lips brushed my face, soft, light, tingling my skin.

And then I reacted.

"What? Actor. You said actor."

Erin stepped back. "I didn't mean anything. I just meant tomorrow, and –"

"No. Wait. That theatre you followed Anita to. What did you say it was called?"

A frown crossed Erin's brow. "Erm... the... Calderón, I think. Teatro Calderón."

I stepped away from the sink. "That's it. Another connection."

"What's it, Matthew? What're you on about?"

"When I was at Ascot, I met an actress... erm, Arabella. Arabella Leslie. She said she was appearing in Madrid. I remember now. That was the theatre she mentioned... the Calderón. It can't be coincidence that Anita went there and Arabella was at Ascot the same time as I was." And then something else struck me. "Neets!"

"Neets?"

"Yes, remember. The YouTube clip with Huguette... she mentioned her agent, Neets. And you worked out it was a nickname for Anita?"

"Uh, yeah. That's right. So?"

"I remember where I heard the name before. From Arabella. She told me that she'd got complimentary Ascot tickets from one of her agents... Neets. I didn't ask anything about it at the time. I was too focused on other stuff and in any case, there must be loads of people in hospitality sections with comps." I paused, letting the Ascot memory flood back in. "I bet Arabella's staying in that hotel you mentioned, next door to the theatre. What was it called?"

"I can't remember. I took a picture on my phone. I'll check." Erin went out to the bedroom and picked up her mobile. As she scrolled through her pictures she said, "You certainly know how to kill a moment, Matthew."

I didn't reply. I thought of Louise back home. Erin was hugely tempting, and I knew my resistance fuelled the challenge for her, but I was pleased I had got through the moment... again.

"There you go." Erin held out her phone. "Hotel Cortezo."

I stared at the picture. The shot showed the entrance to the hotel, its name emblazoned in huge grey letters across the front. "And that's the theatre right next to it?"

Erin looked at the screen. "Yep. It is. So what's your thinking."

I sat on the bed. "We've been looking for connections, looking to see how I was set up. What if Arabella's connected to this drug deal? She might even be the brains behind it."

"Or she might just be a jobbing actor that Anita keeps in touch with as part of her day job cover."

"Maybe, but she was there, at the races. She knew I'd pretended to be Cañizares. She knew Huguette. What if she planned the setup after that once she saw an opportunity to make a deal with Kreshnik work?"

"That's speculation, Matthew. I never actually saw Anita with anyone, and you don't know for sure if this Arabella Leslie is even in Madrid."

I grabbed my shirt. "No, not yet I don't. Look, I have to go. I need to chat with the lads." I pointed to my ear. "Oh, and thanks for this."

"My pleasure."

"Thanks, Erin. I'll make it up to you."

Erin grinned, her green eyes flashing mischief. "How? You've had plenty of opportunity."

"Uh... well, I... err, I'll think of –"

"I'm teasing, Matthew. Go on, go see your mates. Catch up later."

I pulled on my shirt and left the room. As I walked towards the lift, my mind flashed back to my dating days. I remembered my search for love, for that elusive woman that I could build a relationship with, and now that I'd found her, it was ironic how someone as attractive and alluring as Erin was in my life. Back then I'd have jumped at the chance of dating Erin. Now, I was happy with Louise and I knew that things had worked out right. If I'd met Erin first, I'm sure she would have been more than I could have handled. I dismissed the thought from my mind and took the lift down to the lobby. I went through to the bar and found Carlos drinking coffee.

"Where's the other two, Carlos?"

"Ach, lightweights. Gone upstairs for a sleep. Hit the beer a bit hard. Could you nae tell wi'Cecil? The drunker he gets the more cockney he is."

I smiled, knowing that Carlos's own identity swung randomly between his South American and Scottish personas once he'd had a few drinks himself. "Never mind. I'll catch up with them later." I caught the bar man's attention and ordered a coffee. Then I turned back to Carlos. "You remember that girl from Ascot, Arabella, the actress... actor? I think they're all called 'actor' now, man or woman."

"Aye, I do. The lassie with the cleavage. I wouldnae forget her, Mateo. Why?"

"You didn't keep in touch or anything, did you?"

Carlos laughed. "I wish, pal. Nah, I think she had an eye for young Jas. He's the ladies' man and he was giving her his best chat. What about it?"

"Not sure. I think she might be here in Madrid and she's connected to Anita."

"Yeah?"

"Yeah, and now I'm wondering if she's involved in this drug deal. I'll need to speak to Jas."

"But if she is, what difference does it make? You get your passport back tomorrow, you're away back home. Disnae matter about that lot."

The waiter arrived with my coffee. I took a sip and said, "I know, Carlos, but I'm still wondering how they had so much info about us. Ces might be right about social media but I'd like to know for sure. Plus, if we know who's behind this and can prove the connections, it might help me if something goes wrong tomorrow and they backtrack on the deal. Knowledge is power, they say."

Carlos nodded. "Aye, it is, amigo."

"If you see Jas or Ces before I do, don't say anything. I'd sooner be there to discuss it."

"Nae problema, Mateo. You know me."

I finished my coffee and stood up. "Okay, I'm going up to my room. Catch up later. Oh, and what do you think?"

"About what?"

"The earring?"

Carlos stared for a moment. "Bloody hell, Mateo. That ear's awful red. Where'd you get that done?"

"Bloody sore too. Erin did it."

48

I laid down on my bed and fell into a deep sleep.
 The sound of the bedside phone woke me. I ignored it the first time, my mind foggy, my ear burning. I sat up and checked my watch – ten to eight. I had been asleep almost three hours. I went to the bathroom and splashed cold water on my face. The phone buzzed again. This time I picked up.
 "*Mate, where 'ya bin?*"
 "Ces. I was asleep. Long day."
 "*You coming out?*"
 "Yeah, later. I'm just going to get some room service. Chill a bit. I'm not doing a big night, Ces. I have to be sharp for tomorrow."
 "*Nobody's going large, are they? A few quiet ones, chat about the old mumble, how we're gonna plan it.*"
 Cecil knew how to press my buttons. "Okay, yeah. Makes sense. We ought to have a plan."
 "*Good man. See 'ya in the Hemingway Bar nine o'clock, yeah?*"
 "Where's that?"
 "*Here. In the hotel. Round the back. Ask 'em at reception.*"
 "Okay."
 At just gone nine, I strolled into Hemingway Bar. Hemingway Bar had that smoky, jazz feel, almost sleazy but without either the sleaze or the smoke. It told a story of decadent days gone by, and it was red, very red. The furniture, the ceiling and the back of the bar area were a deep dark crimson, the walls and ceiling covered in the same red velvet-like material as the sofas that lined one side. Above the sofas a mirrored wall served to make the narrow room look larger. The overall image was enhanced with wood panelling, a long wooden bar with gold coloured carving along its front and a leopard print carpet. Two rows of dimly glowing lights ran the

length of the ceiling. The perfect hiding place, unseen from the street and neither night nor day encroaching. At the far corner of the bar, a dark alcove suggested more intimate encounters. It was the sort of bar you would have expected to find elegant ladies with cigarette holders and gentlemen in lounge suits. It was already crowded, a mix of age ranges, a laid back, chilled atmosphere.

I found the lads sitting at two round tables that resembled serving trays, complete with raised edges and lifting eyes.

"Got you a Bulleit and coke, mate."

I sat down. "Cheers, Ces. On my tab?"

"You know how it works, geezer. You called the trip and all that. Still coming out of the Ascot cash, ain't it? And without them tips we got'ya, we might be sitting here drinking fucking milkshake. Anyway, Carlos says Erin did the earring. Let's have a look."

I leaned towards Cecil, realising that since my ear was almost as red as the bar décor, it might need a close up inspection.

"Looks kosher. She's done a blinding job." He winked. "You and her… y'know?"

"What?"

"The old hashmadishmalacka mumble. She's got the hots for you, you know that?"

"Not sure about that, Ces. She's a good friend. I like her."

"Mate, I dunno what's wrong with ya. The more you put them barriers up, the more she's gonna wanna break 'em down. Women are like that. Ask Jas. She ain't the sort of girl that's used to being turned down."

"Ces, I don't want to talk about this now. Got too much going on, and you know better than anyone I'm not going to do that to Louise. It's about trust."

Cecil ran a hand through his hair and shot a glance at Jasper. Then he focussed back on me. "Your call, mate, but a one-off with a bird who only wants that too, ain't being unfaithful. It ain't as if your thinking of marrying her after, are'ya? No commitment. Erin's pretty street. She knows the mumble. She knows about Louise. She ain't gonna give you no grief afterwards. I reckon she'd be off your case then."

I raised my glass, hesitated and then slugged back half the contents. The hit went straight to my head. "Enough, Ces. I'm not even going to think about it." I turned to Jasper. "Jas, I need to ask you something."

"Sure, Matt."

"Look, it's no big deal, but you remember Arabella from Ascot?"

"Yeah, course I do. Hot chick."

"Okay. Did you keep in touch with her or anything... I mean... you know, phone numbers?"

Jasper looked perplexed for a moment. "Well, yeah. We exchanged numbers and did the Whatsapp thing for a while. Why, what's the problem?"

"Nothing. It's cool. Did you meet with her or chat on the phone?"

Jasper glanced at Cecil and Carlos before answering. "No. We didn't. Just a bit of WhatsApp banter. I did suggest we speak but she was always too busy, you know... rehearsing, performing. And then she was travelling, Milan or some place. In the end I lost interest. The WhatsApp stuff only lasted about a week... ten days... after the races. No point in all that messaging. For me it's about meeting up."

"Yeah, I get that. So did you ever talk about going to Madrid?"

"Well, yeah, 'specially because she said she was going. I said we were planning a trip but didn't have a date. She was interested. Said it would be good to hook up. Then things just fizzled out. Too much messaging, like I said."

"So let me get this clear. When you first mentioned you were going to Madrid, was that in the first week, ten days, after Ascot?"

Jasper sipped his drink, his brow furrowed in concentration. "Yeah, it was. She asked me to let her know when I knew more so we could get together. But, like I said, I'd lost a bit of interest and hadn't been in touch. Then, when I knew we were definitely coming here, I messaged her."

"You told her the dates?"

"Uh, yeah, I just said we were coming out on the twelfth. She said she'd been delayed in Milan... some shit about permits for work or something. She asked how long I'd be in Madrid. I said a week. She just said she'd be in touch when she'd sorted her stuff out."

"And was she?"

"No. That first night, when we were in the bar, I'd had a few drinks so I thought I'd give her a buzz. So I did, but the number came up as unobtainable. I just thought, fuck it, no big deal and then forgot about it. What's this all about?"

"I think there's a connection between Arabella and Anita. I don't know for sure but I need to find out."

Jasper frowned but didn't respond.

"You reckon her, Anita and Huguette are all in it together?" Cecil asked.

"Could be. Might just be coincidence, but when Erin followed Anita she went to the theatre area that Arabella mentioned."

"What, she seen her and the actress together?"

"No, she didn't. I'm just saying that she followed Anita to the Teatro Calderón area. When we were at the races, that was the theatre that Arabella mentioned. I couldn't remember it before but when Erin said the name, it clicked."

"Is she there now?" Jasper asked.

"No idea. Erin didn't know about Arabella so not something she checked. She just followed Anita."

"What, into the theatre?"

"No, to the hotel next door. The Cort… Cortezio, or something… but she didn't go inside in case Anita spotted her and got suspicious. Anita must have noticed Erin at the café bar, so she couldn't risk getting too close."

Jasper looked puzzled. "So we don't know if Arabella is there or who Anita went to see. I mean, she could have gone there for any reason at all. A hotel next to a theatre might have other actors staying there. She's an agent so she must have contacts."

"Maybe she still does the day job. She might have gone to the hotel on business," Cecil said. "We don't know, do we?" He looked at me. "You're trying to make things fit, mate, I know that, but we ain't got nothing."

I took in Cecil's statement and then turned to Jasper. "Jas, you got on all right with Arabella, didn't you? So, I need you to do something."

"Yeah, no probs, Matt. What do you need?"

"I'm not sure to be honest. I was thinking, maybe tomorrow you could go to the theatre or the hotel, see if she's there. At the very least check if she's in the cast of whatever's on. If she is, even better if you ran into her. I mean, if you did and got chatting, maybe there'd be some giveaway, anything, just a feel for her thinking. She might let something slip… you know, see if she asks you questions that might reveal something."

"Yeah, no worries. I'll go up there, sniff around a bit."

"Good, but if you do see her make out it's coincidence. Don't be telling her too much about us. If she asks about me, just say I'm staying out of Madrid somewhere. You haven't seen me for a while."

I had just finished the sentence when Erin caught my eye, making her way through the bar, her tight jeans and confident walk attracting glances from men and women alike.

"What you drinking, darlin'?" Cecil asked as she sat down.

"A G and T would be lovely."

Carlos jumped up and ordered the drink. Erin focussed on me. "I've been doing some research."

"Okay, anything new?"

"Absolutely. Wait 'til you hear this. So I did a search on Arabella Leslie and it turns out she certainly does know Anita. In fact she was a director of her agency, 'Eliades Elite.'"

"You're joking."

"I'm not. And there's more. The same year Anita's agency went bust, Arabella was convicted of possession of cocaine with intent to supply. She was fined five thousand pounds with a six month suspended prison sentence. I looked into the case and her defence was based on the fact it was a small amount of the drug for private use and intended for private distribution amongst friends. The court took into account that it was a first offence."

"There you go then. She's in it up to her neck, ain't she?" Cecil said. "She takes a five kay hit, the agency goes tits up and she's only a jobbing actress. Don't earn a lot, so goes back to the old dealing. Gets her mate Anita involved who needs the moolah. She's got loads of showbiz contacts who like a bit of the old Charlie, and there you go."

Carlos came back to the table with Erin's drink. I brought him up to speed with Erin's news.

"You know what this means?" he said, as he sat down. "It means the French woman, Hugs, might have nothing to do with any of this."

"What did I see at Ascot then, mate? What was going on with that minder, when he give her something and she went off to the toilets?"

"I dinnae know, Cecil, but it could've been anything. She could've dropped an earring or something. Who knows, but it disnae mean that she's a dealer."

Cecil ran both hands through his hair. "Okay. So what we got? The actress is trying make ends meet by doing a bit on the side. Her business partnership goes bust and she's hit with the fine too. That makes things more intense. So let's say she ramps up the dealing a bit, gets more into it, makes a few connections and starts to make some money out of it. She gets Anita involved 'cos she's got plenty of contacts and she needs cash too. That way the little mumble they got starts to grow. They get more dealing contacts and then they wanna cut out the middle guys, go straight for the bigger stuff. Stands to reason, people get greedy. But the upside is, you distance yourself from the street stuff, you reduce your risk of getting caught. You get other mugs to do it for'ya. But if you wanna go proper big time, you gotta go higher up the food chain."

"How's that fit?" Jasper asked.

"Easy, mate. Anita and Arabella hear that one of the big suppliers got busted and they wanna piece of that action. Get in on the big time, high volume supply. There's huge moolah in it, but they ain't got no money to front it up."

"Yeah, but how'd they work the Ascot thing?"

Cecil's eyes narrowed. "Think about it. They need an angle to get in. Arabella sees one at Ascot. She sees the whole mumble play out with Matt and the footballer, tumbles the double act. She then gets info that Matt's going to Madrid, she picks up all the social media shit, stuff from Fad's and then comes up with a plan to replace the busted suppliers. Risky one, but they're in the risk business and it's a way in if they can pull it off. She gets Anita on it. Anita's friends with the French bird and probably the footballer's missus too, so she knows Sergio and Lucero, who are on the little celeb dealing mumble already. It works, they pull off a big money deal. It don't, they're just back where they started."

Cecil's analysis made some sense, and now that we knew Arabella had history and was connected to Anita, the picture about who was behind the scheme to set me up seemed clearer. But I had no direct proof and even though I knew that I would get my passport back and could get home, I had a nagging fear that I would need some insurance, something on Anita and Arabella in case things went wrong.

"One thing puzzles me," Carlos said. "You're probably spot on, Ces, but how did they get the bent copper on side?"

Cecil picked up his drink and said, "Ain't difficult, mate. Sergio and Lucero. These geezers might be looking after a high profile footballer but they're villains, ain't they. They're gonna know anyone who ain't on the old straight and narrow and that includes cops."

I drained my drink and said, "Another one? I got a feeling tomorrow's not going to be simple."

49

It was 10.30 the following morning when the burner phone rang. I had just come back from breakfast with Erin and the lads. I sat on the bed and answered the call. Anita.
"*The package you asked for is ready. You'll need to collect it.*"
"Where? When?"
"*At twelve-thirty. Go to Sol Metro station and wait by the statue of King Carlos the third. It's right in the middle of the plaza, on Puerta del Sol. He's on horseback. You can't miss it. Wait there and the package will be delivered.*"
"I'm not coming. I don't trust you lot. I'll send Carlos."
I heard Anita's laugh. "*Seems fitting. Up to you, but you have nothing to worry about. We want this meeting to go ahead.*"
"And where is that meeting?"
"*You'll be told that later.*"
"What's the big secret?"
"*Maybe lack of trust works both ways, Matthew.*"
I ignored the remark. "And what about Armendarez? Is he going to be there with my passport?"
"*Yes. He'll be there.*"
Despite the sudden wave of optimism I felt that this could be over by tonight, I said, "He better be or it's not happening."
"*I told you, he'll be there. Just make sure you get your bit right. No cockups.*"
"I will." I was about to end the call when Anita said something I found quite strange.
"*You know something, Matthew. I quite like you. You're a straight-up sort of guy. I think you mean well in life. I just think you don't take advantage of opportunities. Sometimes you have to grab things when they're in front of you. No doubt you've judged me already, but I'm just a working girl trying to make ends meet.*"

So, yes, I'm involved in something illegal, but I didn't start this. Not my fault if people want to shove stuff up their noses. That's their problem. If I wasn't involved, somebody else would be. It's them that create the demand, not me."

I hesitated for a moment, unsure of how to reply. Anita continued.

"Our paths crossed and maybe in another life, things could've been different."

Suddenly I sensed Anita's vulnerability and for a fleeting moment, I felt sorry for her. Maybe life had put her in the position she was in, and her intention was simply to make money, get out and be happy. But that didn't make what she was doing, and how she'd used me, right.

"Who knows, Anita, but we're in this life and things aren't different. You've set me up, using me for your own ends." There was no response. "I'll send Carlos, like I said."

"Okay. I'll be in touch."

At two o'clock Carlos came back to the hotel with the package. I placed it on the bed and opened it to find an Aircast support boot, a sports compression sleeve, two adjustable crutches and a pair of dark blue tracksuit bottoms. I picked up the boot and examined it. It reminded me of a ski boot but it was much lighter than I expected, a grey semi-rigid shell that covered the leg almost up to the knee. It had two straps along the leg and one across the foot. I took out the instruction leaflet and scanned it. The boot seemed easy enough to fit and it was interchangeable, right or left foot. Next, I took the tracksuit bottoms and held them against my waist. They seemed to be the right size. My mind flashed back to the video clip I'd watched of Ignacio Cañizares walking through Madrid airport. The tracksuit bottoms looked identical, even down to the brand logo.

Carlos pointed to the boot. "You should try it on. Walk round the room, get used to it. You'll be wearing it tonight and you want it to feel natural."

"Good idea." I sat on the bed, looked at the instruction leaflet and picked up the boot. I took off one of my trainers and positioned the boot on the floor. It was only a matter of removing the front panel, opening up the sides and placing my foot inside. Then I had to wrap the internal liner around my leg and foot, seal the Velcro ends, replace the front panel and tighten up the straps. It felt snug but the instructions said that I had to inflate the air cells. This was done by pumping an inflation button located on one side of the boot. It caused the boot to tighten and feel even snugger. I stood up.

"How's that feel?"

"Not too bad," I said as I began to pace the room. The boot felt cumbersome at first, but I knew I had to get used to it.

After a few minutes, Carlos picked up one of the crutches. "Here, try it with these."

I took the crutch and adjusted it so it tucked comfortably under my arm and rested on the ground to give proper support. I did the same with the other one. Again I paced the floor, adjusting to the sensation of walking with my new props.

"I'll be fine, Carlos. People don't walk perfectly in these things anyway so the odd fumble won't matter."

"Aye, I s'pose not. Hadn't you better shave that moustache off too."

"I will, later." I sat down on the bed and began to unstrap the boot. "Let me try those track bottoms."

Carlos threw the track bottoms over to me. I put them on and found they fitted perfectly.

"Try the sleeve too, pal."

I unwrapped the sleeve from its package and held it up. Long and black, it looked more complicated than the boot, with its cross straps and stabilisers. I checked the packaging to see how to fit it and found that it was made of a material called neoprene. I slipped it over my left arm and, with Carlos's help, secured it as directed by the instructions. With the strapping done up it felt secure and snug.

"That'll take care of yer tattoo problem, laddie," Carlos said. "How's it feel?"

"All good. Yep, I think I'll manage."

"Good. I'm off to my room then. A wee kip for an hour."

"No worries. I'm going to shower and shave and wait for the call. I'll give you a shout when I hear something."

The call came a couple of hours later and was short and to the point.

"*Matthew, you'll be picked up at Palacio de Cibelis opposite the fountain, at seven o'clock sharp,*" Anita said. "*You wait there, just you and Carlos, nobody else. A black limo will stop and you have just enough time to get in. Be there.*"

Then the line went dead.

I checked my watch – 4.30 p.m. I had two and a half hours to the rendezvous. I called Erin's room. No reply. I called Carlos's room. He picked up immediately. I asked him to round up Cecil and Jasper and tell them to be in the Lobby Bar in five minutes. I asked him to message Erin and tell her we needed to meet and it was urgent.

I sat in the Lobby Bar and waited, my stomach a churning mass of nerves as the reality of my imminent meeting kicked in.

My thoughts were interrupted by Cecil, who strode towards my table followed by Carlos and Jasper.

"Did you hear from Erin?" I asked Carlos.

"She's on her way. Ten minutes. She went shopping."

Cecil laughed. "Typical, ain't it. Don't matter what shit's happening, women still go shopping."

"Ces, if I know Erin she won't be shopping for the sake of it. She'll be up to something." I leaned forward, hands on the table. "I've heard from Anita. Got a pickup time. We need to make some decisions. Let's wait for Erin to get here." I looked at Jasper. "Any news?"

"Not a lot. I went up there, to the theatre. Arabella's there. Her name's in the cast list. I had to look for it though. She isn't exactly the star. She does two performances a day, afternoon and evening so she's –"

"Matinée," Cecil said.

"What?" Jasper asked, looking surprised at Cecil's interruption.

"Matinée. It's an afternoon performance. Just educating'ya, mate."

Carlos laughed. "I didnae know you spoke French, pal. I thought your only language was cockney."

"Geezer, some of us have a bit about us. I mean, what's that mongrel language you speak? Scotspan or something, ain't it?"

"Guys, cut it out. I'm trying to have a serious discussion here," I said. "Go on, Jas. You were saying."

"I was just gonna say, Arabella *is* working here, like she said. I went in the hotel and asked at reception if she was staying there but they wouldn't say. They said they don't give out information about guests unless they can see ID. I reckon it's 'cos they have actors there and you probably get the odd nutter fan showing up. I didn't want to show any ID, you know, not with what's going on."

"They said, 'information about guests'?" Carlos asked.

"Yeah."

"That sounds like she might be there."

"Not necessarily," I said. "It could be just stating hotel policy. Anyway, good work, Jas. At least we know that Arabella's here in Madrid and, maybe, it was her Anita went to see." I checked my watch. "We need to wait for Erin. Ten minutes, you reckon, Carlos?"

"Aye. It's what the lassie said."

Jasper suggested drinks while we waited. Carlos and I had coffee. Cecil and Jasper, a beer each. A few minutes later, Erin arrived. Cecil was right on the case.

"How'd the shopping go, darlin'? Get me anything?"

Erin's eyes narrowed, her frown dark, showing her irritation. Cecil got the message. Erin pulled out a chair. "What's going on, guys?" She sat down and stared at me. "You look a lot better without that moustache and scruffy stubble. How's the ear?"

"It's fine." I ignored the comment about my appearance and told her about the call from Anita and the rendezvous time and place. I then I asked her a question. "You remember yesterday, you said we needed a backup plan and you'd keep an eye on Armendarez? What've you got in mind?"

Erin crossed her legs and sat back, thoughtful for a moment. "I don't trust any of these people. Armendarez can't be trusted. He's a cop and a feckin' bent one at that. You and Carlos are going out there on your own, no backup. I don't like it. You can't do that. You're only there to get your passport and wallet back. That's it. Anita and her crew have a bigger stake in this meeting. If it goes smoothly, we're all done and you're out. If it doesn't, what's your fallback position?" She didn't wait for an answer. "You haven't got one. We need to be there. We're in this together."

"Yeah, I'm up for that," Cecil said. "That geezer with the ponytail needs a slap."

"I think we need to be a bit more subtle than that, Cecil. Now we know where the pickup point is we can follow the car to the venue."

"And then what?" I asked.

"I don't know yet, but somebody needs to be close to it. Nobody knows me, remember. Armendarez could be key to what you want out of this."

"If he shows up."

"He will. This is the pivotal moment for them. They'll all be there." Erin paused. "I need my laptop. Let's go to my room and we can work something out." She glanced at Cecil. "Leave your beer, Cecil. Looks like you might be driving tonight."

When we reached Erin's room she opened her laptop and logged on to Google Maps. "What was the meeting point?"

"Uh… Palacio de Cibelis," I said.

Erin typed the name into the search bar, clicked on the magnifying glass search icon and the map focussed onto the Fuente de Cibeles area with a red marker indicating the precise location. Next, using the 'orange man' symbol, Erin picked out the Palacio de Cibelis on Street View.

"Okay. So it's on the big roundabout with the fountain. That's handy, it's not far from here." Then she moved the view around so we could scan the location. "The car will be approaching from the left. That means we have to find a spot that gives us a good view of the pickup point but still keeps us out of sight and allows us to follow as soon as it moves off."

She moved the picture around again to take us to different parts of the area. A six lane carriageway, controlled by traffic lights, led to the Palacio de Cibelis from the left. There were no parking places and it looked far too busy to stop and wait without causing a hold up and attracting a lot of attention. To the near side of the carriageway, separated by a treelined expanse of paved walkway, there was a smaller two lane access road. At its end, as it joined the roundabout close to our rendezvous point, there was a bus stop on the right and a taxi rank marked out on the left. A pedestrian crossing in front of the taxi rank led from the walkway to the bus stop.

Erin pointed to the picture, focussing on the taxi rank. "That looks like our best option. It gives us a view of your meeting point and it's on the same side."

"Yeah, but what about the taxis?" Jasper said.

"We'll just have to take our chances. Any bother, I'll just flutter my eyelashes and say we had an oil light come on or something and we won't be there long."

Cecil laughed. "Good thinking', darlin'"

Erin smiled. "Okay, when we're done here, I'm going down there to check it out so I get a feel for it. You're driving, Cecil, so you come too, but not with me. Remember, nobody knows me, so I don't want any association with you if we run into one of their lot.

You stay well behind me and just act like a tourist looking at the view."

"Don't worry about that, darlin'. If I'm behind you I'll definitely be looking at the view."

"Cecil, this is serious. I need you focussed. You need to take in the location, be familiar with it. You can't make a mistake. That looks like a tricky junction. Get in the wrong lane and –"

"Yeah, I know that. I'll be on it."

"Good. Matthew and Carlos will go to the meeting point. Jasper, you come in the car as backup with Cecil. Once we're at whatever venue it is, you two stay close but out of sight, okay."

"Yeah, okay, but what if it kicks off?" Cecil asked.

Erin closed the laptop and stood up. She picked up her handbag and pulled out the gun that she'd taken from Vicente in Cartagena. "I'm ready. And, since you're so interested in shopping, Cecil, I bought something today that might come in useful. Here's the plan."

50

We ordered a taxi. The rendezvous point was no more than five hundred metres from the hotel, but there was no way I fancied struggling with my booted foot and crutches any further than I had to. In any case, I didn't want to draw attention to myself out on the street. I wore a loose-fitting blue and white checked shirt, the left cuff undone to accommodate the sports brace sleeve, a casual style that I thought might look in keeping with track bottoms. I had a white trainer on my non-booted foot. The other trainer, I had given to Jasper to keep in Erin's car.

The taxi dropped us at our meeting point. As I stepped onto the street, I glanced up at the impressive façade of the Palacio de Cibelis, its three white towers dominating the pavement, the middle one, the tallest, housing a clockface that told me it was ten minutes to seven. But my mind wasn't on architecture.

I stood close to the roadside edge, which meant my back was to most of the tourists that were pointing cameras at the building. The last thing I wanted was someone to notice my resemblance, enhanced now by my 'injured' leg, to Ignacio Cañizares.

Carlos paced up and down, clearly as nervous as I was. I checked the clock again. Eight minutes to go. The roundabout was a continual stream of traffic, a busy intersection for the city. I looked to my left, past the traffic lights, at the queue of vehicles spread across six lanes of tarmac, each waiting their turn to join what seemed like a free-for-all dash across the junction.

And then I spotted the red Seat Ibiza easing its way into a parking space behind two white Madrid taxis. Erin's hire car. I saw Jasper emerge from the back and walk forward on the central pavement towards the pedestrian crossing, presumably where he could getter a better view of my location. I felt a moment's relief knowing that my friends had my back.

The pickup car arrived at precisely 7 p.m. I have no idea what type of car it was – I was too nervous to take much notice – just that it was long and black with dark tinted rear windows that discouraged the curious. Lucero emerged from the front passenger side. He glowered at me but said nothing and opened the rear door. A final glance in Jasper's direction told me he'd seen us. I made a show of getting into the back, using my booted foot as an excuse for making it look difficult. It was an encumbrance, but my exaggerated efforts were designed to give Cecil time to pull out from the taxi rank and tail the car. Once I was in the back, Carlos clambered in next to me. I didn't recognise the driver. He didn't acknowledge our presence.

The evening traffic was relatively light once we'd left the roundabout, and roughly ten minutes later we pulled up outside the Intercontinental Hotel. There was no time to take in my surroundings. Lucero opened the rear door, and as Carlos and I emerged we were hustled through the entrance by two tall guys in black suits and dark glasses who seemed to have been waiting for us on the pavement. I struggled up the steps from the foyer, attracting a few glances from people milling around, and followed Lucero. He turned to the right, taking us to the bar area. The bar itself was set to one side of a circular lounge, its ornately patterned floor surrounded by marble columns, that led the eye to the disc shaped ceiling, and the huge chandelier at its centre.

We were directed to a small round table that was positioned some way from the bar, on the perimeter of the lounge. A row of mirrored rectangular columns enclosed a seating area that framed the bar front, to our right. The polished wooden tables were vacant, still too early for most Madrileños.

And then I spotted him. Armendarez.

He was sitting at the bar, his demeanour relaxed with no acknowledgement of my presence. I had mixed feelings. At least he had shown up. I wanted to confront him but I knew I had to be patient. Lucero told us to wait where we were and left us.

I nudged Carlos and nodded in Armendarez's direction. "He turned up then."

"Aye, a good sign, Mateo."

"Hope so. Don't know about you but I could do with a drink." I stretched my leg out to relieve the slight ache the tight boot had caused and tried to comfort myself with the thought that my ordeal would soon be over.

And then my attention focussed on the click of heels on the marble floor. Erin Farrell strode confidently towards the bar, a head turning sight in her short white dress and matching shoes, a small blue bag looped on her shoulder by a gold chain. She didn't look in any direction other than straight ahead, but I sensed she was making an entrance.

And it worked. I caught Armendarez's doubletake as Erin reached the bar. I watched as she engaged the barman. I saw the surreptitious tilt of her head in Armendarez's direction, subtle, just enough to cause her hair to flick slightly away from her face, but in body language terms a massive 'look at me' signal. Even though he was trying to remain cool, I sensed Armendarez had taken the bait.

My observation was interrupted by Anita and Lucero.

Anita was matter of fact, no greeting, just a cold smile as she took in my appearance.

"Ready?" she said.

I stood up, picked up the crutches and cast one more glance towards the bar. Armendarez had made his move and had attempted to engage Erin. I turned to Anita. "I see your bent copper friend showed up. Has he got my stuff and the document?"

"Afterwards. Let's go."

I stayed where I was. "No, we had a deal. I get a signed document that states that there are no charges against me *before* the meeting and my passport and wallet back when we leave the meeting."

Anita frowned. "Matthew, you're delaying things here. You'll get everything afterwards. We need some assurance that you'll play this right."

I glanced at Carlos. He shrugged, unsure of how the stalemate could be resolved. "Look, Anita, like I said before, it's not my problem whether your deal goes through or not. I'll do my bit. I'm here aren't I, dressed like a dick with a stupid boot on my leg and my arm strapped up like... like RoboCop. Do I look like I'm trying to screw this up? I don't trust Armendarez. A bent cop, by definition, is untrustworthy. How do I know if he'll refuse to give me my stuff after this meeting? I don't even know if he's got it with him. I need that document. I can get another passport if I have to."

Anita's irritation was evident. "I told you not to get too cocky with your demands. You'll get what you want after the meeting."

"Okay, if that's your attitude then there's no meeting." I sat back down.

Anita scowled and then glanced to her left looking at nothing particular. Then she fixed her gaze on me and opened her handbag. She took out her mobile and tapped the screen a couple of times. When she had found what she was looking for she turned the phone and held it out towards me. A video clip began to play and in an instant I realised what it was. I felt the blood drain from my face as I saw my own image on the screen, in Kreshnik's hotel room. The clip played through, the camera zooming in to show me snorting the lines of cocaine that Kreshnik had made me take. It was the first time I'd seen it and the full implications of the scene suddenly hit me.

Anita saw my alarmed expression. It was impossible to hide. "Like I said, I wouldn't get too cocky about your demands, if I were you. You want this posted to social media?" She nodded in Carlos's direction. "It'd look good associated with his wine bar." She put the phone back in her bag.

It took me a moment to regain my composure, the realisation that the control had shifted away from me. "How did you get that? I thought Kreshnik's people shot it."

Anita smiled. "They did but Lucero asked for a copy. We needed a bit of insurance in case you got difficult. And do you know who else has a copy?"

I shook my head.

Anita glanced towards the bar. "Our friend, Ricardo Armendarez. If the deal falls through because of something you do, it makes no difference to any of us who gets the fallout from the video… you, your friends or the footballer. Put it this way, it won't do you any favours if the charge is applied. Now, you coming to this meeting or not?"

I stood up and reached for the crutches. Lucero, a grin on his face, beckoned me to follow him. He led us back out towards the lobby and we took the lift. The lift doors shut. I didn't even see which floor we were going to. When the doors opened again, we stepped out and followed a long, carpeted corridor, past a number of heavy, oak doors that had their room numbers displayed on brass plates. Lucero stopped at one of the rooms and knocked on the door.

We were shown into what appeared to be an executive suite by one of the guys who had met us at the front of the hotel. Up close,

I noticed the scar that ran from the corner of his right eye to just below his ear. I tried to dismiss the image. It wasn't helpful to my state of mind.

Carlos went ahead of me. I was so focussed on walking properly with the boot and the crutches, hoping that I wouldn't make a stupid mistake and trip over my own feet, that I didn't take much notice of my surroundings until we reached the centre of the room. It was then I realised we were in a sitting room, a plush sofa and armchairs on one side and an elegant wooden desk on the other. Ahead, I could see onto a balcony area, the curtain drawn back to reveal a table and four chairs. In the centre of the table, a champagne bucket with a bottle tilted against the side. I wondered for a moment if we were to be part of a celebration drink and my anxiety soared to 'burst thermometer' level.

The guy who had opened the door indicated the two armchairs on one side of a coffee table. I sat down, awkwardly, the boot making it difficult to ease into the low seat. I stretched my leg out and propped both crutches against the coffee table. Anita sat down in a chair to my right. The silence only served to fuel my anxiety.

And then Kreshnik appeared in the balcony doorway, a glass of champagne in one hand, the remnants of a cigarette in the other. He pressed the life out of the cigarette in an ashtray and walked down the two steps into the sitting room.

"Señor Cañizares. Good to see you again." He stared for a moment at my boot encased leg. "Sorry to hear of this accident... uh, injury. Most unfortunate. I hope you get fixed soon."

Carlos was faster on the uptake than I was. He leaned towards me and unloaded a stream of Spanish. Then he whispered, "Just say, gracias, Señor."

I shifted in my seat, trying to compose myself to respond. I had forgotten that I wasn't supposed to be an English speaker. I mumbled the words, parrot-like. I saw Carlos flinch. He realised that I shouldn't really open my mouth and dealt with it.

"Señor Kreshnik. Uh... this is a sensitive issue for Señor Cañizares. He has a career, as I said last time. If things got out... uh, like your video and a recording of this meeting, it would be, uh, unbelievably bad for him. So, it's not about trust, you understand. More about caution. So, I will speak for him."

Kreshnik took a sip of his champagne and smiled. "It's no problem. I am pleased Señor Cañizares has come for our meeting, even with this injury. This shows me he is serious for our deal."

Carlos spoke in Spanish again translating, I assumed, what Kreshnik had said. But I'd heard what he'd said and his positive tone gave me a lift, a wave of optimism that made me feel that we were nearly there. I glanced at Anita. Her expression gave nothing away. Made sense. Let Kreshnik make the moves. Don't complicate it.

And then I caught Kreshnik's surreptitious nod towards the guy who had let us into the room. I sensed that he responded by moving closer to me, positioning himself right behind me. I took a deep breath, a reaction to the tension.

Kreshnik took a step forward, his gaze first settling on my booted leg and then a glance at my left arm. I was pleased that I'd worn a long sleeved shirt. The end of the compression brace showed clearly enough through the open shirt cuff. A short sleeved t-shirt would have looked like I was trying too hard to emphasise the injury.

Kreshnik sipped his champagne, stared at the bubbles as they fizzed in the glass and said, "A new earring, I see. No need to worry, Señor. We don't steal earrings."

Carlos began to translate but I wasn't listening. I shifted in my seat, aware of the proximity of the guy behind me, so close that I felt his breath on my neck. And then I realised what was happening and I was pleased that the stud showed right through my ear.

Kreshnik turned away and focussed on Anita. He sipped some more champagne and then placed the glass on the coffee table. He nodded at me and then looked back at Anita.

"Okay. Let us waste no more time. Our deal is good."

"Same terms as we agreed originally?" Anita asked. "Fifty per cent up front and then the final payment two weeks after delivery?"

Kreshnik grinned. "Yes. You make first payment by midday Friday and you get your consignment delivered on Sunday. And remember, I still have my surance."

"Insurance," Anita said. She stepped forward, her hand held out to Kreshnik. "We have a deal."

"Yes. A deal. Now, maybe your business partners would like champagne to celebrate, no?"

The last thing I wanted was champagne. Relief was better than champagne. The deal had been done. I was one step closer to being free of my nightmare. I was happy to hear Anita decline, saying that it was important that they got, "Señor Cañizares home."

51

No one said a word as we descended in the lift. It was almost as if we all thought this isn't over until these doors open and we walk out of here. Anita and Lucero stared straight ahead. Carlos kept his eyes focused on the ground. I watched the display count down the floors, knowing that I had one more thing to attend to before I could relax.

When the doors slid open, Anita and Lucero stepped out first. Carlos and I followed. Anita turned to me, a smile on her face. "Well done, Matthew, and thank you."

I ignored the remark and walked straight past her, my gait still slow due to the boot. I turned left, and with the help of the crutches struggled up the steps from the lobby and headed straight for the bar. Carlos followed. As I walked through the circular lounge, I caught sight of Cecil sitting on the far side, his head down, looking at his mobile. He was trying to look discreet, but his white baseball hat and dark glasses seemed a tad inappropriate in the plush surroundings. I stayed focussed on my target.

Armendarez seemed fully engaged in conversation with Erin and didn't notice me until I was almost upon him. He looked up, his expression one of surprise, but that gave way to a smirk.

I propped the crutches against the bar. "I want my passport and wallet. I've done my bit."

Armendarez turned back to Erin. "Excuse this intrusion." Then he stood up and took a step towards me. As he did so, I became aware of Anita and Lucero approaching. Erin took a step closer too.

Armendarez's smirk turned to a look of contempt. "Amigo, you do not make demands of me. You get nothing until our deal is safe."

"That's not what I arranged with Anita. She told me you'd give me back my passport and wallet and I would get a document clearing me of all your trumped up drug charges once this meeting was over."

Armendarez laughed. "It's not my problem, amigo, what you arrange. Your passport is safe. I have it." Then he spoke to Anita in Spanish and she replied.

I looked at Carlos. "What are they saying?"

"He asked her if the shipment has been sorted out with Kreshnik. She told him what they agreed."

Armendarez interrupted. "Your friend here, he is right. Now I know when our shipment is coming, you get your passport and wallet back when it is delivered, understand? Not before. I have to be sure Gustav keeps his side of our deal. Then no more drug charge."

"Gustav? Who's that?" And then I guessed it might be Kreshnik's first name. "That's not what we arranged," I said to Anita. "I've done what you ask. Tell him."

Anita shrugged. "I tried to tell you he wouldn't agree."

"You mean you lied." As I said it I caught sight of Cecil coming towards us. At the same time I saw Erin open her bag. Her hand movement was quick, but subtle. She leaned forward, her voice low but firm.

"Señor Armendarez, what you're feeling in your back is a gun, a Glock to be precise. It's pointed at the base of your spine. If you don't hand over the passport and wallet, you won't be walking out of here. Do you understand?"

Armendarez's face turned pale, shock and confusion registering together. His mouth dropped open and he went to turn around.

"Don't move," Erin said, sternly.

I sensed a movement behind me. Lucero took a step forward but Cecil anticipated the move. He pulled a dark handled object from his pocket, pressed a switch on the handle and flashed a steel blade at Lucero. "You fucking stay where you are, big boy."

I recognised the knife, Erin's switchblade. Cecil tucked the knife back into his pocket but left the blade open. The last thing we needed was anyone seeing a drawn knife in a hotel bar.

Erin prodded Armendarez. "The passport, now."

"I don't have it here," he said. "It's in my office. You don't think I have it if I don't mean to give it tonight?" He spread his arms. "You look."

Cecil stepped forward and searched through Armendarez's jacket pockets. No passport. He pulled out a mobile phone and Armendarez's wallet. "Nothing, the geezer ain't got it."

"Give me the phone," Erin said. Cecil did as Erin asked. She stood up and prodded the gun against Armendarez. "One of us will be at your office tomorrow to get the passport, the wallet and the document clearing my friend of any drug charges. If you want your phone back, and I know you do because it must have quite a few contacts, some that honest police might be interested in, then you'll do as you're asked.

"You cannot do this. You are very stupid. I can trace my phone. My people will find you and you have big trouble. These are not nice people," Armendarez said, his voice shaking with anger.

"Not so stupid, Señor." Erin beckoned in my direction. "Matthew, come here." I moved towards Erin. "Undo the zip on my dress."

"What?"

"Just do it."

I moved behind Erin and lowered the zip.

"Okay, now put your hand inside on the right. You'll find a small microphone clipped to my bra on one side. Unclip it. The other end is plugged into my mobile phone. The phone's taped on my right side, just above my hip. Just pull the tape off."

I eased my hand inside Erin's dress and found the small microphone clipped to the cup of her bra. Then I pulled off the tape that held the mobile and removed it along with the microphone.

"Show him." I held Erin's mobile and the mic in front of Armendarez. "That, Señor Armendarez, has been recording you since you first spoke to me tonight," Erin said. "Yes, maybe it has got your feeble chat up lines, but it also recorded what you said about your shipment. You try anything to harm any of us and this goes to the press."

And then I remembered the video. "He's got a video on there I need deleted." From the corner of my eye, I saw Anita shuffle uncomfortably. "So has she."

Erin prodded Armendarez in the back with the gun and stared over his shoulder at Anita. "Hand over your phone. Now, or he isn't walking out of here."

"You wouldn't shoot me in a public place," Armendarez said.

Erin laughed. "You want to bet on that, Señor? Up to you but I'll just say it was an accident. You threatened me. The gun went off. They arrest me, but you will give your evidence in a wheelchair. Tell him, Carlos, in case I'm not clear."

Carlos turned to Armendarez. "Ella dijo que usted dará su evidencia en una silla de ruedas, mi amigo."

Armendarez scowled. "I heard what the English bitch say."

"*Irish* bitch, Señor." Erin glanced at Anita. "Your phone."

"I know you from somewhere," Anita said.

Erin smiled. "A little café, perhaps? You might have seen me but you don't know me. Now hand over your phone. Don't make me ask again."

Anita looked at Armendarez. He nodded. She opened her bag and pulled out the mobile. Cecil grabbed it.

"Okay, you'll get these tomorrow when Matthew gets his passport, wallet and a letter dismissing all charges against him. No questions asked. You understand?" Erin said. "Now we're leaving. You don't try to follow us." She leaned towards Armendarez. "You stay where you are, Señor."

"Wait," Cecil said. "He pointed at Lucero. "We'll have his phone too."

Lucero hesitated but a nod from Armendarez focussed him. He pulled out his phone. Cecil grabbed it, handed it to Erin and said, "Okay, let's go."

I turned away from the bar, anxious to get out, and then I saw them. They were walking towards us, their approach urgent and determined, the lead guy's eyes fixed on me.

Cecil spotted them too. "Who's that? They look like fucking trouble."

"Kreshnik's blokes," I said, recognising the two guys who had met the car outside the hotel and who were in the room during the meeting.

The guy with the face scar came towards me, intimidatingly close.

"Señor Cañizares, tu pierna está mejor. ¿Ahora te has hecho daño en la otra?" I couldn't respond. He looked at Carlos. "Dile lo que dije."

Carlos's expression told me that something had gone horribly wrong even before he spoke. "He's saying that your leg is better now but asking if you hurt the other one."

"What?"

"Tienes la bota en el pie equivocado," the guy said, his finger jabbing the air.

Carlos translated. "He said your boot is on the wrong foot."

"The wrong…" I stepped back as one vivid image came crashing in on me. Cañizares walking through Madrid airport, his right leg encased in a support boot. His *right* leg. I looked down at my right foot as if expecting things to be fine and saw the white trainer. Detail. Bloody detail. It was all about detail. A wave of nausea and heat shot through my body as more thoughts piled in. The earring. The cause of my last mistake. The conversation with Erin. *"Don't want any cockups with the wrong ear, do we?"* I glanced in Erin's direction. She stared at me, her expression tense, the gun now visible. Anita's face was white with shock.

And then chaos erupted.

The scar-faced guy lunged towards me, grabbing at my arm. I saw the crutch swing in an arc through the space between us, the top end catching him full in the face, Cecil delivering the blow as if swinging a baseball bat. The guy's nose split in a crunching splatter of blood. Lucero sprung forward, a swinging right hook grazing Cecil's head. As Lucero's momentum threw him off balance, Cecil slammed the padded end of the crutch hard into his stomach, sending him backwards onto the floor in a winded heap.

It was Erin who brought an end to the chaos. "Nobody move," she shouted, the gun raised and aimed at Kreshnik's guys. I saw the shocked barman make a move for his phone. Armendarez saw it too. He flashed his police badge and shook his head.

"Let's get the fuck out of here," Cecil said. "Jas has the car. C'mon, move it."

Outside the hotel we spotted Erin's car, Jasper in the driving seat ready to go. We piled in.

"Mate, move it. We got a fucking problem," Cecil shouted.

Jasper hit the accelerator. "What's happened?"

"Don't ask. Matt's fucked up big time, ain't he. We ain't leaving town just yet."

52

Given the stress of the evening, we were all ready for a drink. At the hotel, we headed straight for Hemingway Bar. I had removed the Aircast boot in the car and felt more comfortable. And then, the inquest began.

"So how'd you make that cockup, geezer?" Cecil said once we had four beers on the table and Erin had ordered a large glass of wine.

"I don't know. I must have... I just don't know. I made a –"

"Mate, you do know your left from your right, don't ya?"

"Look, Ces. I didn't do it deliberately. I've been under a lot of stress... kidnapped, threatened with arrest, held at gunpoint... I just, you know... I got confused. I think I focussed on the arm bandage on the left side and... I can't explain it."

"Hey, Mateo. Chill. Don't worry. Anybody could have made the same mistake," Carlos said. He looked at Cecil. "Give him a break, pal. He's had enough bother."

Cecil sipped his beer and smiled at Erin. "You took a chance waving that gun about."

"No choice, had I? And I knew Armendarez wouldn't want any cops there. He's got too much to lose. And fair play, Cecil, you did give that guy a proper whack in the face."

Cecil laughed. "Yeah, probably broke his nose but glad I got that fucking nob Lucero too."

Jasper looked at me. "Still no passport, Matt."

"Tomorrow, I hope."

Erin said, "I've been thinking. We shouldn't give the phones back."

I stared at her for a moment. She flicked her hair away from her face and put her glass down. "Think about it. The phones probably contain information that could be evidence against Armendarez, and maybe Kreshnik, and along with my recording, that might be enough to get them both closed down."

"How do I get my passport back then?"

"You don't. You go to the Consulate. Get a replacement." Erin saw my frown. "Look, Matthew, after all that's happened, do you trust these people? They've set you up and even after you kept your part of the deal, they didn't keep theirs. I think we should go after them. This is not going to end by you being nice. Don't forget Kreshnik still has that video clip, and now he thinks he's been stitched up, he's going to release it. Bet on it. The only way we're going to end this is by exposing them."

I saw Jasper and Carlos nodding in agreement. I turned to Cecil. "What you thinking?"

He ran both hands through his hair. "Mate, I think Erin's got a point. I can't see it ending well. We know too much about them, and their deal's off now. Trust me. There's no coming back for them with Kreshnik. They tried to blag him. He ain't gonna take that too well. And even if the cop gives back your passport in exchange for his phone, you don't know what the others are gonna do."

"That's right, Matthew," Erin said. "We need to take control of the situation and stay ahead." Erin took the phones from her bag and placed them on the table. "We need to move fast on this. They'll be looking for us and they'll be looking to trace these. We need to get them away from here."

And then one of the phones vibrated on the table. Erin picked it up and looked at the screen.

"D. Who's D?" she said to nobody in particular.

"Dunno. Just answer it," Cecil said. Seeing Erin's hesitation, he added, "It's noisy. Blag it."

Erin picked up the call. "Hi."

I moved closer to Erin, my ear almost against the phone. I could just about make out the male voice on the other end of the call. *"Neets, how did it go?"*

Erin glanced quickly at me and then, modifying her Irish lilt and with one hand close to her mouth to muffle her voice, said, "Who's that? Noisy here. Can't hear you too well."

"It's me. David."

"Oh, sorry, David. Didn't check."

"You celebrating?"

"Kind of."

"Must have gone well then?"

Erin looked flustered, unsure of how to respond. She held the mobile away for a moment to pick up the bar noise. "Sorry, I can't hear."

"I said it sounds like it went well. All sorted?"

I nodded in Erin's direction. Her eyes never left mine as she said, "Yes. All good. Your line's not clear."

"Okay. Don't worry. Look, I haven't got long right now. I'll book an early flight for tomorrow morning. Let's meet at the hotel, one o'clock, and we can finalise things. Tell Lucero."

I nudged Erin. "We need more," I mouthed. She nodded.

"Kreshnik's delivering Sunday."

"Sunday. Good. And payment terms sorted?"

"Yes, all sorted."

"Great. Well done. The first payment's good to go. Catch up tomorrow then."

I nudged Erin again. "The hotel… ask…"

Erin held the mobile out again, picking up the surrounding noise, then said, "Sorry, David, meet where?"

"The hotel. The Intercontinental."

Erin shot me a glance, her eyes wide. "Of course. I meant, where in the hotel?"

"My room. I'll send you the number when I've checked in."

"Uh… okay. I'll… "

I pulled the notepad sheet from my pocket that had my burner phone numbers on and placed it in front of Erin. I pointed to the last one of the three. "Give him that. Make something up."

Erin frowned and mouthed, "Why?"

"If we're going to hide these phones we need another option."

"Sorry, David. Can you message me on another number," Erin said, as she nodded her understanding to me. "Just being careful after tonight's deal." She read out the number I'd indicated.

"Got it. No problem. See you tomorrow."

"Okay. See you then." She killed the call. "Who on earth was that? Who's David?"

The boys looked at me. My mind raced through all the faces that I had come into contact with through my unfortunate encounter with Ignacio Cañizares. And then, almost as instant as the spark that had ignited his tie at Ascot, a face flashed through my brain – David Anderson.

"Shit! I think it's… it's *him*! David is David Anderson."

I was met by a sea of blank expressions. Cecil broke the moment. "Who?"

"David Anderson. I met him at Ascot. He was with Cañizares's girlfriend. He's the sponsor I mentioned… aftershave… cologne. The guy whose suit got ruined after I set fire to his tie. Remember?"

Cecil rolled his eyes. "Fuck's sake, mate. I wouldn't be surprised if he's trying to stitch'ya."

I took a deep breath. "I doubt it. None of that matters. It sounds like he's up to his neck in this scam, and it isn't because I set his clothes on fire."

Erin held up her hand, interrupting Cecil who was about to respond. "Matthew's right. It doesn't matter why he's in it, just that he is. I'll see if I can find anything online about him, but first we need to lose these phones before they're traced."

I swigged my drink. "How do we do that? We need them for evidence."

"If you take out the sim card, that works, doesn't it?" Carlos said.

"No, the phone can still be traced through GPS," Jasper said.

Cecil focussed on Jasper. "You sure, mate? The Old Bill can trace it?"

"Yeah, through satellite masts and the internet, as far as I know."

"Well whatever the case we need to conceal them," Erin said. "We can't have Armendarez locating us."

Jasper reached out and picked up the mobile that Erin had just used. "We know this white one's Anita's. It's a Samsung. The other two are both iPhones. I don't know about Samsung but if you back up an iPhone or connect to the cloud, there'll be data associated with the accounts so that's where a lot of our evidence will be. We need to keep the sim cards. If they're out of the phone they're harder to trace."

"Yeah? How d'you know so much about mobile phones?" Carlos asked.

"I don't know that much. Friend of mine used to sell them. He told me loads of stuff, most of it boring shit."

Carlos didn't reply. He took out his own phone and began examining it.

"The video of me will be stored on the cloud too?" I asked.

"I'm no expert, Matt," Jasper said with a shrug. "It depends when they were last backed up. All I know is if we keep the sim cards then the data can be accessed." He fiddled with the phone. "Look, see that hole? Stick a pin in there and it ejects the sim card."

"We have to keep the sims then," Erin said.

"You can wrap a mobile in tin foil to stop it getting a signal or being located," Carlos said, holding out his phone to show a web page. "Says so here."

Cecil took the phone and looked at the text. Then he read it out. "Based on the Faraday Cage principle, wrapped in tin foil or metal, a mobile phone will not receive the signal."

Erin smiled. "Worth a try."

"We can get tin foil in a supermarket, can't we?" Jasper said.

"Jas, yer nae thinking. We're in a hotel. They have a kitchen. I'll ask," Carlos replied.

"Great," Erin said. "Drink up, Matthew. We'll go to my room and take the sim cards out." She turned to Carlos. "Meet us there as soon as you can." She finished her drink and put the glass down. "We need a plan for tomorrow. Cecil, you and Jasper come up when you've done your drinks."

Ten minutes later Carlos walked into Erin's room waving a roll of tin foil, a broad grin indicating his pleasure at achieving his task.

"Well done, Carlos. Any problems?" I asked.

"Ach, nae bother. I just told them I'd bought some Spanish sausages that I wanted to take home and needed to wrap them."

Within a few minutes Erin had removed the sim cards. Then she triple wrapped each phone in tin foil.

I picked up the sims. "Might as well wrap these too. If nothing else it keeps them safe."

Erin took the sim cards, placed them together and wrapped a small piece of foil around them forming a tiny, tight shell. "I'll look after these," she said, and put both foil packages into a drawer by her bed. "Not that I don't trust you boys, but you do tend to screw up."

I couldn't argue that point.

Erin sat on the bed and picked up her laptop. "I've got some wine in the fridge. Pour us a glass," she said as she opened the laptop.

I found some wine glasses in the cabinet next to the fridge, opened the bottle and poured three large measures. I handed one to Erin and one to Carlos and sat down, my mind focussing on the connections we had uncovered.

Anita and Armendarez were definitely involved, but was Arabella? Having a conviction for drugs doesn't turn you into a major coke dealer, although her association with Anita didn't help her case. Huguette bothered me. She was connected to Anita but didn't seem the type to be involved in criminal activity. Now David Anderson was in the mix. I had been too preoccupied at Ascot with keeping up the deception to take much notice of him. I scanned my mind for 'tells.' He seemed normal, a businessman. Possibly a drinker, but who didn't party a bit at a hospitality venue?

A rap on the door brought me back to the here and now. Cecil and Jasper. Cecil wasted no time in focussing on the wine. "Party started? I'm liking it. Fill us up," he said as he sat down on the sofa.

I poured the last of the bottle for the two lads and caught Erin's wink as she told me to open another bottle.

It was Carlos who expressed the urgency. "Boys, we gottae move fast on this. You just pissed off some big time villains. You getting that? They're nae gonna take this lying down. You any idea what half a million spondoolaes means tae some people? We cannae be drinking wine here and chilling. We gottae look at the facts. And I'll tell you, them guys'll be on yer case right now, so get yer shit sorted, lads." The Scot in Carlos was taking precedence over his Spanish side, a sure sign that the wine and the few drinks he had consumed earlier had kicked in.

I glanced at Cecil. For once he had nothing to say. It was Erin who interrupted the moment.

"There are so many feckin' David Andersons on here. It's a bloody minefield."

"He's in the perfume industry," I said. "Can't be many of them."

"Hang on. There was... yeah, on LinkedIn."

We sat in silence for a moment, each of us staring at Erin as she focussed on her laptop. Then she said, "Got something." She looked up from the screen. "What's wrong with you guys? I'm drinking too." She held out her glass. "Top me up. It's my feckin' wine."

I sensed that the stress of the evening had got to everyone. Carlos leapt up, perhaps his bar owner instinct, and filled Erin's glass from the fresh bottle. She smiled at him and took a sip. "I've got a David Anderson on LinkedIn. UK National Account Executive for… 'Chuchoter Sàrl', some French company that manufactures a range of cosmetics for men. Former football agent, he's got quite a bio."

"Chuchoter rings a bell. Sounds feasible," I said. "Is there a picture?"

Erin swivelled the laptop around so that I could see the screen. In the top right corner there was a small image, a formal headshot.

"That's him!"

"You sure?"

"Yeah, absolutely. I won't forget many faces from that day. That's the bloke I saw with Lorena when I went –"

Cecil was on it. "What, the geezer you set on fire?"

"I didn't set him on fire. I told you. It was an accident."

"Mate, only trying to focus'ya. You sure it's him?"

I stared at the screen again. "Yep, hundred per cent. That's him."

Erin read out the bio. "UK National Account Executive for 'Chuchoter'. Usual corporate bullshit. Let me read it all." She waved us away with a dismissive hand.

Cecil sat back on the sofa, his feet finding the coffee table. I caught Jasper's intense look in my direction and realised that he thought I had answers. I didn't. A silence ensued, the boys covering the moment by trying to look chilled. I sensed the tension.

Erin broke it.

"Interesting stuff. I've checked him out elsewhere too." She turned the screen around again, the display showing a different webpage. "Look at that. He's an ex pro footballer, done by the FA for gambling offences. Suspended for six months and in his second game back breaks his right leg in two places."

I stared at the screen. "He certainly wasn't big time. Let go by Arsenal as a junior, ended up in the lower leagues." I scrolled through the text. "Betting on games he was involved in. Got fined heavily by the FA as well as the ban. Didn't have much luck then if he broke his leg straight after coming back from the ban. Had to have it pinned."

"That's game over then for your football career, ain't it?" Cecil said.

"That's exactly what happened. Yeah, he had to pack up. Finished at twenty-six. Looks like he tried to use his football connections to start an agency a couple of years after he finished... 'Star Link', it says, representing pro players, but it went bust eight years later. Now he's in the perfume industry, started in sales."

"You know what I reckon," Cecil said, sitting forward so he was on the edge of the sofa. "The geezer's got a chip on his shoulder about the football industry. Gets let go by one of the big clubs, bang goes all the big money. He don't make it as a top pro, ends up in the lower leagues on a basic wage; gets caught breaking the gambling rules and then his career ends through injury. Then when he tries to get in on the agent act and make some real money on the back of big time players, that goes tits up too."

"Good point," Jasper said. "But I don't see how that's got anything to do with him getting into drugs."

Cecil held out his hands in an open gesture. "It ain't directly, mate, but what I'm saying, he's had knock backs, ain't he? Had his dreams of making it big in football and every time he gets a way in, it gets blown out. The gambling thing shows he ain't afraid to break the rules, and he was looking to make money back then. The drug game is quick money if you get it right. And I'll tell'ya something else. I reckon he knew the old mumble at Ascot, knew what Cañizares was up to with the girlfriend and getting Matt to cover him."

"How come?" Jasper asked.

"Well, for a start the girlfriend was with him when Matt went to see her." Cecil pointed at me. "That's what you said, yeah?"

I nodded.

"Anderson knew Cañizares had brought her, so it makes sense for Cañizares to put him in the picture. Always good to have backup. Then it's only a short step to seeing an opportunity to set Matt up for their little drug mumble. And Anderson don't care about using Cañizares's name. It's kind of payback time for the football industry that's treated him like shit, ain't it."

My mind flashed back again to my meeting with David Anderson. There was nothing about him that seemed odd or suspicious, but then I remembered something he'd said.

"You could be right, Ces. He might have known something. Maybe Cañizares did tip him off about me." I paused while I tried to recall David Anderson's exact words. "I remember he said, 'I know what's going on with Lorena and the wife. You're stressed.' I don't know if that meant he knew that Cañizares was having an affair, or that he knew about me pretending to be Cañizares because Chiara was there."

Then I remembered his angry reaction when I had referred to a 'cheap suit.' *'It's not a fucking cheap suit. I don't do cheap suits,'* he'd said and his bitter remark about thinking *'only famous footballers dress well.'* "You know what, he did seem bitter about something. He was going to a dinner. I remember that now. He mentioned clients too, important people and deals. Could've been anything, but clients, deals… could've been drugs."

Cecil shrugged. "Yeah, I am right, and that phone call just told us he's involved."

"And another thing, I remember he had a limp… well, not so much a limp, but an odd way of walking. His right leg just seemed to move differently. I noticed it as he was leaving."

"Now we know he broke it," Jasper said.

Erin interrupted the discussion. "Let's see what I recorded in the bar." She took out her mobile and played around with the screen. "I use this voice memo app. Let's hope it's clear." She pressed the screen. There was a few seconds of background noise from the bar, then Armendarez's voice came through. We listened to the whole conversation in silence, right up to the point where Erin asked me to remove the phone. The damning bit was Armendarez's reference to the shipment and 'Gustav' and his conversation in Spanish with Anita about the arrangements. I hoped it was enough.

Erin closed the app and put down her phone. "Look, guys, we don't have time for any more guesswork right now. Let's look at what we know and that is David Anderson, Anita Eliades, Ricardo Armendarez, and possibly Arabella Leslie and Huguette de Villiers, are the main players. We need a plan. Let's get to it."

53

I returned to my room and did two things – remove the earring, which had begun to feel more and more uncomfortable, and change the sim in the burner phone to the number I had allocated for my use. I then made two calls, the first to Louise. I finally revealed the full extent of my predicament and the fact that I was being blackmailed by Ricardo Armendarez from the Spanish National Narcotics Agency. Once she had explained to me how stupid, irresponsible and foolish I was for not telling her sooner, a bollocking I took on the chin, her professional approach took over.

"Gustav Kreshnik's been on the NCA's radar for some time and he's also well known to Europol. He's on their –"

"Known to who?"

"Europol. The law enforcement agency for the European Union. Like Interpol. It deals with criminal intelligence, organised crime, that sort of thing. Look, it doesn't matter right now, Matthew. Just take my word for it. Kreshnik's a big player, but he always seems to stay a few steps away from the heat. We believe he's a significant facilitator for the South American cartels' access to European markets. The problem we have is linking him to suppliers or distributors. He uses the encrypted phone service, EncroChat, which makes it very difficult –"

"Uses what?"

"EncroChat. It's a phone system that uses end-to-end encryption, servers that don't store messages and timers to wipe messages and pictures so they can't be traced. It's popular with organised crime gangs and really hard to hack. We're working on it though, that's all I can say. And, on top of that, there was a bust earlier this year, but no-one's talking. So basically there's a lack of evidence to nail Kreshnik."

I thought about what Louise had just said about the phone system and Anita's eagerness to replace the distributors. "I might have something," I said. "We got hold of mobile phones that belong to three of the people involved. They could contain information that could be useful but if they're using that system then –"

"*You did what? How did you do that?*"

"Don't ask. We –"

"*Matthew, I hope you're not doing anything stupid. You can't be getting involved with this sort of stuff. It's dangerous. You need to leave it to the police.*"

"I can't trust the police, can I? I just told you about the bent cop. Look, there's a meeting tomorrow at the… uh, a hotel in Madrid. Something about finalising things for the weekend. Problem is… this David Anderson bloke might get tipped off before that about what happened tonight."

There was a moment's silence on the other end of the line. Then Louise came back on. "*Okay, leave it with me. The phones could well be useful. Not everyone can afford to use the EncroChat system. It's way too expensive for most. Don't do anything stupid. I'll call you back.*"

The second call was to Lorena Márquez, or at least to her TV station. I didn't expect her to be at work at that time of night. She presented the six o'clock news programme, so I wasn't surprised to be told that she was not there. After several questions about my identity and the purpose of the call, I was asked to leave my number and a message. Lorena could decide whether she would call back.

"Tell her it's about Ignacio Cañizares and the disappearing tattoo."

I was asked to repeat my message and my name and then the call ended. I put the mobile down on the bedside table, unsure if the call had been taken seriously. I'd find out soon enough.

At seven the following morning, I called Jasper's room. His sleepy voice said he wasn't expecting telephone calls.

"*Hello.*"

"Jas. It's me, Matt… "

"*Matt. What's happening? What time is it?*"

"Just gone seven." And then I asked him a pointless question. "You up?"

"*Up? No. The phone woke me. Thought it was the middle of the night. These blackout curtains make –*"

"Sorry, mate. Listen, I need you to come and see Arabella with me."

"*What? Arabella. When?*"

"This morning. Now."

"*Hang on, if we do that she'll tip off the others and –*"

"I don't think she's involved. I don't reckon she knows anything about what's going on."

"*Eh? But I thought she'd been done for drugs and was mixed up with Anita? We worked that out, didn't we?*"

"I know, but I've been awake half the night thinking about it and I don't think she's involved at all."

"*How come?*" Jasper sounded a lot more alert than he had done a few minutes earlier.

"Think about it. Remember when I lost my jacket at the races? Who found it?"

"*Uh... Arabella, didn't she?*"

"Exactly. And there was twenty grand in the pockets. If she was dodgy, she'd have taken the money? She needn't have told me she found the jacket. She could've just taken the cash and said nothing. I wouldn't have known any different."

"*Yeah, but that was part of the scam to set you up.*"

I paced the room. "No. The money made no difference. Even if she was involved, she could have taken the cash and still set up the scam. I thought I'd lost the twenty grand. I was resigned to the fact I'd lost it but trying to look on the bright side because I was still ahead on the day. She knew that."

"*Yeah, but maybe she was doing the trust thing. She gives you the jacket with the money in it, and you got no reason to be suspicious about her.*"

"I didn't anyway. She seemed all right to me. We'd got on okay. And twenty grand's a lot of trust, Jas. She'd taken a big hit with that six grand fine a few years back, and like I said, she could have taken the cash and still been part of the set up. Cake and eat it I think it's called. It's just a hunch, but if I'm right, she might know stuff. She knows Anita for a start."

Jasper was silent for a moment.

"You there, Jas?"

"*Yeah... yeah. Sorry. Just thinking. So what do you want to do?*"

"I need to talk to Arabella today before the shit hits the fan. I'm going to the Hotel Cortezo to see if I can find her. The earlier the better. I'd be happier if you came with me. She liked you, so... you know. You up for that."

"*Course I am. What time?*"

I checked my watch. "Meet me at the lift in forty-five minutes. Should give you time to get showered and dressed."

At eight o'clock, Jasper and I set off for the hotel. We hailed a taxi on the main road and pulled up by the Teatro Calderon ten minutes later. We made our way to the Hotel Cortezo and went straight to the reception desk. I put on the spectacles that Erin had bought.

"We're here to see one of your guests, Arabella Leslie," I said to the receptionist. I'd taken a flyer on Arabella Leslie actually being a guest.

He did a double take. "Err... your name, Señor?"

"Matthew Malarkey." I nodded in Jasper's direction. "And Jasper Kane."

"Is she expecting you, Señor?" The response told us Arabella was there.

"Uh... we're friends of hers," Jasper said. "We were just passing –"

I kicked Jasper's foot. "Uh, yes... sort of. We said we'd meet up when we came to Madrid."

The receptionist looked sceptical. "We are careful about security and our guests here. We don't let anyone in without an appointment. Our guests' privacy is important."

"I told you, Matt. Same the other day," Jasper said. "It's got something to do with a lot of actors staying here and strange people bugging them."

I stared at the receptionist. "I understand that, of course, but this is a matter of some urgency."

The receptionist smiled. "Urgency? But your friend said you were just meeting up?"

I decided on another approach. "Sorry, yes. We met at the races in England and now –"

"Hang on. Do you know Arabella Leslie?" Jasper asked the receptionist.

"Si."

"Okay." Jasper pulled his mobile from his pocket and began to scroll through the screen. "There you go. See. There she is."

The receptionist stared at the mobile, smiled and then picked up the desk phone.

I looked at Jasper. "What is it?"

He turned the phone around. "Remember that? We got the betting woman to take it."

I stared at the picture that showed Jasper, Carlos, Cecil and me with raised champagne glasses, and Arabella standing in the middle, a broad grin on her face.

"Oh yeah. Wendy, the lady that Ces gave the champagne to. Yeah, I remember that."

"I forgot about it until you mentioned the races."

It was fortunate that Jasper's memory had returned. Twenty minutes later, Arabella appeared in reception.

54

We sat in a small cafe bar on the Plaza de Jacinto Benavente, just across the street from the Teatro Calderon. We had coffee and slices of tortilla with toast. By then Arabella had gotten over her initial surprise at seeing us and was all smiles at the start to her day. We talked about Ascot and what we'd been doing since. Her demeanour was open and welcoming and it only helped to reassure me that I was right about her. But I tried to remember that she was an actor. Eventually, I decided that it was time to get serious.

I shoved my coffee cup to one side and leaned towards her. "Arabella, we've got something we need to discuss and you may not like what you hear."

Arabella's smiley expression faltered. And in that fleeting moment I realised she wasn't acting.

"Oh," was her response and then, after composing herself, "This doesn't sound like a social visit after all."

I glanced at Jasper who was staring into his coffee cup. I turned back to Arabella. "I believe you know Anita Eliades."

Arabella's eyes widened. "Yes, Neets. Oh my god. You know Neets? How?"

"Long story. So, how do you know her?"

"She's been my agent for the last seven... eight years. We were in business for a while too. She got me this gig here in Madrid. Why? What's going on?"

"Tell me about her. I mean, personal stuff, not the professional stuff."

Arabella sat back. "Personal stuff? What's this all about, Matthew? I'm not comfortable with this. Neets is my friend."

I took a deep breath. "Arabella, I don't have much time today so I'm going to get straight to the point. Anita... Neets... is involved in a serious drug deal and –"

"What? A drug deal? Neets? Is this some sort of joke?" Arabella's expression showed genuine surprise.

"No, I'm serious, and she's got me involved too. I've been set up... blackmailed. Her people are after me right now." I paused and decided to go for it. "And to be honest, I think you're involved too."

Arabella's eyes tightened, a furrow running across her brow. "Is this about what happened to me with the cocaine bust? Is that it? You trying to stitch me up?"

I tried to intervene but Arabella's anger didn't allow it.

"Anita's my friend. You two are scammers, aren't you? Found out some shit in my past and now you're trying to... " She stood up. "Well, you listen to me. That was four years ago. I've put that behind me. I've moved on. It was a mistake. I was stupid... a stupid mistake. I'm not going to let scammers like you fuck things up for me now. I'm working hard and getting on with life."

It was Jasper that rescued the moment. "Hey, Arabella. We're not scamming anyone. We found out about your coke bust, yeah, but we don't care about that. Look, remember, we all got on at Ascot. We like you. Just sit down. Please. Hear us out. Let's get more coffee." Jasper waved at the guy behind the counter and then pointed at our coffee cups.

Arabella shrugged and sat back down.

I had no time to waste. "David Anderson. You know him?"

Arabella's face showed surprise, not shock. "David Anderson? You mean the sports agent?"

I glanced at Jasper. "Uh, possibly. He's with a French cosmetics company now."

"Yes. That's him. I don't know him personally, but I know of him. I mean, I've never met him. How do you know him?" There was something guarded about Arabella's tone.

"I don't. I met him briefly at Ascot, that was it," I said, trying to dismiss David Anderson's burning tie from my mind. I took a deep breath, anxious to make some sort of breakthrough. "Look, Arabella, think back to the races. You remember I asked you to go and find the footballer that time?"

"Yes. So?"

"If you knew David Anderson why didn't you say back then?"

"I just said I knew of him, not that I knew him. I didn't even know he was at Ascot. I was focussed on that footballer and trying to get to speak to him, like you asked. His two minders tried to stop me. I think he likes a nice pair of boobs because he told both guys to go away. Then your friend... the Scottish one... came over, said something to the footballer and off they went."

I sat back, thinking about what Arabella had just said. I recalled my first glimpse of David Anderson. He was on the balcony with Cañizares and Lorena when I'd wanted to talk to Cañizares about the tattoo problem, but decided it was too risky in full public view. It was shortly afterwards that Arabella had agreed to help, but that didn't mean that Anderson was still there when she'd approached Cañizares.

"Okay, you said you know of him. What do you know?"

Arabella frowned. "You sound like a cop, Matthew. I've been there. Look, I don't know that much. A lot of this was before I even got to know Neets. I only know the bits she's mentioned. She's quite private you know."

Jasper leaned forward, his hands spread in an open gesture. "Listen, Arabella. Anything you know could be helpful. Trust me, Anita's in a lot of trouble. She risks going to jail for a long time. Me and Matt are just trying to find out who's behind this. It might be that if the police get the right guys, then things could turn out better for her."

I shot a look at Jasper. He was gambling. There was no way he could know what Anita's chances were, but I said nothing.

"Okay. Let's get some things straight. Neets is one of the good guys," Arabella said, her eyes filling with tears. "All she wanted was to make a living in a business she loved. You know how she started?"

"Uh.. no, " I said. Arabella's sad eyes had thrown me.

"She was a dancer. She performed everywhere, television, theatre, you name it. But, you know what? She realised that most people in that business don't make it, never get further than being the support act. So at twenty-four she started a dance academy. She created opportunities for young people to express themselves. She always said that even if they didn't make it in show business, it gave them a sense of belonging. It was really successful. Then a couple of her girls were approached by an agent and signed up to a contract with a show that was touring the UK. Neets saw an opportunity to get involved in the bigger scene. No point in losing her best dancers to rivals. So she started the agency. I didn't know her back then but I knew about her academy. I'd met several of her dancers in different shows I was involved in. Some of them I knew from drama school too."

"But what about Anderson?"

Arabella sighed. "I don't know much. Neets was seeing him for a while... romantically, I mean. She started her agency about a year or so after they met. Anita made him a partner. Apparently, he borrowed a lot of money on the back of her business. I don't know how much. She never said. He was greedy, a manipulator. Neets used to say he was angry about life."

"So what happened? They split up?"

"Yes, but look, I didn't even know her until all of that was over. I met her some two years later. I didn't get involved in her personal stuff. I was just an actor. We were friendly, sure, but she kept a professional distance. I only know about this because she told me, about a year or so after we'd met, that she'd split up from her bloke because he owed her money and there were rumours he'd had a fling with a footballer's girlfriend."

"What? An affair? Who?"

"She told me that her boyfriend had been –"

Arabella was interrupted by the waiter as he placed three cups of coffee on the table and cleared away the used cups and plates.

"Gracias," I said, and then focussed on Arabella. "You were saying."

"Sorry, yes. Neets told me that her bloke, David, had been trying to sign some Spanish footballer to his agency. The player's girlfriend was a model that Neets had booked for the occasional promo thing. David thought he might be able to get to the player through her."

I listened while the information filtered through. "Wait a minute. You don't mean... uh, Chiara, do you? Chiara... ?"

"Rustichelli," Jasper said.

"Yes, that's right, but at that time she wasn't global like now. Neets was always dealing with singers, performers, models. I didn't think much of it. I can't even remember if she told me who the footballer was. She probably didn't. We're talking over six years ago."

"But look, Arabella, I don't get this. At Ascot you didn't seem to know who Cañizares was but you recognised his wife."

"Yes, she's famous now but I don't know either of them. And at the races, I thought *you* were the footballer, if you recall. My friends said you were. I didn't want to come across as some doe-eyed groupie like he's probably used to, so I was just being myself. And to be honest, when I spoke to you, I didn't make any association with anything Anita had said six or seven years earlier. I didn't even take much of an interest back then. As far as I was concerned, it was just another showbiz fling she was on about, some star struck agent cheating on his partner. It happens. I was too busy trying to get my career on track. And as I told you before, I'm a rugby fan and not that impressed by footballers, let alone know any."

"I played rugby for a while," Jasper said.

Arabella laughed. "I know. You told me." She pushed her hair away from her face and looked at me. "Let's get this straight. I'd never met David Anderson, nor Chiara or her husband, before Ascot, and even then I never actually met them for real. I was there having a good time, not sticking my nose into stuff. Yes, I spoke to the footballer that one time, and Chiara insulted me when she thought I was chatting you up, if you remember, but that was it. Neets got me and my friends the tickets for the races, but she never told us who else would be on the guest list. I just assumed there might be some of her clients there and a few celebs, so I wasn't too surprised to see a footballer and people like Huguette De Villiers."

At the mention of Hugs's name, I focussed on her connection to Arabella. "You said before that you knew Huguette. Is she connected to David Anderson?"

"I've no idea. And I didn't say I knew her, either. I said I'd worked with her, that's all. I didn't move in her glamourous circles for starters. I was a backing singer for her tour, but that's it. When I realised she was at Ascot I spoke to her, but you know that. It's good to network in my business."

"Wait a second," Jasper said. "If you were in business with Anita and Hugs was a client of hers, how come you didn't know her, other than as a backing singer? I mean, she was pretty high profile."

Arabella shrugged, a wry smile playing on her lips. "You sound like a cop now too! Look, it was Anita's agency. She owned it. Yes, she made me a director. She needed help after the bust up with David and she'd got rid of him. My role, other than being a working performer, was to seek out new talent and audition prospective artists for minor theatre parts. I didn't get involved with the big names. Anita knew Hugs way before I came on board.

And, if you check your facts, you'll see that I was only a Director for two years before the agency folded."

"That's fine," I said. "Nobody's trying to catch you out. We're just trying to piece things together." I reached for my coffee. "So, what did you talk about with Hugs at the races?"

"The usual showbiz stuff and the fact I'd worked on her recordings. She was very gracious. She said she remembered me, but I don't know for sure that she did. She's met lots of support artists in her time."

"Did you mention that you were going to Madrid?"

Arabella paused, a thoughtful look crossing her face. "I think so, but only as part of the tour I was booked on. She seemed interested but didn't ask me any real detail."

"Did you talk about Anita?"

"I said that Neets had made the bookings. I knew she was Huguette's agent still, so it was worth dropping that in so she made the connection... future work and all that."

The more Arabella said, the more I was convinced that she had nothing to do with Anita's drug deal, but I had to ask.

"So, are you involved?"

"With what?"

"The drug deal I've been stitched up for."

Arabella picked up her coffee cup, paused and then said, "I'm a singer and an actor. That's it. I take work where I can. I'm not bigtime. I don't get invited to the big award events but I'm happy with what I do. I make a reasonable living from it now. I get to travel and see exciting places and I've moved on from that mistake. I got sucked into something just because of the lifestyle. There were lots of singers and actors using stuff recreationally. Some even used coke to get through the demands and stress of long hours. I saw an opportunity and made some money from it, that's all. I'm not involved in anything like that now. I learned my lesson. And you know what? Neets knew what had happened but stuck by me when nobody else wanted to touch me after the court case." Arabella drained her coffee and put the cup on the table. "I'm not sure how you think I can help you. If you want to know anything else, I suggest you call Anita yourself."

I felt Jasper's gaze rather than saw him looking. I knew what he was thinking.

"Uh... we can't contact her," I said. "She hasn't got her mobile. We've got it."

"*You've* got it?" Arabella picked up her handbag from the seat next to her and stood up. "Call her on her other one then. I have to go."

"Arabella, wait," I called out as she turned to leave. "Her other one?"

"Yes, she's got two – one personal and one for work. Which one've you got?"

"I don't know."

"You have a problem then, don't you?"

Jasper stood up. "Arabella, listen. I'm sorry you've been dragged into this. We believe you. We don't think you've got anything to do with it. Trouble is your friend has, and it's her that's got the problem. We need to contact her. If we can, there might be a chance to sort this out, and maybe the cops will give her a break. They're interested in the big players, not anyone caught up in it. And you said that Anita's one of the good guys. If she is, then she deserves a chance, and the only chance she has right now is if you get hold of her and get her to meet us."

Arabella's expression softened, her eyes dampening again as she looked at Jasper. "Give me a minute." She walked away and went outside.

"That was some speech," I said as we looked through the window at Arabella standing with her mobile to her ear.

Jasper shrugged. "Yeah, winging it a bit, but if we get Anita to talk we might have a chance of getting anyone who's a threat off the streets. We can't risk them coming after us."

55

Anita agreed to meet at the café on Calle del Arenal, where we had met on two previous occasions, at 10.00 a.m. I was happy with the location as it was open and very public. It was a seven minute walk from the Teatro Calderon. Jasper followed the route on his mobile using Google Maps and we arrived early. We sat down outside, ordered two coffees and waited.

Anita showed up right on time. She was dressed in jeans, a black jacket and a grey cotton top that had a button panel collar and a star print design. The top caught my eye because the bold star shapes made me think of the people she represented and how she had put her legitimate business at risk. She said nothing at first, just pulled out a chair and sat down. Her hair was tied back in a tight ponytail. She pushed her sunglasses onto the top of her head and looked at me for a moment, the blue of her eyes exaggerating the intensity of her stare.

"So, Matthew, what do you want?"

Her question took me by surprise, mostly because it was said with a degree of hostility. I had expected her to come with a more conciliatory attitude after what had happened.

"Uh… would you like coffee?"

Anita smiled and glanced to her right. "I didn't think this was a social meeting. Get to the point."

"Okay. I will. I'm not sure what Arabella told you but thanks for coming. I want to discuss a way out for you, but I'm going to need your cooperation."

Anita laughed. "A way out? For me?" "Don't bullshit me, Matthew. You didn't get me here for my welfare. You're covering your own arse and you know it."

"Hey, Anita. Chill! We're not going to get anywhere if we fight," Jasper said. "We're trying to find the best solution we can here, yeah."

She sat back, her lips a tight line that revealed her tension. A waiter approached the table.

"Have something," I said. "Jasper's right. We're not here to fight."

"Café con leche, por favor," Anita said to the waiter. Then she looked at me. "Okay, so… "

"Look, yes, you're right. I want out of this mess and I want to get home, but you know I've pissed off some serious people who will want payback for last night." I noticed the slight downturn of Anita's mouth, an expression I read as agreement. I carried on. "The only control I have is the phones we took. Once they're analysed, I'm guessing your link to Armendarez will be revealed. So will your association with Gustav Kreshnik. I also have the recording my friend made, and I've already taken steps to make sure I protect my position."

Anita said nothing but her face showed her concern. The cool exterior that I'd seen when she was in control was no longer there. My guess about the phones seemed correct. I continued.

"You know something, Arabella said you're one of the good guys. And you know what I think? I think you've got mixed up in something that's got out of control. You don't go from dance academy, to show business agency, to international drug dealer just like that. It's not a recognised career path," I said, my last remark trying to add some levity.

Anita shifted in her seat. The waiter arrived with her coffee. She nodded in his direction but still said nothing. I tried another approach.

"Why don't you tell us how that happened."

She sipped her coffee, her eyes betraying her distress.

"Look, Anita, we know about David Anderson. We know he's involved. As for Arabella, I don't think she's got anything to do with this, but if we don't have the full picture, then we'll need to name everyone, and with her record that could get messy."

"Arabella has nothing to do with this," Anita said, her expression tense, a flash of anger in her eyes. "She's my friend and her work is legit." She put the coffee cup down, sat back and said, "You've found out about her drug bust, haven't you, and now you're putting two and two together? Well, don't. She's not involved."

"Okay, that's fine, I understand you wanting to protect your friend. I believe you, but you need to explain things. Your only chance of coming out of this as best you can is to cooperate, so I'd start talking now and make it quick. We don't have long."

Anita laughed. "I knew there was a bit of alpha bubbling below the surface, Matthew. What do you want to know?"

"The connections. How you got into this? Who's involved?"

She frowned and beckoned to the waiter. "I need a drink. Join me?"

I checked my watch. It was still early, but if it relaxed the situation, I was game. I recalled our early morning wine indulgence at the last meeting and realised that sometimes a distraction was needed. "Go on then," I said, catching Jasper's nod.

"Tráeme una botella del vino de la casa," Anita said to the waiter. He brought a bottle of white wine and three glasses and a bowl of peanuts. We dispensed with the formalities of tasting and told him to pour it. Anita took a sip, screwed up her face as the liquid caught her palate and let out a deep sigh.

"It's David who started this. He's fucked up basically, bitter about life. Always trying to hit the big time just because his football career failed."

"David Anderson?"

"Yes. I first met him at a charity event. I was impressed by him. I liked his alpha male persona, his ambition. But he had no business sense, always trying to shortcut things, trying to get the main prize without the hard work. His dream was taken away, the money, the cars… the women too, I guess. So he was always chasing it. Footballers seem to get it all very easily and he missed out. When his playing days were done, he thought he could still make money off the back of football through his agency. But the reality is, it's extremely competitive and only a few get the top players. And that still needs hard work.

"When I started my agency, he wanted to merge his business, Star Link, with mine. I wasn't sure as I didn't see any compatibility between what he was doing and my direction. But, stupidly, I made him a partner but with the proviso that he kept the sports side separate." She took another sip of wine, this time the hit seemed more agreeable.

"That's how he met Hugs. He showed a lot of interest in her, but it was mostly because he knew she was still friends with Ignacio Cañizares. Hugs and Cañizares had a thing when he played in France. Did you know that?"

I nodded. I wasn't going to interrupt Anita when she was on a roll.

"David knew Cañizares was going to be a star so he was keen to sign him. Saw him as a future ticket to riches. He also knew that Hugs was friends with Chiara Rustichelli who was seeing Cañizares, so he was always asking to meet her – Chiara was a bigger celeb than Cañizares at that time. Then he borrowed money against my business – a hundred grand. He convinced me it was to invest and expand, get bigger, more high profile clients. Once the money was available, he wanted half as a cash transfer for his business expenses. The rest was invested in renting out trendy offices in London.

"Hugs introduced him to Chiara and he thought he was in. He told me he was on the brink of signing Cañizares and a couple of other big name players. But it was bullshit. He spent loads on wining and dining Chiara in the hope that she'd get Cañizares to sign with Star Link. He even paid for her to go to the Cannes film festival, top hotel, all expenses and lots of other things… gifts, travel. And she rinsed it. Why not? He was playing the big shot. She didn't know any better. He got so focussed on Chiara that people thought they were having an affair. They weren't. Chiara wasn't interested, but Cañizares got wind of all the attention she was getting and put a stop to it. Then Cañizares went and signed for a Spanish club through another agent… can't even remember which club now."

"Madrid," I said.

"No, it was before that," Jasper said. "He only moved to Madrid six years ago."

"That's right. This was nearly ten years ago. Anyway, David was totally pissed off, blamed Cañizares for everything. The reality was Ignacio knew nothing about Star Link. I don't even know if Chiara ever tried to get him to sign with David. She's a very focussed woman, looks out for whatever is good for her career." Anita gulped down a couple of mouthfuls of wine, her face tense as she unloaded her story. Then she lowered the glass and stared into it for a moment before looking up and continuing.

"David and I split up soon after. I didn't believe all the nonsense about an affair, but I couldn't forgive him for wasting my money the way he did. His agency went bust the following year. He only had a few low profile players at the time. He then took a job in sales and eventually he got the job with Chuchoter, the French perfume and cosmetic company. It was Hugs who put a word in for him."

"Why would she do that?"

"After her last hit record, sales dried up. She's always stayed friends with Cañizares, so when he was looking for a new business manager, he asked Huguette to join his team."

"What, Huguette became Cañizares's business manager?" I thought back to Ascot. That was who he was referring to when he said his wife and 'business manager' had surprised him. Not David Anderson.

"Yes, she still toured as a singer from time to time, but she kept a lot of commercial contacts from her modelling days. Cañizares knew she could open doors for sponsorship contracts and commercial deals. It turned out to be a really successful arrangement. It wasn't long before she had sole charge of all his business affairs outside football."

"Yeah, but what about the Anderson thing? Why did she back him?"

"She'd worked a major deal with Chuchoter and Cañizares became the face of Attaque, their bestselling aftershave brand. She thought that if David had a better income he might be able to pay back the money he owed me. The weird thing was, eventually, the company gave David the Attaque account and he ended up with Cañizares as the brand ambassador."

Attaque. I recalled the name from my conversation with Lorena at Ascot and the confusion about cologne. I let it go. "Didn't Cañizares object, given what you said about the issue with Chiara?"

"No. He didn't care. He was married to her by then and the aftershave thing was easy money. He didn't have to do much. Just show up now and then and make an advert or do a photoshoot. David never really liked him after his hopes of signing him fell through. He knew that Cañizares only tolerated him because of the sponsorship."

"Fair enough. So how did David get involved in cocaine dealing?"

Anita smiled. "Through Lucero."

"What, the minder… security guy?"

"Yes, Lucero Garrido. He was a footballer at one time, a teammate of Gustav Kreshnik's son, Gezim, when they played amateur football in Spain. Lucero came to England to play in one of the lower leagues and David signed him to his agency. He played a few seasons but then got banned for a year after he failed two dope tests for recreational substances. He didn't play again after that and ended up in security work. Gezim never made it as a player. He drifted and then started working with his father. He's based in South America now coordinating the supply chain, although he often visits Spain to liaise with syndicate people in the ports."

"That's the connection then to Kreshnik? So Lucero knew of Kreshnik's drug smuggling operation?"

"Of course, but he wasn't involved with it. Lucero did his own thing, small time, dabbled in marijuana and coke. After he failed the dope tests he got more into it. His job in security took him around the showbiz scene so he had readymade customers. Nothing hardcore, just those who liked to party and who used recreationally. He kept in touch with David. Lucero supplied some of David's contacts on the celeb scene and they'd split the cash. It was David who got Lucero the security job with Cañizares. Plus it opened up some higher profile customers for Lucero's sideline."

"What about Huguette? Did she use?"

"Occasionally. Not that often, maybe when out partying, but she's not involved in any of this. She knows nothing about it."

I glanced at Jasper. Maybe Cecil had been right when he said he'd spotted Lucero passing Huguette something before she went off to the toilets at Ascot. "And Arabella? Was he supplying her?"

"No, Arabella never met Lucero. She made a mistake. She thought she could make some extra cash with her friends. It's tough being a jobbing actor. You know what, for all her up front, larger than life attitude, Arabella is pretty naïve. She just covers it well."

"So if Lucero wasn't working with Gezim, how did he get involved in your distribution plan?"

"Gezim had always kept in touch, so Lucero knew that Kreshnik was looking for new distributors after the arrests. He saw a way into the bigtime, but he knew it would need a huge investment of cash to get involved and none of his contacts, including David, had that sort of money."

"So who set this scam up then, with Matthew?" Jasper asked.

Anita frowned and tapped her fingers against her wine glass. "It kind of evolved. David knew about Cañizares's affair with that newswoman... can't remember her name. Cañizares told him what was going on with you at the races, and that he had to play along. Then Lucero found out about your trip to Madrid because Hugs had given him your mate's wine bar cards –"

"What, MacFadden's?" I said, thinking back to the moment I had given the cards to Huguette.

"Yes, maybe. She thought it might be somewhere for him and Sergio to go when they were in London. Lucero checked online and then followed all the Facebook posts and social media stuff. It was then that him and David came up with the plan. They knew you'd managed to pull off the double act thing at Ascot. They checked your pictures in the wine bar posts and became convinced they could use you. The more they found out online, the more credible their plan looked. Spain is one of the key cocaine import centres for mainland Europe so it all seemed to fit."

Jasper took a long swig from his glass. I almost felt his discomfort at the mention of Facebook and social media. I ignored it and focussed on Anita. "How did you get involved then?"

Anita let out a long sigh and glanced to her right. She stayed silent for a moment, her eyes closing as she tried to deal with whatever turmoil had entered her head. Then she turned back to face Jasper and me.

"David persuaded me. He said there was big money to be made and that if they could pull off the deal, he could pay back the rest of my money and he'd give me an additional fifty grand to restart my agency." Anita looked into her glass again, contemplating the contents before continuing. "You have to understand, I was nearly bankrupted. I had to mortgage my house to pay back the money David had taken. I'd not had a mortgage before. My house was my own."

"Why didn't you just sue him?" Jasper said.

"I... I didn't want the aggro and the bad PR, and to be honest, I couldn't see what I could sue him for. We were business partners at that point, and he'd started paying me back once he got his sales position. He paid about fifteen thousand over the next four or five years but I was still eighty-five down. Then my agency went bust a few years ago and I was really struggling. I was up to my neck in debt. So when David came up with the distribution plan I thought, why not? I assumed he was already paying me back with money he was skimming from coke with Lucero, in any case. And look, there aren't many ways to make quick money... sex maybe, but I wasn't going on the streets... or crime."

Jasper shrugged. "I s'pose it makes sense if you're willing to take the risk."

"Massive risk though," I said. "And, you know what, when you first stitched me up with this, you were talking like you were in it big time, doing, what was it? Oh yeah, twenty kilos a month and expanding to the Côte d'Azur. It didn't sound like you wanted cash just to restart your agency."

Anita shrugged. "Look, I had to convince you that you were dealing with serious people. I may have wanted out quick, but David didn't."

I sipped some wine and tried to focus my thoughts. David Anderson was a chancer, prepared to take risks and prepared to risk someone else's money. And then something occurred to me. I leaned towards Anita.

"You told me you were putting up half the money to finance the deal, right? Two hundred and fifty thousand or something wasn't it?"

Anita nodded.

"So what I don't get is how a bloke who's business went tits up and who's borrowed a hundred grand, can come up with a quarter of a million quid to front up a drug deal. How's that work?"

Anita looked furtive. "I don't know. I didn't ask."

"You didn't ask?"

"Not exactly. He said he had a consortium, people putting up the cash. With the numbers he was floating around, it seemed to make sense. Everybody'd get paid back and then it was up to him what he did. I didn't want to know, to be honest. I just wanted to clear my debts and have enough left to get my agency going again. I was pretty desperate."

"Yeah, but you seemed pretty cool about it all."

Anita shrugged. "David said I'd be perfect as the face... the face to deal with you, Matthew. I got sucked in. I thought it'd be easy money, get in, get out, job done. If David wanted to carry on after he made money, that was up to him. I wanted no more than that."

'To deal with you.' The words hit a nerve. David Anderson obviously thought I was some sort of mug. Time to show him that was not the case.

56

The sun had begun to warm the front of the café. The wine had begun to fuzz my thinking. I needed to keep a clear head and focus on our next move. Time was running out and I realised that the small advantage we had gained in taking some control may well be lost if we didn't have a workable plan for the hotel meeting.

The shrill tone of my burner mobile caught my attention.

"Hello."

"*Buenos días. Señor Malarkey?*"

"Uh, yeah… sí."

"Lorena Márquez. You left a message last night." Her tone was matter of fact, teetering on 'this better be good or I hang up.'

I stood up and moved away from the table. "Lorena. Buenos días. Thank you for calling back. We met at Ascot horseraces in England. I was the one who –"

Her tone softened. "*I know who you are. I know your voice. I had to make sure it is you. I get funny calls.*"

"I'm sure you do, but it's definitely me."

"*Ignacio told me about you. He said that you were… un embaucador… in English… uhm… a cheat, trickster.*" I hesitated, unsure of how to respond. Lorena continued. "*But I make up my own mind and I do not forget what it is you say to me. You remember?*"

I tried to collect my thoughts, scanning through what I'd said at Ascot, but my mind was a jumble of blurred discussions from that time, and the chaos that surrounded me in the present. "No, sorry."

"'*You don't have to have what belongs to someone else.' This is what you say to me. And you are right. I realised that Ignacio was not good for me and that he belong to someone, not me. Now I am happy and my life is not so… complicada.*"

I smiled. I had managed to annoy Ignacio Cañizares that day but at least I had made somebody happy. "Good, I'm pleased," was all I could say.

"*Your message was funny. The disappearing tattoo. Can I help with something?*"

I got straight to the point about the video that Kreshnik and Armendarez had. I told Lorena that I'd been set up by criminals wanting to use Cañizares's image to blackmail me into cooperating with them.

"*We received a video file at the newsroom this morning,*" Lorena said. "*Our lawyers are checking it now to see if we can use it.*"

Even though I knew it was likely to happen, I still felt the shock. "You can't! I just told you, it's not him. It's me. Either way, you can't use it."

"*It's a news story, Matthew. That's what we do... news. And it will come out on social media anyway. I think the reason it is not out already is because... uhm, the someone who sent it wants to make sure it is not traced to them, or somebody connected to them, through the IP address.*"

I began to pace up and down the pavement. "If it gets out, Cañizares will sue me."

"*Not if we manage it.*"

"Manage it? How?"

"*You come to the studio, we do an interview and you tell your story.*"

"Interview? I can't do that. I haven't got –"

"*Okay, we can come to you. You do something to camera. It will help you.*"

Help me. I needed help... and soon. "Lorena, call me back in an hour. There's some things I have to sort out first, some things that'll help your story. I'm sure you'll want proof."

"*¡Vale! I will call you later.*"

I cut the call and walked back to the table.

"Who was that? The police?" Anita asked.

"Uh... no, the press. Somebody's sent the video."

"Shit. Who?" Jasper asked.

"Don't know yet, but it has to be Kreshnik." I sat down. The call from Lorena had worried me. With the video already sent to the TV station, I realised that Kreshnik would be expecting the media to act on it. The sooner it was broadcast, the sooner he got his revenge on me, Cañizares and whoever else he felt might get burnt by the fallout. I realised too that he would be impatient. If the media sat on it, he would try other avenues. Exposure was the name of the game.

Anita interrupted my thoughts. "What's the plan then, since you seem to be in control now?"

My mind began to race, churning over the discussions I'd had with Erin and the lads the night before. The only plan we had was to get Anita to cooperate. She was key. I was mindful of Louise's point that the police had next to no evidence against Kreshnik. We had the mobile phones but it was important to pinpoint the leading players. I'd heard enough from Anita to feel sure that she realised things had shifted, that the deal could never happen and that her best option was to distance herself from the whole plot. My biggest concern now was convincing her to turn David Anderson in. I had to gamble.

"David's coming to Madrid today. You know that?"

Anita nodded. "Yes. He said he'd call."

"He did. Last night, on your mobile. He thinks everything's cool. There's a meeting today at the Intercontinental. One o'clock. You need to be there."

"Why?"

"I need to know you're going to cooperate. It's the only option you have now if you want to save your future. You don't cooperate, then I talk to the press and I'll make sure you're implicated."

Anita lifted her glass, drained the contents and held it out across the table. "I need a top up."

I picked up the bottle. "What you really need is to come clean. You going to do that or do we end this conversation here?"

It was a smirk, not a smile, but a resigned expression, one that said, 'game over.' "What do you want me to do?"

"To start, you need to confirm that meeting with Anderson. Reassurance." I poured Anita's wine, pulled the burner phone from my pocket and called Erin. I told her where I was and to come and meet me. I asked her to bring Anita's mobile and sim card and the microphone she'd used to record Armendarez.

When I'd finished, Anita said, "You know David's expecting Lucero at the meeting."

Suddenly, I remembered what I'd overheard in Erin's call from David, '*Tell Lucero.*' "Fuck, no, he can't be there. He knows what happened last night." And then I had another thought. "Is Armendarez likely to have called David?"

Anita played with her ponytail, tightening it, an act of security perhaps, or maybe comfort. "No. Armendarez always went through me. He's got no direct contact with David. He wanted it that way. He's a cop and has to protect that cover. David only speaks to me. He would never call Armendarez unless there was a major failure with the plan. The fewer the connections the better. We set this up to minimise interactions and protect ourselves. Lucero talks to me and I'm the go between for all of them. I make the arrangements, so I guess if mobiles are analysed I'm the one right in the shit."

"But you said that Lucero always kept in touch with David and with Gezim," Jasper said.

"That's right, but once this plan started he was told to keep to the contact rules and, anyway, you've got his phone now, haven't you?"

Anita had a point. We took Lucero's phone but that only bought us some time. "Does Lucero know where the meeting is today?" I asked.

"No, he doesn't even know there is a meeting. I normally contact him and let him know if something's been set up."

"Okay. Good." I thought about the phone connections. Lucero had an association with Gustav Kreshnik through Gezim. Anita was connected to all the main players and that meant that a link could be made between the others. But if they kept the contact limited it would be hard to prove. It was vital that we got Anita to cooperate.

Erin showed up soon after my call. She pulled out a chair, sat down and stared at Anita.

"You!" Anita's face tensed.

"Yes, me. We didn't get properly introduced last night, did we? I'm Erin. I'm friends with these guys, but I'm nowhere near as reasonable as they are. I can't stand eejits and people who can't make a decision. So if you're messing with them, we'll have a major big feckin' problem. Oh, and did I mention that I'm Irish and I can smell bullshit from several miles away? So, in case you didn't get it, straight talking works for me."

Anita looked at me, her expression asking, 'Who the fuck is she?' Then she turned to Erin and said, "I knew I'd seen you somewhere. You were here before, a couple of days ago."

Erin smiled but said nothing.

I tried to ignore the tension between two feisty women. It wasn't helpful. I focussed on Anita. "You need to make that call to David. He's on a plane right now but leave a message and confirm today's meeting. Just say you were a bit drunk last night, or something, and you wanted to catch up. And say that Lucero has been delayed and might not be there."

Anita nodded.

"Oh, and one other thing, tell him to make sure he uses the other number from now on."

"What?"

"We gave him a different number last night so he can text his room details." I turned to Erin. "You got the phone?"

She opened her handbag, took out Anita's foil wrapped phone and placed it on the table. Then she reached back into her bag and pulled out a gun – the Glock. She laid it on the table next to the mobile. She'd made her point.

I nudged her. "Erin, put that away."

Anita had got the message. She stared at the foil package. "What's that?"

"Your mobile."

Anita picked up the package, removed the foil, switched on the phone and stared at the screen. Then she tapped a couple of buttons. With perfect voice modulation, she confirmed the meeting, said that Lucero may not be there and then added something about partying the night before. She ended the call saying that she should be contacted on the other number. When she'd finished, she pushed the mobile across the table towards Erin.

"Good, that's great," I said. "Now, you'll need to make another call. Call Armendarez. Ask him if he's traced the mobiles. Tell him to sit tight, you're on the case. Tell him that nothing happens until you get back to him. Give him some bullshit, stall him. Make it sound like it's under control."

"Okay, but I don't have his number and you took his phone."

"Uh, good point. Call him at the station but keep it brief."

Anita reached out for her phone.

"No, not that one. It was taken last night, remember?" I dipped into my pocket. "I'm going to give you this mobile, and from now on –"

"Hang on a minute, Matt," Jasper said. "What about her other phone?" He looked at Anita and said, "You contacted anyone on your work phone?"

Anita smiled. "No, I haven't. I keep that separate. It's only for the artists I work with and theatre people. Here, have a look at my call list and contacts." She took the mobile from her bag, unlocked it and handed it to Jasper.

Jasper rolled the screen with his index finger, checking the contacts. Then he did the same with the 'recent calls' log. "Only Arabella and a Lorenzo since yesterday. Nothing else. Lorenzo was yesterday morning."

"Who's Lorenzo?" I asked.

"Lorenzo's part of the music arrangement team for the show that Arabella's in. It's business, like I said."

"Okay. Does Anderson have that number?"

"No, I got that phone after the agency went bust. It was my way of trying to start again with the few contacts I still had. I didn't want him anywhere near it."

I looked at Erin. She just shrugged. I knew I had to put some trust in Anita. "Okay." I placed the burner phone on the table. "You use this from now on." I took the envelope that contained the two other sim cards from my pocket and checked the numbers on my piece of paper. I removed the sim card from the burner and put the one that had the number Erin had given to Anderson into it. I checked it for messages. There were none. I gave Anita the phone. "Okay, call Armendarez."

Anita made the call. It took a few minutes to reach Armendarez at the police station. At the start of the call it was clear he was agitated. She kept having to interrupt him and tell him to calm down. Eventually, she was able to tell him that she had a plan and that he had to wait to hear from her. It was also clear he had not been able to trace his mobile.

When she'd finished, I said, "Good. Now, you need to be at that meeting with David today as if nothing happened last night. And I need you to collect information. I need you to record whatever happens."

Anita looked taken aback. "What?" She took a deep breath, and then a shrug of acceptance. "Okay. Tell me how."

"It'll need the 'Voice Memo' app, Matthew," Erin said, reaching out for the burner. "I'll download it. We got wi-fi here." She took the phone and stared at the screen. When she'd done, she handed it to Anita along with the microphone. "Just click on that app, then press the red button and it's in record mode."

"You need to get whatever you can," I said. "If this works out, we'll make sure you get credit for cooperation. I've already spoken to my contact in the National Crime Agency in London. They're in touch with Europol. Things are moving. There's no going back." I caught the concern on Anita's face. "You need to choose sides."

She drained her glass and stood up. "Already have done. I want out of this, no comebacks. I'm taking a huge risk."

57

When Anita had gone, we left the cafe and headed down Calle del Arenal. We found a shop and bought another cheap burner phone. I loaded the sim card that I'd used to call Louise and Lorena. I had four missed calls, one from Louise and three from Lorena. I decided that three missed calls was more urgent than one.

I called Lorena. She was straight to the point. *"Matthew! Where have you been? You need to come here."*

"Sorry? What's going –"

"The video is online. It was posted on Twitter thirty minutes ago. Cañizares's people are already dealing with calls from the press."

"The cocaine video?"

"Yes. How do you say in England? The... the stink has hit the fanny."

"Eh? Oh... you mean the shit has hit the fan?"

"I don't care what has hit what. We need to be in front... ahead of this. When can you come here?"

"I... I thought you said *you* could come to me. I'm not sure I –"

"There is no time to put a location crew together. You need to come to the studio. I will get a pass for you."

Erin tugged at my t-shirt. She beckoned me towards a taxi she'd flagged down.

"Lorena, listen. If you want to get the full story, you need to wait. There's something happening this afternoon in a... " I looked at my watch. 11.15 a.m. "... a couple of hours, that will make things clearer."

"But we have no time. The other stations and the newspapers will be on the story. I know what it is like. We cannot be... behind... late."

331

"Trust me, Lorena. You need to be patient. They'll all be chasing it. If this goes right, I'll give you the proper story, an exclusive. Just manage things right now. Better to get the facts than all that speculation."

"*Yes, but –*"

"Look, the media will just have the bare detail... what looks like Cañizares doing cocaine. They won't be able to do much with it other than report that it's appeared on social media."

"*¡Vale! But we have to be fast.*"

"I know. I'll call you. If things go well, I can be at the studio later."

Lorena sounded concerned. "*Okay, but we have the six o'clock news tonight. I want us to be... in front.*"

I finished the call and jumped in the taxi. Ten minutes later we arrived at our hotel. Carlos and Cecil were already in the bar area ordering coffee.

"Where you bin, geezer?" Cecil asked.

I pulled Cecil to one side and sat down at one of the tables. Carlos pulled up a chair. As succinctly as I could, I outlined my theory about Arabella, told them about the conversations with her and Anita and the contact with Lorena.

"Mate, we gotta be on top of that meeting. That Anita might go fucking rogue on'ya. She's into that David geezer. You can't trust her."

"Ces, she wants out. She ditched him a long while ago. She knows this is her only chance. She either cooperates or she's screwed."

Cecil shrugged and ran a hand through his hair. He beckoned to Jasper who was standing at the bar with Erin. "We need to be there. Keep an eye on things. Me and Jas'll just hang about in the lobby."

"Why?"

"You ain't getting it, mate, are'ya? You're hoping Anita's just gonna go in with your wire and get evidence. But s'pose something goes wrong and she gets tumbled? You don't even know who else's gonna show up, do'ya? I wanna be there to make sure she gets out. That way we get what we're after."

I thought for a second. There were no guarantees. I'd placed my trust in Anita. "How're you going to do that?"

"Mate, the minute she leaves, I'm on her case. I'll get the phone off her soon as she's out."

"You're call, Ces, but we can't have any screw ups."

Cecil laughed and I knew what he was thinking. "There won't be. It's me on the case, ain't it."

Erin came over carrying a tray with five cups of coffee on it. As soon as she sat down, Cecil ran through his plan again. Erin agreed that we needed back up.

I got up from the table. "I've got a call to make," I said and went outside.

Louise answered straight away.

"Sorry, missed your call. What's happening?" I said.

"*It's fine. You okay?*"

"Yeah. Yeah… all good. Well, except the video of me has been sent to the media and it's online."

"*I wouldn't worry about that right now. That can be sorted out. We've been liaising with Europol. They've confirmed with the Spanish police that Ricardo Armendarez is a real police officer, but there's no such thing as the Spanish National Narcotics Agency. It doesn't exist. Illegal drug activity is investigated by the Servicio de Vigilancia Aduanera... the Customs Surveillance Service. So he was bullshitting to stitch you up. And what he told you about not being entitled to a lawyer is not right either.*"

"I should've guessed, I suppose. But why didn't he just say he was with the, uh… Servicio… customs people?"

"*I don't know. Maybe he thought you'd look them up and call to check on him. If he made up an agency you couldn't find, he was probably banking on you thinking they are incredibly secretive or something.*"

"Maybe. So what happens now?"

"*Nothing yet. None of the law enforcement agencies have anything on Armendarez. On the face of it, he's squeaky clean. We need something to connect him to anyone involved in drug trafficking. Can you get the mobiles to the police? We'll get forensics and our Encrochat team on them. They might be encrypted.*"

"No idea if they are."

"*Doesn't matter. We need to see the phones. Then you can name names and –*"

"No, I can't trust the police right now. Look, I've got to go, Louise. I'll call later."

At that moment I realised I needed to bring the police something credible and the only way to stop Armendarez shutting me down was to go public. Lorena was key.

But first I had to have something concrete on David Anderson.

58

I knew that turning up at the hotel was a risk but we had agreed that it was one worth taking. If it was just Anita and David Anderson at the meeting, it was less of a worry but we had no idea who else might be there. And although the bar area had been clear the night before, if the incident had been spotted by a guest there could be repercussions. We had assumed that Armendarez, having flashed his police ID, had satisfied any witnesses that the police had things under control. But we knew it was best to keep a low profile.

My resemblance to Ignacio Cañizares had already got me enough trouble so I decided to revert to my disguise. I left the stubble look and sprinkled talcum powder through my hair as Erin had done before. Next, I put on the spectacles. Through the slightly blurred view that the glasses created, I checked my look in the bathroom mirror. The disguise was good enough.

At 12.25 p.m. we piled into Erin's small Seat Ibiza, Carlos, Jasper and I squeezed up on the back seat, Cecil in the front passenger side with Erin driving. It took around twelve minutes in the daytime traffic to get to the Intercontinental. Erin parked in a street along one side of the hotel.

As we approached the entrance we split into groups – me and Erin, Cecil and Jasper, and Carlos on his own. The thinking wasn't too sophisticated. If none of the key players knew about the meeting then discovery was not a big concern, but we needed to be careful. Cecil and Jasper, with their baseball hats and dark glasses, would look like a couple of friends just chilling, especially as both had pulled out their phones as soon as they sat down on one side of the circular lounge; Carlos, with his deep tan and Latin looks would look like a local having a lunchtime drink; Erin and I were supposed to look like a couple, but with my talcum powdered hair and unfashionable glasses, I felt more like her dad. We positioned ourselves close to the entrance but strategically enough so that we could maintain visual contact with the others.

A waiter brought a coke for me and a glass of water for Erin. I noticed that the two lads each had a small beer. Seated at the bar, Carlos ordered a coffee. I sipped the coke, saying little to Erin, feeling the tension. I knew it should be straightforward. Anita would show up for the meeting. When she left, we'd collect the phone with its recording. Simple enough, but I still had a feeling that things might not be that straightforward.

At five minutes to one, Anita entered the lobby. Her stride was purposeful, her gaze straight ahead. She disappeared from view as she approached the lift. Erin had seen her walk in too and winked at me. I looked across at Cecil and Jasper. Cecil nodded and then looked back at his phone. Carlos's position at the bar meant he couldn't see into the lobby. He would need to react to any signal from one of us. I gulped down some more coke and checked my watch. Just gone one o'clock. I glanced at Erin. She looked calm, unfazed by anything, probably revelling in the moment, her thirst for excitement not new to me.

At twelve minutes past one, a woman entered the lobby, flanked by two tall guys in dark suits. She was pulling a small blue suitcase, the type that fits in overhead aircraft bins. Her hair knotted in a French plait; big dark glasses concealing half her face; her lips a deep, eye-catching red. She wore a light, loose-fitting white coat and red heels. A woman pulling a suitcase as she entered a hotel, even a glamorous woman, might have attracted minimal attention, but the two guys either side of her focused the mind. It took a few seconds to make the association.

"Erin. It's her. I'm sure of it. You need to go. The lift."

"Who?"

"Huguette de Villiers. Quick. Follow her. She doesn't know you. Find out where she goes. Text me."

Erin stood up, grabbed her bag and headed for the lift.

I got up and beckoned to Cecil. In a few strides he was across the floor, Jasper right behind him.

"I think I've just seen Huguette come in," I said.

"What, the French bird, the singer?"

"Yep. Erin's following her, see where she's going. Can't be coincidence she's here."

"Nah, it ain't. Something ain't right. Thought you said the meeting was Anita and that Anderson geezer?"

"Yeah, it was."

"Mate, this is fucked up. We gotta get up there. Erin's on her own."

I held an arm out to stop Cecil heading for the lifts. "Hold it, Ces. Erin's on it. She's not stupid. Let's wait for her message. And Huguette came in with two big guys who look like they mean business. Just cool it a minute."

"Fuck 'em. I ain't worried about no fucking big lumps. They wanna bring it on, let's do it."

"Ces, we don't even know what room they're in or what's up there."

"Geezer, roll the dice, see where it goes," Cecil said as he pushed forward.

Jasper grabbed him. "Chill, Ces. We'll take them if we have to but let's not screw this up. There's a bigger picture here, mate."

Jasper's intervention seemed to calm Cecil. Jasper was strong and muscular and could handle himself, but he had a bit more calmness about him than Cecil did when things got tense.

Cecil shook Jasper off and sat down. "All right, all right. I'm good. Chill."

Carlos appeared just as Cecil began to calm down.

"What's going on? What're you fighting about?"

"We're not fighting, Carlos." I motioned to Jasper. "Tell him, Jas."

Jasper had barely finished when the message came through. *'on floor 5. come up.'*

"Let's go, guys. Keep it cool."

We got out on the fifth floor. Erin came to meet us. She pointed down the hallway towards the heavy oak door that was a feature of the guest rooms. "She went in there."

"What about the two guys?" I asked.

"They went in too. I listened at the door for a while but it's too muffled to make anything out."

I thought for a moment, trying to convince myself that Huguette's appearance might just be a coincidence and we were overreacting. If we'd got it wrong and she was simply a guest, it could cause a scene. If that happened, it could unnerve Anita and she may change her mind and disappear. I couldn't afford that.

"Jas, I need you to go back to the lobby and look out for Anita. We might have the wrong room."

Cecil pointed to the end of the hallway. "What you on about, geezer? She's in there with the French bird, trust me."

"Ces, there's enough of us here. Just in case."

"No worries," Jasper said. "I'll do back up." He turned and went back to the lift.

With Jasper gone, there was a moment's hesitancy. It was Erin who broke it. "We're not standing here all feckin' afternoon are we? They've had long enough. Let's knock and find out what's going on." She opened her bag and pointed to the gun. "We've got back up here too."

Cecil strode forward and rapped on the door.

It seemed like a minute went by and then a response. "¿Quién es?"

I looked at Carlos. "What's that?"

"They're asking who it is."

"Tell them it's maintenance or something."

Carlos leaned towards the door. "Mantenimiento. Problema eléctrico."

There was a pause and then the door opened. Cecil pushed hard against it, sending the surprised looking guy who'd opened it stumbling backwards.

My adrenalin was in supercharged mode and I absorbed every detail in an instant. David Anderson, Huguette de Villiers and Anita stared in surprise at the sudden intrusion. The other guy hadn't even reacted. Maybe an electrical problem didn't galvanise everyone into action. Cecil strode forward. A flicker of recognition played in Huguette's eyes. My heightened state of alert somehow transferred to Erin. She shot me a look and reached for her handbag. She was getting used to handling the Glock. In one deft movement she swivelled it into a threatening position, pointed straight at David Anderson.

"Open the case."

Nobody moved. I wondered why the case was Erin's first thought.

"Open the feckin' case or I'll shoot your feckin' dick off and open it myself."

Anderson reacted, clearly sensitive about his dick. He'd probably had enough setbacks in life and a gun threatening his manhood was one too many. He unzipped the blue case that I'd seen Huguette towing into the hotel. As he flipped it open, I stared for a moment, trying to absorb what I saw before me. It was an instant mass of colour, organised colour, bundles of patterned paper. And as my mind began to focus, I saw the detail. Stacks of money, two hundred euro notes arranged in neatly wrapped piles. And in that instant, I knew it was two hundred and fifty thousand in cash. The upfront payment.

Huguette!

I had no time to dwell on it. Cecil leapt forward and grabbed the case. Just as he did, one of the suited guys lunged towards him. In a swift movement that said he was ready for any aggro, Cecil pulled the knife from his pocket. The movement was one continuous action as the blade slashed across the guy's front, ripping his jacket collar and tearing into his white shirt. I saw the streak of blood paint itself in a trail behind the blade, a flesh wound rather than a stab, but enough to make him recoil.

Cecil, stood up, looking taller than I'd ever seen him. "Any of you fuktards wanna play? Yeah? I'm game. What you got?"

Erin's gun reinforced the message. Nobody moved.

Without taking his eyes off the startled group in front of him, Cecil said, "We need a picture. The case. This lot."

Carlos reacted. He pulled out his mobile and took a couple of shots of the case with Anderson and the others in the background. When he'd finished, Cecil zipped up the case. Casually, he extended the handle, as if he was just checking out of his room. Then he focussed on Anderson. "You're gonna have to explain this. Better be good."

Anderson smirked. "Explain what? You just robbed us. We're doing a legitimate business transaction. I'm calling the police." He pulled out his mobile.

"Who you gonna call, nobhead? Let me guess. Armendarez?"

Anderson went white. That was the only way to explain his face. I thought he was going to faint. Anita had said that he'd never call Armendarez unless there was a major failure with the plan. Too late now.

Cecil stepped forward, the knife poised, his bravado bolstered by the fact that Erin could train the Glock on anyone. "Tell you what, geezer. Why don't you gimme that phone. Looks like a nice one."

Anderson looked at Cecil, glanced at the knife and then at Erin's gun. His face tightened, an expression that said he had nowhere to go. I noticed the tiny downturn of his mouth as he handed the phone to Cecil. Defeat? I hoped so.

Cecil grinned. "If it makes you feel better maybe you can add mugging to your robbery complaint. Yeah?"

There was no response. Erin trained the gun on the room. Cecil put the phone in his pocket. "While we're nicking phones, might as well have 'em all." He nodded towards me. "Get 'em, mate." Erin pointed the gun at the wounded guy. He pulled out his mobile and put it on the table. His companion did the same.

Cecil looked at Huguette. "I don't speak French, darlin', but you know what I'm saying. Hand over your phone."

Huguette's eyes flashed defiance but she knew she had no choice. I took the phone.

"Yours too," Cecil said to Anita

"I don't have one," she said. I knew she had to bluff. She couldn't risk the microphone being seen.

Cecil caught on. "Don't gimme that bollocks. Everybody's got a mobile." Again he nodded towards me. "Search her."

I approached Anita making sure she had her back to Anderson and Huguette. I made a pretence of searching her pockets. As I did, I caught the surreptitious downward movement of her eyes towards her left. I held out the side of her jacket, making sure that it screened what I was doing as I disconnected the mic from the mobile and then took the phone from her inside pocket. I pushed the mic cable back down into the pocket.

"Got it," I said.

Cecil beckoned to Carlos. "Get them others," he said, pointing to the table. Carlos picked up both phones, his eyes fixed on the two minders.

Cecil turned and walked towards the door, dragging the case. I followed him. Erin backed up, the Glock in two hands, her expression intense, not one you could second guess. She waved the gun and zeroed in on the bodyguards. "Take your trousers off."

Carlos caught on. "Quítate los pantalones."

The guys hesitated. Erin took a step forward, aiming the gun at the wounded guy's crotch. He got the message and undid his belt. His partner did the same. Both of them had to remove their shoes as well to get their trousers off.

Erin nodded at Carlos. "Get them."

Carlos scooped up the trousers and the shoes. He wrapped the trousers around the shoes to form a bundle, tucked it under his arm and headed towards the door.

Erin backed up again, the Glock held out in both hands. "Stay where you are. Any of you try to follow, you're feckin' over. If you're feeling brave, try it, but I suggest you don't fuck with the Irish unless you like playing dangerous."

She reached the door. As she backed out, I pulled it shut. We ran for the lift. The display showed floor '1.' We couldn't afford to wait.

"The stairs," Cecil said, pointing down the corridor to the gold balustrade ahead. We legged it to the curved staircase, the four of us reaching it at the same time. With my adrenaline almost at panic level, I tried to take the first two steps in one. I don't suppose the stupid glasses helped. My heel caught the edge of the third step. The loss of balance threw me sideways. I pitched off the wall first and then forward, down six steps of the first flight. Carlos was first on the scene as I lay in a heap clutching my right leg.

"You okay, Mateo?"

"My ankle. I think it's busted."

"You cannae stay here, pal. We gottae get you out."

Cecil handed the case to Erin. "Here, take this, darlin'. We gotta get this geezer outta here. Call Jas."

Between them, Cecil and Carlos got me upright, but I could hardly put any weight on my right foot. Cecil took my right arm and dragged it across his shoulders. Carlos did the same with my left arm, and between them, they managed to bundle me down the winding staircase. Jasper came bounding up the other way and took over from Carlos.

"What happened?" he asked.

"Let's just get him in the car," Cecil said, glancing towards the lift doors as we reached the bottom. There was no sign of activity.

The guys shoved me into the car, this time the front seat. Carlos ran across the road and dumped the rolled up trouser package in a waste bin. Then he jumped in the back of the car. Jasper hit the accelerator. We sped off.

"You need to get that leg looked at, Matthew," Erin said from the back seat.

"I'm okay," I said, although the pain was excruciating and my ankle had begun to swell.

"But you can't walk on it. I've found a hospital. Hospital Universitario… err, Ramón y Cajal… ten minutes away."

"I'll be fine. We need to get this case hidden and I have to –"

"No, the hospital. I got it on Google Maps. Jasper, follow these directions."

59

We arrived at the hospital within twelve minutes. After my details were taken, I was wheeled from the reception area into the X-ray department. One of the nurses spoke excellent English. She said her name was Alethea. She put me at ease. I checked my watch – 2.12 p.m. I had plenty of time before the six o'clock news. I realised I was in the right place. It was best to get my injury looked at.

One of the staff wheeled me back out to a waiting area while the x-ray was processed. I stared at the white tiled floor and white ceiling, my mind buzzing. I was close to ending my nightmare. I needed to get things out in the open. I needed to get home.

I called Lorena.

"Lorena. Matthew Malarkey."

"*Hola, Matthew. Have you information?*"

"Yes, I do. But I need you to guarantee some things before I speak to you."

"*Guarantee? Erm... garantías?*"

"Uh… yeah. First, I want you to book flights for me and my friends to London at your expense."

"*I don't think that is possible.*"

"You pay for interviews, don't you? I don't want payment. All I want is some costs covered."

There was a pause. "*I will have to speak to my colleagues. I will try for you.*"

"Try is no good. I need someone to sort this out."

"*Okay.*"

"Then I want you to cover our hotel costs for the extra stay in Madrid. It's only six nights if you can get us on a flight tomorrow."

There was another pause. "*Okay, this should not be a problem. But you must come to the studio for an interview. I need this to run on the six o'clock news.*"

I gave Lorena the address of our hotel. She said we'd be picked up at four-thirty. I called Louise. I told her what had happened at the Intercontinental. I left out the bit about my injury.

"The Policia Nacional and the Customs Surveillance Service have been alerted by Europol officers, Matthew. The Customs people have some intelligence about drug shipments moving through A Coruña, a port in Galicia in the north-west. You need to hand over any evidence you have as soon as possible."

"I know. I've got eight mobile phones, two recordings, a case full of cash and a photo. That enough for starters?"

"What? How did... where'd you get all this?"

"I'll explain, but right now I need a bit more time. I promise I'll get all this stuff to your guys, but I need you to do something, Louise. I need you to use your contacts to get my passport back, or sort it out with the consulate. I told you Armendarez took it. I have information now that will discredit him and his attempt to stitch me up. They need to start investigating him. If I can get a passport, I can leave Spain tomorrow."

"Okay. There's a team on this right now. Where are you staying?"

I ignored the question. I knew that Louise would want me to lay low, but I'd come too far to let go. I had to finish it, and with Erin and the lads on the case, I felt confident we would succeed.

"I need a few more hours, Louise. I have to clear some things up. Soon as that's done, I'll call you. I'll tell you where your Euro police guys can find me. Trust me... please."

I didn't wait for 'trust' confirmation. I was focussed on clearing my name and negating the video for me and Cañizares.

Alethea returned from the x-ray room just as I finished the call.

"Good news, Matthew. Your ankle, it is not broken. You have torn ligaments and a lot of swelling. You will need a support boot to... err, how you say this... make stable your leg and help with swelling."

"Stabilise."

"Sí. Stabilise. I will take you to have it fitted." She wheeled me to a small room and shut the door. "I have a question for you, Matthew."

"Sure."

"Why do you have this powder in your hair?"

We got back to the Casa de Suecia hotel at 3.50 p.m. On the journey back, I had to deal with the banter about ending up in an Aircast support boot again. It was fortunate that I already had the experience of walking in one and I seemed to adapt very quickly to it and the crutches that the hospital gave me. And then it was time for the serious business.

We went to Erin's room where we opened the blue suitcase. We stared at the neatly organised bundles of two hundred euro notes, each of us aware that it was more money than we were ever likely to handle again.

"It's the coke deposit, ain't it?" Cecil said.

"Yeah, has to be," I said. "But how come Huguette had it? And where'd she get it? Anderson's skint and Anita said Huguette knew nothing about what was going on."

"Let's count it," Cecil said.

I checked my watch. "We don't have time. We're being picked up at half four for the TV thing."

"Not all of it note by note, mate. We can work out what's in there but we need to know if it's the two-fifty kay."

"Aye, we need to find out, but go careful. We don't want everybody's fingerprints all over it," Carlos said. "It's evidence."

Cecil took out one of the bundles and removed the wrap. Then, carefully to minimise handling, he flicked through the notes. There were twenty-five in the bundle. He tapped the numbers into the calculator on his mobile. "That's five grand and they're all the same." He emptied the rest of the case contents on to the bed. There were forty-nine more wrapped bundles.

"That's it, ain't it. Quarter of a million euros. That's the coke upfront payment right there."

"Yep, it certainly is," I said. "We got to make sure this gets to the police... the organised crime guys. And the phones and the picture we took."

"Hey, let's have a listen to what Anita got," Erin said.

She found the burner phone and clicked on the app. It started with general chat between Anderson and Anita. He asks where Lucero is and Anita says that he's running late and may not make it, but she'll update him on the meeting. Then Anderson asks about the arrangements for the handover of the upfront payment to Kreshnik's people. Anita confirms the arrangement for 'tomorrow' but says she's waiting for confirmation of where the handover will take place and the time.

Good bluff, I thought. She seemed to be keeping her nerve.

Then she asks how Anderson has managed to get the cash together. He seems to stall, saying that the cash is on its way and he'll tell her how he raised it after he's checked it's all there. That confirmed for us that the cash in the case was intended for the deal. It was shortly after that exchange that Huguette arrived. Anita seems surprised that Huguette is there. It was either more bluff because she knew she was recording or what she had said about Huguette not being involved was what she believed to be true.

Anderson greets Huguette but then focusses on the money asking if it's all there and if there were any issues. Huguette answers saying that it is and there are no problems, her distinctive French tones reminding me of our Ascot meeting. After that she says very little. Anderson appears to be checking the case contents as there is only background noise until he confirms to the group that the money is fine. He starts to speak directly to Anita, but at that point, a knock can be heard on the door and he stops. There's a moment's silence before the knock is responded to, in Spanish – "¿Quién es?"

The next sound is Carlos's muffled voice coming from outside the door.

"I think there's enough there to interest the cops, don't you?" Erin said.

"Definitely," Jasper replied. "Up to them how they deal with it, I s'pose."

"Okay, we need to get sorted here," I said. "With a bit of luck we'll be rid of all this in a couple of hours."

We put the euro bundles back into the case and closed it. Carlos went downstairs and managed to get a whole roll of tin foil. He covered each phone separately and then wrapped all eight of them up together in one of the bathroom towels. When he'd finished, he said, "I dinnae know about you lot, but I could do with a wee drink."

Erin laughed. "I got wine in the fridge. Hang on."

I decided that I needed to shave and to wash my hair if I was going to be making a TV appearance, but a drink would calm my nerves. Erin poured us a glass each and called a toast to what she declared a 'successful operation.'

There was still a bit to do, but it was good to know that we were close.

60

At 4.30 p.m. a call came through to my room. A car was waiting for us. I was nervous, but I knew that this was my chance to set the record straight and clear my name. Cecil took the blue suitcase and Carlos had the towel full of mobile phones in a carrier bag that Erin had from her shopping trips.

In the car, I made a call to Louise. She didn't pick up. I left a message to say where I was and gave her the TV studio address. I asked her to tell the Policia Nacional and Customs Surveillance Service that I would meet them there at six o'clock.

The car arrived at the studio entrance and, after a check at the gate, we drove through. At the main building we were shown into a plush suite that had long trailing plants on shelves and colourful floral displays on low wooden tables. There were several leather sofas positioned around the room. I chose a chair as it was more comfortable to sit on – and get up again – with my injured ankle. A smiley female member of staff brought coffee.

A few minutes later Lorena entered the room, followed by a guy with a clipboard. Her greeting was expansive.

"Hola, Matthew. Me alegro de verte… good to see you." She embraced me and kissed me on both cheeks. Then she held me at arm's length and gestured to my foot. "But you don't have to pretend to be Ignacio anymore!"

I laughed. "I'm not. An accident. It's… it's nothing."

"Okay." She looked at the clipboard guy. "Es una coincidencia." Then she turned back to me. "But you look so much like him. I was a fool at the races but, you know, these things… they happen for reasons, yes? So I thank you. You give me good advice."

I smiled. "Uh, let me introduce my friends. This is Cecil. He's –"

Lorena held out her hand. "I think I have seen you at the race, Señor."

Cecil grinned, a swagger as he took a step towards Lorena. "Yeah, we met briefly, darlin'. All a bit short. Maybe we... y'know, next time."

I directed Lorena away before Cecil could get into his patter. "Jasper, Carlos and Erin," I said.

Lorena shook hands with each of them, said a few words and then turned back to me, her demeanour more business-like. "Okay, Matthew, we interview to camera and record it. It is not live, so you don't worry. Then we edit and broadcast in the six o'clock news. We will like to use the recording again in a bigger programme when we know more things."

"No problem."

"¡Vale! And now I need you to sign a document." She gestured towards the clipboard man who stepped forward and gave Lorena the clipboard. "This is just your permission to be interviewed and to use the recording."

"That's fine." I signed. "One thing, Lorena. Can you just do an upper body shot?" I pointed to the Air Cast boot. "I'm embarrassed about this. I don't want people to think that I'm still copying Ignacio Cañizares. They'll think I'm a complete weirdo if they see it."

"Weirdo?"

I pointed to my head, twirling my index finger.

Lorena giggled "Ah, lunático... loco! Okay, no problem."

The interview went well. Lorena referred to the internet video which would be shown ahead of the interview. And then I told my story.

I revealed the plan to set up a cocaine distribution network that would continue the supply from South America to Spain and the Balearic Islands, and the plot to replace the former distributors. I explained how the perpetrators had tried to use Ignacio Cañizares's name to guarantee their funding, and that they had used me to facilitate this. I left out the whole of my Ascot encounter with Cañizares. There was no point in bringing it up as it would only reveal his marital infidelity and implicate Lorena. I was not there to destroy him. Instead, I started from Madrid.

It was clear that I resembled Cañizares so it was credible that the bad guys had used that to form their plan. It didn't matter to the public when the plan had begun to take shape, just that it had. I said that I had been set up on a false drug charge and blackmailed into cooperating. I cleared Cañizares's name in relation to the coke snorting video and explained that the perpetrators had threatened to implicate Cañizares by releasing it if I didn't cooperate; I didn't reveal names – information on who was involved would be for a police investigation. I gave a detailed account of my kidnapping and captivity in Cartagena; I revealed that I had recordings and mobile records that would be given to the authorities as evidence.

Lorena's approach was sympathetic. She understood that the interview was difficult for me, and her questions were probing but without pressure. As she said afterwards, the intention was to reveal the facts behind the released video and it was up to the authorities to take the appropriate action.

The interview concluded at 5.25 p.m. When we'd finished, Lorena handed me details of flight arrangements back to London. I only needed to supply travel details, namely passport information. She said that her office had been in touch with my hotel and the TV station would settle the account. I thanked her and told her that the police and customs people were coming to the studio to meet me. She was happy for us to use the room.

At just before six o'clock, two officials, one from the Policia Nacional and one from the Servicio de Vigilancia Aduanera, arrived at the studios. To my delight they brought an Emergency Travel Document to replace my missing passport. They said the fee had been paid – I assumed Louise had sorted it out and supplied the photo – but I wouldn't get my original passport back until a full investigation had begun and there was evidence to make arrests. With Armendarez now aware he was on the police radar, he would probably destroy my passport. It didn't matter to me what document I had as long as I knew I could leave and go home.

I handed over the case of money, the bag with the mobile phones and the recording Erin had made. I got Carlos to send them the pictures he'd taken in the hotel room. And then I named names.

When it came to Anita, I told the officials that she'd helped obtain the recorded information from the meeting with David Anderson, and she was willing to cooperate with any investigation. They said that this would be taken into consideration. Their main objective was to get Gustav Kreshnik, cut off his supply line and arrest anyone connected with drug distribution.

The discussion lasted almost an hour. When it was over, I signed a statement. I was allowed to leave but told that I might be contacted again if further information was required. The officials then took statements from Erin, Cecil, Carlos and Jasper.

Back at the hotel Cecil was in party mood. "Boys and... girl, time for a little celebration."

I fancied a drink and liked the word 'little', but I knew that where Cecil was concerned that description meant nothing. "I know we should celebrate, Ces, but we have a flight to catch tomorrow and I don't want anything going wrong. Been here long enough now."

Cecil glanced at Jasper and Carlos, then back at me and winked at Erin. "Mate, we'll have an easy one, nice and civilised. You ain't gonna wake up feeling like you got an axe through your head."

The following morning I woke up feeling like I had two axes through my head. The partying had gone on until the early hours in Hemingway Bar.

Erin called my room and we arranged to have coffee and croissants. She was due to leave later that morning and drive to Bilbao. We were joined a bit later by Carlos, Jasper and Cecil, each of them looking the worse for wear, but in good spirits. If we hadn't been booked on a two o'clock flight, I guessed I might not have seen the three of them until well after midday.

Before Erin left, I told her how grateful I was for all her help. If she hadn't been there things might have gone very differently. She'd rescued me more than once, especially with her timely intervention in Cartagena. She said she'd keep in touch, and I knew that even if we didn't call one another frequently, our paths would always cross, just as they had several times already.

At eleven o'clock, we checked out of the hotel. The bill had already been taken care of by the TV station, as Lorena had promised. The receptionist called a taxi and we headed for Barajas Airport.

As we left behind the urban sprawl of the city and eased on to the motorway, I had mixed emotions. Regret at leaving the beautiful city of Madrid, but excited about returning home to normality.

61

Madrid airport was busy, but the check-in process went smoothly. It's always a relief to get rid of baggage, get through the security checks and find somewhere to sit and have a drink in the departures area. Cecil and Jasper went to the bar, Carlos wandered off in search of an English paper. I sat down at a table, mainly to rest my leg.

I felt a tap on my shoulder. I turned to find Anita standing next to me.

"Hello, Matthew."

"Anita!"

She smiled and glanced away for a second. "Can I sit down?"

"Uh, yeah... yeah. Sure."

She pulled out the seat opposite. "I'm going back to London. I guess you are too."

"Yeah, I am. Which flight?"

"Stanstead. I took a chance and showed up this morning. I managed to get a seat. You?"

"Gatwick."

"Okay." She shifted her gaze downwards towards my outstretched leg. "Why have you got the boot back on?"

"Uh... I haven't. It's for real... an accident." I didn't want to go through the embarrassing explanation. I changed the subject. "So what happened yesterday? What was Huguette doing there? You told me she knew nothing about what was going on."

Anita sighed. "I wanted to explain. I was going to call you at some point, so I'm glad I've run into you." She looked away again and then brushed her hair from her face. "Look, Matthew, whether you believe me or not I had no idea Hugs was involved. I was shocked to see her yesterday. David never mentioned anything. He didn't –"

"But she was there and had a bag full of cash. Two hundred and fifty grand to be precise. We counted it."

"I know. It was the upfront payment."

"I guessed that. But where'd she get it? Anderson's skint. Is she part of the consortium he told you about?"

"No, she…" Anita's voice faltered. And then she said, "The cash belongs to Ignacio Cañizares."

"What? He's involved? You're joking me!"

"No. Hang on. You're getting ahead of –"

I felt the thud against my booted foot and became aware of Cecil stumbling forward and slopping beer onto the floor. "What the fuck, geezer? Ain't you caused enough bovver with that boot? What you doing sticking it out where people can trip…?" And then he spotted Anita. "Well, look who it ain't?" He put two glasses of beer on the table. "What you doing here?"

"I was just explaining something to Matthew," Anita said.

"I'm all ears meself. You want a drink?"

Anita nodded. "Please. Large white wine."

Jasper placed the two beers he was carrying on the table and said, "I'll get it. My shout."

Cecil sat down. "So what's the mumble?"

"I was telling Matthew about Hugs… the money she had yesterday."

"Yeah, two-fifty kay. Was wondering about that."

"It belongs to Ignacio Cañizares. She borrowed it."

"Borrowed it? What, from Cañizares?" Cecil said.

"No. She…" Anita's expression tensed, her lips tight as if she didn't want to say whatever was on her mind. She leaned back in the chair and looked towards the bar area. Then she put both hands on the table and focussed on me. "You know I told you Hugs was working as Cañizares's business manager for his commercial stuff? Well, he has a company for that side of things and channels income and expenses through it. Hugs is a signatory and has access to two of his company accounts. She moved the money out and took the cash to make the upfront payment for David."

"So she nicked it then," Cecil said. "Not borrowed."

"No. She was going to return it once they started selling the product."

"Oh, that's all right then, ain't it." Cecil lifted his beer glass. "Yeah. 'Cept for one thing. Did Cañizares know about it?"

"Uhm… no, he didn't but –"

"Then she's nicked it. Ain't no way you can take money that ain't yours from someone else's account without them knowing, and then say you borrowed it. Don't matter what way you spin it, she stole it."

Anita looked downcast. She knew Cecil was right but loyalty to a friend was hard to ditch. I assumed that the surprise of finding that Huguette was involved had been hard to take and somehow she wanted to give her the benefit of the doubt.

Cecil brought her back to reality. "Two hundred and fifty large is a lot of money to nick just to help out some fuckwit who wants to be a billy big bollocks drug dealer. What's in it for her?"

Anita sighed. "David said he'd invest in her career. She wanted to start her own record label. He said he'd finance it. The money he stood to make straight away, and long term, would mean he could help her. He told me the same about my agency. He duped us both."

"He's a fucking con artist, darlin'. You're well shot of him."

"Wait a minute," I said. "So if she had access to Cañizares's business accounts, why didn't she take all of the deposit you needed? That way you wouldn't have needed me."

"She couldn't. Cañizares has monthly transfers of any business profits to a Swiss account and has a cap on the amounts kept in the two accounts that Hugs controlled. She had to borrow the amount from both accounts to make up the two hundred and fifty thousand."

"Nicked," Cecil said. "Not borrowed."

Anita wiped her eyes. "She had to leave working capital too. She had no way of knowing how long it would take to recover the amount she borrow… took… and had to make sure the business could trade normally."

Jasper came back with the wine. He noticed a tear on Anita's cheek. "What's going on?"

"Tell you later, Jas," I said. "So where's Anderson now?"

Anita picked up the wine glass and took two long sips. "He was arrested last night at the Intercontinental. I was at the Cortezo. I went to see Arabella. I needed to talk to somebody." Anita took another gulp of her wine and continued. "After you left yesterday, David was in a state. At first he thought you were muggers, opportunists, that followed a woman with a suitcase just because she looked the part… you know, well to do, two big guys escorting her. He didn't even focus on you, Matthew. He just didn't connect what he thought was a robbery with the cocaine plan. Hugs was in shock. She couldn't speak. Two hundred and fifty grand... gone." Anita, looked at Cecil. "It was only when David focussed on what you'd said about Armendarez that he started to realise the seriousness of the situation. Hugs thought she recognised you and... and your other friend... "

"Carlos," I said.

"Yes. David knew then the game was up. I played along. I said nothing about what happened with Kreshnik or Armendarez the previous night. I didn't want him to get suspicious of me. I knew you had the recording I made. I know it'll all come out in the end that I set him up, but I couldn't handle it right there in front of him... and Hugs. I was shocked in any case about Hugs. David thought about going back to London, but he couldn't get a flight. Then he saw the six o'clock news with your interview and he knew there was no point in running. You had his phone, all his contacts.

"Anyway, turns out the police came to his hotel at around seven-thirty last night. I don't suppose they expected to find him so easily, but after seeing the interview he assumed you'd spoken to the police and would have told them where he was. They could have traced him through his flight and hotel booking in any case. He rang me on that phone you gave me and told me he'd been arrested. The police were questioning him. They were going after Lucero too. I told David where I was and he said I'd have to talk to the police. They came for me about eight... eight-fifteen... last night, and I was taken to the station and interviewed. I was there a couple of hours. They released me because I said I was under threat from Kreshnik's people if I stayed in the country, but I have to report to the UK police on my return. I said I was willing to cooperate, and they also had the information from you about how I'd helped."

Carlos came back to the table. He was surprised to see Anita there. I told him that we'd fill him in.

"Makes sense to play ball with the cops," Cecil said. "Bottom line, they're after the big boys. And if you look at it, you ain't done that much wrong. Yeah, you got involved in a plan to move drugs, but you ain't done that yet. Would've bin worse had you bin handling the shipment already." Cecil stroked his stubbled chin. "I s'pose they could get you on conspiring to nick Cañizares's money."

"I knew nothing about that," Anita said, the intensity in her eyes emphasising her point.

"Yeah, I know. I'm just looking at what they might wanna do'ya for."

"What about kidnap?" Carlos said. "Yer gang abducted Mateo here and took him away against his will. The polis cannae ignore that."

Anita looked at me.

"I won't pursue the kidnapping thing, Anita, if you cooperate. I get that you kind of fell into this for your own reasons. You do what you said you'd do… make sure they get that bent bastard cop, Armendarez, and we're square. Once he starts blabbing, trying to save his own skin, it won't be long until they get to Kreshnik and his outfit."

"What about Hugs?" Anita asked. "I think she just got caught up too. She's not a bad person."

"Nothing to do with me. Not much I can say. She took the money from Cañizares. Whatever way you look at it and whatever her thinking, it's still theft, and there's also the trust thing with Cañizares. I suppose it'll be up to him what he does."

Anita brushed her hair from her face. "I know. It's a mess. I'm sorry. I shouldn't have… look, thank you, you've tried to help me when you didn't need to. I appreciate it. I'll cooperate, don't worry. I just… just want to go back to what I do."

I nodded. "Yep. Better to be tied to a mortgage than a prison sentence."

She glanced up at a flight information monitor. "I have to go. They're calling my flight."

"Hey, one thing. Banging flake? Remember, when you were telling me about your product that time? That doesn't sound like something you'd come out with?"

Anita laughed. "No. That was something Lucero picked up from some English guy he was selling to. I thought it would make me sound more, you know… into it." She stood up, looked away for a moment and then said, "I like you, Matthew. You're a decent guy." She glanced around the bar again, then looked back at me. "You know, when a lady does something to you or says something, it's more to do with how she would like you to react than anything negative. Take care." She smiled and left.

With Anita walking away, the four of us sat looking at one another for a moment, mystified by her last comment. It was Cecil who broke the silence.

"Women, mate. No bloke knows what the fuck they're thinking half the time."

We raised our glasses in a toast. It seemed like a good idea to leave it there.

62

I had been back at work almost a week, my head down, working flat out to convince the boss that my additional five days absence hadn't just been an extended 'jolly', when a call came through to my office desk.

"*Señor Matthew?*"

I was taken aback at being addressed with the formal Spanish title. "Uh, yes. Speaking."

"*Hola. It is difficult to find you, Señor Matthew. My people have big trouble to find you.*"

"It's just Matthew. Who is this?" Even as I asked, the voice sounded familiar.

"*It is your friend, Ignacio. Ignacio Cañizares.*"

I was shocked, and not only by the 'friend' reference. "Oh... err, how's your leg?" was all I could think to say.

He laughed. "*Still bad, amigo. No play for me but, you know, this is life.*"

"I suppose so." The small talk had helped me regain some composure. "I wasn't expecting to hear from you."

"*Hear?*"

"Uh, yeah... your telephone call, I mean."

"*Sí. I understand. I want to say, muchas gracias. You help to get my money. Lorena telephone to me and she say what has happened to you in Madrid. I see the television so I understand too. I... uh... lamento que esto haya sucedido... how you say?*"

"Sorry? I don't under –"

"*Ah, sí. Sorry this happen to you. You have big trouble in Madrid, no?*"

"I did, yes." I had a sudden feeling of regret. "Look, Ignacio, I'm sorry too for what happened at the races... at Ascot. It got out of hand."

"*What is this out of hands?*"

"Erm, out of control."

"*Sí, I know. Fuera de control, sí. But this my problema too, you know. I should no ask you to be me. It is bad thing. It make big, big problema with Chiara, but now is okay. I tell her that Lorena with you at races, no me, and it a television like looker promotion. But it make me think. So, Lorena and me, we finish, but now amigos. You are right, Matthew. It no good to have too many women. Chiara, she a good woman. She always with me when problema. She my friend too. She help me. Ella es mi apoyo... my support. Mi refugio. How is it they say en inglés? Like a stone?*"

"Your rock?"

"*Sí. This is it. And I no lose her. I make sense now and this is because you make me see. If you have good woman, you must keep.*"

I hesitated as I considered the advice of an arch philanderer. But he sounded sincere. I was glad he'd seen sense.

"*Okay, so more, I say gracias. You save my wife, you save my money. And, you know, my two security, Lucero and Sergio, I do not know about this drug thing. Now I throw them.*"

"You mean, sack them... err, get rid... fire them?"

"*Sí. I think this is it. They no good... pandilleros!*"

"Sorry, I don't –"

"*You know. In the gangs, criminal.*"

"Oh... yes, like gangsters."

"*Eso es correcto. And you help me with this too.*"

The reference to money brought Huguette to mind. "What will happen to Huguette, Ignacio?"

"*Hugs, she make big mistake, but she is my friend and I understand why she did this. I no take her to police, but now she no can be my business person.*" And then there was a burst of anger in Cañizares's tone. "*This David Anderson, he is a bad man... un criminal. He must go to prison.*" There was a pause, presumably while he tried to regain his earlier calm. "*But we no speak of this now, Matthew. I call you because I want to make gift to you. I make ten thousand euros to your banco, is okay?*"

Ten thousand euros. The words rattled around in my head. A gift. No catch. He hadn't said there was a catch. And then, for some reason, natural British politeness kicked in.

"Uh... no, it's okay. I can't take your... " 'Money' was the next word but I hesitated. Why couldn't I take it? He was offering. I'd been through quite an ordeal.

"You no want the money? Why not? It is no much. I do not worry about ten thousand euros. You bring back my two hundred and fifty thousand. I am paid good for my football and my business. Recompensa. I like to give you."

He had a point. Small change, pocket money to a superstar footballer. It had cost me enough in Madrid already. I'd paid Carlos back for the hotel and expenses in Cartagena; Armendarez had taken a thousand euros off me with my passport and wallet, money I was unlikely to see again. Luckily, the TV station had covered the additional hotel costs, but a gift of ten grand would still be welcome. "That's very kind of you, Ignacio. Thank you. Gracias. I accept your generous offer."

"¡Vale! This is good. I give you email for my assistant and you send banco numbers, sí?"

"Sí. Okay." I wrote down the email address and thanked him again."

"Adios, Señor Matthew. Buena suerte. You have good luck, amigo."

I finished the call and sat back. Ten thousand euros was quite a bonus. Just as I was absorbing the information another call came through.

"Matthew Malarkey?"

"Yes, speaking."

"Rob Black."

Rob Black. My mind did a quick search and then settled. "Rob Black? The reporter?"

"Yep, that's me. The Post. You're a difficult man to track down."

"So I've been told. What can I do for you, Mister Black?"

"Rob. Call me Rob. It's about this drug bust and Ignacio Cañizares. How do you fancy telling your story to the Post?"

I was taken aback for a moment but I'd done the Spanish television thing so why not. In for a penny, in for a pound. "Did you say 'telling' or 'selling' Mister... uh, Rob?"

"Telling. I said telling."

"Okay, but I thought national newspapers pay people for stories, especially if they're given exclusivity."

"*Well, yeah, sometimes, but you kind of owe me a favour after selling me a pup with them stories about Cañizares going to United and then to Cologne. Remember? Ascot?*"

I knew I didn't owe Rob Black any favours. And then I remembered something that Cecil had said at the races when he was trying to get me to relax and blend into the environment. '*Plug yourself into their DNA.*' Rob Black was in the cutthroat world of journalism. Every man for himself. That was his DNA. He wanted a story or he wouldn't have called.

"Look, Rob, it's payment or no story. You don't want to do a deal, there'll be plenty others who will." I was chancing it. No one else had approached me, but after Cañizares's call, I was on a high. Nothing to lose.

There was silence on the line. Then a question. "*Okay, what we looking at?*"

Something else that Cecil had said clicked in. '*Roll the dice, see where it goes.*' I took a deep breath. "Fifty grand."

"*What? You're having a laugh,*" Rob Black replied, his voice almost scornful.

"I'm not, Rob. You'll sell a lot of newspapers. Take it or leave it. Makes no odds to me."

"*Tell you what, how about we call it twenty and you got a deal.*"

I was shocked. I thought he'd leave it. One more roll of the dice then. "Rob, you know what? I'll factor in that favour you reckon I owe you, and we'll split the difference. Thirty-five."

His response was instant. "*Done. I'll draw up a contract and email it. I need it signed off today. We'll serialise this over three days.*"

I gave him my email details and then said, "One other condition, Rob."

"*What's that?*"

"You don't make up any nonsense about Cañizares. He had nothing to do with this." I'd decided the Ascot fiasco wouldn't be part of what I told the paper. What happened in Spain was all they would get.

When the call ended, I sat back in my chair and tried to let the afternoon's turn of events sink in. With Cañizares's gift, almost forty-five thousand pounds had, unexpectedly, landed in my lap. And I still had the expensive designer outfit that Anita had bought in Madrid to give me some football star credibility. And then I thought of someone who had helped me when things looked grim, when I was desperate, alone and scared. A man who gave me twenty euros to 'set me free.'

I clicked on Google and typed in 'Mugga Transport, Mazarrón.' A single page website appeared. The number I wanted was clearly displayed, and so was the owner's name – Muggabusca.

Mugga was surprised to hear from me but seemed happy that I was okay and had made it back to England. I told him I wanted to send him something as a special thank you for his help. In much the same way that I'd initially declined Cañizares's offer, Muggabusca shrugged it off, saying that it would be a bad thing if one man could not help another in times of trouble.

I tried a different approach. I said that I wanted to contribute something to keep his van on the road. After all, if his van hadn't appeared that day, battered as it was, things might have turned out very differently for me. And it was about keeping his business going too. He was happier with that and gave me his bank details. I didn't say how much I was going to send, but I knew that five thousand euros would go some way to helping out.

I put the phone down and went to see Jasper in the sales office. A celebration was in order. I didn't say why. I just asked him to message Cecil and get him to meet us at MacFadden's Bar. We left work right on five and headed for Fad's.

Cecil was already there. "Gotta get ahead of the after work lot," he said, as we walked in.

I couldn't wait to tell the lads about my calls from Ignacio Cañizares and Rob Black. When I'd finished, Carlos sprang into action. "I cannae think of a better reason to have a wee glass of the bubbly stuff, boys. And it's on the house."

"Forget your 'wee' glass, geezer," Cecil replied. "You need to get a few bottles out that fridge, at least. Let's do this thing proper."

"Alright, pal. Keep yer hair on," Carlos shot back. He placed four champagne flutes on the bar, cracked a bottle and poured. "Cheers, boys."

Cecil grinned and slapped me heartily on the back. "Shows'ya, mate, don't it? Gambling pays off. You go racing, win a shed load of moolah, then get a nice little bonus on top."

I didn't quite see it the way Cecil did. I would've gladly exchanged my experience in Madrid for a quieter life.

He raised his glass, slurped a mouthful of champagne and said. "When's the next one, mate? You're wedged up again, ain't ya?"

I stared at him. "The next one?"

"Yeah, the next road trip?"

"Yeah, Matt. Gotta be done," Jasper said, his eyes bright with enthusiasm.

I smiled at my friends. Much as I enjoyed their company and the adventure, I'd had enough for a while.

"That's not happening, Ces."

FIVE WEEKS LATER

It was almost five weeks later that the following news item appeared on the major news websites and national papers.

Spanish authorities carry out a major operation against a prolific drug syndicate in Europe.

Reports are coming in from the Spanish authorities that the Spanish National Police and the Mossos d'Esquadra, have carried out one of the biggest European drug operations against an organised gang operating on Spanish territory. Supported by Europol and information gathered by the UK's National Crime Agency (NCA) through Operation Venetic, raids across Spain in several locations, ranging from Cartagena in the south to the Galicia region in the north and Tarragona in the North-eastern Catalonia region, resulted in the arrest of nearly one hundred people. Arrests were also made in the capital, Madrid, following raids on several private properties. Police are investigating links to the notorious gang boss, Gustav Kreshnik. Sources indicate that 250 kilos of cocaine, worth a street value of 23 million euros, was seized at various port locations, along with significant quantities of cash and firearms.

Kreshnik, an Albanian national, has been tracked for some time by Europol officers from the Serious and Organised Crime Department. Said to have links to organised crime groups in a number of countries, Kreshnik has, to date, evaded arrest and prosecution. However, it is believed that his son, Gezim, was amongst those arrested in the operation in Northern Spain. Sources also indicate that a Spanish police officer may be linked to the criminal group, but no details have been released as yet.

Once the news had broken, Louise filled me in on some of the detail. Operation Venetic, led by the NCA, had led to numerous arrests both in Britain and Europe, after agents infiltrated the encrypted telephone system, EncroChat, used by organised crime bosses; the authorities were close to linking Kreshnik to the syndicate now that his son had been arrested; Gezim Kreshnik had been brought in from South America to coordinate the shipments into Spain in the absence of a new and trusted distributor; Anita Eliades had cooperated fully with the investigation and would not be prosecuted, although she would be required as a witness in any subsequent trial; Huguette de Villiers was fired from her job as Ignacio Cañizares's business manager, but he decided not to take any further action against her; Ricardo Armendarez was being held and charged with corruption and conspiracy to commit a crime; David Anderson was being held on a criminal conspiracy charge too, and the intent to supply illegal narcotics; Sergio Colas and Lucero Garrido had been arrested, questioned and charged with various drug offences and conspiracy.

And then Rob Black published my story.

Spanish to English Translation

Spanish	English
¿A qué hora ?	What time?
adiós	goodbye
¿Adónde vas, inglés?	Where are you going, Englishman?
ahora!	now!
amigo	friend
apasionado	passionate
apostar	to bet
aquí	here
buena suerte	good luck
buenas noches	good evening/good night
buenos días	good morning
cervezas	beers
complicado/complicada	complicated
confundido	confused
¿cuándo viene?	when is he coming?
cucaracha	cockroach
delicado	awkward/delicate
dice que también es un placer conocerte	says it's also a pleasure to meet you
dile lo que dije	tell him what I said
discúlpeme un momento	excuse me a moment
¿dónde estás?	where are you
el quiere ver tu tatuaje	he wants to see your tattoo
ella es mi apoyo	she is my support
ella habla mucho en inglés	she speaks in English a lot
en inglés	in English
¿entiendes?	you understand
es una coincidencia	it's a coincidence
eso es correcto	that's correct
esta mañana	this morning
el hombre del teatro	the theatre man
fuera de control	out of control
gracias/muchas gracias	thank you/thank you very much
gusto de conocerlo	nice to meet you
hablar	speak
hasta luego	see you later

Spanish	English
hola	hello
laboratorio	laboratory
lamento que esto haya sucedido	I'm sorry this happened
las diez de la mañana	ten o'clock in the morning
llamada telefónica	phone call
las manos	hands
lunático… loco	lunatic… crazy
mañana	tomorrow
Mantenimiento. Problema eléctrico	Maintenance. Electric problem
me alegro de verte	nice to see you
¿me comprendes?	do you understand me? (implication)
¿me entiendes?	do you understand me? (general)
me entró el pánico	I panicked
mi amigo	my friend
mi refugio	my refuge
No hablo español muy bien	I don't speak Spanish very well
número	number
pandilleros	gang members
¿para él?	for him?
pepino	cucumber
¿perdón?	sorry?
perfecto, mi amigo	perfect, my friend
pin del teléfono	phone pin
por casualidad	by chance
por favor	please
problema	problem
prueba	test (proof)
público	public
¿Qué?	What?
¿Qué está pasando?	What's going on?
¿Qué pasa? Soy su representante	What's the matter? I'm his agent.
¿Quién es?	Who is it?
Quítate los pantalones	Take off your trousers
Quítese la chaqueta	Remove your jacket
recompensa	reward

Spanish	English
resolver esto?	solve this (sort it out)
¡salud!	cheers!
sí	yes
supermercado	supermarket
Tráeme una botella de Rioja Blanco	Bring me a bottle of Rioja Blanco
Tráeme una botella del vino de la casa	Bring me a bottle of house wine
un café con leche por favor	coffee with milk please
un embaucador	a swindler
un momento	just a moment
un paquete	a package
una ambulancia viene por ti	an ambulance is coming for you
usted no debe hablar así	you mustn't speak like that (as in insulting)
vacaciones	vacation/holiday
¡vale!	okay (regional)
¡vaya! ¿Estás loco?	wow! Are you crazy?
venga aquí	come here
¿Y vosotros quiénes sois?	And who are you?

Italian to English Translation

Italian	English
capisci?	you understand?
Che cosa hai fatto?	What did you do?
Ciao, tesoro mio. Come stai?	Hello, my darling. How are you?
Felice di vederti. Sei sorpreso di vedermi?	Happy to see you. Are you surprised to see me?
finito	finished/over *(as in our relationship is finished)*
impostore	imposter
Non è una cosa di cui ci si debba vergognare	It is not something to be ashamed of
puttana!	bitch/whore
Questo è stupido. Dici al tuo dottore che è un idiota	That is stupid. Tell your doctor that he is an idiot!

Italian	English
un idiota	an idiot

French to English Translation

French	English
adieu	farewell/goodbye (final or permanent)
arrête	stop
au revoir	goodbye
bonne chance, mon ami	good luck, my friend
bonjour	hello
C'est comme ça!	That's the way it is!
C'est bien!	Well done!
et aussi	and also
Je m'appelle	My name is
merci	thank you
mes amis	my friends
peut-être	perhaps
santé!	cheers!
se sépare de sa petite amie	separates from his girlfriend

Author's Note and Acknowledgements

For the sake of authenticity, this work includes a number of venues and place names that are genuine and actually exist. The rationale for this is should the reader be familiar with, or visit, for example, the city of Madrid, the locations will be realistic and give the story some context. Where real venues have been used, I would like to point out that none of them have any connection whatsoever to the production of this book or indeed to any of the entirely fictitious events and characters that appear in the plot.

With that in mind, however, I would like to acknowledge the following venues which I visited during the course of my research: The NH Collection Madrid Suecia hotel (Madrid); the Intercontinental Hotel (Madrid); Hotel Cortezo (Madrid) and the Hotel Los Habaneros (Cartagena). In each case I was treated superbly and with the utmost hospitality. In addition my research took me to Circulo de Bellas Artes and Teatro Real, both excellent Madrid venues well worth a visit.

Another venue that provided me with both a location for the story and inspiration, is Tara Casa, in La Magdalena (Murcia). I enjoyed several days of peace and tranquillity at Tara Casa, in excellent surroundings, where a writer, or any creative soul, can have time to think. A big thank you to the proprietors, Vivienne and Dan, for their hospitality too.

I would also like to mention, and give a special thank you to, a venue that I had not intended to visit and which was not even a consideration for this book. That is the Hospital Universitario Ramón y Cajal where I was taken after a minor 'mishap.' The staff at the hospital were superb, attentive and extremely efficient. I am grateful for their assistance and, as a result of that unplanned visit, the hospital has made a brief appearance in the text.

I must acknowledge too, Ascot Racecourse where part of the story is set. Ascot has no connection to the production of this work nor indeed to any of the entirely fictitious events or characters that appear in the book. However, I am grateful for their permission to use the venue name. My visits there on various occasions have been extremely enjoyable and confirmed my opinion that it was an ideal starting point for this work.

There are a number of football clubs in Madrid, many more well-known than others. The references to 'Madrid' in the football club context is a general one and is not intended to depict any specific club or to imply any connection to, or any endorsement by, any club in the city or the immediate environs. This too, is true of the reference to 'Paris' in the same context.

Finally, a big thank you to the following people for their assistance in one way or another. Steve Skarratt for his insight and scrutiny of the text; Gaspar Weiss for guidance on the Spanish translation; Giuseppe Morreale for guidance on the Italian translation; Eve Hepworth for her technical help; Shellee Evans for her character inspiration; Jem Butcher at Jem Butcher Design, for the cover design and artwork. It really doesn't matter whether that assistance or input is big or small. It all helps to form the final result.

Patrick Shanahan

Patrick Shanahan is the author of four novels in the Pursuit Series of books, each of them featuring his main creation Matthew Malarkey.

Patrick was born in South West London and now lives in Gloucestershire where he continues to write and is working on new titles.

Other Titles by Patrick Shanahan

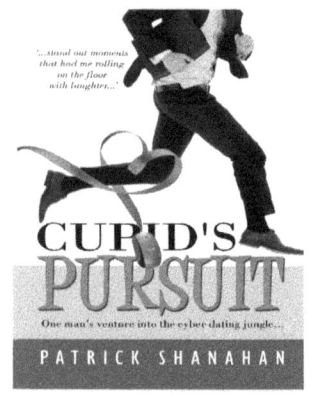

"An extremely humorous insight into the world of internet dating."

"Excellent writing, great characters... lots of laughs... "

"This book is full of humour and intrigue that keeps you guessing until the end... "

For more information please visit www.pursuitseries.com